ISLE OF
BLOOD
AND STONE

ALSO BY MAKIIA LUCIER

A Death-Struck Year

ISLE OF
BLOOD
AND STONE

MAKIIA LUCIER

HOUGHTON MIFFLIN HARCOURT
Boston New York

Copyright © 2018 by Makiia Lucier

Map art © 2018 by Leo Hartas

For information about permission to reproduce selections from
this book, write to trade.permissions@hmhco.com or to Permissions,
Houghton Mifflin Harcourt Publishing Company,
3 Park Avenue, 19th Floor, New York, New York 10016.

hmhco.com

The text was set in Adobe Jenson Pro.

Library of Congress Cataloging-in-Publication Data:
Names: Lucier, Makiia, author.
Title: Isle of blood and stone / Makiia Lucier.
Description: Boston ; New York : Houghton Mifflin Harcourt, [2018]
Summary: When two maps surface, each bearing the same hidden riddle,
nineteen-year-old Elias, a royal mapmaker, sets sail with King Ulises to
uncover long-held secrets behind the mysterious disappearance of the
king's two young brothers eighteen years earlier.
Identifiers: LCCN 2017015656 | ISBN 9780544968578
Subjects: | CYAC: Kings, queens, rulers, etc.–Fiction. | Missing
children–Fiction. | Secrets–Fiction. | Maps–Fiction. | Fantasy.
Classification: LCC PZ7.L9715 Is 2018 | DDC [Fic]–dc23
LC record available at https://lccn.loc.gov/2017015656

Printed in the United States of America
DOC 10 9 8 7 6 5 4 3 2
4500715723

For Mia

It is not down in any map; true places never are.

— Herman Melville, *Moby-Dick*

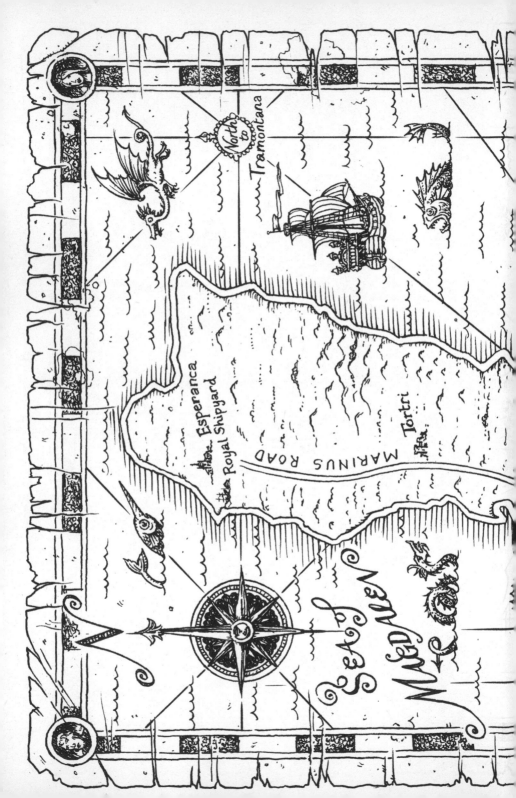

PROLOGUE

The outing had been planned on a whim; an afternoon lesson up in the hills, away from the smoke and stink of the city. Antoni hauled himself over the ledge and caught his breath — Saint Mary, he had grown soft — then reached down and instructed the child below to hold fast. When Bartolome's small hand grasped his, Antoni swung him up onto the rocks by his side.

Prince Bartolome landed on his knees with an *Oof* before scrambling to his feet. He was seven, tall for his age, dark hair pulled back in a queue. The boy looked around with an expectant air, but as he surveyed the area — a flat hilltop covered entirely in black rock, barren of even a single bush or shrub — his anticipation quickly turned to bewilderment.

"But, my lord Antoni . . . there's nothing here."

"No?" Antoni rose, wincing as the muscles in his back twitched in protest. "What is that on your feet?"

Bartolome wore a loose white shirt and trousers that fell just past his knees. Attire far less formal than his nurse, the lady Esma, would have liked, but Antoni had insisted on comfort for this outing. Strapped to the prince's dusty feet were open leather sandals, the kind the fishermen wore. And around their outer edges, black pebbles had stuck fast.

Frowning, Bartolome attempted to shake off the stones,

lifting one foot, then the other. They did not budge. More loose pebbles rose from the ground, as if coaxed by a sorcerer's magic, and flew toward the sandals. The child stumbled backward with rising panic, shaking his feet wildly, and soon after fell onto his backside with a yelp.

"Stop." Antoni crouched before the boy. Careful not to laugh. Mindful of a young prince's dignity. "They're only magnets. There's nothing to be afraid of."

"Magnets?" Bartolome bent one leg for closer inspection, bringing his foot an inch from his face.

Antoni could not remember a time when he'd been that limber. "Look." He scooped the pebbles away from one sandal, holding the stones in a closed fist. When he opened his palm, the rocks flung themselves once again at the prince's foot. Bartolome laughed, then glanced in puzzlement at Antoni's boots, which the stones had left alone.

"Your shoes were cobbled with nails," Antoni explained, tapping the bottom of the sandal, where the iron nail heads could be seen. He held up a rock the size of a pea. "This is called a leading stone. It's an explorer's greatest treasure. We use them to build —"

"Compasses! Is that why we're here? To build compasses? But that's grand!"

Antoni smiled, with amusement and some regret. Such enthusiasm. Such a curious mind. Bartolome would make a fine king someday, but for him, St. John del Mar's Royal Navigator, it was a pity and a shame. A good apprentice was hard to come by.

The thought came to him unbidden, unwelcome: *Jonas would have turned thirteen this year.*

Carefully, Antoni pushed the memories back toward the far recesses of his heart. Every day came easier. Today, he would think of only the living.

He said to Bartolome, "We'll build one when we join the others. But first" — he handed the boy an empty sack pulled from his belt — "let's gather some stones. The small ones only, as many as you can carry."

A picnic had been arranged on a meadow at the bottom of the hill. Spread across the grass was a colorful assortment of blankets — reds, golds, oranges — giving the space a festive air. A lemon grove bordered the meadow on three sides, a far more welcoming sight than Javelin Forest, which loomed just beyond the bright green leaves and fragrant fruit. Smoke floated high over a pig turning on a spit while nearby, soldiers in pale green and silver congregated around a game table. The air was filled with laughter and cursing and the tumble of dice across wood. Summer had come to del Mar at last, after a long and stormy spring.

Antoni and Bartolome made their way down the hill with a sackful of stones. Neither was surprised to find five-year-old Teodor being scolded by his nurse. Lady Esma wore a dress as blue as the afternoon sky. She was young, her black hair hidden beneath a butterfly wimple, hands planted firmly on her hips. "I won't have your lady mother see you in an intoxicated state," she was saying. "There will be no wine for you."

Teodor slunk toward his elder brother and Antoni. Esma rolled her eyes heavenward.

Amused, Antoni tossed the sack onto a blanket. "Troubles?" he asked.

"Never." Esma inspected Bartolome with a critical eye. "And how was your adventure? You've brought the dirt with you, I see." She reached out with a handkerchief to wipe a smudge from his nose.

Bartolome dodged the cloth, exclaiming, "We found magnets, Lady! Look." He held out a handful for her scrutiny. Rough and unpolished, glinting dully in the sun. Teodor poked his head close before drawing away, unimpressed, but Esma was suitably admiring. "And Lord Antoni is going to show me how to make a compass!"

"Is that why we're here?" She glanced over at Antoni, holding his waterskin high over his mouth only to discover there was not a drop left to drink. She laughed. "Stop, Antoni. That is pitiful. I'll find a cup for you, too. Cider for everyone."

"Thank you, Esma."

With one last warning look aimed at Teodor, she strolled off, calling for a servant.

Teodor made sure his nurse was well out of earshot before he kicked at the grass. "I hate cider," he grumbled. "Why shouldn't I drink the wine? It's only grapes, after all."

"Because it will stop your growth." Antoni repeated the lie

told to del Marian children for a thousand years. "And we can't have a prince who is only three feet tall."

Offended, Teodor glared up at Antoni. "I'm already taller than three feet."

"Oh, yes?" Affectionately, Antoni tousled the boy's hair. "Never mind, then. Plenty of time for wine when you're older."

"*When?*"

Always so impatient, this one. "Later."

Bartolome eyed his brother with disfavor. He pointed toward the edge of the meadow. "Master Ruy is tending the horses. Go and be useful."

One injustice after another. It was too much for the king's second son. "I will not!" Teodor cried. "You can't order me about. You're not king yet." He ran off in the direction opposite the one Lady Esma had taken, sidling around the wine barrels and disappearing from sight.

Bartolome watched him go. "He is my burden," he said with such weary resignation that Antoni had to laugh. His own boy was a year old, only a day younger than the king and queen's third son, Ulises. What manner of child would Elias be at Bartolome's age?

After Bartolome followed his brother across the meadow, Antoni considered the supplies he had set out earlier on the blanket. A small wooden bowl, squares of sheepskin the size of his thumbnail, a tinful of needles. And now the leading stones. All he needed to show Bartolome how to make a compass was water.

A serving girl appeared and offered a drink. Her eyes were red, and the cups on her tray performed a precarious dance, the result of a trembling hand. She could not be more than fifteen or sixteen. A decade younger than he. Antoni thought he knew all the servants in the castle, at least by sight, but she was unfamiliar.

He steadied the tray. "What is the matter?"

Her gaze was fixed firmly on his boots. "A speck of dust in the eye only, my lord Antoni. May I bring anything else?"

A blood-red vintage filled his cup. Not cider. She had brought wine. "Some water, please."

The girl curtsied. Before he could think to ask anything more, she was gone.

Troubled, he kept watch as she dispersed drinks among the soldiers. Had one of the men been too free with his hands? Too coarse with his compliments? But no, they barely acknowledged her, grabbing at mugs without looking up from their game, and within moments her tray was empty.

Well, there were a thousand reasons for a woman's tears. He would not try to untangle that riddle today. He caught a glimpse of blue skirts disappearing into the lemon grove. Esma, presumably gone to answer nature's call, for the trees offered the only measure of privacy in these parts. He had just raised the mug to his lips when he heard the first scream.

Seconds passed. A servant was on his knees, clutching his middle as he vomited onto a blanket. Horse Master Ruy convulsed on the ground. The soldiers at their dice game spun in their seats. One broke from the group and ran toward the horse master before stopping dead in his tracks. His eyes bulged; he clutched at his throat, then collapsed facefirst onto the grass and was still. Soldiers and servants fell, one by one, and as the cup tumbled from Antoni's limp fingers, he saw Bartolome at the far side of the meadow. The prince knelt with his brother in his arms. He was looking directly at Antoni and crying for help.

Antoni raced across the meadow. Shock sped his feet, along with a terrible, hideous fear. *God blind me. The wine.* Teodor was not moving. The screams engulfed him, along with the sad, piercing cry of a warbler. He had nearly reached the boys when he heard the horses in the distance.

A mad thundering of hooves.

Coming closer.

EIGHTEEN YEARS LATER

ONE

N THE SQUARE, just off the harbor, Mercedes heard the cockfight long before she saw it. A crowd of men gathered in a circle. Thirty deep, they occupied nearly the whole of the small plaza, their shouts reverberating off gray stone buildings. All around them was seawater: salty, pungent, and a little bit rotten, mixed with the smell of fish frying and bodies gone too long without a wash. And rising above the din was the distinct, high-pitched crowing of a rooster.

Dubious, she turned to the man standing beside her with his arms crossed, his expression darkening as he surveyed the scene before him.

"You're certain we're in the right place, Commander?" she asked. "He cannot be here." But even she heard the lack of conviction in her voice. This square, so near to the harbor, was a favorite haunt for pickpockets, charlatans, and travelers lured by cheap lodging and strong drink. They were in an ill-favored part of her cousin's kingdom, surrounded now by the lowest form of men. Mercedes had known Elias all her life. It was likely they were in exactly the right place.

Apparently, Commander Aimon agreed. "Oh?" was his reply. He pulled her aside as a man stumbled out of the throng, cheeks flushed, reeking of spirits. After the inebriate tripped past them, he released her arm. "You are all diplomacy, my lady Mercedes. But let's not fool ourselves." With his face the picture of resignation, he added, "Stay close. Follow me."

Commander Aimon forced his way through the crowd. He was a big man wearing the king's colors and a ferocious scowl; the mass yielded easily. Mercedes kept her head down and her elbows out, absently noting that the oaths and insults thrown their way were in many different languages. These men were Hellespontians and Lunesians and Coronads. A smattering of Caffeesh so far from home. Very few Mondragans, however. They had long since learned the dangers of lingering where they were not welcome.

Someone grabbed her arm. A man with very few teeth grinned and sniffed her hair. His breath stank of garlic and rot. She heard "What a pretty piece! Let me —" before her fist came up, sharp with rings, and connected with the underside of his chin. A pained grunt emerged. Her admirer fell back into the throng and was lost. Onlookers laughed and hooted, but no one else tried to touch her. She continued after the commander and, after much shoving, found herself before a small, dusty clearing.

Her suspicions were confirmed. It was a cockfight. To the right, a bald man with a stained leather apron held up a rooster, turning it this way and that while a second rough-looking character pointed out scratches and gaps in the feathers. She paid them only a cursory glance, her attention captured entirely by the young man to the left.

Elias.

Or, formally, Lord Elias. Only child of Lady Antoni and Lord Antoni, the long-departed Royal Navigator for the island kingdom of St. John del Mar. The last surviving son of a powerful noble family knelt in the dirt, a rooster cradled in his arms like a newborn babe. He wore a loose-fitting shirt and dark trousers, both now encrusted with muck and what she suspected was bird blood. His hair, a rich brown lightened by the summer sun, had grown overlong, so that it settled about his shoulders in thick waves, like a woman's. A battered leather map carrier lay against his back, cylindrical in shape, three feet long. Of his sword, there was no sign. As was usual.

Her breath caught. He'd been hurt. A bruise spread across one cheekbone, mottled and yellow. *What else?* Her inspection was swift: He had all his fingers, his limbs. He moved easily; no obvious injury, then, hidden beneath his clothing. One never knew with Elias, who collected wounds the way she collected secrets and enemies. It was his least endearing quality, this skill he had in making her worry.

Who was that man with him? He hovered over Elias with an anxious expression and deep smudges beneath his eyes. Similar in age and vaguely familiar; his identity poked at the very edge of her memory. Whoever he was, he was out of place: well-groomed and dressed in the dark tailored clothing of an upper tradesman.

The bird was motionless. A lock of hair fell forward as Elias placed his open mouth over its beak and blew gently. Miraculously, the rooster's chest expanded. Wings fluttered, then flapped. Cheers and curses erupted from the crowd. As she watched with appalled fascination, Elias lifted his head and spat out several feathers before sharing a grin with his neatly dressed companion.

She slid a glance toward Commander Aimon. The poor man rubbed his temple with his fingertips as he always did when trying to ease head pains. She could not help but smile, though it felt wrong, knowing what lay ahead. This morning was not going to end pleasantly.

Elias's bald opponent did not look pleased by the bird's quick recovery. "Chart maker!" he shouted, his guttural tones and dull features marking him for a Coronad. "You bird swiver! That rooster is dead. I have won!"

Elias laughed. "It's not dead yet, my friend!" he yelled back. He set the bird on the ground, his hands preventing it from taking flight. "Do you forfeit?"

The Coronad sneered. "We come here; we see del Marian men, even prettier than their women. With soft hands and flower oil in their hair. What do you know of cockfights, pretty del Marian?"

Elias's grin widened. His answer was to blow the man a kiss. Amid the laughter, the other man scowled even more. "Bah!" he said before snatching his own bird from his companion and setting it down in the dust.

A girl ran to the center of the clearing, barefoot, the tattered red kerchief covering her hair a perfect match to her skirts. The child raised an arm high, counted to three, then brought her hand down with dramatic flourish. Elias and his opponent released their holds on their roosters. The girl jumped aside as the birds flew at each other, feathers thrashing.

Commander Aimon's voice was an irritated rumble. "That boy sounds like a lord and looks like a vagabond."

Mercedes leaned close so that she could be heard above the shouting. "He's at ease in any setting. Have you noticed? He blends in without effort. I wonder why Ulises doesn't make use of it."

The commander made a skeptical noise. "Lord Elias isn't like you, Lady. He isn't made for intrigue."

"No?"

"Look at him." They watched Elias cheer on his bird. One arm was hooked around his friend's neck, and they were both jumping up and down and hollering like small boys at the bullfights.

"Hmm," she said.

"You see? Everything he thinks and feels is written on his face for the world to see. A dangerous trait for a king's . . . emissary."

She supposed that was true. Elias in a temper was a rare thing, but it was always memorable, and when he learned of the maps, outrage and insult would be within his rights. Not for the first time, she wished Reyna had not gone to the harbor that day and stumbled upon the map. She wished she herself had not traveled to Lunes and found the other. But what use, wishes? They would do her no good today.

Commander Aimon made to signal Elias. She placed a hand on his arm, stopping him. "We might as well wait until he's finished."

"Must we?"

Another quick smile emerged at his aggrieved tone. "He'll learn why we're here soon enough," she said. "And I've never seen an actual cockfight, have you?"

The commander answered her question with one of his own. "Do you think he can solve it?"

She knew Elias was capable. She wondered only if he would be willing. "It concerns him as much as the king."

The commander studied her with dark, kohl-rimmed eyes, a common trait among the men and women of del Mar's native population in the east. His hair was long and straight, black shot through with gray, and pulled back into a queue. He looked more like a pirate than the commander of the king's armies. "True," he acknowledged. "But that was not my question, Lady."

She didn't answer straightaway, but watched as Elias smoothed the rooster's feathers and whispered what looked like soothing, encouraging words to it. His hands were beautifully shaped. His fingertips, as always, bore the faintest trace of blue paint. Elias cared little for gloves or for the cleansing potions used by most mapmakers. And why was she standing here admiring his hands? She found herself frowning.

"You underestimate him," she said finally. "He's smarter than he looks."

The commander turned away and went back to his mutterings, this time something about being damned by faint praise. She let his words wash over her. Someone prodded her in the back so hard she fell forward a step. Slowly, she turned her head and gave the man behind her a gimlet-eyed stare. Fair hair, blue eyes, skin peeling from the sun: almost certainly a Mondragan.

"Apologies, miss . . ." His smile turned to puzzlement as he took in her own unusual appearance: black hair, golden skin, but with the green eyes and dreadful freckles that no full-blooded del Marian would ever proudly bear. The man glanced at Commander Aimon and then back at her, and she knew from the stranger's reaction that she had been recognized. His eyes widened. Prudently, he inched away until he was gone from view.

She watched him go. Stupid to feel this way, this terrible, skin-crawling shame, when there was not a thing to be done about it. She could not change the blood flowing through her veins. Half Mondragan, half del Marian.

A curse.

Turning back to watch the fight, she held herself apart from the crowd, as she always did, and waited.

The opposing bird lay dead on the ground, his master mourning above it. There was laughter and groaning as wagers were paid. As the crowd loosened, the stink of men dispersed into something that was, while not exactly pleasant, at least far more breathable.

Elias brushed the feathers from a shirt that had once been white. A futile effort; they merely fluttered about in the air before settling onto a different part of his person. Beside him, Olivier danced a small victorious jig, his rooster clutched under one arm.

It was a ridiculous sight, and Elias laughed. He heard "Chart maker!" and looked up in time to see a pouch sailing through the air toward him. He caught it with one hand and held it out to Olivier. "Your winnings."

Olivier took the pouch, unable to hide his relief as he felt the reassuring weight of copper sand dollars and silver double-shells. "You'll take half? It's only fair."

Elias refused. "It's your bird. Give it to your wife, with my compliments."

Elias had just disembarked from the *Amaris* when he'd caught a glimpse of Olivier, a parchment seller by trade, standing at the back of the crowd with a birdcage in his hand. Elias knew desperation when he saw it. He suspected its reason. Olivier's daughter suffered from a prolonged illness. Keeping his workshop profitable and paying off the leeches could not be a simple thing. Everyone knew these fights were a quick way to make money. Or lose it.

"You're certain?" Olivier asked.

"Yes, take it. I can't afford to lose your services. I don't care for the way Master Hernan prepares his sheepskin."

Olivier tucked the pouch away, then knelt to place the bird in its cage. "I'm grateful that you happened by, Lord Elias, and that you know so much about gamecocks." He eyed Elias curiously. "*How* do you know so much? It's an odd talent for a geographer."

"Most of my talents are considered odd. Or worse."

Olivier laughed. He shut the cage with a snap and, with final thanks, hurried off, the rooster swinging in the cage by his side.

Elias hitched his map carrier higher on his shoulder and glanced up, still smiling. Cortes was the capital city of St. John del Mar. An ancient settlement built on a hill with a round, walled castle at the very top and the parishes, or neighborhoods, spilling downward on slanted streets. The castle was his home. He had not seen it in months.

In his mind, he ticked off all he would do as soon as he reached the tower. First he would bathe, then eat. He would find out if Mercedes was on island, report to Lord Silva, deliver his maps to Madame Vega. Ulises would be in some council meeting or another at this hour of day, but he could visit his mother and the rest of—

He felt her before he saw her, absently touching the back of his neck, then turning fully when he glimpsed pale green silk at the edge of his vision.

Mercedes.

She stood among dust and abandoned feathers, watching him. Dark hair coiled over her ears like ram horns. A belt made of pearls, looped around a slender waist. A silver circlet above her brow. Her eyes, the green of the sea before a storm.

Unfortunately, he also saw Commander Aimon, who hovered behind her like some enormous dour shadow.

With dark humor, Elias looked down at the feathers stuck to his shirt. He saw the caged rooster disappear around a corner. Well. They had seen him do worse.

"Your ship is a month late, Elias," Mercedes said when he walked up to them. She pronounced his name the del Marian way, *EE-lee-us*, and she was soft-spoken. Frequently, it lulled strangers into thinking she possessed a sweet nature. "What happened to your face?"

"Mercedes." He kissed her on one cheek and the next, a ritual practiced on both women and men after a long absence. *Most* men, he amended after another glance at Aimon. There would be no kisses exchanged with the commander, today or any day. "It couldn't be helped. Did you worry for me?"

"I prayed for you, if that is what you're asking."

He laughed. "It's not." He had missed this, this type of conversation, or whatever it was they shared. He had missed her. Looking over her shoulder, he said, "Commander, I've just come off the ship. I haven't had time yet to cause you grief."

"Don't disregard your talents so quickly." Commander Aimon reached out and plucked a feather from Elias's shirt. He held it up, unsmiling. "And so. You've taken up cockfighting for charity?"

They had heard his exchange with Olivier. Elias shrugged. "It's true. What are you both doing here? Are you lost?"

The commander's answer was to bring his fingers to his lips in a sharp, piercing whistle. Elias nearly jumped from his skin. From a side street, three soldiers on horseback appeared and cantered toward them, scattering what was left of the crowd. Like Mercedes and the commander, they wore royal green and silver. Each led a riderless horse. One of them was Pythagoras.

Not a coincidence, then. They had come looking for him, if his horse was here. Elias had been away for months with little news of home. Sharply, he asked, "What's happened? My family —?"

"Is well, everyone is well." Mercedes's hand on his chest was fleeting, but enough to assure him the worst hadn't occurred in his absence. "Ulises would like a word."

Relief turned into puzzlement. That was all? The king would like a word? He was distracted for a short time by Pythagoras, who nudged his ear in greeting. "Fine. I'll get out of these rags and —"

"No time for that." Commander Aimon was already on his horse. "The *Amaris* was spotted on the horizon hours ago. The king has waited long enough."

Elias looked from the commander to Mercedes. They had been watching for him. Why? There was nothing unusual about a ship arriving late. A month's delay was later than he would have liked, but it should not have caused too much concern.

He thought about that as he helped Mercedes onto her horse. Light green skirts spread about a white mare. Keeping one hand wrapped around her ankle, he asked quietly, "Since when is a watch put out on my ship?"

"There wasn't."

"No? Since when am I met at the docks with personal escort? What aren't you telling me, Mercedes?"

Once, they had been close. When they were children, it had been simple to know how she'd felt and what she'd thought. She'd worn her heart on her sleeve for friend and foe to see. Mostly foe. But that was then. In the years since, Mercedes had become very good at hiding her thoughts, even from him.

She looked at him. Beautiful green eyes. Giving away nothing. "I'm not trying to be mysterious," she said. "It's simpler just to show you. Will you come? And let go."

He stepped away before she could kick him. She rode off with Commander Aimon and his men, and Elias was left with no choice but to follow — up toward the castle, up toward his king — at a complete loss, and with a very bad feeling.

TWO

I T WAS NOT the first time someone had spat at Mercedes, or even the fifth, but it had been some years since Elias had witnessed the insult.

Just before they reached the raised portcullis, Commander Aimon broke off with a salute and rode toward the arena with his men. Elias followed Mercedes into the castle's courtyard, a large circular space open to the sky. The sea air was faint here, high on the hill, overpowered by bougainvillea and the blood oranges growing in the nearby orchard. An ancient olive tree dominated the center: two hundred feet tall and growing, its thick, gnarled roots bursting from the ground and creeping along the surface.

The ladies of the court strolled about, weaving their way among soldiers and servants and robed scholars deep in conversation. Many called out greetings to Elias, welcoming him home. A few clucked at his appearance. And they swept low in deference to Mercedes, second in line to the throne.

All of them bowed, that is, except one.

The courtyard was surrounded by an arcade three stories high. An old woman stood just inside the ground level, partially concealed by the crimson bougainvillea cascading off an upper balcony. As Mercedes rode past, the woman spat, missing the horse's rear hooves by a hand's width.

Anger tightened his stomach. A quick glance at Mercedes dashed any hope that she had not seen what happened. She stared straight ahead, her face composed. But her shoulders had stiffened, and her chin had lifted up, up, in that way he recognized.

This he had not missed. He nudged Pythagoras forward until he had placed himself between Mercedes and the old woman. He did not know her. She was dressed as a tradeswoman. Old enough to have remembered that day eighteen years ago. Bitter enough to blame Mercedes for it, though she had still been in her mother's womb. He said nothing, only watched and waited and wished it were a man standing there by the bougainvillea. One did not have to be so polite with a man.

Mercedes was King Ulises's cousin, his only living relative. Her father, Augustin, long dead, had been the old king's younger brother. Her mother, Alyss, a beautiful noblewoman from Mondrago. Her parents had fallen in love and married long ago, when it was still acceptable for a del Marian to marry a Mondragan. Before the kidnappings and the murders. Before the two kingdoms had gone to war.

Conversation trailed away as others turned to see who it was Elias watched, stonefaced. The old woman must have gained some sense, seeing his expression, because she curtsied, quickly but correctly, and scurried off toward the gates.

Mercedes would not look at him. There was the familiar crush of white pebbles and seashells beneath his boots as he dismounted. He handed his reins over to a groom.

"Who was that, Marco?" Elias asked.

The boy glared after the old woman. "I've never seen her before, Lord Elias. Should I find out? I'll follow her."

"No, you won't." Mercedes handed her reins to the boy and said firmly, "Thank you, Marco."

The boy looked from Mercedes to Elias and sighed. "Yes, Lady." He took himself off, leading the horses behind him.

Once the boy was out of earshot, Elias frowned at her. "I didn't know this still happened. How often, Mercedes?"

"It's nothing to do with you." She turned on her heel and marched off toward the door that led to the king's chambers.

He caught up with her easily. "Does Ulises know?"

"Why would I tell him? So he can punish an old woman?"

"Yes."

Mercedes threw a dark glance in his direction. "Leave her alone. She's entitled to her rage."

She didn't truly believe that? "No, she isn't. Not toward you."

Mercedes stopped directly beneath the archway, ignoring the curious stares turned in their direction. "I don't need a champion, Elias. And I won't have you running to the king and telling tales. I can fight my own wars."

He would have argued his point forever had she not lifted her eyes to meet his. There was the anger he expected, but just beneath, nearly hidden, a bone-deep mortification.

All at once, the fight left him. He said only, "Mercedes. You should not have to." He motioned for her to precede him, and they made their way through the castle in silence.

The king's chamber was a vast room dominated by a long table. At the far end, conversation broke off and three pairs of eyes turned in their direction: those of Lord Silva, Royal Navigator; his young granddaughter, Lady Reyna; and Ulises, del Mar's king of one year.

Ulises was nineteen — only a day older than Elias — and, though the official mourning period for his father had passed months ago, still dressed entirely in black. Black trousers, black boots. Even his crown was black, a thin band of onyx with an emerald at its center. Taller than Elias, but only slightly, with black hair cropped close to his head and a face that could be thought of as melancholy but that Elias had heard more than one lady describe as "poetic."

Ulises did not look melancholy just now as he shoved his chair back and rose, smiling. "You found him, Mercedes. Good." His smile faded somewhat as he studied Elias's shirt front. "Whose blood is that? Not yours?"

"It's better not to ask, cousin." Mercedes took a seat. Behind her, a series of doors had been flung open, offering a staggering view of the harbor and, beyond that, the Sea of Magdalen.

"It isn't mine," Elias said after a quick bow. "Forgive me for coming in my dirt. I was told to hurry."

He did not miss the raised eyebrows exchanged between Ulises and Lord Silva. Mercedes and Elias had dragged their tension into the chamber, dampening the air around them like fog.

Ulises said only, "We were starting to worry." He clasped Elias's forearms in greeting. A kiss on each cheek, a grin, then, "Old friend, it's good to see your face, battered though it is."

"And yours." Still it gave him an odd feeling to see Ulises as king. To bow and address formally, at least sometimes, the boy he had grown up beside. Ulises returned to his seat as Elias greeted Lord Silva.

His former teacher was nearing seventy, a neatly kept man of middling height with a gray triangle of a beard and pleasant features. He looked like someone's gentle grandfather. Which he was. But no other grandfather Elias knew could speak a dozen languages. Or sail past the Strait of Cain's turbulent whirlpools without ever once losing his supper. Or outrun an entire tribe of cannibals with a terrified seven-year-old Elias clinging to his back. Lord Silva was thinner than Elias remembered, but his grip was still strong, his eyes still bright and sure.

"Elias. Welcome home." Lord Silva reached up and patted Elias's unmarked cheek. As usual, the pats felt more like a couple of brisk slaps. "What happened to your face?"

"A miscalculation." Elias didn't like to think about it: the *Amaris* and the jutting rocks that had sprung from nowhere.

"That sounds ominous. Is everyone alive, at least?"

Elias smiled. He could always count on Lord Silva to ask the important questions and disregard the rest. "Mostly."

"Good." Lord Silva stepped back and examined him. "I don't want to know about the blood. Or the . . . are those feathers?"

"Ah . . ." Elias saw Mercedes smile despite herself. "You don't want to know about those, either."

"Hmph." Lord Silva returned to his chair.

And Elias turned to Reyna. How old was she now? Nine? Ten? As small as Mercedes was at that age. Why would she be here, at this urgent, mysterious summons?

He asked, "Have you taken up fighting, Lady Reyna? You've lost a few more teeth since I last saw you."

Reyna smiled shyly at his teasing, displaying two late missing incisors. Her black hair fell in two braids that disappeared below the table's edge. "Welcome home, Lord Elias."

"It's good to be home." He set his map carrier on the table and threw himself into a chair. Curious, he eyed the two scrolls that lay in the center of the table, both about four feet in length, rolled, and tied with black ribbon. Too large to be the king's typical correspondence. They looked like maps.

"The king spoke for all of us," Lord Silva said. "We were starting to worry. What took you so long?"

Months ago, Elias had been dispatched to Hellespont, an island along del Mar's trade route, to survey its coastlines after a series of earthquakes had altered its topography. But at this moment, he didn't care the least bit about Hellespont, though it had occupied his every waking thought for many weeks. Now all he wanted to know was why he'd been summoned here before he'd even had a glimpse of his chambers and an opportunity to bathe. He glanced at Ulises, whose expression gave away nothing, and checked his impatience.

"Parts of the island are unrecognizable," Elias answered Lord Silva's question. He uncapped his carrier and removed the contents. Sheets of parchment were spread across the table. They varied in size, each a specific rendering of Hellespont. A few sketches showed the entire island, others primarily the northern half. Others magnified an even smaller portion: a harbor, a peninsula, a stretch of coastline. Everyone leaned forward for a closer look.

"The earthquakes transformed the northern edge," Elias continued, "and there are islets on the west side that have sprung right out of the sea. I've redrawn the area." He addressed Lord Silva. "I wouldn't have our captains attempt that route without these maps. There are new shoals in place, and rocks that will take the bottom right out of our ships."

Shoals and sandbars were a danger to every seagoing vessel. There was the risk of grounding or capsizing. Unlike Elias, most of the men aboard a ship could not swim.

Mercedes pulled a chart closer with a fingertip. "These whirlpools are new?"

"Yes," Elias said.

"Was the *Amaris* damaged?" Ulises asked.

"Yes," Elias said. "We hit some rocks. A few of us were thrown. One shipman broke his leg, and we were delayed for weeks with repairs."

"Thrown?" Mercedes eyed Elias's bruise with a frown. "What about the serpents?"

"There were none. We were lucky."

"You've a gift for understatement, Elias," Ulises said. To be thrown from a ship usually meant one was the next meal for the water monsters that lurked beneath the surface, waiting for just such an opportunity. "Were there any signs of surveyors from Lunes?"

Elias smiled. "None."

Ulises looked satisfied. "Then we have the advantage." To Lord Silva, he said, "We'll need copies made."

"Quickly," Lord Silva acknowledged. "Several ships are sailing within the week. I'll see to it."

"I'll help," Elias offered.

In a far-off corner of the castle, mapmakers, painters, and calligraphers copied the charts sketched out by the kingdom's explorers, men like Elias. They also drew maps using the information brought home by captains, shipmen, and other travelers who were met at the ports. But when time permitted, Elias preferred to draw his own maps. It was the only way to ensure that the copies looked exactly the way he wanted them.

Lord Silva studied one of the charts with a distracted air. "No, you won't have time, I suspect."

And Elias could be only so patient. "Won't I?" he asked politely. "Why not?"

Silence fell. Lord Silva set the map down. Glances were

exchanged all around. It grated on Elias, the feeling that everyone in the chamber knew something that he did not.

Mercedes stood. "If I may, Lord Silva?"

"Certainly, my dear."

Mercedes reached for one of the scrolls, tossed the ribbon aside, and unrolled it. Also on the table was a shallow bowl filled with conch shells. Without a word being exchanged, Elias and Reyna used the shells to secure the four corners. Elias glanced down at the scroll, and then looked again, startled.

It was one of his father's maps. A rendering of del Mar in its entirety, from the village of Esperanca in the north to the southernmost city of Alfonse. Five compass roses dotted the surface, and a maze of rhumb lines crisscrossed the sheepskin. He saw the harbor, the mountain ranges, the rivers, and waterfalls. Even the sea serpents, slithery monsters painted just beyond the harbor, were given their due in brilliant blues and greens and purples. But most splendid of all was a large inset of Cortes, showing the hilltop castle and the individual streets and storefronts. There were people, even animals. Pigs caged in pens and stray dogs roaming the streets. The detail was remarkable.

The only thing missing was a cartouche with the mapmaker's name and kingdom of origin. But this was his father's, Lord Antoni's, work; Elias knew it without question. And it was in fine condition: the parchment untorn, the paint vivid. He had never seen this particular chart before, but that was of no significance. His father had painted thousands of maps. Why was this one here now?

"Several months ago," Ulises said, "just after you left, in fact, a merchant tried to sell this map at the harbor. He claimed to have won it in a tavern game of chance on Oslaw. He knew nothing of its provenance, and could only say that the man he won it from was a Coronad shipman with arms like tree trunks."

"Helpful," Elias commented. Show him a Coronad shipman who did not fit that description. They were few and far between.

Ulises half smiled. "Quite," he agreed. "The map is unsigned, but Reyna is familiar with Lord Antoni's work. And there were other . . . elements she thought curious. She bought the map."

Elias's attention shifted to Reyna. "You've graduated to the mappers' booth?"

The child looked uneasy to have all eyes on her. "It was only that once. I help with the ledgers, usually. Madame Vega says I'm too young to barter."

Lord Silva said, "The child, correctly, thought discretion might be in order. She purchased the map using her own funds so that it would not appear in the official records. And she brought it directly to the king."

"Mercedes was there as well," Ulises said. "It was just before she sailed to Lunes."

Discretion? Curious elements? And what did Mercedes have to do with anything? Utterly lost, Elias turned to her as she spoke.

"While I was on Lunes," she said, "I came across a chart hanging in the king's map chambers." She unrolled the second map beside the first and secured it with more shells. "One chart among a hundred others. I would not have given it a second glance if I had not seen Reyna's copy first. It's also missing a cartouche. You'll see that they are nearly identical."

"Nearly?" Elias leaned close, comparing the two. Some time passed before he saw that yes, there was a telling difference. Unlike the first map, the second featured the beacon on the cliffs of Alfonse, at the very southern tip of the island. These maps were clearly painted by the same artist, but it could not have been his father. Lord Antoni had died eighteen years ago. The beacon was only ten years old.

Elias sat back, disappointed. He had been so sure. "Fine copies, then," he conceded. "It's not uncommon to learn from the masters. What of it?" He glanced at the first map.

And saw it.

In the top left corner, hidden along a thick border made up of olive trees and lemon groves. He brought his face down to the map, so close that his nose nearly touched the parchment. He glanced quickly at Lord Silva, who said, "The child saw it at the harbor."

"Her eyesight is sharp," Mercedes said.

Elias's was less so. To him, the words were like the footprints of ants, barely recognizable as lettering. A small glass dish had been placed halfway down the table. He shoved his chair back and retrieved the bowl. It was filled with dried orange blossoms and lavender. He returned to his seat and without ceremony upended the contents beside the maps. Immediately, Mercedes sneezed.

"Apologies," he said absently. He cleaned the dish with the end of his shirt. Mercedes and Ulises were frowning, at a loss, but Reyna was already on her feet and reaching for a water pitcher. When Elias held out the bowl, she filled it with small, steady hands. Carefully, he placed the bowl on the map, over the border. He peered into the glass and read the tiny print that had been drawn there, now magnified by glass and water.

> *Adventurer, two princes lost but not gone.*
> *Follow the path of the ancient mariners, Tramontana to Ostro.*
> *Look not to what is there but to what is not.*

He felt a sharp prickling along his scalp. No one made a sound. He moved the bowl over the second map. The wording was identical to that on the first. He straightened, anger simmering. "Someone is having their fun with us."

He expected Lord Silva to agree with him, right then and there, without the slightest hesitation. And so he was stunned when the silence inched along even further before Lord Silva said, "Elias, I taught your father how to hold a brush. How to mix his paints. I have seen him cast a thousand rhumb lines across the page. I know his work, child. As well as yours, as well as my own."

And from Ulises, "What if these are his?"

"The beacon —" Elias began.

"I know what it means." Ulises regarded him, unsmiling. "Whoever painted the maps was alive ten years ago."

"What are you saying?" Elias rose slowly, not taking his eyes off his king. He sounded to himself unnaturally calm and detached. "And how dare you say it?"

"Elias . . ." Mercedes said. His eyes flashed to hers; she looked away first. He began to understand now what she would not tell him in the square.

The king's voice remained even. "I'm saying nothing. Only that there is a riddle. I'm asking you to solve it."

"I see." Elias's temper unraveled faster than he was proud of. "You want me to solve this riddle. And prove what? That my father is alive somewhere, painting maps" — he sent a scornful glance toward the charts — "and *choosing* not to come home?"

Ulises opened his mouth, then shut it. Elias stared at his friend, infuriated, then swung around to glare at Mercedes. "You found this on Lunes, you said?"

Her hands were folded on the table. She was pale and set, but she met his eyes squarely. "Yes."

"What did Lamech say when you asked for the map?"

"I did not ask for it," Mercedes said.

"The king offered it to you?" Elias asked with a skeptical air. The king of Lunes was a stingy old miser. He would not hand over anything valuable without expecting something in return.

"I'm certain he would have, had I asked."

Her meaning became clear. Incredulous, Elias said, "You *stole* this map? From the royal map chambers on Lunes?"

Mercedes glanced at Reyna. The child's eyes were as large as twin moons. Likely this was the first time she was hearing of Mercedes's more colorful diplomatic responsibilities. "What would you have had me do?" Mercedes countered. "I couldn't have anyone wondering at my interest. The last thing I wanted was for someone else to take a closer look."

"How did you—?" Elias stopped. He didn't want to know how she had stolen the map. Turning back to Ulises, he said, "This is ridiculous. How can you give this credence?"

"How can I not?" Ulises snapped. "*Two princes lost but not gone?* These are not strangers in a fairy story, Elias. They are my brothers!" Ulises rose, facing him across the table. A pulse beat at his temple. "Lord Antoni's skill is not something that can be copied, as simple as that. Look at them. This is the work of a master. Are they not worthy of a look, at least?"

"No." Elias grabbed his carrier. Better that he go before he really said something he shouldn't. The Hellespontian sketches were left scattered about the table.

"These were painted years apart," Ulises continued, urgent. "And they've turned up on opposite sides of an entire sea."

"A coincidence."

"Two coincidences?" Ulises shot back, gesturing toward the maps. "There may be more. Why would someone go to this much trouble?"

"Because he is mad!" Elias's voice rose. "Because he is cruel. Or bored. There are a thousand, thousand reasons why. Have you not considered them?" Bitterly, he added, "Was this ambush simpler? *Old friend?*"

A slow flush crawled up Ulises's neck. *Good.*

"Sit down, Elias. Listen to me. I am your friend —"

"My king," Lord Silva broke in. He, too, was on his feet. "Elias. Please . . ."

Elias paid him no attention. "And this is how you show it?" he demanded of Ulises. "By besmirching my father's name? By bringing fresh grief to his widow —" Another shock coursed through him as he thought of his mother.

Mercedes spoke quickly, "She won't learn of it. No one knows of the maps except us."

He glared at her. Hurt unfurled in him. He let her see it. She had known of this all along, at the harbor. She could have given him some warning. He asked, "What about the man who sold Reyna the map?"

"He's gone," Mercedes said, frowning. "Sailed off. What of him?"

"That doesn't mean he won't return, or speak of it," Elias said. "What about Commander Aimon?"

Her hands were no longer folded before her. They were fists. "That is unworthy of you. You know he can be trusted."

Elias's laugh held little humor. "A secret is safe, Mercedes, when one person knows it. Not seven, or more. You of all people should know that." He turned his anger back to Ulises. "Did you spare a thought to what this will do to my family?" He jabbed at one of the maps. "Even a whisper of it?"

"Listen to me," Ulises said. "I mean no insult —"

"I am insulted!" Elias slapped both palms flat against the table, hard enough to rattle the seashells.

Their raised voices had not gone unnoticed. The doors swung open, and two guards stuck their heads in.

"*Out.*" The order came from Ulises. That, and the cold look he shot their way, had the men stumbling over themselves as they backed away. The doors slammed shut.

It was only then that Elias became aware of Reyna huddled in her chair and Lord Silva's lips pressed thin. A child. His teacher. A spark of shame ignited within him. He forced his breath to slow, and tried to pull his anger back inside of him.

"My father," he said quietly, "was a lord of del Mar. A man who served his king and kingdom and died for it. I am insulted." He slung the carrier over his head and stalked out of the chamber, leaving behind a thick and muffling silence.

THREE

ELIAS HAD BEEN only an infant when it happened, but he knew the tale as well as any, and better than most. Eighteen years ago, on the island of St. John del Mar, two princes vanished, never to be seen again.

Prince Bartolome and Prince Teodor, ages seven and five, had traveled outside the city in the company of Lord Antoni. As Royal Navigator, Antoni oversaw del Mar's School of Navigation, along with its considerable network of explorers, mapmakers, instrument makers, and pilots. Bartolome had developed a fascination with the navigator's arts, and anyone looking for the prince knew to look for Antoni, for he had become the man's shadow. The outing was meant to show the princes the magnetic compass rocks that could be found on a hill near Javelin Forest. Accompanying them were their nurse, Lady Esma; servants; and two dozen of the king's finest guards. In the end, their strength and numbers mattered not.

When the party did not return by nightfall as planned, King Andrés and more soldiers rode out to find them. They came upon an unspeakable sight. Beneath a full moon, lying scattered across the meadow like broken dolls, were two dozen dead soldiers. Servants, too. There was no sign of the princes or Lord Antoni. The nurse, also, was missing.

The king launched a frantic search. Spies and emissaries, one and the same, were sent to kingdoms near and far to ferret out the truth. After many months, a Mondragan soldier was questioned. And slowly a crime was uncovered, layer by layer, exposing a rotted core at its center.

Five island kingdoms dotted the Sea of Magdalen like steppingstones. Each with its own language and customs. Each with its fortune tied in some way to the sea. The largest and most powerful stone was St. John del Mar, followed by Lunes, Mondrago, Hellespont, and Coronado.

Mondrago lay to the east of del Mar, at that time ruled by the newly crowned King Marius. Marius lived far more extravagantly than he ought to have, supplementing his treasury by imposing crippling taxes on his people. When that was not enough, he hatched a plan.

Bartolome and Teodor were to be snatched and held for ransom. The kidnapping of royals or noblemen was not unprecedented. They were on occasion waylaid, though returned unharmed once payment was made. The boys were to have been smuggled to an undisclosed location while terms were being negotiated between del Mar and an anonymous envoy representing Mondrago. Only something went wrong. The ship carrying the princes was lost in a storm.

Retribution was brutal. The grief-stricken King Andrés

gathered his forces and sailed to Mondrago. King Marius denied having anything to do with the boys' disappearance and, when that did not work, begged for mercy for himself and his family. His pleas fell on deaf ears. After an endless siege, Marius and his family were put to death, scores of nobility slaughtered, citizens scattered to the wind, castles and estates burned to rubble. Mondrago was now a del Marian possession. What remained of a once-picturesque island kingdom was an impoverished wasteland, a ruin.

The people of St. John del Mar settled into a prolonged period of mourning. The queen died the following spring, many said of a broken heart. And a third son, Ulises, only a babe when his brothers were lost, was named heir to the kingdom of del Mar.

That was where the story ended. Always.

Until now.

Elias strode across a different courtyard this time. One smaller than the other, and without an olive tree, but still remarkable. Beneath his feet was an immense compass star constructed of tilework in blues and greens and golds. The compass filled the entirety of the open courtyard. Eight wind points led directly to stone archways that, in turn, led to eight separate doors for the School of Navigation. The Tower of Winds rose directly ahead, its exterior not smooth and curved but octagonal, each side depicting a famed explorer. His father was up there, map carrier strapped to his back, his likeness facing the sea. The courtyard was empty except for a lone servant who swept the tile with a palm frond. Elias had just stomped past the compass's northern point when he heard Lord Silva calling behind him.

"Elias! Stop."

He did as he was told. Reyna had accompanied her grandfather. Lord Silva said something to her, and after an uncertain look in Elias's direction, the child took herself off whence she had come.

When Lord Silva was only a few feet away, Elias said, "I'm done speaking of it."

"And I'm not," Lord Silva said mildly. "Come, let us go where we can talk frankly." And he walked off into the tower, fully expecting to be obeyed.

Old habits died hard. Elias followed, trying to ignore the rolled maps Lord Silva had tucked beneath his arm.

The School of Navigation was housed along the castle's northern walls. Books on geography, cosmography, hydrography, astronomy, navigation, and foreign kingdoms were stored here. A vast quantity, though, far outnumbered by maps. Scroll upon scroll of rolled parchment could be found, maps and sea charts depicting every part of the known world.

A marble statue of Saint Cosme stood in the center of the main floor: forty feet tall, head and shoulders bent to carry the heavens on his shoulders. Tables were scattered around him. Mapmakers hunched over parchment, working shoulder to shoulder with the painters and miniaturists. In one corner, Lord Braga's son Jaime shaved away a length of wood that was beginning to resemble a cross-staff. He grinned as they strode past and returned Elias's salute with one of his own. Through an open door, Madame Vega instructed a group of boys on the use of an astrolabe.

Lord Silva's work chamber was also filled with books and charts. A map of the world dominated one wall, nine feet by twelve feet, framed in gilt. This map had a cartouche. The signature read, *Vittor, Tower of Winds, Kingdom of St. John del Mar.*

Elias had never met Lord Silva's eldest son. Vittor had died the year Elias was born, buried in an avalanche along with most of his expedition. His death had broken his widowed father, who had retreated to his home in Alfonse. Lord Silva had never intended to return as Royal Navigator. His former apprentice Antoni had assumed the role. But when, only months later, Antoni and the two princes disappeared, the king had summoned Lord Silva back to Cortes.

Lord Silva set the maps on the table. The parchment unfurled slightly; he had not bothered replacing the ribbons. Joints crackled as he lowered himself into a chair. He waited until Elias had paced the length of the chamber before he spoke. "You should not have lost your temper."

Elias swung around. "Why not?" he burst out. "He was being absurd."

Lord Silva rested his chin on steepled fingers. "He may be absurd if he wishes," he said with some asperity. "You forget he is no longer just the prince, or just your friend. Elias, he is your king."

To this, Elias said nothing. He understood his teacher's full meaning. *He is your king. And that position demands loyalty and respect, at all times.* He tried to fight off a twinge of conscience. When that failed, he resumed his pacing.

"What would you have done in his place?" Lord Silva asked. "Ignored the maps? *Could* you have?"

Elias gestured toward the parchment. "You think my father painted those?"

Lord Silva did not answer right away. In the silence, Elias could hear the boys in the next chamber with Madame Vega, reciting the same chant he had learned long ago:

"You, adventurer who boasts of being
quick-witted and a good troubadour,
would you make me a song
that the eight winds call?"
"Levante, Scirocco, and Ostro,
Libeccio, Ponente, and Maestro,
Tramontana and Greco:
Here you have the eight winds of the globe."

Levante was the ancient del Marian word for the wind from the east; *Scirocco,* from the southeast; *Ostro,* from the south. And the five remaining winds were *Libeccio,* southwest; *Ponente,* west; *Maestro,* northwest; *Tramontana,* north; and

Greco, northeast. *Follow the path of the ancient mariners, Tramontana to Ostro*, the maps stated. *Tramontana to Ostro:* north to south. *What did that mean?* he wondered, and then was angry at himself for wondering.

"Do I think Antoni painted the maps?" Lord Silva asked with a thoughtful expression. "I can't say yes. I can't say no. One possibility leads to another, and my mind is left tangled by the conclusions I draw."

Elias did not try to conceal his dismay when he asked, "If he were alive, why would he stay away?"

"I don't know." Lord Silva raised his troubled gaze to Elias's. "But there's something strange about those maps. You know it as well as I do. The king knows it. Lady Mercedes, too."

Mercedes. His scowl deepened just hearing her name. "And Reyna," he reminded Lord Silva.

Lord Silva's expression turned blank, as if he'd forgotten who Reyna was. "Yes, yes. And the child."

The boys in the next chamber laughed, and it occurred to Elias that he should not have been able to hear them. Not with Lord Silva's heavy door and thick walls. He glanced over, saw that the door had not been shut completely. A crack could be seen, and he thought he heard . . . He was across the chamber in an instant, startling Lord Silva as he yanked the door wide. And groaned.

Madame Grec's nose was suspiciously close to the threshold. She jumped a foot when Elias appeared, embarrassed color sweeping her features. "Lord Elias. Welcome home."

"Madame Grec." Elias tried to hide his consternation. The school's language master was not quite as old as his own mother. One of del Mar's rare tall women, she stood across from him, nose to nose, eye to eye. Dark hair caught beneath a wimple and a gleam in her eye that said, *I have just heard the most interesting things!*

What could she have heard? Elias thought back.

You think my father painted those?
If he were alive, why would he stay away?
There's something strange about those maps. . . .

Lord Silva had risen behind his desk. His eyes had narrowed, though his tone was courteous. "Madame Grec, was there something I can do for you?"

Madame Grec had been staring at Elias's bruise. She dragged her gaze away and smiled brightly at the Royal Navigator. "My lord Silva, yes. I'd hoped to discuss Hector." She glanced at Elias, her smile fading slightly. "But if you're engaged . . ."

"As you see," Lord Silva said with some dryness.

". . . I'll return later," Madame Grec finished reluctantly.

"Please do."

This time, Elias made sure the door shut completely. He looked across the chamber in mute dismay.

"She heard nothing." Lord Silva returned to his chair and held up one hand wearily. "And don't start pacing again. It's exhausting to watch."

Elias stopped before the desk, too restless to sit. "What's wrong with Hector?"

Hector was the Grecs' only son. He had been admitted to the school earlier this year, when he turned five, the youngest age possible for acceptance.

"Nothing is the matter with Hector," Lord Silva said. "Only he's not meant to be an explorer, and his mother will not see it."

Elias had not been taught languages by Madame Grec but by a previous language master now retired. The Grecs had returned to del Mar a year ago after living among the Bushidos.

"Where is Master Grec?" Elias asked.

"In Caffa. Visiting his brother."

A dull pain had worked its way behind Elias's eyes. He lost interest in the Grecs. "I don't like riddles. Why don't people just say what they mean?"

Surprisingly, Lord Silva smiled. "I know you don't. And yet your father loved them." His smile faded. "We could be mistaken. These maps could be nothing more than some fool passing the time. A very skilled fool . . ."

Elias waited. "But?"

Lord Silva said, "If there is someone out there who knows a different truth, do you not want to learn of it?" He slid the maps across the desk toward Elias. "Not for me, not even for the king. But for your own sake?"

Elias rode hard, leaving the walled city in his wake as the afternoon sun beat down upon his shoulders. A farmer with ass and cart approached from the opposite direction. Seeing Elias bearing down on him, he clattered to the side of the road in alarm. The explicit nature of his curses jolted Elias from his reverie. He looked over his shoulder to see the man shaking a meaty fist at him, then turned away, filled with grim humor. Another person upset with him. Well. What was one more?

The ride did not clear his thoughts as he had hoped. Pythagoras's mane whipped against him as he rode lower, faster, down the king's highway, Marinus Road.

Follow the path of the ancient mariners.

Ancient mariners.

Marinus Road.

Around in his mind the riddle went, until a cluster of cypress appeared to the east. He rode beneath a triple archway that marked the entrance to a graveyard, with its ancient landscape and stone sarcophagi. The chapel doors were shut. There was no one about.

The graves lay to the right, the dead bordered by spindly columns of cypress. He left Pythagoras by a tree and made his way to the far end of the grounds. The marker he sought rose six feet high, as tall as he, inscribed with nothing more than a name and an image of a compass rose.

He laid his hand on the marker. Why did he come back to this place? There was no one here beneath the dirt. Only a memorial stone placed by his mother. His map carrier, normally a pleasant weight against his back, felt like a millstone. He took it off and laid it on the grass.

If there is someone out there who knows a different truth . . . do you not want to learn of it? Not for me, not even for the king. But for your own sake?

What did he know of Lord Antoni, his father? From his mother, he knew that he had grown up in Antoni's image, so alike in manner and appearance that he would hear her catch her breath sometimes, and when he turned to face her, she would have her hand pressed over her heart and a look in her eye that said her thoughts were not on her son but on someone else entirely.

From Antoni's friend Lord Braga, Elias knew his father had been a man quick to laugh and slow to rile. An explorer with an adventuresome spirit and a curious nature, whose respect for the traditions of others had gained him entry to the world's mysterious kingdoms: the Pyrenees tribe of the Western Angolas, the Bushidos in the east, and, Lord Braga's favorite, the unnaturally tall race of women who lived in the forests and swamps of the Inner Jangas.

From Lord Silva, Elias had learned Antoni had been a gifted mapmaker, a fine artist, and a brilliant man of science, who, at the age of twenty-five, had given up many of his travels to become del Mar's Royal Navigator so that he could remain close to his wife and son.

Husband. Friend. Explorer. Father.

What did Elias know of Lord Antoni? He knew many things.

And he knew nothing.

A sound had him looking up. A holy man approached, wearing a black robe and holding rosary beads.

"Lord Elias," the priest said, "it has been some time since your last visit. You look well."

"Father," Elias said in greeting. He indicated the marker. "You've kept it tended. I'm grateful."

The priest gestured toward the chapel. "There's food inside . . . and counsel, should you need it." The last was a question.

Elias hesitated. "No. Not this time."

The priest stepped back, beads swaying from long, bony fingers. "Then I'll leave you to your prayers. Your horse will be tended to." He left as quietly as he'd come.

Elias waited until the priest had disappeared into the chapel before kneeling and bowing his head. He stayed there, by his father's empty grave, for a long time.

And then he opened his carrier and spread the maps upon the grass.

FOUR

OR THE FIRST time in his life, Elias found himself barred from the king's chambers. A change of guard had taken place. Clearly, they had heard of the earlier altercation. At any other time, Elias would have simply strolled past. This evening, the guards looked uneasy, but they blocked his path and made him wait while they sought the king's permission.

Embarrassment crept along his neck and warmed his ears. He and Ulises had fought occasionally, as friends do, as boys do. But not once had they fought since Ulises had been crowned, after the old king had fallen from his horse and snapped his neck. Elias had not been on island enough in the past year to wonder how a kingship would affect their friendship. Standing here, still covered with the dust and dirt of travel, he had to admit it did not look promising.

And then he smiled to himself, for within the chamber came a testy "And? Why is he being announced? Do you know something I do not?" followed by the guard's mumbled apology. Elias was allowed to enter.

Inside, five of the king's scribes gathered their belongings and made to depart. Chairs scraped against stone; parchment crinkled. They passed him with murmured greetings — "Welcome home, Lord Elias" — and a few censorious looks. The guard shut the doors behind them.

Ulises was at the table, quill in hand, scrawling his way across parchment. He did not look up at Elias's approach. Before the king were stacks of what looked to be very official documents and six inkpots. Six! Through open balcony doors, Elias could see a full moon settled high in the night.

Silently, Elias pulled the carrier over his head and placed it on the table. Ulises continued to ignore him, so he sat opposite and reached for a fig from a bowl. Then five more figs. He had not eaten since early this morning aboard the *Amaris*. The minutes ticked by.

Elias used the time to study his king. With his serious expression and that quill, Ulises reminded him of a scholar or one of those monks who shuffled down from the monasteries in his robe and sandals. With a start, he realized that had Bartolome and Teodor lived, Ulises likely would have made his home in the church, for it was the traditional expectation of a third son.

Ulises glanced up and caught him staring. "What is it?"

You forget he is no longer just the prince, or just your friend. Elias, he is your king. Lord Silva's words. Elias remembered them and shrugged. "I was thinking you would have made a very good monk."

Silence, followed by a sour look. Ulises tossed the quill

aside. "It's a good thing you chose to be an explorer. You'd have made a poor diplomat."

Elias held up his carrier. "I found something."

Ulises's eyes widened. The scowl vanished. "Show me."

Together, they shoved aside the parchment and inkpots. The first map was unrolled, anchored by the shells. Elias said, "We're told to follow the path of the ancient mariners, north to south. And we're told to pay attention not to what is there but to what is not."

"Yes, I know," Ulises said, impatient. "What does it mean? It couldn't be less clear."

"Look close. Right there."

Javelin Forest was a massive woodland north of Cortes, off Marinus Road. A cluster of green marked its existence. In the center of the forest was a clearing, and within it, the map-maker had painted a woman seated on a tree stump. She was dressed in white, her hair covered by one of those cone-shaped wimples his great-aunt Fabiana still wore on occasion. If one squinted and strained, one could see the red cross painted over her chest. Clinging to her skirts were two children. Their faces were turned outward, toward the viewer, but their features had been left unpainted, so that they were merely blank white circles. It was an unnerving image, one that had sent the hairs dancing lightly along his arms when he'd first spotted them.

Ulises was frowning. "Javelin? It's exactly where it should be. He's even painted in the spirits."

He spoke of the children. Centuries ago, the forest had been home to a thriving orphanage run by nuns. The girls were raised to be royal woodcarvers. Once, their work was admired in the intricate carvings of the figureheads that graced del Mar's royal fleet. Until one summer night a mysterious fire had broken out, destroying the buildings and leaving no survivors. There were some who whispered of the abbess, and a doomed affair, and a rejected lover who had taken his revenge. But no one knew for certain, and there was none left to tell the tale. Since then, very few entered Javelin Forest. It was not a welcoming place for the living.

Elias prompted, "Look at the trees."

Ulises leaned closer, and closer still. He glanced over in surprise. "These are oaks."

"And alder," Elias said. Javelin was an anomaly in the Sea of Magdalen, a dense forest made entirely of palm trees and anchored by white sand.

Ulises looked skeptical. "It could be an error. It's a small detail, easy to miss."

"It's not a mistake." Of this, Elias was certain. He pointed to the inset of Cortes. "See here? He's painted the exact number of archways in the arena. I counted. Who takes that much care? Who is that obsessive?"

"You are," Ulises pointed out.

A quick grin. "True, but it's uncommon. And outside the maritime courts, that fat figure there in red. Do you recognize him?"

After a moment, Ulises said, "It's Judge Piri."

"Yes." Piri had worked for the maritime courts for decades,

most recently as a judge. He was a corpulent man, fond of his meals and wine, and always wore a red robe. Elias continued, "Whoever painted these knows del Mar like the back of his hand. It's not a mistake he would make." He could not help feeling a sense of professional admiration for the unnamed mapmaker. He found himself irritated by it.

"An orphanage that burned down hundreds of years ago," Ulises mused. "What does it have to do with anything?"

That, Elias could not answer. But . . . "Javelin is next to the meadow where your brothers were taken. You see?"

"Yes." Beside the forest was another clearing, this one bordered on three sides by a lemon grove, and on the fourth side by a hill covered in black rock.

Elias said, "It was the only oddity I could find before I lost the light." And finding more would take time. The images were so small that to study them for any length of time left him with a violent headache. It was almost as if the painter had not intended for anyone to actually see his work.

Ulises returned to his chair and propped his chin on his fist. "No one with any sense enters Javelin. Unless they have a death wish. Perhaps it is a trick."

Isn't that what Elias had said all along? "I'll find out."

Ulises heard what was not said. He asked carefully, "Then you'll see it through?"

Elias sat, weary beyond all measure. He was filthy; he was hungry. This day had gone on forever. "Are you giving me a choice?"

Ulises looked away, studying the moon for some time. Then, quietly, "I know what is said about me. That my reign is one born of tragedy. That I am king by default, the prince of mischance. Cursed."

For the first time, Elias saw a trace of bitterness around his friend's mouth. "Ulises —"

"And I know you've had your fist bloodied more than once in my defense," Ulises said. "Don't think I don't know what a friend you've been to me."

When they were boys, a fellow explorer, Luca, had repeated something about this supposed curse within his hearing. Elias had bloodied his nose and made him take the words back. It wasn't just Luca. He had not known Ulises was aware of what others said. It made him angry to think of it.

"Who cares what anyone else thinks?"

"I do," Ulises answered. "I know my skin is supposed to be thick. But I care what my kingdom thinks of me."

"It's not your kingdom that thinks these things," Elias said. "It's only a few, and they can go to the serpents."

Ulises looked over with a half smile. "We can't feed them all to the serpents. But if possible, I would have the truth, one way or the other." He rubbed his face with both hands. Elias was not the only one who was weary. "How can I look at these maps, see this riddle, and do nothing? They are my brothers."

Elias felt a tightness in his chest, even as he said, "They are dead."

"It's likely," Ulises acknowledged. "Prove it, and we'll never speak of it again."

Elias reached across the table and flicked aside two shells with a fingertip. The map curled into itself. "It's bound to be a goose chase. You know that?"

"Or a treasure hunt," Ulises countered, "and you've always been good at those." A lengthy pause. "I meant no insult to you, or to your lord father. That was not my intent."

Elias nodded, saying nothing. And when that did not feel sufficient, he cleared his throat and offered, "I shouldn't have spoken to you that way, in front of others."

Ulises smiled. As an apology to a king, it was a sad, feeble thing. But to a friend? Well. It was good enough.

Elias returned his smile, the tension easing from his shoulders. A thought occurred to him. "Why did Reyna bring her map to you, and not to her grandfather?"

Ulises thought back. "He wasn't in Cortes that day," he said, then surprised Elias by laughing. "You should have seen her. She didn't send a note asking to speak to me. She gave her name to the steward and waited in the queue with everyone else."

Elias thought of Reyna purchasing the map with her own coin, and he pictured her sitting quietly in the king's antechamber along with councilors and scribes and merchants, anyone seeking an audience with the king. The chamber was a daunting place for adults, all booming voices and men constantly speaking over one another. Reyna was only nine. Or ten. Whichever. Sitting in one of those chairs, her feet would not have even touched the ground. The image made him smile.

Glancing at the parchment and the inkpots scattered around the maps, he asked, "What are these?"

Ulises grimaced. "Everything you can imagine. Land disputes in the north. Tax disputes in the east. The head monk on Valdemossa needs funds for a new hospital. And you should see what our emissaries claim they need. You would think we send them off without a single gold squid to support them."

"You'll sign all of them?" Elias asked.

"Yes."

"Why can't the scribes do it? Or Mercedes? She's an excellent forger."

"She's already offered," Ulises said. "I'd rather do it myself. I want to know what has my name on it."

Elias was quiet. They lived by the sea, where the sun shone bright most of the year. Yet Ulises wore the pallor of a full-blooded Mondragan. How much time did he spend trapped in here with his inkpots and his councilors? Elias indicated the stacks of parchment and asked, "You enjoy this? Governing?"

"Most times I do."

"So did your father," Elias remembered, "but even he took a day for himself now and again. Del Mar would not collapse if you eased off a bit."

"An empty day?" Ulises looked baffled by the notion. "I wouldn't know what to do with it."

"Do what all kings do. Go to your summer palace. Hunt wild pigs. Lie on the beach and have a pretty girl feed you grapes."

Ulises snorted, and Elias said, "No, I'm serious. In Hellespont, King Ari took his afternoon meal on the beach, every day, and grapes were fed to him."

"By a pretty girl?"

"By a man." Elias frowned at the memory. "He looked like me somewhat. It was disconcerting."

Ulises laughed, a generous, rolling sound that was contagious. "Maybe later." He looked down at the map, his amusement fading. "Javelin, Elias. Of all places. How will you get in safely? How will you get out?"

Elias had been wondering the same thing, ever since he had spotted the abbess and her faceless wards. And because it was just the two of them, he answered honestly.

"Old friend, I'm damned if I know."

Elias owned two estates: one in the central mountains, the other on the northeastern coast. But when he was in Cortes, he lived in the castle, on the uppermost level of the Tower of Winds. These chambers had been empty for some time before he'd taken them over four years ago. The last person who'd lived here had been Lord Antoni, before his marriage.

Elias's work chamber was as he'd left it, filled with globes, sundials, and, to anyone but him, a seemingly endless collection

of compasses. Dry compasses and wet compasses. Crude compasses fashioned from halved coconut shells. Another set within
an ivory box. There were maps everywhere, framed on walls
or rolled into teetering pyramids upon every surface. A single
candle burned on a table, but the chamber just beyond, his bedchamber, was brightly lit.

He found Basilio kneeling beside his open trunk, feeding
his clothes into the fire. Elias could not help a laugh. "Those are
usable still," he said in greeting, tossing his carrier onto the bed.

When Elias had moved from the family home into the castle, Basilio had come with him. Reluctantly. Elias's mother had
known that if left to his own whims, her son would gladly spend
his days in what she called his "mapper's rags," frayed clothing
stained with ancient paint and charcoal dust, and bring her an
everlasting shame. Basilio had accepted his new responsibilities
with the squared shoulders and stoicism of a man wrongfully
condemned.

Basilio continued to feed the flames. He was several years
older than Elias, short and round-faced, as neatly dressed as
Elias was not. He said, "There are washerwomen in Hellespont.
Seamstresses, menders . . ." He glanced across the chamber at
Elias and closed his eyes briefly. "There are people to trim your
hair. Surely it did not need to come to this."

Elias ran a hand down his face, so rough it could sand driftwood, and offered the same words he used whenever he returned
from off island. "Apologies, Basilio. I'll try to do better next
time."

Basilio sighed, knowing he was being humored. "Welcome home, Lord Elias," he said. "Supper or a bath. Which would you like first?"

At the word *bath*, Elias raised one arm and sniffed, rearing back in disgust. Basilio was already heading toward the adjacent bathing chamber when Elias said, "A bath."

For Elias, the long night was not over. Basilio had long since retired to his own chambers one level below when his master dressed in dark clothing, grabbed his carrier and his dagger, and headed out into the night. Early summer brought with it warmer days, but nightfall still carried a chill, and he was left wishing he had thought to bring a cloak.

At the castle gates, he ducked beneath the portcullis just as it began a slow, rattling descent. When one of the guards called down a warning, "Lord Elias, the gates will be closed until sunrise," Elias raised a hand in acknowledgment, said "Then I'll see you tomorrow," and continued on his way.

It was for the best. The angry words he'd thrown at Mercedes bothered him, and even now it was tempting to steal away to her wing of the castle and pound on her door. He kicked at a rock, sent it spinning down the street. Better the gates were locked behind him. Better he stayed away tonight.

Like most large cities, Cortes's parishes were shaped by profession. In one quarter, he passed the shuttered storefronts of fabric sellers and purse makers, hatters and glove makers. In another, the goldsmiths and silversmiths. Rings and necklaces would be on proud display in the daylight hours, alongside delicate cups and bowls painted with images of the sea: sirens, serpents, a storm-tossed ship. Near the harbor, merchants catered to travelers by selling maps and compasses and the services of guides and translators.

He wandered through narrow, mazy lanes, guided by the moon and the flickering of candlelight in the windows. A solitary figure in the night. Or nearly so. As he turned down one street, a dark form held up a wall, eyeing him from the shadows. Elias placed a hand on the hilt of his dagger; he made sure the stranger saw him do it. "I would not try it," he advised, and after a brief, considering moment, his would-be robber melted back into the stones.

After a time, he found himself on the edge of town in the parish of St. Medina, home to many of the island's noble families. The streets were wider here, cleaner, with high sandstone walls shielding the luxury within. He stopped before one wall and ran a hand along the stone. The notches were where he remembered. Grabbing hold, he climbed up and over, dropping lightly to his feet. A large house rose before him, windows shuttered and dark. A fountain trickled quietly in the courtyard. Circling the house, he made his way around to the back and let himself in, expecting to feel his way about in blackness. To his surprise, the kitchen fireplace gave off a faint glow. Immediately, he felt a knife at his jugular.

"I'm tempted to slice your gullet first, then ask questions

second, thief." The voice was the scraping of a blade against stone. As familiar to Elias as his own.

"Papa, it's me."

"Elias?" The knife disappeared. "What are you doing, skulking in the dark?"

"I wasn't skulking. I didn't want to wake —" he managed, before his mother's husband grabbed him up in a bone-crushing embrace.

Lord Isidore was del Mar's Lord Exchequer, principal guardian of the royal finances. He was a big man, taller even than Elias and twice his width. A full, bushy beard showed more black than gray. His stepfather was considered a stern, intimidating figure to many. But most did not have the pleasure of seeing him as he was now, dressed in a voluminous white night robe with lace at the sleeves. He had come into Elias's life when the boy was nearly five, wooing both mother and son with such single-minded determination that Sabine, Lady Isidore, laughingly referred to their courtship as a siege.

Lord Isidore stepped back and inspected him, frowning. "Your *maman* is not going to like what's happened to your face."

"I know it. I wasn't sure I'd find you here."

"You nearly did not. We leave in the morning. Are you hungry? Come, help me eat this."

This was a feast. In the center of the kitchen was the cook's worktable. Lord Isidore had pulled from the larder bread, lobster, fish eggs, and crab legs the size of a man's forearm. So much food that Elias could almost believe he had been expected.

At the very edge of the table was a straw basket. As he watched, a small, dimpled leg poked straight up in the air before dangling over the side.

Lord Isidore looked over his shoulder at the basket. "He's just over a fever," he said in a low voice. "Let's speak quietly here."

Elias propped his carrier against the table before leaning over Jonas, the youngest of his three siblings, who had passed his first birthday while Elias was on Hellespont. A thumb was planted firmly in his mouth. In the time Elias had been gone, his brother's cheeks had hollowed out some, so that he looked more child than infant.

"He looks just like Nieve," Elias said quietly, with some surprise. Nieve was his sister closest to him in age, at twelve. Lea was six. "He's twice the size I remember."

Lord Isidore had settled comfortably into a chair. He pointed a crab leg at Elias in warning. "Don't say that to your *maman*. Please. She's already hinting at another."

Elias grimaced at the thought, then kissed Jonas on the forehead. "You're both too old to be having babies. I'm embarrassed every time another appears."

His comment provoked a low rumble of laughter from Lord Isidore, who said, "Sleep in your old chamber tonight. Don't argue. You give me gray hairs, wandering the streets at this hour."

Elias smiled. Already he was glad to have come here. Almost, he could forget the maps in his carrier with their unsettling riddle. He said, "I've wandered through worse."

"Don't remind me." Lord Isidore gestured toward the food. "Eat, and tell me why you're a month late returning home. You know your *maman* worries."

Elias *was* hungry, though he had eaten his fill just hours ago. He was also chilled; the fire was in danger of disappearing completely. A leather tub filled with water and dwarf sea serpents occupied its usual place in the corner. The serpents were about three feet long. One had to be mindful because they resembled the harmless sea worm, but these were malicious, with sharp teeth and nasty dispositions. Delicious, though. Most had drifted to the bottom, where they curled around one another in sleep, blissfully unaware the cook intended them for supper. Only one remained on the surface, jade green in color and swimming the edges of the tub in slow, desultory circles.

Elias shoved his sleeves past his elbows and reached into the tub, snatching the snake just behind its mouth and grabbing its tail with his other hand. Ignoring his stepfather's terse "For pity's sake, boy, have a care!" he strode toward the fireplace. Aiming the snake at the embers, he gave the tail one swift yank and loosened his hold on the jaw, enough so that the snake, riled and indignant, spewed forth a single stream of fire. Instantly the fire crackled and burned with a welcoming heat. Satisfied, Elias tossed the snake back into the tub. It gave off one last resentful hiss before slithering beneath the surface.

Lord Isidore was torn between consternation and amusement. "You could not use a poker like the rest of us?"

Elias grinned. "This was quicker."

"I've missed you, boy." Lord Isidore shoved the platter of lobster his way. "When does your ship leave next?"

"Six weeks."

They stayed up for a time, sharing their news. Lord Isidore did not live in the city during the summer months but conducted his affairs from the family home outside the northern village of Esperanca. Elias had never been more grateful for its distance. Any news and gossip they received from Cortes would be few and far between. It would be better if his family was away, safe from any whispers that might stray to their ears.

A memory came to him, of sitting outside Lord Silva's chambers for the first time, no older than five, watching the geographers hard at their work and the giant, brooding statue of Saint Cosme.

The door had been left ajar. From Lord Silva, Elias heard, *Of course we'll see to the child's training. Nothing would give me greater pleasure. But are you certain, Isidore?*

I am.

Truly? Elias is your son now, under the law, to follow whatever path you choose for him. It is your right.

A rueful laugh from his stepfather. *That may be, but the boy isn't meant to live his life indoors, with an abacus.* A chair scraped. *Do you know . . . he spends his days copying Antoni's maps? He's quite good at it. And last week, he disappeared after supper. We turned the parish upside down searching for him. Sabine was frantic.*

Where was he?

I found him on the roof. He was trying to chart the stars. A brief silence fell before Lord Isidore continued, quieter, so Elias had to lean closer to the door to hear. *I have a wife and a son now, Lord Silva. I won't begrudge Antoni this. Please, I would like you to train the child.*

Very well.

What would happen to Elias's family if the existence of the maps became known? Even if nothing were proven, the validity of Lord and Lady Isidore's marriage would be called into question, as well as the legitimacy of their three children. The world was an unkind place to bastards. His sister's marriage prospects would suffer greatly. And his mother . . . he looked away from the carrier propped against the table and tried not to think of the maps rolled within. Resenting their very existence.

Ink and paint and parchment, a threat to his family.

Jonas stirred in his basket. Elias gathered him up before he could wake the entire household, cradling him against his shoulder and walking the length of the chamber, over and over, until his brother settled. He was comforted just being under this roof, knowing his family was safe within, and passing the small hours of the night with the man who had raised him.

Lord Isidore, the only father he knew.

FIVE

I N THE MORNING, Elias descended the staircase into chaos. Servants rushed through the front doors, loading trunks and baskets onto carriages. His stepfather was by the fountain, speaking with a guard. Lord Isidore's white sleeping lace had been replaced with practical traveling clothes: a leather doublet and black cape; a sword on his back and a dagger at his belt. Elias leaned out the door, the early summer sunlight pleasant on his skin. A good day for travel.

He called out, "When do you leave?"

Lord Isidore looked over and smiled. "Momentarily," he answered. "I want to be in Tortri before sundown. We'll stay the night with my brother."

A sensible plan. Only the foolish braved the roads at night, when thieves waited patiently beyond the bend, their movements masked by cricket song. But it would leave Elias with very little time to say goodbye. He squinted up at the sun, goggling as he realized the hour.

"Why didn't anyone wake me?"

"We tried," Lord Isidore said with some dryness. "Nieve

found Lea jumping on your bed and you right beside her. She had to check to see if you were still breathing."

Elias laughed. "No."

"Yes. You sleep like the dead, boy." Lord Isidore turned away, distracted by a question from the guard, then added over his shoulder, "Your *maman* is in the solar."

From deep within the house came a burst of feminine laughter followed by a baby's high-pitched screech. Elias followed the sounds, pausing long enough to accept a cup from a passing servant. He downed its contents — Lunesian coffee, thicker than tree sap, the way he liked it, and strong enough to set his heart racing. He handed the empty cup off to another servant.

Elias had to make a conscious effort not to tug at his clothing. Basilio had tracked him to his parents' house with scary efficiency, something he would have to accustom himself to again after months of living in the rough. Now he wore a leather vest over a white shirt and trousers that were more constricting than he was comfortable with. He knew he wasn't imagining it; the fashions on del Mar grew tighter each year. He wondered who made these decisions, and thought perhaps he should have a quick word with them. Basilio had also forced on him a summer cloak in a green so dark it appeared nearly black, further embellished with a gold compass pin.

It was customary for female family and friends to send a woman off when she departed for any significant length of time. His family would be gone for three turns of the moon, returning when the early autumn rains began to fall. He found his mother reigning over a visiting chamber full of relatives. Women and children, from his great-aunt Fabiana to Jonas, who toddled frantically across the chamber as a cousin pretended to chase him. The older women draped themselves over chairs and settees while the younger sat upon the rugs, dressed so colorfully that they reminded him of a bowl of fruit. Here was an entire room filled with grapes and jujubes, pomegranates, lemons, and mandarins.

Nieve spotted him first. "Elias!" His sister ran across the chamber and flung herself at him. He caught her, laughing, then waded in, greeting aunts, nieces, and cousins. It took some time. He made sure the carrier strapped to his back did not inadvertently strike someone. Returning home always gave him a jolt, for his family was never exactly as he'd left them. His elders changed in subtle ways: the curve of a back a little more pronounced, the lines about the face more settled. But the transformation among his siblings and younger cousins was the most dramatic. They sprang up like sageweed, one day as tall as his knees, the next his chin, their faces thinner, or not, or full of spots, but never quite the same.

He bent to kiss his mother — Sabine, Lady Isidore — on both cheeks. "Maman."

Lady Isidore's face was wreathed in a smile. Her skin, barely lined, contrasted sharply with hair that was a pure white. Elias had never known it to be any other color. Aunt Fabiana had told him that once it had been a rich brown streaked with gold, like his, but had turned white during those terrible months following her husband's disappearance.

"How tired you must have been," his mother said, "that you did not hear the stampede in your chamber this morn —" Her smile faded. She took his chin and turned it, first one way and then the other. "What has happened to your face?"

He pulled away slightly. "A scratch."

She gave him a look. "It is far larger than a *scratch*."

"It doesn't hurt. . . ." He trailed off, startled. Nearly hidden behind his mother, her red skirts spread about the rugs, was Mercedes. She sat patiently while his youngest sister, Lea, knelt behind her, attempting to gather her waist-length hair into a braid. A red peony the size of a Coronad's fist was tucked over one ear. Mercedes smiled at him pleasantly; the ugly scene yesterday might never have taken place. His mood soured.

"You're looking much cleaner today, Elias," Mercedes commented. "Basilio must have found you."

"Mercedes." He leaned over to accept Lea's damp kisses and give Mercedes a dark look. She pretended not to see, turning her back to allow Lea a better grip on her hair and to strike up a conversation with his cousin Dita. A cheerful argument ensued about the superiority of Lunesian versus Oslawn silk.

"Wasn't it kind of Mercedes to see us off today?" His mother smiled. "Such a lovely surprise."

"Yes. Kind." He managed to keep his voice even, though he knew exactly why she was here. Not to bid his family farewell, at least not entirely. Their mothers had been friends. This home had been Mercedes's refuge after the lady Alyss's death. But unlike Ulises, who had accepted Elias's word that he would give the maps every consideration, Mercedes would stay close to his side to make sure he did. She was first and foremost the king's man. Or woman. Whichever.

Annoyed, he turned back to his mother. "I'm sorry to be missing you."

"Well." Lady Isidore placed a hand briefly on the gold compass pinned to his cloak. Once, it had belonged to Lord Antoni. "I'm grateful to catch a glimpse of you when I can. When will you visit?"

He sat on his heels, trying to think things through as the conversation and laughter continued around them. In six weeks' time, five ships would sail west past the Strait of Cain on expeditions that would last anywhere from six months to three years. The *Aldene*, the *Amaris*, the *Nina*, the *Palma*, and the *St. Clementina*. On every ship, in addition to captain and crew, would be a pilot major to navigate the vessel and a geographer to survey the land and people. Elias was to take on his usual role as geographer for the *Amaris* and was expected to be gone two years at least.

His original plan had been simple. Upon returning from Hellespont — an unexpected trip: no one could have anticipated those earthquakes or the destruction they would cause — he would travel to his family's home in Esperanca and stay a month. Enough time to ensure his sisters at least recognized his face when next he appeared. Then he would return to Cortes to prepare for the expedition. There was parchment to acquire, paints to mix, equipment to ensure was in working order: compasses, astrolabes, chronometers, quadrants . . . a hundred things to do.

Now what? His plans were thrown into uncertainty with these maps. When would he have the time to visit? "There are things I need to finish here, Maman, that I had not planned on. I'll come as soon as I can. I'll send word."

"I promised your father I wouldn't hover." She studied him, her gaze lingering on the bruise. "But you'll be careful?"

He smiled. "Always." Unsurprisingly, his mother did not look reassured by his promise.

Against his will, his attention returned to Mercedes. She was different here with his family. Her smile unguarded and Jonas on her lap. Assuring Lea that her handiwork was quite fine, she would wear her braid all day. She was very pretty with that flower in her hair. His thoughts were interrupted when Aunt Fabiana rapped his shoulder twice with her fan.

"How old are you now, boy?" His aunt wore purple, her hair covered by a black lace headdress, her face a maze of wrinkles.

He bit back a sigh. He didn't need a compass to know where this was headed. "Nineteen, Aunt."

"Nineteen? And still not married?" A quelling look was sent to his mother, whose expression said, *I agree, but what is to be done?* Aunt Fabiana swiveled back to him. "When I was nineteen, I was married already. Three babies."

Mercedes looked over at that, eyes widening.

"I'm never home," Elias reasoned. "It wouldn't be fair to find a wife and then constantly leave her." He ignored the snicker from Dita, who, at eighteen, was betrothed and therefore no longer a target for their great-aunt's questioning.

"What is this reason?" Aunt Fabiana was unimpressed by his argument. "You go on your ship. You come back; you make babies. You go. That is how it was with my Henri."

Despite his best efforts, Elias could feel his ears turning red. "*Maman*," he whispered in desperation, and his mother laughed.

"Oh, look," Lady Isidore said, glancing past him. "There's Isidore."

His stepfather stood in the doorway, showing no interest in entering farther. A wise man. "My lady wife, we're off."

Lady Isidore smiled across the chamber at her husband as a mass exodus took place around her. Skirts rustled and children were gathered as everyone made their way outdoors. Most would be fleeing the city themselves in the coming days, Elias knew. *Good.* Better they were gone. Relatives always knew more than you wanted them to.

Mercedes kissed his mother on both cheeks. "You'll be missed, my lady Isidore. Safe travels to you and your family."

"I will see you in the fall, child." Lady Isidore patted Mercedes's cheek. "Unless my son has the good sense to bring you with him for a visit." She looked at Elias, eyes merry. "So pretty," she added, provoking good-natured teasing from those within hearing.

Both Elias and Mercedes were careful not to look at each other. His mother had never been subtle when it came to the king's cousin. By unspoken agreement, he and Mercedes stayed where they were until the chamber emptied.

Unsmiling, Elias said, "You're following me."

"You are all things suspicious. I'd planned all along to send your *maman* off today." Mercedes flicked her braid forward over a shoulder. The end unraveled slightly. "However, since you are here . . ."

He turned on his heel to leave. Her words came to him quietly.

"I should not have let you walk into that chamber blind."

With his back to her, he asked, "Why did you?"

"I didn't know what to say."

He turned to face her and saw the apology in her eyes. "You always know what to say, Mercedes. That is your gift."

It was why she was so rarely on island. Ulises sent her everywhere. To reassure allies and to treat with enemies. To use words, not weapons, to ensure the continued well-being of their kingdom. He wondered if Ulises sensed she was more at ease abroad than at home. More comfortable with strangers than among the del Marians, whose heritage she shared.

"Not this time," she answered.

She said nothing more, only stood there waiting for his response, and he found he could no longer hold on to his annoyance. A leather string kept his own hair off his face. He pulled it free as he approached her.

She stepped back, startled. "What are you . . . ?"

He indicated the braid in her hair. "Did you wish to keep it?"

"Oh." She glanced down at the lumpy, untidy braid. "Yes. I promised Lea I would."

He did not rush, tying the braid. Her hair smelled like the blood oranges that grew in the royal groves. "I'd forgotten how sweet you are to my sisters."

She had kept herself perfectly still and silent while he took his time. Now she said, "It's nothing unusual. I'm sweet to everyone."

Elias met her eyes, not saying a word, and saw her answering smile.

"What were you doing on Lunes?" he asked. "You weren't there just to steal maps."

"Vashti's wedding. What else?"

"Ah." He had forgotten about the Lunesian princess's wedding. The sounds of laughter in the distance reminded him he was ignoring what little time he had left with his family. He offered Mercedes his arm as they left the chamber and headed toward the main doors.

She said, "You've never been able to keep a grudge."

"Lucky for you."

"Yes," she said with a smile in her voice. She glanced at him, turning serious. "I'm glad. It would have hurt him to lose your friendship."

Elias was quiet. "Ulises has plenty of friends."

"No," she said with certainty. "He has people who wish to be close to him because he is king." Her hand tightened ever so slightly on his arm. "When things are peaceful, everyone dances attendance, everyone makes promises, and everyone would die for him so long as death is far off."

Amused, he said, "You're a cynic, Mercedes."

"It's true." She shrugged. "It's also true that I wouldn't have your family hurt for anything. So let's solve your riddle, and be done with it."

"As simple as that?" They passed a life-size painting of the fifth Lord Isidore, the present lord's grandfather. Not Elias's ancestor, but a reminder, in oil and wood, that for all his step-father's affection, he was no blood relation. Unlike Nieve and Lea and Jonas, Elias was the cuckoo in the nest.

Mercedes studied the painting, then looked up at him, and he had the unsettling feeling that she knew what he thought. But she said only, "Why not? I'll help. Ulises told me of your creepy forest. That is unfortunate."

"You didn't see it?" The map had been in her possession for some time. She could have studied it on the voyage home from Lunes.

She shook her head. "It makes my head hurt to look at it for more than a few minutes. It's all so tiny." Then, in a softer voice, conscious of passing servants and lingering relatives, "Have you never wondered?"

"No." Yes. Of course he had wondered. Once or twice over the years, a little more than that over the past day.

"Elias," she said, only a hint of exasperation in her voice. "An entire kingdom sacked, based on one man's word?"

She spoke of Felip of Mondrago. The captured soldier, who had spilled his king's secrets . . . and started a war.

"He confessed," Elias reminded her.

"I've heard many confessions," she said. "Enough to know that they are not all created equal." She would have said more, but two serving girls bustled by, arms full of baskets, and the moment was lost. Mercedes turned the conversation back to the forest. "What about Javelin? What is your plan?"

To call what he had a plan was ambitious. He would describe it more as grasping at straws. He said, "I'm going to have my hair trimmed."

She stopped. "What?"

Through the front doors, from Nieve: "Elias! We're *leaving!*"

They joined everyone on the steps, but it was some time before the family actually departed. There were delays. A horse had to be exchanged; a crack had been found in its shoe. Lea refused to leave until a beloved toy was found, a wooden monkey Elias had brought back from his travels several years ago. Eventually, it was discovered in a trunk above the third carriage.

Elias was accustomed to farewells. They were second nature to him. But today it gave him an odd feeling to kiss his mother one last time and watch the carriages rumble around the fountain and through the gates. To see Lord Isidore on his horse raise a hand in farewell. "Mercedes," he called, "watch after my boy." And then he, too, was gone, riding alongside his guards and leaving a cloud of white shell dust in his wake.

SIX

N THE PARISH of St. Soledad, just outside the barber-surgeon's shop, a piper played a lively tune. He was Nieve's age, and so scrawny that when he kicked up his heels to add dancing to his repertoire, Elias was reminded of a puppet on a string. Mori often hired musicians to perform outside his shop so as to mask the sounds of agony. It made good business sense, he'd once told Elias. Screams scared away the customers.

Not that it always worked. As they crossed the square toward the shop, Mercedes said what he was thinking. "It sounds like someone is being murdered in there."

The piper's music was loud, though he could not drown out the muffled cries from within. It was not for lack of effort. As the yelps and moans grew noisier, he piped louder and danced faster. Off to the right, a cluster of urchins gathered by the window, lured by the blood and gore that was the barber-surgeon's trademark. A wooden sign hung above Master Mori's door. Painted on it was an arm, bent at the elbow and bound in a white sling.

The piper brightened when he saw them. He paused long

enough to pocket the copper sand dollar Elias tossed his way, then danced from the open door so they could enter. Elias followed Mercedes, pulling up short when she stopped abruptly just inside the doorway.

Over the top of her head, he saw a crowded chamber with low wooden beams. A man occupied a chair, his mouth open at such a wide angle that the pink toggle at the back of his throat was clearly visible. Mori stood behind him. He held a pair of wicked-looking pliers and, as Elias looked on in mute sympathy, did his best to yank a tooth while his poor patient struggled weakly beneath him and moaned.

Mori was a slender man with black hair, stubble, and an apron splattered with blood. Elias had told Mercedes some of their history on the walk over. They'd met when Elias was a boy on his first expedition aboard the *Amaris* and Mori was the ship's surgeon. A few years later, during a storm, Mori had been thrown overboard. He was rescued eventually, but not before a sea serpent had given him a nasty bite on his lower back. Shortly thereafter, the barber-surgeon had declared his sailing days over. He'd returned to del Mar and set up shop near the waterfront.

Mori had yet to see them, so preoccupied was he with the inside of his patient's mouth. "Be still," he commanded. "You're only making it worse." A string of terse mutterings ended with a "*Why* is this tooth so stubborn?"

The patient's legs twisted and flopped and his feet tapped an unnerving tattoo upon the floor, like fish flailing upon a ship's deck. One boot rapped a nearby table leg, rattling an assortment of scissors, pincers, and saws. Flies buzzed around a heap of bloody rags flung across the tabletop.

Mercedes said in an undertone, "You have interesting friends."

He spoke close to her ear. "You're my friend," he pointed out, making her laugh.

Which Mori heard. "Elias!" His gaze swept over Mercedes and pinned Elias in the doorway. His greeting consisted of a barked, "Don't just stand there, man! Hold his boots."

Obliging, Elias sidled around Mercedes. He crossed the chamber and knelt before the patient, grabbing the man's boots and holding fast. It must have rained early this morning. The shoes were caked in a foul-smelling mud. The man gave a half-hearted kick, one Elias dodged. He watched Mori wrestle with the patient's insides — more rotted teeth and soured gums — and found he did not have the stomach for surgery so early in the day. He turned his head. Mercedes had made herself at home on a stool at the opposite end of the table, safe from any splatter, blood or otherwise.

"Ha!" the barber announced as he finally managed to pull the tooth out. It sailed through the air, joining the scattering of teeth among the rushes. Mori grinned at Elias, all surliness gone now that his task was accomplished. "Just like old times, eh?"

"I remember differently." Elias moved away from the patient. He grabbed a somewhat clean cloth from the table and wiped the mud from his hands. "Remind me never to come to you with a sore tooth."

"Ha," Mori said again. His grin disappeared as the patient slid off the chair. He landed on his knees, holding his jaw and moaning. "Oh, get up, man," Mori said to him. "It was only one tooth. No need to be such an old woman about it. Here, take this." He hauled the patient off the floor with one hand and grabbed a flask from the table with the other.

The patient cast a doubtful look at the flask. "Whath ith it?" The left side of his face had already begun to swell. A thin line of blood trickled down his jaw.

Elias had caught a whiff as the flask passed him by. He offered up a "Smells like poppy juice and cat pi —"

"It's *ground yarrow.*" Mori sent an irritable look Elias's way before shoving the flask into the patient's hand. "Gargle once a day. Do *not* swallow. You'll feel excellent in a day or two."

The patient turned obediently and stumbled through the door. Past the piper playing a cheery tune.

Mori cleaned off his hands with another rag. "When did you sail in? Hellespont, was it?"

"Just yesterday."

"How's the old man?"

He meant Lord Silva. "Still strong enough to box you if he heard you calling him an old man."

Amused, Mori glanced past Elias to Mercedes, perched on the stool and watching their exchange. His mouth fell open.

Clearly, he'd only now recognized the king's cousin. He bowed. "Lady Mercedes! I did not see you. Please forgive . . ." He looked down at his apron, at the gory condition of his tabletop, and winced. "Everything. You are welcome here."

"Master Mori." Mercedes looked perfectly comfortable; she might have spent every morning surrounded by teeth carpeting the floor and chatting with men covered in blood. "Elias tells me you sailed together on the *Amaris*. You must have some tales to tell. Though maybe only one or two you can share with company, knowing Elias."

She had hoped to put the barber at ease, Elias knew, and it worked. The stiff formality, which sat unnaturally on Mori, melted away.

Mori laughed. "Two would be ambitious, Lady," he agreed. To Elias: "Are you hurt?" Mori half-circled around him in the manner of a customs inspector. "You've the bruise there. What else?"

"No, there's nothing . . ." Elias looked at Mercedes, brows raised. *How much to tell him?* He trusted Mori, but the fewer people who knew about the maps, the better. She lifted one shoulder in response to his silent question — the decision was his — and fiddled with the gold chain encircling her waist.

Mori saw the exchange. His gaze followed Mercedes's hands, settling briefly on her stomach. He turned sober. "I see," he said.

Elias looked at his friend, perplexed. What did he see? They hadn't told him a thing.

"It's a romantic problem you have." Mori leaned against the table and scratched his jaw. "Well, it's happened to the best of us. I'm glad you came to me, but I have to tell you, Elias, I'm no lady barber. I can recommend a good midwife, though, discreet —"

Mercedes snatched her hands away from the chain. Elias could feel the fire on his face. He groaned, *"Mori."*

"What? No?" Mori looked from one to the other. He smacked his forehead. "I'm an idiot —"

"Yes," Elias said.

"An imbecile. My sincerest apologies, Lady —"

"There's no need." Mercedes would not look at Elias. High color swept her cheekbones. "We're here for information, Master Barber, nothing more."

And because Elias knew Mori would not accept coin without performing some sort of service, he added, "And a grooming, if you've time. Basilio's away." Mercedes glanced over at the lie, casually told, but did not give him away.

"Ah." Still chagrined, Mori lifted a handful of Elias's hair and let it fall back to his shoulders. "You've let it grow too long. Like a woman. Sit."

Mercedes rose and held out her hand. When Elias gave her his carrier, she wandered the shop's edges, where Mori kept his curiosities on display upon high tables. Human skulls resided by animal heads in varying shades of brown. A delicate blue bowl held a small mountain of teeth. Elias watched her. She wore his carrier as he did, resting across her back with the strap diagonally across her chest. It felt intensely personal to see it on her, as though she wore a shirt that belonged to him. A small sound had him turning to find Mori eyeing him with amusement.

"Sit," Mori repeated. When Elias settled on the stool Mercedes had left, Mori selected shears from the instruments on the table. He said, "So. What sort of information do you need?"

Elias said, "You told me once you grew up near Javelin."

"I did." Distracted, Mori looked across the chamber. Mercedes studied a painting on the wall of a serene-looking woman dressed in a white robe and holding a pair of pliers. "That is Appolonia, Lady."

Mercedes smiled. "Patron saint of dentists? Yes, I recognize the pliers."

"Have you studied the saints?" Mori asked, surprised and pleased. "Very few people do anymore."

"I know a little." Beside the painting was a glass cage on a shelf. The glass was cloudy, difficult to see into. She leaned in for a closer look.

"Careful," Elias said.

The warning came too late. What looked like a fat red worm the size of a man's foot thumped against the glass, hard enough to rattle the cage and send a tremor throughout the entire shelf. Mercedes sprang away like a startled cat, causing both men to chuckle. The creature squirmed against the glass — it looked as though it were stuck — before sliding slowly to the bottom, leaving a thick trail of blood in its wake.

"*Ugh.*" Mercedes turned to them, repulsed. "That is the biggest worm I've ever seen!"

"It's a Bushido fire leech," Elias said. When he'd last visited, it had measured the length of his thumb. "It's growing fast, Mori. You're going to need a bigger cage."

"I'm having one built. They're very good for cleaning wounds," Mori said to Mercedes. "For getting rid of poisons. You can't keep more than one in a cage, though. They tend to eat one another."

"*Ugh.*" Mercedes shuddered and moved off. As she circled the chamber, Mori stepped behind Elias, grabbed a handful of hair, and twisted. He answered Elias's earlier question. "We lived on the southern edge of Javelin, outside Montserrat."

"Your father was a healer also, wasn't he?"

Mori made a sound of agreement. "A better one than I could ever be."

"Is it true he would travel within the forest? On his own?"

A startled silence from Mori, but Mercedes looked across the chamber at Elias, and on her face was a sudden understanding.

Mori released Elias's hair and came around to face him, the shears dangling from his hand. "Where did you hear this?" he demanded.

"You told me," Elias explained. "On the *Amaris*. I was seven, maybe. You said there was a rare plant that grew there. Plants that lessened a person's chance of infection."

Mori frowned. "I don't remember telling you this. I don't remember telling anyone."

"It was during your fever." The serpent bite on Mori's back

had caused a sweating sickness that had lasted many days. Elias and the rest of the crew, including Lord Silva, had taken turns by Mori's side, keeping him fed and watered. Listening to his ravings.

Mercedes came over. She gave Elias a strange look. "You recall something Master Mori said during a fever twelve years ago?"

Mori didn't give Elias a chance to answer. "And I spoke of my father wandering through a forest?" A mottled red had spread across his face. "Saint Mary. What else did I say?"

"Mori, this is important," Elias said. "Was the part about Javelin true? Men aren't supposed to go anywhere near that forest. Do you know how he did it?"

Mori whistled through his teeth. "Is that what you need to do?"

"Yes."

Mori didn't say anything right away. He disappeared behind Elias, who felt his hair sliced off with the shears.

"Much better," Mercedes commented.

Mori continued his trimming. *Snip snip* as locks of hair fell to the floor. The chamber was noticeably brighter. The urchins had little interest in watching a hair trim and had abandoned their post by the window. A cheerful sunlight filtered in. Mori said at last, "My father walked into Javelin once. My *maman* was ill from childbirth, and her only chance came from the minna bush that grew there. He had no choice."

"I don't think I do either." Elias had made his king a promise. There was no going back on his word.

Mori set the shears aside. He perched on the edge of the table. "Elias, I would wish my greatest enemy into that forest and no one else. It's not a friendly place for people like you and me."

"Men, you mean?"

"That's right," Mori said. "There were no men in that abbey. Only nuns and girls. They're not happy when we enter their space. What's in Javelin that you need?"

Elias glanced over at Mercedes with his carrier. "It's not something I can tell you. I'm sorry."

Mori did not appear offended, only thoughtful as he rubbed his chin. "When will you go?"

"Now if I can."

Mori made a disagreeable sound. "You won't have as much daylight if you leave now. And who knows how long you'll be there doing whatever it is you're doing? Better to go first thing."

Elias had wanted to get this over with quickly, but Mori's words made sense. "Tomorrow, then."

Mori said, "I've seen men enter Javelin and never return. But that was because they didn't follow the rules."

So there was a way. Hopeful, Elias asked, "What rules?"

"You'll have to recite the *oratio*. Do you remember it?"

"Yes." Lord Silva had taught the prayer to him. *May the guardians of old protect me in daytime, and at night . . .* It was the kind of prayer one uttered during a storm at sea, when the ship was in grave danger of capsizing and drowning appeared imminent. Or when being chased unexpectedly by wild pigs. It had happened. To Elias, more than once. Who knew if the prayer actually worked, but it made him feel better to say it. And he was still here, wasn't he, mostly in one piece?

Mercedes looked skeptical. "A simple protection prayer? Surely that isn't all?"

"No," Mori agreed. "He'll need some sort of offering. They may be spirits, but they're children still. Girls."

Elias shifted uncomfortably at the mention of spirits, but he said evenly enough, "Dolls, maybe?"

The look Mercedes sent him was pained. "That is your first choice? Not every girl enjoys playing with dolls."

Elias gave her a considering glance. He guessed again. "Knives?"

Mori started to smile and then thought better of it. Mercedes ignored Elias, instead addressing the barber. "Sweets?"

"Yes," Mori said. "My father brought small cakes and ribbons. And a few toys. Those little carved whistles you can find at market."

Mercedes frowned, committing his words to memory. "That is simple enough. Is there anything else?"

Mori hesitated. "My father . . . he brought a lucky charm with him."

"What, like a fish bone?" Elias asked.

"Like a female," Mori corrected. "A girl would be preferable, but a woman should do. You cannot enter that forest without a female presence. We would never see you again."

A silence fell.

"Who was your father's charm?" Mercedes asked.

"My sister," Mori answered quietly. "She was three days old. He strapped her to his chest, and off they went. That was the worst day for me, waiting to see if they would come back. And watching my *maman* grow sicker."

Elias wasn't sure he wanted to know the end of this story. What had happened to Mori's poor sick mother? He would not ask.

Mercedes felt differently. With one hand pressed against her heart, she demanded, "And? What happened to your *maman*? Did they return in time? Did the shrub work? Where is your sister now?"

"Mercedes," Elias muttered, "for pity's sake —"

"It worked." Mori's smile was faint. "My mother is healthier than I am. She lives with my sister and her husband. And their six children."

A happy ending. Perhaps tomorrow would be the same for Elias. But first, he needed a prayer, a present, and a lady. He looked at Mercedes. Not a flicker in those green eyes, but he knew her thoughts as clearly as if she'd spoken them aloud.

"No," he said.

They were still arguing as they left Mori's and made their way through the parish's narrow streets and twisting alleys. St. Soledad was a mariner's neighborhood. All around them, Elias recognized the boatmen and porters and sailcloth makers who earned their living by the harbor. Rich and poor called St. Soledad their home: the sea captains at one end behind walls and gates; the rest above ground-floor shops, three or four generations of a family packed into tight quarters.

"You heard what Master Mori said. It makes sense for me to go."

"I'm going alone." Elias pulled Mercedes aside as a cart rolled past. Large barrels were packed in behind horse and driver, each piled high with freshly caught fish. "I'll find another way."

But he was afraid he was out of luck. He'd gone to Mori because he'd trusted what the barber would tell him. Unfortunately, Mori's advice was to use Mercedes as a shield. He would not do it. What's more, she could not make him.

"You'll cut off your nose to spite your face." Her cheeks were as red as the flower at her ear. "Or worse, something will cut it off for you, because you're foolish enough to walk into that forest alone."

He scowled at her. "What would have happened if you'd been caught stealing that map?"

It took her a moment to separate their current argument from their previous one. "We are back to that? I didn't get caught."

"But you could have been."

She stopped in the middle of the street and threw up a hand, not caring that they were attracting attention. "Have you seen your face?" she demanded. "You, of all people, will scold me on danger?"

"It's not —"

"It is the same thing! You are like one of your precious leading stones, Elias, only you attract trouble instead of iron." She stopped and took a deep, steadying breath. Almost, he could hear her counting to ten. She asked, "What precisely are we arguing about?"

"Nothing, because you're not going."

A muffled cry drew their attention down an alley between a cookhouse and a rope maker's. Two boys threw rocks at a cloaked figure cowering against a wall. They were laughing. Elias, already riled, felt his temper spike.

He wasn't the only one. "Little beasts!" Mercedes said under her breath. And louder, "Stop that!"

The boys spun around. They were twelve or thereabouts, just like Nieve and Mori's piper. One had collected an armful of rocks in his tunic. He gave Mercedes an admiring glance as she approached, then yelped when she reached out and smacked him on the side of the head. The rocks tumbled to the ground.

"Oy!" The boy clutched his head.

The other miscreant jumped beyond her reach. "We weren't bothering anyone! It's only a leper."

Elias had brushed past them on his way to help the stranger, but at the word *leper*, he froze. A closer look into the shadows revealed little more than a cloak made of a dark winter wool, far heavier than necessary for this time of year. It concealed the stranger's face, hands, everything.

"Are you hurt?" Elias asked.

"No," the stranger said in a perfectly ordinary male voice.

"I'm grateful for your assistance. I'll be on my way now." The man's movements were slow and stiff as he struggled to his feet. And as he did, his hood fell away.

Elias heard Mercedes inhale sharply even as a terrible pity filled him. He was no stranger to leprosy, so common it was at every port he'd set foot on, including del Mar. Men and women huddled by the beggars' wall. Ringing their bells and shaking their castanets. Shouting *I am unclean!* because the law said they must. But those unfortunates had been in the early stages of the curse. Repugnant, yet tolerated still on the fringes of society.

This leper was different, his disfigurement so advanced that he was more monster than man. The bridge of his nose had collapsed in upon itself, leaving two small holes in its place. He had no hair on his head, no eyebrows or eyelashes to hint at the color he had been born with. He could have been Elias's age, or twenty years his elder. There was no way of telling one way or the other.

The leper continued, "I have my papers and my castanets, you see?" Misshapen hands, like claws, shook the wooden shells. The instrument rattled cheerfully.

The pleasant sound did not match what Elias was feeling, standing here in this filthy alley with this ruined man. He was not proud of his first instinct — to grab Mercedes and put as much distance as possible between them and him. He stood his ground and said quietly, "There's a hospital nearby." The Brotherhood of our Lady of Fair Wind. Only two streets over. "Is that where you were headed?"

"Yes," the leper said.

Mercedes came to stand by Elias's side. She took his arm long enough to pull him back a few steps. He had been standing far too close. Close enough to see the mucus running down the man's face. Near enough to smell the misery and decay.

She spoke calmly. "Sir, my name is Mercedes. This is Lord Elias."

There was a short silence before the stranger understood she meant to observe the usual pleasantries between strangers. "I am Rafael, Lady."

If she heard the slight tremor in his voice, she gave no sign of it. "Master Rafael. You've not been on the streets very long. Do you have family?"

Rafael lifted his chin, and it occurred to Elias that a man's eyes appeared less human without their lashes. "They left, Lady. My wife and mother. Two days ago."

Elias and Mercedes avoided looking at each other.

"I see," was her quiet answer. "May I ask . . . when did you last eat?"

"Two days ago." Rafael addressed his feet, as though the answer shamed him. Elias had to strain to hear his next words. "I'm not a beggar. I have coin. No one will take it."

There was a retching sound behind them. The two boys watched from the street; one pretended to be ill while the other laughed, the high-pitched braying of a jackass. Elias fought the urge to chase after them and wring their necks. A malevolent light had entered Mercedes's eyes. He could see her remembering their faces, for next time. She'd always had a gift for patience, and vengeance. It made him feel better.

A shudder racked the leper's frame, from pain maybe, but Elias wondered if he might still be cold, despite his layers and the pleasant day.

Elias shrugged out of his green cloak and held it out. "Here, take this." Rafael did not move. "Take it," he said again. "We'll see you to the Fair Wind. No one will harm you." The man would never make it to the hospital without further abuse. Elias hoped onlookers would see him, or at least Mercedes, and think twice before reaching for rocks and rotted food.

Tentatively, Rafael reached for the cloak. He wrapped it over his own and pulled the hood over his head so that only the bottom half of his face was visible. A muffled "Thank you" emerged.

The trio made for a strange processional. Mercedes led the way down the street, with Rafael following behind at a safe-enough distance. Elias brought up the rear. The leper's casta-nets rattled as everyone around gave them a wide berth. Just as they reached the hospital steps, a red object sailed through the air. Elias caught the apple before it could strike Rafael and snapped it back where it came from. It hit the thrower — a man clutching a second piece of rotted fruit — right between the eyes; he windmilled backward and cracked his head into a wall, stunned.

Which set the crowd laughing. Elias did not have time to enjoy it. A rock streaked by and struck Rafael square in the back.

There was a sharp cry of pain as he pitched forward. Unthinking, Elias leaped ahead and grabbed him even as Mercedes cried out, *"Elias, don't!"* A collective gasp rose from the onlookers. As soon as the leper had steadied, Elias snatched his hands away.

"What is this?" A robed monk had rushed down the steps from the hospital, alerted by the noise.

Mercedes did not take her eyes from Elias. She said, "Take him inside, Brother." And to Rafael, "Go inside, please, Master Rafael. They'll take care of you here."

For a short time, at least. To the south of del Mar, just beyond its shores, was the leper island of Valdemossa. Every del Marian afflicted with the curse eventually made his way there. By force, if necessary, since banishment to Valdemossa usually meant a lifetime of separation from loved ones. The island was run by monks of the Order of Saint Lazarus and was considered an asylum for those with or without coin, for leprosy did not discriminate. Rafael had known that by seeking out this hospital, he had taken the first step to leaving del Mar forever.

The monk scrambled to do her bidding. As he hurried his new patient along, Rafael looked back at Elias and whispered, "Forgive me."

"Don't apologize to me —" Elias nearly choked on his words. He had forgotten. His compass pin was attached to his cloak, the one he had handed over without any intention of asking for it back. It was made of gold with tiny emeralds to mark the wind points. But that was not where its value lay. The pin had belonged to Lord Antoni, a gift from his wife. It felt small and mean to ask Rafael to remove it. He said, "I'm so sorry this happened to you."

Master Rafael and the monk disappeared behind the hospital doors. Mercedes asked for the second time that day, "You will scold me on danger?" Then, "What am I to do with you?"

Uneasy, he answered, "I don't know."

They both stared in consternation at his arm. Master Rafael had not worn gloves. His remaining fingernails had been jagged. One had caught Elias when he'd reached to break his fall, scratching him and leaving a thin strip of blood along his wrist.

"Here, Lady, hold his hand down," Mori instructed. "Best if he doesn't move. Elias!" he snapped. "Be still."

"I'm trying," Elias said through gritted teeth.

They were back in Mori's shop. Elias on the stool, arm extended along the table. Mercedes remained on her feet, anchoring his hand to the table with her own. Mori held his Bushido fire leech over Elias's forearm, where it had attached its fangs to the cut left by Master Rafael. To Mercedes, the creature was even more loathsome up close. Short, bristly hairs covered its plump, wormlike body. The noise it made feasting on Elias's blood was stomach-churning: wet, pulling, filled with gluttony.

Best not to look at it. She studied Elias instead. Sweat beaded his forehead. He swallowed convulsively. For both their sakes, she tried not to look anxious. "Does it hurt?" she asked.

"No."

Clearly, he was lying. She wanted to yell at him. But for what crime? Trying to protect a sick man? If he had been careless, he had also been kind. She asked the barber-surgeon, "Will this work, Master Mori?"

"I can't say, Lady," Mori said, his hands preventing the leech from sliding off Elias's arm. "No one knows how the leper's curse is spread, and for every claim, there's argument against it." He shifted the leech a quarter inch to the left. "Some believe leprosy is a sign of demonic possession. Others will insist a leper is born a leper, and that the poison manifests itself over time. In which case" — he shrugged — "there's nothing to be done."

Elias hissed sharply, making Mercedes jump. Because both of Mori's hands were occupied and only one of hers, the barber-surgeon said to her, "Grab the shears there. Give its head a sharp tap."

Mercedes did as she was told, rapping the leech on its head with the handle and thinking she would not do this for anyone else. The leech flinched under her assault, then resumed a less aggressive feeding. Elias's shoulders relaxed.

"Better?" she asked.

Miserable brown eyes met hers. "Yes. Thank you."

Mori went on. "Many doctors insist it is caused by breathing the same air. This I don't believe. There are lepers everywhere. If it were true, surely there would be more of them."

"You think it could be passed through the blood?" Elias eyed the leech with revulsion.

"Maybe yes, maybe no," Mori answered. "Sharing a spoon, a kiss, a home. It's possible. But I've heard stories of lepers remaining with their families where no one else grew ill. Ever. There are lepers being cared for at the Fair Wind, but only one monk in the last fifteen years had to follow his patients to Valdemossa."

Master Mori's words made her feel better. She said, "Then this scratch . . ."

"Probably means nothing," Mori said. "If there were something new and foul in Elias's blood, the leech has taken care of it. It was a smart thing, coming back here. There's no use in worrying." He lifted the creature off Elias's arm. Mercedes stepped away hastily. It was plumper than it had been when they'd first arrived. Two small holes had been left beside the original scratch. Elias's skin was shiny and wet and, grimacing, he grabbed a cloth from the table and scrubbed away.

Mori crossed the chamber and lowered the leech back in its glass cage. He said over his shoulder, "*Unless* you wake one day and your arms and legs have gone numb. That's the first sign. Then I would start to worry plenty."

SEVEN

ELIAS STRODE INTO the arena, trying not to think of plagues and lepers. He found Ulises just finishing sword practice. The field was open to the heavens, and the sun blazed directly overhead without a single cloud to temper its brilliance.

"What is the score now, Lazar?" Ulises handed his sword to Commander Aimon's second-in-command and collapsed onto a bench. Both men were drenched in sweat.

"I'm one over you, my king."

"Ha." Ulises leaned his head against the stone wall and closed his eyes. "Only until next time."

Lazar grinned at the challenge. "We will see. My lord Elias," he added as he walked away.

Ulises opened his eyes. Elias joined him on the bench, elbows on knees, his carrier behind him. "You've left it too late," Ulises informed him without ceremony. "Mercedes has beat you to it. She's going with you."

Silently, Elias cursed her sneakiness. How had she found Ulises so quickly? They had barely gone their separate ways.

Ulises answered his unspoken question. "She's smarter than you. Simpler just to accept it." The look Elias sent him earned a laugh in response.

Elias said, "You'll send her into that forest to face who-knows-what. What sort of relation are you?"

"The realistic sort," Ulises answered, unoffended. "You need a female, and you need someone who can keep secrets. Mercedes will do both." Ulises studied him. "She was as insistent about going as you are about her staying. What is between the two of you?"

"Nothing."

"Oh, yes? If that is what you wish me to believe, I'll pretend to believe it."

Brooding, Elias studied his boots, no longer gleaming from Basilio's care, but splattered with mud and sand. The words nearly stuck in his throat. "I want her safe."

An endless silence, followed by a sigh. "She would kick you in the teeth if she thought you were trying to protect her."

Elias didn't bother to deny it. "I know."

Ulises took a cloth from beneath the bench and mopped his face. They were alone in this corner of the field. The arena was rapidly emptying as men headed to their midday meal. A handful of soldiers remained in place on the perimeter, keeping company with Commander Aimon's training catapults and trebuchets pushed up against the walls. The king's personal guard. Never too far away. Elias wondered what it must feel like to be constantly watched, and he said so.

Ulises glanced at his men and shrugged. "Most days I forget they're there."

"What about other days?"

"It's like having bearded nursemaids," Ulises confessed, then returned to the topic at hand. "Even with Mercedes, I would feel easier if you took more people. Trusted men. Commander Aimon could choose."

"No."

Ulises scowled. "It's madness to go into that forest, Elias, without more men to watch your back." Whatever he saw on Elias's face made him throw his hands up in irritation. "I could order you to do it; you realize that?"

"*Would* you order me?" Elias demanded. Is this what it would be like for the rest of their lives? Ulises would spring his kingship on him with a threat?

Ulises didn't answer straightaway but scowled off into space with his arms folded, one finger tapping against his arm. "Do you trust your friend Mori?"

"Yes," Elias said without hesitation.

"Then I do, too. Reyna is your only other choice, and that is no choice at all. So. You and Mercedes will watch over each other." He held up a hand as Elias opened his mouth to speak. "No, *listen* to me. I'll have both of you safe. The sooner we decipher these maps and learn what happened to my brothers, the bet —"

A sound came from behind them. The inhalation of breath so faint, Elias would have dismissed it as the wind . . . except Ulises had heard it, too. They turned.

The arena's curved wall was inches away. Several feet above their heads, rectangular openings had been left in the stone to better circulate the air. On the other side of the wall, he knew, was a long tunnel that led to work chambers used by the kingdom's weapon makers: sword makers, crossbow makers, shield makers, engineers, armorers. Anyone passing by could have heard their conversation. He saw that Ulises had come to the same conclusion.

They waited, unmoving, but there was nothing: no voices, no footsteps, no ill-timed sneeze to give anyone away. Finally, Elias stood. "We're being careless."

"Or maybe high-strung, imagining ears at every window." Ulises tossed his cloth onto the bench. "Stop looking so suspicious. There was no one there."

Elias found the navigation chambers empty save for Luca, who worked at a table covered with parchment, paints, and ink.

Those admitted to del Mar's School of Navigation were a mix of noblemen's children and those less wealthy whose intellect had earned them royal patronage. Luca was the fifth son of a cobbler, who, from an early age, had shown far more interest in longitude and latitude than in the soles and arches of a man's foot. He was Elias's age, with a brawler's build — thick arms and rolling shoulders — which made the delicate, round spectacles perched on his nose all the more incongruous. He would also be sailing off in six weeks, as geographer for the *Palma*.

Luca wiped his hands on his apron, smearing ink across the white cloth. "I'm relieved to see you here," he said, by way of greeting. He clapped Elias on the shoulders, kissed him on each cheek, and grinned. "I heard you were in the dungeons after challenging the king yesterday. I heard it was over a woman."

"You think everything is over a woman." Glancing around the empty chamber, Elias added, "Since when are you so industrious? I've never known you to miss a meal." Everyone else must have gone to seek their lunch in the great dining hall.

"I blame you." Luca gestured toward the parchment spread across the table. Elias recognized his maps from Hellespont. "Madame wants these copied. She didn't say so outright, but I don't think I'm supposed to stop for meals or rest." He looked Elias up and down, noting the bruises. "I heard about your ship. How many lives do you have left, I wonder?"

Elias shrugged. "Seven, maybe."

Luca made a rude sound. "More like three. Where have you been all morning? Your friend has been very patient."

"My . . . ?" Only then did Elias notice the small face peering at him from across the chamber, nearly hidden behind the immense statue of Saint Cosme. Reyna. When she saw that he had spied her, she ducked behind the marble.

"I told her it could be hours before you turned up," Luca said, "but she wanted to wait."

Elias walked over, footsteps echoing, and rounded the statue. Three wide marble steps served as a base. Reyna sat upon the top step, her back pressed against the long-suffering

Cosme's ankles. A white, dust-covered apron protected her blue dress. She was industriously polishing an astrolabe with a rag. More astrolabes were piled around her on the steps in a tangle of metal.

Elias leaned one shoulder against Cosme's bared, muscled legs. "Hello, Reyna. Are you being punished for something?"

She looked up from her polishing, startled. "What do you mean?"

He indicated the astrolabes. "Whenever your grandfather disapproved of something I did, I found myself here. Scrubbing the astrolabes."

She did not smile exactly, but at least she no longer looked afraid of him. "I like to scrub them. It helps me think."

Not something one usually heard from a nine-year-old. He asked, "Did your grandfather send you?"

She shook her head. "He's having his meal with Lord Braga. Master Luca said I could stay as long as I wasn't idle." She glanced at Elias's carrier and then looked away, her gaze dancing about his shoulders, his hair, before finally meeting his. "I'm very sorry for yesterday."

She spoke softly; still, he glanced over at Luca, whose back was to them. Elias kept his own voice low. "Why should you be?"

"I didn't think about how much trouble the map would cause," she confessed. "I shouldn't have told anyone of it."

He had frightened her with his temper — snarling at Mercedes, snarling at Ulises — and had likely caused a sleepless night.

There were shadows beneath her eyes that he didn't remember seeing yesterday. He felt like a horse's ass.

He moved a handful of astrolabes to the bottom step and sat beside her. "You did right, showing it to the king. I was surprised yesterday, but I still shouldn't have lost my temper."

"But what about your family? I like your sisters. And your *maman*, very much."

He'd spent his own restless night, imagining the malice that would spread if these maps came to light. His poor *maman*, with two husbands living. "I'll just have to make sense of these maps quickly, before anyone else learns of them."

"Do you think you can?" She did not sound skeptical, only curious.

"Absolutely." He offered up the lie with a smile.

He plucked one of the disks from a step. The instrument, with its scales and symbols etched onto the brass, gleamed. She was thorough. A thought occurred to him. "Reyna, did you see anything else on the map? Something out of place?"

She rubbed a stubborn smudge from the brass before answering. "The forest at Javelin . . . there's a mistake."

She had seen the trees as well. He didn't know why the thought pleased him so much. "The oak and alder."

She returned his smile with a tentative one of her own. "Yes."

"Anything else?"

She looked apologetic. "I didn't have it for very long."

That, at least, he could do something about. "Do you know where my work chambers are?"

"Yes."

"I'll leave one of the maps there. Your map. And I'll tell Basilio that you're free to come and go as you please. If you've time, I could use your eyes."

The map would be safe in his chamber. No one entered except Basilio. He trusted his steward without question.

"I'll try, Lord Elias." She still looked worried, and he could no longer ignore the dull throbbing behind his eyes. It had been with him, off and on, since yesterday. Maybe they both needed a distraction from their thoughts. Something normal and familiar, something that made sense.

Luca hummed while he worked. Contrary to Elias's earlier remark, Luca was a diligent worker. Also the fastest painter Elias knew. Even so, Madame Vega had given him considerable work. His friend would be working late into the evening for several nights to come.

Elias asked Reyna, "How precise are your sea monsters?"

"Madame says they give her nightmares. It was a compliment, I think."

Amused, he assured her, "It was. Madame's tightfisted with her praise." He set the disk aside and stood. "The maps from Hellespont need to be copied. There's no time for color, but that doesn't mean they have to be dull. You can add the embellishments."

Reyna brightened. "These will be real maps? Not just for lessons?"

"You can deliver them to the captains yourself, if you want," he said, and was rewarded with a smile. Over his shoulder, he called, "Master Luca?" using full address for Reyna's benefit.

"Lord Elias?" Luca responded amiably enough.

"Do you need some help?"

At that, Luca looked around and smiled. "The lead's over there."

Elias helped Reyna gather the astrolabes and return them to a large chest set against the wall. He placed his carrier beneath the table, pulled on an apron, and adjusted his sleeves. And for a short while he was able, slowly, to return to himself. To forget everything but the work itself.

He remembered every instant of that first morning in the tower. When he was a boy. Beams of light through the windows, dust motes gathered around Cosme's head like a crown. The painters, four to a table, quietly at their work. Madame Vega, unsmiling but not unkind: *And so you are Elias. You are most welcome here.* Luca sweeping the wood shavings from the floor. And Lord Silva leading him around the tower and answering every question Elias asked. Patiently, as though there were nowhere else for him to be. Elias had not known most of their names. Not then. But he had known *who* they were, *what* they were. Mapmakers and artists and navigators. These were *his* people, a different kind of family.

Now he drew the compass stars onto the sheepskin. He cast rhumb lines across the parchment. Gradually, the chamber filled with others returning from their meal, and he stopped often to greet them and exchange news. Beside him, Reyna knelt on a chair and leaned over one map, her brows knit in concentration. With painstaking care, she sketched in the most vicious-looking sea monsters he had ever seen, in person or on a sea chart.

"That is terrifying," he commented. When she smiled at him, he asked, "Have you seen the finned lion in person?" Her drawing was very realistic and macabre for someone still wearing double braids. The creature bore the head of a lion, a spiked fin on its back, and a long, curving serpent's tale. An unlucky shipman dangled from the lion's jaws, his mouth opened in a scream and his ropy innards spilling onto Elias's shoreline in black ink.

"Only a baby one. Grandfather and I saw it from the cliff tops in Alfonse."

Luca reached around her for some lead. "Have you traveled beyond del Mar, Reyna?"

"No, sir. Never."

Elias caught Luca's eye. They had both heard the wistful note in her voice, and on her face was a look they both recognized and understood. How could they not? They had felt it themselves, all their lives.

Wanderlust.

Once, Lord Silva had three sons living on del Mar. The eldest, Vittor, was killed in that long-ago avalanche. The second, Ginés, sailed off as a young man and chose never to return, the occasional letter home proof he still lived. Silva's youngest son, Tomas, had been Reyna's father. Reyna's parents had died three years ago when their ship was lost in the ferocious whirlpools along the Strait of Cain. Leaving her an orphan and in her widowed grandfather's care. She was the only female enrolled in del Mar's School of Navigation, but there had been others before her. Girls received a nearly equal education to the boys, on land. Geography, history, painting, mathematics, astronomy, linguistics. But to join an expedition, one must be selected formally as an apprentice by a master geographer. Of course, girls were never selected. Most went on to marry and have children. Others became royal painters, copying maps that the male geographers brought home. Or teachers; Madame Grec served as language master. And then there was Madame Vega, Lord Silva's assistant.

Elias found himself curious. He asked Reyna, "If you could sail off today, where would you go?"

She set aside her lead as she thought about his question. Her face took on a dreamy quality, and her answer, when it came, did not surprise him.

"I would go everywhere."

To enter the stairwell that led to his tower chambers, Elias first had to pass Madame Vega's open doorway. He walked quickly, with his head down, in the hopes he would not be seen.

"Just because you hide does not mean I do not see you, Lord Elias."

Sheepish, Elias stepped back into view. Del Mar's geography mistress eyed him from just inside the chamber, where she stood on the top step of a ladder. She was small in stature — on solid ground, her head reached the pit of his arm — and wore a midnight-blue robe with black lace at the collar. Like most del Marian women, her hair was elaborately done. Thick braids coiled above her head, embellished with silver plum-sized pins shaped like the moon and the stars. He'd found her reshelving scrolls. Her arms were full of them.

"Madame Vega," he said, "forgive me. My mind was elsewhere."

The look she gave him said she'd been lied to by better men. "Then it's a good thing I watched for you." She studied his bruise. "I heard about the rocks. Is that your only injury?"

"Yes, Madame."

"Good." Because her arms were full, she pointed to her desk with her chin. "Bring those charts here, if you please. The ones by the pilots."

Madame Vega's work chamber, a fifth the size of Lord Silva's, was a stone cave lined with bookcases and hung with maps. A small round window offered a blurred, distorted view of the harbor. Elias swept up the requested scrolls and glanced at the pilot book she was copying. He could just make out the sailing instructions, though they were upside down: *From Santequer to Donille is twenty miles east-northeast, quarter east. Santequer is a good port-facing town where you may anchor. In case you come from the east, take care of a shoal that is close to the point. From Donille to* . . . He found himself smiling. The words were his, written during a brief excursion to the Outer Islands last fall. It gratified him to see them here, being copied, where they would be used officially for the crown. It was only in the last year that his work had been judged skilled enough to be distributed throughout the fleets.

When he returned to the ladder, he made sure to set a boot on the lowest rung to hold it steady. It would be worse for him if Madame Vega were to fall and crack her head open on the stone. For him, and for every other geographer and apprentice within these walls. Lord Silva was the head of the school, its public face, but Madame Vega was its backbone. Its spine. Nothing would get done without her.

She took the scroll he held up to her. "Lord Silva tells me you've been given a special task by the king." Before he could think what to say, she added, "There's no need to explain. It's no concern of mine. I've been assured it won't interfere with your placement on the expedition." This last was a question.

Just the thought of the *Amaris* sailing without him turned his stomach. "It won't."

"You're certain? King's task or not, you'll be expected to prepare for the journey. See to your own trunks, charts, et cetera, et cetera."

He knew what needed to be done. "I understand. I don't expect a problem."

"Good," she said. "Now, there's another matter to discuss, one we both know you've been avoiding."

"Of course." He cast a longing glance at the open door. "I'll need more time to consider —"

"That time has passed." She shook a scroll at him before placing it on a shelf. "You were awarded master status months ago. Your duties in Hellespont caused an understandable delay, but it's time for you to choose an apprentice."

"With the utmost respect, Madame, I'm not sure I'm meant to have an apprentice. I work better alone."

She said evenly, "With the utmost respect, Lord Elias, *you* were an apprentice, as were your father and grandfather and many generations before them." She snatched the scroll from his grip. "Would you say your instruction under Lord Silva was invaluable?"

"Yes, but —"

"Good. Then you cannot now say 'I work better alone' and break five hundred years of tradition. You must give back. This expedition will be an opportunity for you to train one of the boys, and train him thoroughly."

Every word she spoke was reasonable. "I understand my responsibility," he said. "I know I've been lagging. It's just . . . an apprentice is . . ." He groped about for the right words. "A nuisance."

Something — it might have been amusement — flickered in her eyes before she said, "And you were not?"

He had the grace to smile. "A fair point."

She continued, "Men are not born brilliant explorers. That will be your task. To mold them into someone del Mar can be proud of. What of Jaime? He's a good boy. A rough diamond perhaps, but there's hope there."

Jaime? Lord Braga's son? Her words had barely settled when he heard a sharp cry from the hall and what sounded like a stampede growing closer. A mass of children erupted into the chamber like dervishes, all of them speaking at once. The youngest was the Grecs' son, Hector, age five, who clutched his nose and looked panic-stricken.

"What happened?" Madame Vega demanded, at once off the ladder and in the middle of the fray.

"There's a rock in his nose," Reyna explained, one arm protectively around Hector's shoulders.

Another boy, Mateo, added, "Jaime dared him to shove a leading stone up his nose, and now it won't come out."

"I didn't think he would do it! Why would anyone do it?"

"Why would anyone dare it?" Reyna glared at Jaime, who had sprouted several inches in the months Elias had been gone. "You're a lump, Jaime."

"Reyna! Language!" Madame Vega's scold was lost beneath Hector's piercing wail. Now would be a good time for Elias to leave. The matter of an apprentice could be put off yet again, maybe even until after he returned from the expedition. He looked at Hector with his nose the color of rubies and tears streaming from his eyes.

And sighed. "There now, Hector," Elias said. "Let's have a look." He lifted the boy onto a ladder step and tipped his head back for inspection. Gray eyes like his mother's. Arms and legs like twigs. The children gathered around in a tight circle, Reyna on one side of Hector and a shamefaced Jaime on the other.

Madame Vega peered around Elias. "How far back is it?"

The stone was lodged good and tight. He was not about to say so in front of poor Hector. "I've seen worse." A leather pouch hung from Elias's belt. He fished around inside it before producing a small round tin and a slim iron pincer.

Reyna eyed him curiously. "You carry pincers and sheep fat with you?"

"Don't you?" He smiled at her, then uncapped the tin. Scooping a pea-sized amount with his little finger, he held it up for Hector to see. "This won't hurt, but try not to move, hmm?"

Hector's response was a dry, shuddering breath. There was a snicker in the crowd, silenced quickly as Madame Vega's head whipped around.

"Sheep's fat," Elias explained, working the lard into Hector's right nostril and ignoring the chorus of giggles that followed, "can be used as a balm for scrapes, burns, bites, rashes, whichever. An explorer learns quickly never to be without it."

There was a whimper from his patient.

"Courage, Hector," Reyna soothed.

Elias shared a glance with Madame Vega and looked away before he laughed. He used the pincers to rotate the stone within the nostril in order to spread the balm around.

"What is the meaning of this?" a female voice demanded, so loud and so unexpectedly that Elias nearly pierced Hector's brains with his pincer. Madame Grec stood inside the doorway with Lord Silva. The children scattered, making way for her to loom, incensed, over her son.

"Maman," Hector said in a small voice.

"Perfectly still, Hector, remember?" Elias said. "It's a small stone only, Madame. I nearly have it."

"A stone! Who put it there?" Madame Grec glared at the other children. They had gone mute and terrified. Her gaze narrowed on Jaime, who had sidled over so that he was half hidden behind Lord Silva.

Madame Grec pointed an accusing finger at Jaime. "You—"

"Genevieve," Madame Vega said, exasperated, "leave the boy alone."

And Hector said, "I put it there, Maman. It's my fault."

Hector had not tattled. Lord Silva turned his gaze heavenward and said nothing.

Elias said, "As I was saying, pincers are excellent for slivers and . . ." He plucked the stone from Hector's nostril with an audible sucking noise, which brought forth cheers. Elias offered it to Jaime. The boy grimaced but took the stone. ". . . removing stones from peculiar places."

Madame Grec did not have a chance to do more than bristle. Madame Vega took over, sending Hector off with his mother and the rest to their lessons in mixing paints. Lord Silva held Jaime back long enough to deliver a mild admonishment: "Be kind to the younger ones; they look up to you. And stay away from Madame Grec for a day or two. There's a good boy." To

Madame Vega, he asked, "Lena, have you seen my pilot book on Caffa? The one with the illustrations?"

Madame Vega didn't have to think before answering. "It's in your work chamber, on the ledge by the silver globe."

"What about my pipe? It seems to have gone missing. I've looked everywhere."

"I've sent it to be repaired, remember? There's a crack in it. I left another by your bed."

They were like an old married couple, Elias thought, together forever. Though Madame Vega was decades younger, the same as Madame Grec. Not for the first time, he wondered . . . and then he stopped wondering. The romantic lives of his elders were never something he wished to consider.

Lord Silva's expression had cleared. "Ah. Thank you, my dear." He turned to Elias. "Stones in noses. You're a man of rare talent." And when Elias laughed, he added, "I'd like a word."

"Yes, sir." Elias turned to follow him out but was stopped at the door when Madame Vega called his name.

She had taken up a quill behind her desk. "It's settled, then. I'll have your answer a week before you depart and no later."

"I . . ." He looked to Lord Silva, who spread his hands. Elias was on his own.

"These are the rules," she said firmly, "if you wish to board that ship. If I change them for you, I must change them for everyone, and that is unacceptable. Every master has an apprentice, Lord Elias. That includes you."

EIGHT

HE RED ONE or the yellow one?" Mercedes asked. "Which is best?"

"Yellow," Reyna answered. "I've never worn it before. We should offer something new, shouldn't we?"

They were in Reyna's small bedchamber in the Tower of Winds. It was nearly time for supper, and Mercedes had come here, thinking to rummage through the child's clothing chests for a dress that would please, or at least placate, a young female ghost. Reyna had been more than obliging when Mercedes had explained her mission, and now they stood at the foot of the bed, eyeing the assortment of dresses that covered every inch of bedspread.

"The yellow, then," Mercedes decided. "You're certain you don't mind?"

Reyna spoke with all seriousness. "You can have them all, if you think they'll keep you safer."

Mercedes found herself smiling as she gathered up the dress, lemon cotton with white lace trimming. Had she ever been as sweet at this age? As kind? She thought back, over years past, and then decided no, not ever.

"Should I go with you tomorrow?" Reyna had climbed onto the edge of the bed, watching as Mercedes folded the dress and wrapped it in linen. "I could help."

What had Master Mori said? *A girl would be preferable, but a woman should do. You cannot enter that forest without a female presence. We would never see you again.*

Mercedes set the package aside. "You're brave to offer. But not this time."

"I—"

"I won't risk you. And neither will your grandfather, or Lord Elias, or the king."

Reyna's shoulders drooped as Mercedes listed one daunting obstacle after the other. And when laughter drifted in through the open window, her expression turned gloomier still.

"What's this?" Mercedes crossed the chamber, knelt upon the blue tufted window seat, and peered out the window. There was enough light in the day for her to see the ten or so boys in the courtyard below with its giant compass underfoot, waving wooden swords at one another and causing general noise and mayhem. One of the smaller boys tripped, landed on his hands and knees, and let out a wail. The Grecs' son, Hector.

Reyna remained on the bed with her chin propped on her hand. "My friends," she explained. "They've just finished sword lessons."

Mercedes thought she understood. "No lessons for you?"

"Master Giarrat won't train a girl. He says it's unseemly."

A spark of annoyance at that. "Do you wish to learn how to fight?"

"No, not really."

Mercedes was lost. "Then why the long face?"

"I don't want to stick a sword into anyone," Reyna said. "Not ever. But I would like to know how to defend myself. And . . . I don't like knowing less than the boys, just because I'm not one."

Something unfurled in Mercedes, something that made her think her own unseemly thoughts about Sword Master Giarrat. She returned to the bed and, pushing aside some dresses, sat beside Reyna. "And that's all?" she demanded. "You'll sit here and be sad while they're out there learning more than you?"

Reyna's brows furrowed, taken aback by Mercedes's lack of sympathy. "What else is there?"

"Reyna," Mercedes said, "if you don't like the answer to something, you must find a way around it." As she herself had earlier, ignoring Elias's refusal and going to Ulises instead. She had found him in his chambers selecting a sword for his own practice. "It's too dangerous," Ulises had said.

"For him, not for me," she'd insisted. "These maps are not just about his family. You said so yourself. How can we send him into Javelin without lifting a finger to help?"

Ulises had not put up much of a fight. But he had wanted something from her as well, waiting until she'd reached for the door before asking, "Were you going to say nothing? About the old woman in the courtyard?"

Fighting a sense of betrayal, she'd turned to face him. "Elias told you."

"He was not the only one there." The sword had slid into its carrier with more force than necessary. "He told me nothing. You should have."

She was tired of being reminded about the spitter in the courtyard. "It wasn't important."

"You're wrong," Ulises had snapped. "We're the only family you and I have left, and when someone insults you, they insult me. That must be made clear. *Every* time."

Mercedes had felt her eyes sting. She had gone to her uncle once to ask for more guards for her mother. He had refused. *We all have our crosses to bear,* he'd said. Mercedes and her mother should spend their days in prayer, grateful that he still offered them shelter. Mercedes loved Ulises as much as she'd hated his father. Now she said to her cousin, "What will it change? Nothing."

"You're wrong," Ulises had said again, but in a far gentler tone. "I'm not my father. We stand back-to-back on this, Mercedes. No more secrets. Agreed?"

This was not an argument she would win. "Agreed."

Mercedes pushed aside the memory and brushed her palms down her red dress briskly, smoothing out the wrinkles. She said to Reyna, "Girls are not taught to use weapons, it's true. But there have been exceptions. In Cortes. In this very castle, in fact."

Reyna took her meaning. "You, Lady?"

"And who do you think taught me?"

That was no great mystery. "Commander Aimon?"

"Yes." She had gone to Commander Aimon when she was eleven, after a wealthy merchant from the east had tried to corner her in a dark corridor. It had been a terrifying experience, a very close call. The commander had not laughed at her request, but had taught her how to protect herself, even if she was small. Especially because she was small. And now that she thought about it all these years later, she realized she had never seen that particular merchant in Cortes again.

Reyna looked uncertain. "I don't like to trouble you. I know you're very busy and important."

"I'm both these things," Mercedes said with a smile. "That does not mean I won't help a friend. Especially one who would give over all her dresses to keep me safe."

Reyna returned her smile and thanked her, and after a thoughtful pause, said, "I would like to go with you tomorrow. How do I find my way around that?"

"You don't." Mercedes nudged Reyna's arm with her own. "Don't press your luck."

Mercedes heard a loud click as part of the wall swung open and a woman walked through it.

"Reyna," Madame Vega said, "have you seen my — oh!"

Mercedes did her best to hide her own surprise. Madame Vega had entered, not through the door that led to the corridor and stairwell, but through a panel beside Reyna's bed that connected to another chamber. Mercedes had never seen her in such a state. Her severe teaching robes had been replaced with a white silk bathing gown full of frills and lace. Black hair, damp from a recent bath, trailed to her knees. Madame Vega had beautiful hair. Her face had been scrubbed clean, and without her kohl-lined eyes or blood-red lips, she looked far younger than Mercedes had imagined. Younger . . . and *female*. She had never thought of Madame Vega as a female before.

"My lady Mercedes, forgive me. I didn't realize Reyna had a guest." Madame Vega pulled at the belt of her gown, clearly discomfited and wishing she was more formally dressed.

"Madame," Mercedes said, "please don't apologize. I've only come to invite Reyna to sit with me at supper this evening."

"Oh!" Reyna looked delighted. Children rarely dined at the king's high table. She turned to Madame Vega and asked, "May I go?"

Madame Vega wore a bemused smile. "You don't need my permission for such an invitation. It's kind of you to think of her, Lady." She noticed the great pile of dresses on the bed. "What has happened here?"

"Reyna is growing too fast for our seamstresses," Mercedes said. The lie rolled off her tongue easily. She ignored Reyna's sideways glance, adding, "We're trying to decide which of these to let."

"I did not realize . . ." Madame Vega trailed off, mortified. "Please don't trouble yourself, Lady. I'll have the nurses see to it."

"It's no trouble," Mercedes assured her.

"Well . . ." Madame Vega backed away toward the panel. "I won't keep you."

After Madame Vega closed the panel behind her, Reyna said, "I forgot to ask her what she needed."

Mercedes left the bed and crossed the chamber. She ran her hands along the panel. When closed, one could not tell it was an entryway. It blended seamlessly with the rest of the stone. She said, "Reyna?"

"Yes, Lady?"

"How long has Madame Vega lived here?" She had been a young widow when she had joined the School of Navigation as a painter, before Lord Silva had taken her on as his assistant. And she wasn't from Cortes, Mercedes remembered, but from some town in the north. Or was it the south?

"Since forever," Reyna said. "Before I was born."

Mercedes smiled. "That long?" And at Reyna's questioning look, she added, "It's nothing. Only she reminds me of someone, though I can't think who."

"Alder and oak." Lord Silva studied the map Elias had left on his worktable. "That is extraordinary. I could have looked at this forever and never noticed."

"Reyna saw it, too." Elias propped his carrier against the table and helped himself to the coffee Basilio had left for them. The cup was slightly larger than a thimble.

Lord Silva glanced over, unsmiling. "Did she? She did not mention it." He refused the coffee Elias offered. "Do you think it wise to leave it here? In the open? Anyone can see it."

"Basilio and I are the only ones with keys." Elias came to stand beside Lord Silva, thimble in hand. "The locks were rusted when I first moved here. He had new ones fitted."

"Are you certain of his loyalty?"

Elias lowered his cup, smiling a little. "To me? Oh, who knows? But to my mother? Yes. Absolutely."

Lord Silva did not return his smile. "What do you expect to find when you get there?"

"Not one thing," he admitted. "But I promised Ulises. And you, remember? You told me to do this. You said—"

"Yes, yes." Lord Silva frowned at the map. "I didn't realize . . . I don't like the thought of you walking into Javelin alone."

"I won't be."

Lord Silva's head came up sharply. "Who—? Lady Mercedes is going with you? Elias, I have to object."

"She's not." He set his cup down and crossed the chamber, kneeling before a chest placed beneath a window. He rummaged around within and pulled out a small leather bag. "Gold," he explained, dropping it onto the map table. "The plan is to meet Mercedes at the stables at sunrise. I did not make this plan," he added dryly. "And I'll be gone before then. Montserrat is near Javelin. I'll offer payment to one of the village women there if she'll ride into the forest with me."

There was a good amount of gold squid in that bag. Someone would take the offer, and the risk.

Lord Silva was silent. "She'll be furious."

And hurt. Elias could stomach the first easier than the last. "She'll be safe."

Lord Silva lifted the bag, appalled at its heft. "Surely you don't need to offer so much?"

"I didn't think it was the time to be tightfisted."

A *hmmph*, followed by, "A woman. Can it really be so simple?" He did not appear to expect an answer. "You've only Mori's word that a woman will protect you."

Elias was surprised. Lord Silva had known the barber-surgeon even longer than he had. "You think he would lie to me? Why would he?"

"Not lie, of course, but he could be mistaken."

Elias tried to make light of it. "It's only a forest full of spirits. We've seen scarier, I think."

Lord Silva's smile, when it finally came, was rueful. "I forget sometimes that you're no longer my apprentice and are perfectly capable of taking care of yourself." He gave the map one last look. "Even so, I will pray a little longer tonight." Elias laughed, and Lord Silva added, "Now, then. You're not one to avoid your responsibilities. Why are you kicking and screaming with this apprentice business?"

It was Elias's turn to frown. It was uncomfortable sometimes how little he could hide from this man. He busied himself, fetching his carrier and unrolling the second map beside Reyna's. He poured more coffee and drank it. Lord Silva waited patiently.

Finally, Elias said, "I'm not my father."

A small silence. "No. I can see that."

Elias set his thimble onto the tray. "An apprentice of mine would have . . . expectations. That I be like him. That I be wise and courageous, like he was."

Understanding dawned. "And you don't think you could meet those expectations?"

"I know I could not."

Lord Silva was quiet, his expression thoughtful. He reached around Elias and pulled a book from a shelf. Bound in leather, edged in gold; the title read: *The Travels of Antoni, Lord of del Mar*. It had been written after his death by his friend and fellow explorer Lord Braga.

Lord Silva placed the book on the table beside the maps. He said, "I spoke to a man at the harbor some weeks ago who knew Antoni. Or so he claimed. He recalled, quite vividly, the time your father rescued a village girl by wrestling a crocodile and killing it."

"I've read that story. It's here." Elias opened the book, turning the pages until he found what he was looking for. The illustrator had captured the tale at its most dramatic point. A twenty-foot crocodile, its body rearing out of the swamp's muddy shallows. Jaws gaping. Teeth like freshly sharpened daggers. Lord Antoni clung to the animal's back, his own teeth bared as he plunged a knife directly into the creature's eye. The artist must have been given a generous paint allowance. Expensive red blood spilled everywhere. In the background, a woman fled the scene with a crying child in her arms. *Lord Antoni and the Great Crocodile Rescue.* It was one of Elias's favorites.

Lord Silva studied the painting for some time. "Antoni was scared to death of crocodiles. You could not drag him near the eastern swamps."

Elias stared at him. "What?"

Lord Silva smiled at him. "Perhaps he did fight off one in order to save the child's life. But he never said so. And you won't convince me of it."

Elias found himself deeply offended on his father's behalf. And this from Lord Silva. "You're saying these stories are false?"

"Some almost certainly," Lord Silva confirmed. "Not all. Your father was everything they say. Wise and brave and full of adventure. But death can transform a man into a myth. A legend even he would not recognize." He turned the page. And fell silent.

The next story was not a happy one. A long-ago expedition, men crushed to nothing beneath an avalanche. The artist had not considered a father's grief when he had painted the accompanying illustration: a mountain pass, the snow settled peacefully over the landscape, the avalanche long since over. But the tranquil image was shattered by a pair of arms reaching straight out of the snow, hands like claws and frosted over, the only reminder of the bodies buried there.

It was a chilling picture. A story Elias had never liked, even though his own father had survived, had led the surviving men to safety. It had been his final expedition. He watched as Lord Silva's palm flattened over the image. The desperate, clawing hands could have belonged to any of the dead, but Elias imagined he thought only of his eldest son, Vittor.

"My lord Silva," Elias said when the silence had gone on for quite some time. Lord Silva's hand trembled. And the mountain pass was no more as he ripped the image from the book and crumpled it in his fist. He stepped away from the table, as if the story were a living thing that could harm him still. The torn page fell to the floor.

Lord Silva said very, very softly, "Don't worry so much about what others think. Choose your apprentice, Vittor. You'll do fine. I'm certain of it."

Elias spoke past the stone in his throat. "Yes, sir."

Lord Silva left. Elias picked up the page, smoothed it as best he could, and tucked it back into the book. He circled the chamber, lighting more candles. Lord Silva had not noticed his mistake, calling Elias by his dead son Vittor's name. His mother forgot his name all the time, pointing at him and calling him Isidore and Jonas and Nieve and Lea and even Dita before finally remembering Elias. These lapses greatly entertained her children.

This was different. It was not a good feeling to return home and realize that Lord Silva, his Royal Navigator, his hero, had grown old.

Elias stayed up late into the night with the maps. Frustration simmered as he studied first one image and then another, considering each and dismissing all.

Surely it should not be this difficult. Locating the first clue had been a simple matter. An entire forest painted in error. Which meant that any other clue should follow the same rule. A detail drawn with a subtle but undeniable mistake. But that was supposing the mapmaker had constructed the maps based on logic and not simply mischief or trickery. And how many clues were there? One? Two? Ten? Elias wished he knew who this mapmaker was, so that he could show him with his fist just what he thought of him.

He was missing something. He started again, from the south. Churches, castles, parishes, rivers, and coves. All were where they should be. Nothing was out of place. He worked his way north. Every town and village and city had been identified, the villages with a simple name marker, the larger towns with a structure that easily identified it. A church, a castle, the ancient ruins of the amphitheater in Portras.

He was vaguely aware of Basilio coming and going. He ignored the dull throbbing behind his eyeballs, continuing on until finally exhaustion overcame him and he fell into bed.

Long before dawn, he woke. After inspecting his wrist — the scratch looked no worse than it had yesterday — and checking to make sure his arms and legs hadn't gone numb, he dressed and packed a single map in his carrier. The other he left behind for Reyna. He took his dagger. As an afterthought, he took his sword. Passing Basilio on the stairs, he said, "I'll be home tonight," and hoped that his words would prove true.

NINE

AN UNPLEASANT SURPRISE waited for Elias at the stables. Her name was Mercedes. Though it was still dark outside, she was there already, sitting on a white mare, surrounded by the smell of horse and hay and oiled leather.

"You decided to make an earlier start of it also?" she asked, watching him with narrowed eyes. "Good. I thought the same."

Beside her, Ulises strapped a saddlebag onto his own glossy brown horse. "You're ready?" he asked Elias. They were dressed similarly in plain traveling clothes and dark cloaks to fight the morning chill. "Let's go."

Bleary-eyed, Elias said, "What?" The groom, Marco, came forward with Pythagoras. Suddenly wide awake, Elias grabbed hold of the reins. "You must be joking. You can't go gallivanting outside the gates without the commander. You've no guards." There was no sign of additional horses being readied. There was no one else about.

"First," Ulises said evenly, "I do not gallivant. And second, I do have a guard. Or have you forgotten how to use that sword?"

Ulises swung onto his horse. To the boy, "Marco, wait until mid-morning . . . no, midday, then inform Commander Aimon we'll be returning tonight. Late."

The boy stammered, "Yes, my king."

Elias felt sorry for him. He doubted Commander Aimon would hold his wrath in check simply because the messenger was a child. He kept his voice low, out of Marco's hearing. "You're sneaking out of your own city," he pointed out, and saw the flush rise over the king's neck.

"And you need someone to guard your back," Ulises said. "We're going with you."

Elias stared at his friend, touched and dismayed in equal measure. "But Commander Aimon —"

"Commander Aimon, Commander Aimon," Ulises said, testy. "Who is king here?" And without another word, he spurred his horse through the doors. Marco prudently disappeared into one of the stalls.

Mercedes wore a forest-green traveling dress. A single thick braid fell to her waist, intertwined with streams of emerald ribbon. Elias said, "Don't look at me that way, Mercedes. I only wanted —"

"I know what you wanted, Elias, you wretch!" she burst out. "What was your plan? To pay some poor village girl to take my place?"

The pouch hanging from his belt felt heavier than it had a moment ago. Guilt gave him a surly edge. "Since when did you become a mind reader?"

"It's a simple thing to read your mind," she retorted. "You'll risk a stranger but not me?"

"You're the last person I'd risk," he said, not meaning to say it, and watched as all expression fled her face. Marco peeked over a stall, ears straining.

"Enough," Ulises said from the stable doors, his horse stamping impatiently. "We're wasting the sun. If it makes you both feel better, we can argue on the road."

Once the city walls were behind them, Ulises pulled up sharply and swung his horse around to face his companions. To Elias's complete and utter bewilderment, he started to laugh. Even Mercedes gave her cousin a worried look.

"What is so funny?" Elias demanded.

Ulises grinned. "Do you know, I don't remember the last time I've left Cortes without an army at my back. This I could grow used to!"

Elias held Pythagoras's reins loose in his grip, struck by his friend's words. He thought of the soldiers at the arena the day before. Always watching, always near, out of necessity, and his aggravation vanished like the morning mist. It was early enough that the path north up Marinus Road was deserted as far as the eye could see. They were alone with the cypress and the yew and the purple orchids that grew in clumps by the roadside. Mercedes made sure Ulises was not watching, then mouthed a single word in Elias's direction.

Peace?

And what could he say to that?

"Fine," Elias said, resigned. "If the commander is going to have our heads, we might as well make the most of it. A race to Portras?" Before his question was even finished, Ulises and Mercedes had flown past him.

"Cheats!" Elias yelled. He urged Pythagoras on to the sound of their laughter.

From Cortes, the landscape gave way to rolling pasture and fields covered in red poppies. The sky was an endless canvas of blue. A stream offered respite for their horses. On the opposite bank, a herder waited as his goats took turns in the water, oblivious to his king across the way. In their garb, well-made but simple, and without guards, they warranted no special attention.

Elias crouched by the water's edge, a waterskin in one hand. A goat lifted its head out of the stream and shook itself dry. He heard the cicadas among the branches. Unlike most places he'd visited, the tree crickets on del Mar chirped not only at night, but throughout the day. He listened to their rhythm; it reminded him of Lea's old wooden rattle. Something tickled his consciousness.

Just there.

So close.

Now lost.

"What do you have against goat herders?" Mercedes knelt

beside him to fill her own waterskin. When he glanced at her in question, she added, "You're glaring at that poor man like he stole the silver."

The herder eyed him nervously, pulling goats from the stream before they'd finished and hurrying them on their way, even after Elias checked his scowl and raised a hand in greeting. "I saw something on that map last night," he said. "Something out of place. And I can't think what it was."

Several feet away, Ulises fed his horse an apple. "It might need fresh eyes. Mercedes and I will have a look when we've left Javelin."

If *we leave Javelin*, Elias thought, though it felt surly to say so out loud when Ulises was so clearly enjoying the day. He held his tongue. They rode on, abreast of one another, Mercedes in the center.

They had not gone far when she said, "Elias, you've been to Mondrago. What do you think of it?"

A question out of nowhere. Elias glanced quickly at Ulises, who was quiet. He answered, "What makes you think I've been there?"

Travel to Mondrago was not exactly forbidden, but neither was it encouraged or looked upon with favor. After King Andrés had laid waste to the island, burning the crops, destroying the bridges, setting fire to the grand homes, he had placed a del Marian governor in charge. The man's duties were simple: he and his soldiers were to leave the island as it was. Nothing was to be rebuilt; no roads were to be repaired. Collapsed bridges were left fallen in the rivers. Ulises's father had wanted Mondrago to remain a wasteland, an example of a king's might and a king's grief.

"Elias," Ulises said in a matter-of-fact tone, "if someone tells you that you cannot do something, you'll do it. It's simply your nature. And if you haven't set foot on Mondrago, I will give you a thousand gold squid."

Mercedes smiled.

"Wait a . . ." Elias said, offended, before his words trailed away. Grudgingly, he said, "The castle was spared. But the rest . . . it's not a place you'd want to linger."

Mercedes was no longer smiling. The Mondragan king had been a distant relation of hers on her mother's side. "It's uninhabitable?"

He considered her question. If del Mar was celebrated for its explorers, then Mondrago, it could be said, had been equally known for its artists. Painters, sculptors, skilled artisans who had crafted exquisite stained glass and intricate mosaics. All gone now. Its people were allowed to live, but only just. Certainly they did not thrive.

"You could see what it had been once," he answered. "It's primitive now. Most of the people have left, and the ones who've stayed are just . . . downtrodden."

Ulises looked thoughtful. "What about the roads?"

"Rubble," Elias said.

"The bridges?" Mercedes asked.

"Rubble."

"And the governor?" Ulises asked. "What sort of man is he?"

Elias shrugged. "Competent enough. He does what he's ordered to do."

"Which means he does nothing," Mercedes said.

"Yes," Elias said. "This feels like an inquisition. What are you two up to?"

Ulises was blunt. "Mondrago's a waste as it is. We can't have it sit there for another twenty years, rotting away to nothing."

"It's like a fairy-tale kingdom that's gone to sleep," Mercedes said, and when they both looked at her, eyebrows arched, she turned defensive. "What? It's true."

Amused, Ulises said, "That is unusually whimsical of you, cousin. But yes."

Elias understood. A kingdom's true wealth was not measured by the amount of gold stored in its treasury. Like so many others, St. John del Mar was judged by the extent of its possessions abroad, its territories. These acquisitions were the driving force behind the School of Navigation. The ambition behind every expedition that sailed past the great harbor and into uncharted waters. Mondrago, as it stood now, was a worthless possession. Producing nothing.

"What will you do? Rebuild?" Elias asked. He thought of what that would mean and felt an unexpected excitement creep into him. The most current maps of Mondrago were two decades old. And, just as quickly, he remembered that if Mondrago was to be rebuilt, he would not be around to see its beginnings. He would be long gone, sailing west on the *Amaris*.

"I'm planning many things," Ulises answered. He might have read Elias's mind, because he looked over with a smile. "You can't be in two places at once, old friend."

Elias frowned. "What will happen to the governor?"

After a pause, Ulises said, "It might be time to bring him home."

From Marinus Road they turned onto a path far less traveled, bordered by cypress and winding downward into a valley known as the Cicada Pass. They skirted the village of Montserrat, Mori's boyhood home, the peal of church bells trailing after them, along with the bitter perfume of peppers drying in the sun. Elias was coaxing Pythagoras around a pile of sharp rocks when Ulises said abruptly, "I found one of my mother's letters yesterday. Among my father's things. She wrote it when Teodor was an infant."

Elias and Mercedes looked at each other. They had never known their queen. She had died when they were babies.

"What did she write about?" Mercedes asked softly.

"Small things," he said. "What she did during her day. My father had gone to Hellespont to attend Ari's wedding — his third one." Ulises frowned as he avoided a second clump of jagged rocks. Elias could almost see him taking note of the road conditions. He wondered how soon it would be before workmen were sent here to begin repairs. "She would spend afternoons outside the castle visiting with the townspeople. And she would toss sweets to the children. From great sacks of it in the square. It was a tradition." He turned to Mercedes, who had gone quiet. "I'd never heard of anyone doing that before. Have you?"

Mercedes shook her head.

"Well." Ulises spoke almost to himself. "It would be nice to see something like that again in Cortes."

Ulises did not look as if he expected a reply. Just as well, because Mercedes did not offer one. As the road narrowed, Ulises nudged his horse forward so that he rode ahead of them, alone in his thoughts. Elias kept pace beside Mercedes.

He had watched her as Ulises spoke. Had seen the dread in her eyes and knew what spooked her. Until Ulises married, she was the kingdom's highest-ranking female. She would be the one expected to maintain such traditions. It would be Mercedes in Cortes's main square, tossing great handfuls of sweets to the children. Would they dive for the treats, laughing and screaming? Or would the children remain silent and disappointed, their shoulders anchored by their mothers' disapproving hands? He pictured Mercedes standing alone, humiliated once again by someone who held her Mondragan blood against her. He nearly broke out in a sweat thinking about it.

Waiting until Ulises had moved well out of earshot, Elias said to her, "He would never force you to do it."

She gripped her reins tight. "He should have someone who will do these things for him, and do them gladly. Someone the people admire. I need to find him a wife."

That seemed to Elias a drastic measure. "You could do that," he agreed. "It might be simpler to ask others to help you. You wouldn't have to do it alone."

She sent him a blank look. "Who would I ask?"

Did she really not know? He started with his cousin. "You get on with Dita, don't you? With most of my family. And there's Reyna." When she did not answer, he said, "Mercedes." He waited until her eyes lifted to his. "Not everyone is like that old woman. Especially the little ones. They would not turn away sacks full of candy and shame you. Especially if you gave them . . . more."

"More sweets?"

"It doesn't have to be just sweets, does it? Make it so they can't say no to you. Make it so they have no wish to."

There was small silence. "Bribery? You think I should throw coins along with the sweets?"

He shrugged. "I would never turn down silver."

She was startled into a laugh. At the same time, Ulises slowed his horse and said, "Look."

They had come upon a meadow surrounded by a lemon grove on three sides. On the fourth side was a hill Elias knew was covered with leading stones. It had once been the compass makers' main source for magnetic stones, but no one ventured up there anymore, instead traveling to the hills on the opposite end of the island. They stopped their horses at the edge of the meadow. A plain white cross, twelve feet high, had been erected at the center.

"I've not been here in years," Ulises said quietly.

"No," Elias said. The sadness was thick here — it clung to his clothes and skin, pushed its way into his lungs as he breathed. He could almost picture the outing: soldiers and servants and princes, his father, colorful blankets thrown about, pigs roasting. A happy place, once.

They had all lost something that day. Not just Ulises and Elias. Mercedes's father, the old king's beloved brother, had died at Mondrago before her birth. A battle that never would have taken place but for what had happened here during that fatal picnic. And beyond even them, the widows and orphans and parents left to mourn the poisoned soldiers and loyal servants. Mercedes rubbed her arms, her skin having turned to goose flesh.

In the distance, the cicadas buzzed and rattled. And again, Elias had that feeling that he was missing something right in front of him. They did not linger, but turned their horses north, toward Javelin.

TEN

THEY WOULD HAVE to leave the horses behind.

As they approached the forest, with its graceful palms anchored in white sand, all three horses revolted. They pranced backward in nervous circles, nearly unseating their riders, and their neighing reached a pitch that sent a nest of warblers fleeing the treetops. No amount of coaxing or soothing would calm them. Only distance helped. They were led to a nearby copse of cypress where they could graze. Elias tried not to think of what the horses had sensed that he had not.

At the very edge of Javelin, Mercedes unfolded a yellow dress with lace trimming. "From Reyna," she explained. She laid it on the sand and smoothed out the creases. Ulises followed with miniature lemon cakes wrapped in wax paper. Elias, for his part, scattered about carved whistles shaped like the more common sea creatures: serpents, fish, molluscs. Beside them he placed a compass he had built himself. It wasn't really a toy, but some of the girls would have been the daughters of mariners, he'd reasoned. It could not hurt.

With that done, he knelt in the sand and steepled his hands

before him in prayer. His companions followed suit. A full ten seconds of silence passed before Mercedes looked past Ulises to frown at Elias. "What is the matter?" she asked.

"Nothing." Elias was sure, but it had been some time since he'd recited the *oratio*. Once again, he ran through the prayer in his mind. *Begin with the tree; end with the curse.*

Mercedes was not helping. "Then why do you look like you've swallowed something sour? Surely you haven't forgotten it?"

Both Ulises and Mercedes stared at him now with identical incredulous expressions.

"I'm *thinking*," Elias said, exasperated. "I haven't spoken it in months. Give me one moment to be sure I have it right."

"To be *sure*?" Mercedes echoed. "Wouldn't it have been simpler to write it down? What happens if—?"

Ulises held up a hand, weary. "Mercedes, let him alone. Elias, get on with it. Already this place makes me uneasy."

Elias answered Mercedes's huff with an unfriendly look, then bowed his head and tried to concentrate. He recited, "*From Saint Matthias, honored son of del Mar, I beg protection in daytime, and at night . . .*" He paused, continuing only after his companions had repeated each line:

> "*That no tree fall upon me,*
> *No flood rise against me,*
> *No weapons, no steel, no iron cut me,*
> *No fire burn me,*

No enemy hinder me,
No witchcraft, spell, or enchantment curse me."

And that was all. Within moments of entering the forest, the densely packed palms blotted the light, pitching them into semidarkness. Elias turned full circle, taking in their surroundings. The old paths had crept in on themselves, leaving little room for two people to walk side by side. Just as well, then, that the horses had stayed behind. He could hear water trickling from a stream and birdsong in the trees. Pleasant, peaceful sounds, even as every nerve within him was pulled tight. The air had a faint smoky quality to it. He breathed deep, feeling the slight tickle in his lungs.

Ulises spoke in a hush. "Something's burning."

Elias said, "Mori says it always smells like this. Ever since the orphanage burned down."

Ulises was dumbfounded. "That was two hundred years ago."

"I know it."

"Where do we go now?" Mercedes asked.

"The orphanage was built northeast of here," Elias said. A small box was strapped to his hip. He removed the compass from within and studied it. "That way," he said, pointing.

Ulises led the way. Their pace was swift and silent, helped along by the powdery sand cushioning their footsteps. With their swords, they beat back the grass and brush. Tension had coiled around Elias like a noose, but when an hour passed with nothing more alarming than a brown tree snake crossing their path, he found himself breathing easier. He could kiss Mori. He *would* kiss Mori, the next time he saw him. His friend had kept them safe.

Just ahead, Mercedes slapped uselessly at the summer gnats feasting on her arms. Red welts appeared on her skin. Elias offered her the tin of sheep fat. "It will keep the bugs away."

She took the tin. "What is it?"

"Better not to know." Elias tried to gauge the position of the sun through the tree cover. Even with the *oratio* and with Mercedes as their talisman, he had no great desire to linger in this forest come nightfall.

The palms were nearly identical, but the shrubs and grasses surrounding them were not. One in particular caught his attention: a waist-high plant with glossy green leaves and blue flowers. Mercedes stopped to watch him tear off a handful of both and crush them in his hand. When he opened his palm to show her, his skin was smeared in plant juice, a brilliant midnight blue in color. He smiled and explained, "It's an indigo plant. I'd no notion they grew on del Mar."

She touched his palm with the tip of her finger. "It's like sapphire. Is it for your paints?"

"When I can find it. It grows everywhere on Caffa. They use it with their beacons to send messages from the king."

Ulises had been keeping watch ahead. He retraced his steps at the mention of Caffa. "I've heard of their color fire. Do you know how it works?"

"I've never actually seen it done, but I think" — Elias crushed another leaf — "you throw the whole bush into the flames. It turns the smoke blue, bright enough to be seen at the next watchtower." He dusted the leaves from his hand. "The larger cities are assigned a specific color, and when it appears in a beacon, the soldiers know where the message came from."

Ulises plucked a leaf of his own but did not crush it. "The king's color is blue?"

"Yes." Elias inspected the immediate area to see what other plants were to be had. With growing enthusiasm, he said, "The saffron plant is used to burn yellow. And hematite is crushed into a powder for their reds. You can also burn green by stirring copper and vinegar, but the mixture is tricky. It must be precise. . . ." He trailed off at their glazed expressions and laughed. He had lost them so quickly. Too bad Luca wasn't here. Or even Reyna. He gave the bushes one last regretful look. He was not here to gather rare shrubbery. "Another time, maybe."

Once again, Ulises led the way. They had not gone far when he stopped dead in his tracks. Something about the line of his body gave them warning. He stepped aside so they could see what lay at his feet.

A worn leather glove. Its pair, and owner, nowhere to be found. Or at least not all of its owner. A hand remained in the glove, severed at the wrist. The stump was covered with sand and worms. Elias felt his stomach take one slow, sickening turn.

They drew their swords.

Mercedes, ever practical, spoke first. "Where is the rest of him?"

They searched, careful to stay within sight of one another. From nowhere, Elias remembered something Lord Silva had told him when they had ventured into the jungles of the Inner Jangas, known for its cannibals. *If you feel that you're in danger, Elias, it's likely because you are. Humans are the only animals that stop to think about their situation, to weigh the possibilities. Am I in danger? Am I not? The other animals? They just run.*

There was no sign of a body. No bootprints in the sand or even a break in the shrubbery to suggest the glove's owner had been carried off by a wild animal. Or something else. Finally, Elias dug a hole beside a palm. He laid the glove inside and covered it with rocks. After a brief prayer spoken by Ulises, they walked on in utter silence.

They might have missed the orphanage had they not been searching for it. It crept up on their left: three crumbling walls nearly hidden by palm cover. The clearing it had been built upon had long since been taken over by the forest.

"No one has been here in years," Ulises said, misgiving clouding his voice.

"It's smaller than I imagined," Mercedes said.

And sadder. They had not felt real to Elias, the girls and the nuns who had lived and died here. Until now, they had simply been the tragic figures in an old del Marian ghost story. He said quietly, "This was the main house." The remnants of a fireplace jutted from the center. "There would have been a chapel nearby and stables. Maybe a separate building to teach the girls their trade. The carvings would have been too large to keep here." He peered into the shadows and saw more crumbling stone in the distance. "You see there?"

"Yes," Ulises said. "I wish we knew what we were looking for."

Elias said, "If there's anything to find, I think we'll recognize it."

Mercedes was already pushing aside the tall grass and stomping through. "I'll start over there," she said, indicating one of the outbuildings.

Ulises chose to search the main house. By default, Elias found himself in the ruins of an old warehouse. The smell of smoke was stronger here. The original structure had been long and narrow, with arched windows, like a church without the altar and pews. The glass from the windows was gone, as well as any furniture and tools, but he was astonished to see that one of the ship figureheads had survived. It lay toppled on its side. Part of the wood had rotted through, though enough remained that he could see what it had once been. A seahorse, partially complete, carved by someone with great skill.

He spent some time among the rubble, trying to find anything that would bring clarity to the riddle. *Look not to what is there but to what is not.* He inspected what was left of the walls, inside and out. Perhaps a message had been carved there or left in a crevice. He knelt, tried to turn over the seahorse, and earned a nasty sliver in his finger for his trouble. He was attempting to remove it with his pincers when Ulises appeared.

"Anything?" Ulises asked.

"No" was his curt response. He pulled the sliver free and inhaled sharply. It had always been a mystery to him how such a small injury could smart so badly.

"I feel like a fool, Elias. This has been for nothing."

The embarrassment in Ulises's voice was enough to distract Elias momentarily from his own personal anguish. "What has it cost us?" he reasoned. "A day? A finger?" He held up his pained finger to show his friend, who gave it a disinterested glance.

Ulises said, "I don't know what I thought we'd find here. Stupid."

"It wasn't." Elias stood. "The maps together are hard to ignore. Reyna came to you with the riddle, and you have always been willing to listen. It's simply in your nature."

Ulises heard his own words tossed back at him; a small smile emerged. Elias could hear Mercedes on the other side of the half-crumbled wall, speaking to herself and trying to commit the *oratio* to memory. "*No weapons, no steel, no iron cut me. No fire burn me —*"

"*Flame,*" Elias called absently. He returned the pincers to his pouch and sucked on his finger.

Mercedes appeared over the wall like a springing toy. Only her head was visible. "What flame?"

"*No flame burn me,*" Elias corrected. "Not *fire.*"

Her brows drew together. She vanished, reappearing a moment later by squeezing through an impossibly narrow gap in the stone. "That is not what you said."

"It is." Elias glanced from Mercedes to Ulises and back again. An odd prickling sensation crawled along his neck. "Of course it is."

"You said *fire*." Ulises had knelt to give the seahorse a closer look. "Does it matter? One word?"

"It matters very much."

Everything around Elias became small and still. The voice had come from above their heads. A girl sat high in the cradle of a broken window, her bare feet dangling. She wore Reyna's yellow dress. In her hands was the compass he'd left at the edge of the forest.

Slowly, Elias bowed at the waist. "Forgive —"

The girl did not look at him. She spoke to Mercedes in a soft voice that echoed over the stone and through the windows and between the palms: "We do not like them. They are not safe."

We?

If Mercedes were rattled, she did not show it. "They mean you no harm." She spoke quietly, calmly. "I promise you. But we will go now, if you do not wish us here." She took a step back. Elias and Ulises followed, taking one cautious step and then another. The girl did not move, only watched them with wide, unblinking eyes.

They did not get far. A low rumble, like thunder, emerged from nowhere, followed by a whistling among the trees. In the distance, palms fell to the side, a pathway cleared by some invisible force. Clumps of sand flew up. As something drew closer and closer.

And closer.

From Ulises, low and urgent: *"Run."*

Elias grabbed Mercedes's hand. They ran, jumping over the seahorse and tripping over stones. The side walls were too high to climb in a hurry. The only opening beckoned from the far end of the warehouse. Elias's heart beat faster than the drumming in his ears. *Fire. Flame. A stupid mistake.* It was his last thought before they were surrounded.

By eight spirits who had once been little girls. Several of them looked as solid as the one in the yellow dress. Others shimmered and faded, so that he could see the palms behind them and the moss-covered stones. The youngest looked to be around six, with curly brown hair and dimples. Elias had time enough to think, *Why, they are not so scary,* before the curly-haired spirit stepped forward, snatched him by the front of his vest, and threw him straight up in the air.

She was stronger than any living being. His world spun upside down; it turned sideways. Ulises flew right past him. Elias tumbled into another child's arms, recoiled at the toothy grin inches from his face, and was once again tossed high. The spirits laughed.

Where was Mercedes? His senses were muddled, but he thought he saw her standing beneath the girl in yellow. Mercedes, with her arms gesturing wildly, arguing with a ghost. A thought flitted by: *You should not argue with a ghost.* Ulises was on his hands and knees in the sand, heaving. Elias lost sight of them both.

It dawned on him. They were playing catch, only they weren't very good at it. Both he and Ulises were dropped. Elias landed on his arms, his face, his back. His mouth was full of sand and twigs. He tasted the sharp tang of blood. The spirits giggled hysterically, their laughter growing higher and higher in pitch, so that he thought his ears would burst. And that is how it continued, for how long, he had no notion. Until he landed on the ground beside Ulises, and Mercedes was there.

She flung herself on top of them both, her green skirt swirling about like a protective cape. Elias grunted as her knee dug sharply into his gut. "Please!" she cried. "Stop! These are my friends."

Surprisingly, the spirits stopped. They retreated into a half circle, watching as Mercedes pulled Elias and Ulises to their knees. Ulises spat out a mouthful of dirt. The circle opened, and the girl in Reyna's dress stood looking down at them. Even with his pounding head, Elias could see the difference. The other spirits looked happy, bouncing on their toes and eager to continue what they thought was a game. This one . . . she did not smile at all, but watched them with the saddest eyes he'd ever seen. Brown eyes. Was she the only one who remembered what had befallen them?

The sad spirit said, "We do not like them. They are not safe."

"Get behind me, Mer—" Ulises began.

"Be quiet!" Mercedes hissed. Then, louder, "This is not the man who harmed you. This is Ulises. He is your king." When they looked at Ulises uncertainly, she added firmly, "You are del Marians, are you not? Loyal citizens. You would not hurt your king."

The spirits turned to the girl in yellow. Clearly, she was their leader. Her gaze shifted reluctantly to Ulises, who did not look so kingly, covered in dirt and scratches. She studied him for the longest time, saying nothing, then turned to Elias. "*He* is not our king."

Mercedes's gaze shot to his, long enough for him to see the panic in her eyes. For him. She turned back to the spirit. "No," she acknowledged. "However —"

"We do not like him. He is not safe."

Elias remembered the hand covered in sand and worms. He held himself perfectly still.

"Please," Mercedes said gently. "I am sorry you were hurt, but he is not like the man who hurt you. His name is Elias, and he has two little sisters. Just like you. He is kind to them. He brings them gifts, like the compass you have there. It is a good compass, is it not? He made it himself." Mercedes's words were like a melody, soft and soothing.

The girl looked down at the compass. She cradled it closer.

Mercedes said, "He is safe."

The spirits looked at one another, engaging in some sort of wordless communication. The girl in yellow said, "Words matter very much."

Everyone, living and dead, turned to Elias. He understood. She was giving him a chance to fix his mistake. *Flame*, not *fire*.

He would never again forget this particular prayer. He bowed his head, steepled his hands, and recited with some difficulty:

"From Saint Matthias, honored son of del Mar, I beg protection in daytime, and at night, that:
No tree fall upon me,
No flood rise against me,
No weapons, no steel, no iron cut me,
No flame burn me,
No enemy hinder me,
No witchcraft, spell, or enchantment curse me."

They were gone. Leaving no trace. Mercedes collapsed onto the sand beside Ulises, who slung an arm around her shoulders and gave her a smacking kiss on the head. "Well done!" To Elias, he added a less friendly, *"Fire. Flame.* Fool."

Well, he deserved it. Elias rubbed a sore arm and groaned, "Apologies."

"Is anything broken?" Mercedes asked them.

Gingerly, Ulises inspected his ribs. "No."

Elias felt around his teeth with his tongue. Nothing loose or chipped; good. "Just bruised. I'll live. Peace, Mercedes. You can say it."

"What can I say?"

"That you were right to be here, and I was wrong. I know you want to say it."

She rose, dusted the sand from her green dress, and looked

down her nose at him. "That would be petty. And childish. I would never say something like that." She offered her hand. "But know that I am thinking it."

He laughed and kissed her hand, which she snatched away from him. He got to his feet without her help. His sword and carrier lay undamaged by the seahorse. He gathered them up and said, "There's nothing to find in this godforsaken forest. We've made a mistake, Ulises."

Ulises grimaced. "Agreed. Let's go."

"Sound advice," said a voice above them.

They spun. If there had been a warbler speaking to them, Elias could not have been more astounded.

Before them was a crumbling wall, eight feet high. Standing on it was a woman. She looked wild. Silver and black hair unbound and flowing down her back. Dressed as a man in dark trousers and a vest cinched tight over a shirt. One trouser leg rolled up to reveal a wooden stump in place of a leg. And a crossbow aimed directly at them. "Your swords," she said. "On the ground, if you please."

Mercedes stood to Elias's right. Ulises to his left. Nobody moved. Elias's thoughts were churning, and not just because of her crossbow. Her voice. It was not the rasp of a crone, some madwoman in the forest. It was not even that of a common peasant, but smooth and learned. A voice of privilege. The strange woman shifted her bow so that it pointed directly at Elias's heart.

Ulises began, "Who are —"

"My arms grow weary, young masters. I would not like to kill you by accident."

Elias and Ulises held on to their swords. Somehow, Mercedes's sword had ended up on the sand against the opposite wall.

The woman raised an eyebrow. "No? You prefer an arrow in your gullet?"

"A crossbow is a fine weapon, Madame," Elias answered, his voice cold. "But you'll only have time to shoot one of us."

She considered his words. "That is true," she admitted, before slowly aiming at Mercedes. Fear sliced through him, sharper than anything he'd ever felt. He was afraid to move, did not want to provoke her in any way that meant Mercedes would be hurt. "But you can be very sure that your charming companion will feel the first shot. And then won't your conscience sting?"

With a curse, Elias flung his sword onto the sand. Ulises did the same.

The woman was studying Ulises, head cocked, a look of puzzlement on her face.

"You." She pointed with her arrow. "Come closer."

"Do *not*," Mercedes breathed.

Ulises walked forward until he stood in a square of light.

There was a gasp. The woman lowered her crossbow an inch. And her voice, when it came, was no longer assured, but shaken.

"Bartolome?"

Ulises stiffened. He glanced wide-eyed over his shoulder at

them, then turned back and said, cautiously, "My brother's name was Bartolome. I am Ulises."

"Ulises." The crossbow lowered, its end touching the wall. All color had leached from her face. "One day an infant, the next a grown man. Have the years gone by so quickly, then?"

A strange feeling settled over Elias. He thought of the maps, and of the woman with a cross surrounded by children. Not an abbess. A cross symbolized many things, and many people. A nun, a healer.

Or a royal nurse who had accompanied two princes on a picnic. One day, long ago, never to be seen again.

"My lady Esma?" Elias asked, and felt Mercedes start beside him. The strange woman flinched, and he knew with a terrible certainty that he had spoken true.

ELEVEN

ADY ESMA LED them deep into the forest, responding to their uneasy looks with a "Be at ease. They won't harm you now." True to her word, the spirits stayed hidden, but Elias knew they were there. Their presence was palpable — in the shifting shadows of the trees, in the screeching silence of the birds.

The sea air came upon them. They broke through the palms to find an old cottage balanced precariously near the cliff's edge. The ramshackle structure looked as though it were held up by nothing more than crumbling stone and daily prayer. Off to one side was a pen where a pig the size of a small horse watched their approach. The surf could be heard far below, crashing against the rocks.

They ducked into the cottage: a single chamber, surprisingly comfortable, with a bed against a far wall, a fireplace, and clean rushes on the floor. The chamber smelled pleasantly of the red oleander drying above a window. Lady Esma set her crossbow against the wall and indicated a scarred wooden table with four chairs. "You may be yourselves here."

Elias caught Ulises's eye. They did not sit in her chairs, nor did they set their weapons aside. Instead, Elias swung the door shut, the thud causing Lady Esma's head to whip around. Her three visitors stood with their backs braced against the wall, tense and watchful. As the princes' trusted nurse, Esma of Cortes had once been an important member of the royal household. Who knew what she was now? Her body had not been among those discovered in the meadow on that long-ago fateful night. She was assumed to have been kidnapped along with the boys and Lord Antoni. She was thought to have drowned when their ship was lost at sea. Elias could not think of a single satisfactory reason for her presence here, and until he did, he would not let down his guard.

"Perhaps you're right to be mistrustful." Lady Esma also remained standing, her hands on a chairback. They had discovered earlier that her leg, far from being a plain wooden stump, had been carved into the shape of a seahorse. Just like the figurehead inside the old warehouse.

Lady Esma studied Mercedes with a peculiar expression on her face. "Who are you?"

"My lady Esma." Mercedes spoke formally; they might have been strangers greeting each other at the king's high table. "My name is Mercedes. My mother was the lady Alyss, wife to Prince Augustin, brother to King Andrés."

There was a sharp intake of breath. "*Was* the Lady Alyss? She is no longer?"

"My *maman* has been gone two years."

Clearly, Mercedes's mother had not been a stranger to the lady Esma. Tears sprang into the older woman's eyes, which she tried fiercely to blink away. "Of what ailment?"

Mercedes did not answer. It was Elias who responded, his tone brusque. "An accident." This was not the time to speak of Lady Alyss, or of how she died.

Lady Esma's gaze fell on Ulises, who'd placed an arm around his cousin's shoulders, then on Elias, whose words were so obviously a lie. But all she said was "I grieve for your loss."

"And my mother grieved for yours" was Mercedes's cool response. "She spoke of you often as a dear friend. Your death was felt keenly in our household." Her unspoken words lingered. Esma's assumed death had caused her mother unnecessary sorrow. It was not something Mercedes would easily forgive.

If Lady Esma heard the rebuke, she gave no sign of it. She glanced at Elias's map carrier, the brown leather battered from years of abuse. "You're a mapmaker? A geographer?"

Elias bowed. "Yes, Lady. My name is Elias, son of —"

He was stopped by her laugh, short and humorless. "I know who your parents are, Lord Elias." She pulled out a chair. "Sit. If I wanted to harm you, I would simply call out. The children have always been very . . . protective of me."

It was a warning of her own. As if to underscore the threat, Elias saw a flash of yellow at the window, followed by giggles and an indignant squeal from the pig.

They sat.

Lady Esma placed a bowl on the table. She poured water

into it from a pitcher, then submerged several white cloths and wrung them out. She handed them to Ulises and Elias. Not Mercedes; she was not covered in dirt and scratches as they were.

"Mind your lip," Lady Esma said to Ulises, who pressed the cloth to his face and winced. "You showed foresight in bringing a woman with you." Lady Esma took the chair beside Ulises. "I've seen the men who venture into Javelin on their own. They believe the old stories of pirate gold buried here and decide the risk is worth taking. A few of them are still here, somewhere."

She spoke in a matter-of-fact tone. To her, the dismembering of men was something unremarkable. Elias found her just as unsettling as the spirits lingering outside.

"My lady Esma," Ulises said, "how are you here? The entire kingdom, including your family, thinks you're dead."

Lady Esma looked as if she was having some sort of silent argument with herself. The crease between her brows deepened. "I should start from the beginning," she said.

"It's as good a place as any," Mercedes said.

Lady Esma folded her hands on the table. They were rough, with skin like tree bark, and unlike those of the ladies of the court, bare of even a single piece of jewelry. "First, will you tell me . . . what has become of my family?"

A brief silence. Mercedes said, "Your sister is Lady Bernat?"

"Yes. She was not Lady Bernat when I left. She was betrothed. Is she well?"

"Quite," Mercedes said, still wary, but her tone was not

unkind. "Lord and Lady Bernat have three children. Two boys and a girl. Their eldest son is nearly grown."

Lady Esma was quiet. "And my parents?"

Mercedes said, "I am sorry, Lady, we never knew them. They passed on long ago."

Lady Esma did not look surprised, but her voice was more subdued when she said again, "I should start from the beginning."

"Please," Ulises said.

"Bartolome was seven years old," Lady Esma told him, "and at that age, he had no interest in becoming king. He wanted to be an explorer, an adventurer. Just like Antoni. To find out for himself what lay beyond the Strait of Cain." To Elias, Lady Esma said, "Your father promised to show him some magic compass rocks that could be found on the hill by the lemon groves."

"The leading stones," Elias said.

"Yes." Lady Esma glanced down, noting, "You have his hands."

Elias's fingers curled reflexively. "Lady?"

"Your father's hands were always covered in paint, usually blue," Lady Esma explained. "Strange. I haven't had that thought in years. Why that color?"

Everyone was looking at Elias's hands, freshly stained by the leaves of the indigo plant, like his father's. It was a detail he'd never known, some small connection to a man he did not remember.

"I use it to paint the sea," he said. "The rivers, the lakes. Blue is the color a mapmaker uses most." Uncomfortable, he let his hands drop beneath the table, out of sight, and felt Mercedes's hand slip into his. They did not look at each other, but instantly he felt better.

"I see." Abruptly, Lady Esma stood. Her chair scraping. Her leg scraping, too. They watched as she busied herself in filling four mugs. They were passed around; Mercedes and Ulises eyed their drinks with dubious expressions. And no wonder — the liquid was thick and green, like pea soup, and smelled curiously of limes.

"Verboun?" Elias asked. The brew was popular in the roughest of ports. Once, on Coronado, he'd made the mistake of drinking his fill in a single evening, and he had paid the price for it all the next day.

Lady Esma said, "We'll need something stronger than water for the conversation we're about to have, I think."

Ulises looked into his cup, then at the red oleander drying above the window. Oleander was a well-known poison. He said to their host, "You first."

A half smile formed. What might have been approval flickered in Lady Esma's eyes. She tossed back her cup.

Elias was impressed. He took a delicate sip, then set his cup down and rubbed Mercedes's back while she gagged and coughed. "It's an acquired taste, Mercedes. Take a breath."

"Is that what it is?" Mercedes breathed in and out, and said, "I don't think I'll be acquiring it again."

Elias shared an unexpected amused glance with Lady Esma, who asked, "Where was I?"

Ulises's face was fiery, but he answered evenly enough, "The picnic."

Lady Esma's hands tightened around her empty cup. "We decided to make a day of it. We brought a feast, games. Prince Teodor came along only because he wanted to be wherever his brother was." Elias would reflect on it much later, her flash of pain at the mention of the younger prince. "When we left that morning, it was with more than enough guards to protect us. Or so we thought. We did not expect danger to come from within."

"Someone had poisoned the wine barrels," Mercedes said.

"Yes. Not the cask belonging to the boys. Their cider was kept separate. They'd had their fill already."

"You didn't drink the wine?" Elias asked.

"No. Though I would have, eventually." Lady Esma's eyes had taken on the stare of someone recalling a nightmare. "I went into the grove for privacy, and it was not long before I heard . . ."

This time, the silence went on for such a time that Ulises prompted, "Lady?"

"People screaming," she said. "Being sick. And then the horses coming fast. There were five men wearing masks that covered the lower half of their faces. They swept in and snatched the princes by their necks. As if they were kittens." Anger threaded its way around her words. "Antoni tried to stop them, but it was five against one. They beat him, and when he fell, they threw him over a horse."

Elias could feel his heart hammering in his chest. "He was alive when he left?"

"All four of them were."

"Four?" Ulises asked sharply.

Lady Esma said, "Yes. One of the servants, I believe. A girl."

Elias sat back. It made no sense. The only people missing were the boy princes, Lady Esma, and Lord Antoni. Everyone else had been accounted for, claimed among the dead. Every servant, every soldier. What girl did she speak of?

Mercedes had visibly thawed toward Lady Esma during the retelling. "You were right to stay hidden," she said. "The . . . Mondragans would have killed you, too."

Lady Esma turned to her, perplexed. "Mondragans? Those men weren't from Mondrago. They were del Marian." The silence was absolute. Even the ghosts were quiet, peering in through the window.

Ulises found his voice first. "You're mistaken," he said, his tone flat. "A Mondragan soldier confessed. He was following his king's orders."

"Confessed? What became of him?"

Ulises said, "He was hanged."

Lady Esma's hand went to her throat. "And Mondrago?"

"Is ours now."

Lady Esma's eyes never left the king's. "I heard them speak," she said, insistent. "I will never forget it. They sounded as del Marian as you and I. It was their native tongue."

Elias said, "I know several languages, Lady. It would be a

simple thing for me to pass for a Lunesian or a Caffeesh if I wore their clothing and hid my face behind a mask."

But Lady Esma was shaking her head. "That was not all. Two of the men stayed back while the others . . . did what they were told. I heard one of them say, 'We will not speak when they are near. They will know my voice.' And the other said, "Don't you want them to know?' 'No,' he answered. 'It will be worse for him . . . the wondering.'"

Neither of Elias's companions looked capable of speech just then, so he asked, "Did you recognize their voices?"

Lady Esma hesitated. "One sounded like you. A nobleman. The other was rougher. He said, 'The king won't stop looking until someone is punished for this.' And the first man . . ."

It was Mercedes who filled the void with a quietness steeped in ice. "Don't stop now, Lady Esma."

Lady Esma looked at her without expression. "He said, 'Coronads, Mondragans, Bushidos . . . I don't care who they blame. I've done what I came to do.' The other man answered, 'I don't care who they blame either, so long as it isn't us.'"

Mercedes had gone very still, and her face . . . Elias stood; he could not sit while Lady Esma threw one revelation after another at them. He paced to one end of the chamber, turned, paced back.

Among the three of them, Ulises was the most composed. "How did you come to be here?"

"Once they'd gone," Lady Esma said, "I looked to see if anyone had survived. There was not one living soul there. I was not myself after what I saw. I ran into the woods and wandered for some time, eating what I could find." Her lips twisted at the memory. "I knew nothing about surviving in a forest then, and I ate berries that were not meant to be eaten. The spirits carried me here to this cottage. It had been abandoned."

"They cared for you," Ulises said.

"Yes," Lady Esma said. "Much later, they told me the bad men had returned the next day. The girls could hear them calling my name, though the men would not come into the woods. They must have realized by then that I was missing. Not among the dead, and certainly not with them."

"And your leg?" Ulises asked. "You did not carve that yourself."

"There was an accident, years ago. The carving was a gift."

She had left a lifetime out in the telling. And Elias could see from her expression that her story would stop there.

He reached for his carrier and tried to calm his racing thoughts. "My lady Esma, you've told your story, and I thank you. May I tell you another?"

"Yes."

Elias showed her the map and explained all they knew. Reading aloud the riddle in the border. Pointing out the alder and oak, not palms, that made up Javelin Forest. He finished with "Whoever painted this map knew you survived that day, and that you were somewhere in these woods. Can you explain how that could be?"

Lady Esma looked at the image of herself on the map. A

woman with a cross, surrounded by her faceless wards. Elias held his breath, waiting for an answer.

Her eyes lifted to his, stunned. "Antoni saw me," she said quietly. "He was beaten, badly. But as they were riding past, he looked straight at me. One eye swollen shut, the other bloody. He mouthed one word only."

"What word?" Elias asked.

"*Hide*. He told me to hide. And he pointed toward the forest." She wrapped her arms around herself and, though the chamber was warm and pleasant, shivered. "Do you know, I hear their screams sometimes, in my head? It was so many years ago. And yet I hear them still."

Barely a word was spoken as Lady Esma saw them back through the forest. Whatever Ulises thought was tucked away behind a stony expression. Mercedes was the quietest of them all. She walked beside Elias, ashen but for the two spots of color on her cheeks. A smoldering torch.

As for him, the spirits that trailed after them were the least of his troubles. A thousand questions ran through his mind, every one of them unanswered. If the Mondragans were not behind that long-ago crime, who was? And if his father and the princes had not died a watery death, where had they gone? They must be dead, for how does one keep the presence of two royal princes and a lord of the realm a secret without a whisper making its way home? There was no place so isolated. Why had they not sent word? He thought of the maps and felt himself a fool. Perhaps they had, the only way they knew how.

Another horrible thought: if the Mondragan king had spoken true, then del Mar had laid waste to a kingdom wholly innocent. Killed the royal family and scores of their countrymen, ravaged their lands, destroyed their heritage.

For nothing.

"Your horses are just there," Lady Esma said.

Pulled from his grisly thoughts, Elias saw that they had reached the edge of the forest. It was early evening, though the sun was bright. The days were growing longer. If they hurried, they would be able to travel most of the way home with enough light left to guide their way. Elias gathered the horses. He handed the reins to Mercedes, murmuring, "Mercedes, are you all right?"

"Why shouldn't I be?" she said, and did not meet his eyes.

Ulises reached for Lady Esma's hands, stopping when she drew back sharply, her leg digging a shallow trench in the sand. Elias saw the sympathy in his friend's eyes and wondered when Lady Esma had last touched another human being. Eighteen years?

Ulises said, "Come with us."

"No."

"Then I'll speak with your sister. She must be told —" Lady Esma's horrified look silenced him.

She said, "You think you're doing me a kindness. You're not. My family remains safe because I'm dead."

Elias had been tightening the strap on his saddlebag. At her words, he looked over. Not *because I am thought dead,* but *because I'm dead.* She had chosen her words deliberately. Lady Esma had no intention of ever returning to her old life in Cortes.

Ulises would not give up so easily. "It's been eighteen years, Lady."

"What does time matter?" Lady Esma asked. "My king, you must take care. You've said you are not the only ones who know of the maps."

Lord Silva, Reyna, Commander Aimon.

"They're friends," Elias said. "Not anyone who would wish us harm."

Lady Esma said, "Friend or foe, it takes only one to speak carelessly, and if the wrong person suspects you know more than you should, your life . . . your lives will be forfeit." She turned to Mercedes, who was sitting marble-faced on her horse and staring off into the distance. "You're angry. I do not blame you."

Mercedes looked down at her. "Angry," she repeated in a tone that had both men exchanging alarmed glances. "My father died before I was born," Mercedes continued. "He fell at Mondrago. Did you know this, Lady?"

"No."

"Of course you would not, cowering here in your forest." Mercedes brought her horse forward so that it was within inches of the lady Esma, who, to her credit, did not flinch. "Once, when I was very young, I visited the market with my *maman.* She did not venture out often, but I had begged her to go, and finally she said yes. Our guards were not quick enough to protect her from a man who appeared from nowhere, who hit her in the face and called her names . . . names no child should ever hear her mother called."

Lady Esma had fallen back a step. Mercedes pressed on. "He had lost his son during the siege, you see. He had lost his wits to grief. And that day . . . it was the first time I understood that there was something wrong with being part Mondragan, and that being part del Marian mattered not at all. Because of what had happened to my dear lost cousins. It was the first of many insults I've witnessed, Lady. And my *maman* was so gentle and kind, every word against her was like that man's fist. You would know this."

By now the tears were falling unchecked from Lady Esma's face. "Yes."

"Shall I tell you how she died?" Mercedes asked. "You wanted to know."

Lady Esma said nothing. Her eyes were red with sorrow.

With her face devoid of color, Mercedes's freckles stood out in stark relief. "I am an emissary for the royal house of del Mar. Two years ago, she saw my ship off as she always did and waited until it had disappeared from the horizon. And then she filled her skirts with rocks and walked into the sea."

"Mercedes," Ulises said, his voice strained. "Dearest."

Elias did not try to silence her. He had been the one to tell her of her mother's death. The nature of it. Sailing off even before Lady Alyss's funeral, he had caught up with Mercedes on Lunes. She had smiled when she'd seen him riding into the castle courtyard. Surprised and delighted to see him. After that day, she had not smiled again for a very long time.

Lady Esma said, "I am sorry —"

But Mercedes was not finished. "Lord Antoni could not have meant for you to hide forever. You tell us this fantastic tale, Lady Esma, and I wonder now how different our lives would have been if you'd come home and spoken the truth. Words matter very much. That is what your little friend said, isn't it? Well. You ask if I am angry. Perhaps there's another word for what I feel. A stronger word."

Behind Lady Esma, at the edge of the forest, figures emerged. Mere pinpricks of light at first, like fireflies, before they grew larger and once again took on the appearance of children. They formed a protective half circle around Lady Esma. The girl in yellow stood just behind Esma, glaring at Mercedes. "Hush!" the girl warned.

All three horses reared back in fright. Mercedes lifted her chin in defiance, and then she turned and raced away.

Elias found Mercedes by the lemon groves. Here, the cicadas sang freely. She sat on the ground, peeling a blade of grass to shreds. Her horse nuzzled her hair, perhaps sensing she needed comfort.

"I wish . . ." Her voice was low and scratchy with unshed tears.

He sat beside her, close enough that his arm touched hers. "I know it."

"She was my *maman's* friend, and an elder." She flung the grass aside. "I should not have shown her such disrespect."

"Stop." Something heavy pressed against his heart. "I hate that you've always felt this way. That when you see yourself in a looking glass, you see someone who is . . . not enough. Someone not worthy of calling herself a del Marian." He pulled her close and rested his chin on her head. "Do you know what I see when I look at you?"

She shook her head and sniffled into his shirt.

"I see Mercedes," he said quietly. "Not your parents, not your bloodline. I have only ever seen you." He pulled back slightly, waiting until she lifted her face to his. Eyes like sea glass, bright with tears. "I would cut down every person who's hurt you if I could. If it would make you feel better."

Another sniffle, then, "Every person? With your sword?"

The pressure in his chest lightened. Almost, she sounded like her old self. "What else?" he asked.

"You forget to bring your sword half the time."

He smiled until she said, "Elias, I miss my mother." This time, when her tears came, she did not try to stop them.

He held tight, overcome by an angry helplessness. She did not notice his sudden start. Over her head, not twenty feet away, he spied soldiers dressed in green and silver. A handful only, surrounding a game table. Elias could see right through them to the lemon groves. Dice tumbled across the table. The soldiers were laughing, though he heard nothing except the cicadas buzzing and the horses shuffling and Mercedes weeping quietly in his arms. One man in particular sent a frisson of recognition up his spine. Head shaved bald, eyes lined in kohl, he bore an uncanny resemblance to Commander Aimon. Elias had forgotten; the commander had also lost a father that day. Too many ghosts. He closed his eyes and pressed his face into Mercedes's hair, breathing in the warm orange scent. When he opened his eyes, the men were gone.

Mercedes had nearly cried herself out when they heard a horse approaching. Appalled, he thought, *Ulises*. Elias had left him behind with Lady Esma to chase after Mercedes and had forgotten all about him. Some guard *he* was. They were both on their feet by the time Ulises dismounted. He said nothing of Mercedes's tear-stained face, only brushed a hand against her hair and said, "It will be dark soon. We should go." To Elias, abruptly, "I've asked too much of you."

"You ask more of yourself," Elias said.

He had seen Ulises the day King Andrés died. His friend had been stoic and kingly until the crowds had gone and there was no one but Elias and Mercedes to witness his grief. Since boyhood, he had seen Ulises pleased, angry, bored, curious, insulted, indifferent — every feeling under the moon and the stars. Elias had never seen him as he was today, could think of no other word to use than *staggered*.

"I didn't take it seriously," Elias admitted. "I thought I would humor you by coming to Javelin. And then we could leave it alone."

Mercedes dashed more tears away with the back of her hand. "They're alive, aren't they? Somewhere. After all this time."

Ulises spun around and was thoroughly and violently ill. Warblers broke through the tree cover, flying away as the smell of limes and sickness engulfed them.

TWELVE

I**T WAS A** grim ride home. By the time they stopped by the river, dusk had settled, and above them the sky was a somber intermingling of orange and gray. Mercedes and Ulises filled their skins by the water, each silent and preoccupied.

Elias skipped stones across the river. His own thoughts kept circling back to the forest. When the sixth stone disappeared beneath the surface, he asked, "Who gained the most?" Then, when his companions turned to him, "If what Lady Esma says is true, and if Mondrago had nothing to do with what happened, we should look at things a different way." He said to Ulises, "Your brothers. Who would gain from their deaths?"

"Besides me, you mean?" Ulises answered with bleak humor.

"Yes," Elias said, and then fell silent as he remembered the soldiers in the meadow playing their game of dice.

"What is it?" Mercedes asked.

Another stone skipped. "It's just . . . twenty dead soldiers," Elias said. "It would leave a hole in the ranks, wouldn't it? And with the king's guard. Men would have to be promoted quickly to replace them."

Ulises's expression darkened, but Mercedes looked thoughtful.

"That's true," she acknowledged. "But the same could be said for any profession, not just soldiering."

"What are you thinking?" Ulises asked, low and angry. "That we should suspect every high-ranking soldier in Cortes? Every weapon maker who turned a profit because of Mondrago? What cynics we've become." He tossed his waterskin to the ground and rose, his expression one of weariness and disgust.

As far as Elias could tell, Ulises had thrown up everything he'd eaten today and had refused the supper Mercedes had tried to press upon him. He said, "Ulises." The king faced him. "Should I stop looking?"

Mercedes made a small sound: dismay, consternation. Elias did not look at her. No secret had been made of his wishes. He had wanted to tear up the maps and forget their existence. But that was before they had met the lady Esma. Now a powerful longing filled him — to follow the bread crumbs hidden in the maps, to discover what had befallen the father who had been taken from him. Despite the danger.

But it was not only about his wishes. Ulises was his friend. And of anyone on del Mar, Ulises stood to lose most of all.

"Would you stop?" Ulises's expression was impossible to read.

Elias answered quietly. "For you, yes."

Ulises had been holding his breath; he exhaled in a great sweeping rush. "No," he said. "I would regret it forever. So would you. We need to find out what happened. . . ." His eyes flickered to Mercedes. "The three of us. And let the stones fall where they may."

Mercedes went to tuck her waterskin into her saddlebag. She looked over suddenly. "Who was the girl?"

Elias had nearly forgotten about the servant who had ridden off with the men.

"Lady Esma could have been mistaken," Ulises said. "Or maybe someone couldn't stomach killing a female. They decided to take her with them instead."

"They had no trouble killing the other female servants," Elias pointed out. He said to Mercedes, "You think she was an accomplice."

"Why not?" Mercedes asked. "It's what I would do. Have someone at the picnic to make sure everyone had their share of wine and wouldn't cause trouble."

Dubious, Ulises said, "It's a cold woman who would pour out poison to all those people."

"Women can be as cold as men," Mercedes insisted. "Colder, even." She cinched the tie on her saddlebag, gave her horse a pat. "It would be a matter of wooing the right person on the inside. A servant wouldn't have much coin. Think of it. A young woman, poor, vulnerable, without family and male protection, perhaps, made to feel loved and important. She would do anything you asked if you made her feel like a queen."

Elias said, "If she worked inside the castle, why didn't anyone know she was missing? Every person that day was claimed."

Mercedes frowned. "That part escapes me."

The buzzing of the cicadas had grown louder, causing the horses to lift their heads from the water. Elias could only hear them, not see them, but he knew they were gold in color, and with their wings spread, they were often mistaken for butterflies.

Gold cicadas . . . He grabbed his carrier and removed the map.

"What is it?" Mercedes said as he unrolled it onto the grass. All three knelt by the parchment, squinting in the near darkness.

"A tree cricket." Elias sat back on his heels, marveling. "It's been bothering me all day. Look here." Within the inset that showed Cortes, the mapmaker had painted in great miniaturist detail the castle and the narrow lanes that crisscrossed the parishes. He'd also drawn the squares and public gardens. With his finger, Elias followed the familiar street names out loud, naming the guilds associated with each. Butchers, tanners, scriveners, parchment makers, fishmongers. Every street accurately depicted, save one.

The parish of St. Cruz of the Mountain, in the far northern corner of the city, was where many of the soldiers' families lived, along with the sheriffs, bailiffs, and judges. A small grassy knoll had been painted at the end of one street, along with a giant cicada, the color of the sun, perched at its crest. He had thought it a butterfly, a fine embellishment on a fine map.

Mercedes said, "There is no grassy knoll in the parish of St. Cruz."

Elias smiled at her. "No."

"But what is there?" Ulises asked.

Elias thought about this, running through his memory street by street, house by house. The answer came to him, and he said, "It's Judge Piri's home." He looked at his friends. "Why would his house be on this map? And look, he's here also." He pointed to the fat figure in red painted outside the maritime courts. He had shown the image to Ulises two days ago.

Ulises was quiet. Mercedes looked as if she'd bitten into something rotten.

"What?" Elias demanded.

"Piri was an officer for the maritime courts back then," Ulises said. "Not yet a judge. Some of his responsibilities weren't known to many." He glanced at his cousin. "You could say he and Mercedes have much in common."

So Piri had been a spy for the king. Elias said, "Should Mercedes speak with him? It might be simpler."

"I think not," Mercedes said.

"They don't get on," Ulises explained. "Best to question him yourself."

Elias was lost. "What would I question him about? How does he fit into any of this?"

"It must have something to do with the prisoner," Ulises said morosely. "Piri was the man who captured Felip of Mondrago."

The night deepened as they rode home, a dangerous time to be about. But as they turned off the coastal segment of Marinus Road, they found the highway bathed in torchlight.

Soldiers lined the road on horseback. When the trio was spotted, there was a shout, and one of the soldiers came forward. It was Lazar, Commander Aimon's second-in-command.

Ulises demanded, "Why are you here, Lazar? All of you? Who is guarding the city?"

"My king," Lazar responded, "Commander Aimon ordered us to watch the highway for your return. There are men stationed the rest of the way to Cortes. We're to escort you home." He lifted his torch higher. Shock and anger registered on his face. "You're wounded?"

The light had picked up the faint bruise beneath Ulises's eye. He touched it briefly. "It's nothing." He looked down the line of soldiers waiting to accompany them home, seeing what Elias saw. By restricting his men to the main road, Commander Aimon had made sure no one could guess what direction the three returned from. Keeping their secrets even though he must have been furious with them. "Let's go home."

Every mile added more soldiers to their retinue. It was the opposite of how they'd left the city at dawn. By the time they entered Cortes and saw Commander Aimon standing upon the walls, waiting for them with his arms crossed, there was an army at their back.

Twenty dead soldiers. It would leave a hole in the ranks, wouldn't it? And with the king's guard. Men would have to be promoted quickly to replace them.

Men like Commander Aimon.

It was a dark thought, come out of nowhere.

When Elias returned to the tower, he found the courtyard filled with people. Pilots, astronomers, mapmakers, painters — they had poured out of their chambers to enjoy one another's company on a warm summer evening and to gaze at the stars that showed like ice fire across the sky. The spiced wine flowed freely. Conversation was amiable. The laughter rang loud.

Beneath their feet, the mosaic compass that filled the courtyard was clearly visible. The artist had crushed the scales of a lightning fish into his tiles as a form of illumination. As a result, the eight-pointed star was outlined in shimmering green and silver. Lord Silva had gathered the children to the compass center. They lay on their backs on the tiles, arms pillowing their heads, as the Royal Navigator pointed out the various constellations. To the west, the first King Ulises on his throne. In the northwest, Saint Marco the Adventurer's three-masted carrack. To the south, the ancient waterfall of Mira, its cascade of stars disappearing beneath the horizon.

Elias kept to the shadows, watching Lord Silva, imagining Lord Antoni in his place. *Where he should have been.* A bitter anger swept over him. Lady Esma had painted a terrible, vivid picture. His father bloodied and beaten, thrown onto a horse like a captured animal. Elias would find out who had hurt him. If it took a lifetime, he would find a way to set this right.

Lord Silva sat up then, chuckling, and spotted Elias across the courtyard. The only person standing alone. His smile faded. He called out to Lord Braga, Jaime's father, who ambled over and gamely took Lord Silva's place, flopping down between Reyna and Hector and making the children giggle.

Lord Silva came to stand beside Elias in the shadows. He saw the new scratches, the bloodied lip. "You've been hurt. Where are the others?"

"They're here. They're safe."

Lord Silva looked as though he braced himself for something terrible. "Elias, what did you see?"

Elias kept his words low and close to Lord Silva's ear. He told of the spirits and Lady Esma. He spoke of the unknown del Marian attackers. Their callousness, their cruelty. Lord Silva said nothing, only listened. Cries erupted from the children, and Elias looked up in time to see a star shooting across the night sky. A single pearl cutting through a field of diamonds. He watched in wonder, until a strange, rough sound drew him back. To Lord Silva, whose face was lifted to the sky, his skin the color of ash.

He was weeping.

THIRTEEN

TWELVE APOTHECARIES SERVED the city of Cortes. Eight were of the general sort, dispensing everything from incense for lung ailments to fig poultices for rash. But four, including the one Mercedes entered, specialized solely in the needs of women.

The front chamber was typical of most apothecaries: a long mahogany counter with shelves behind. On the shelves were hundreds of glass jars lined up like Commander Aimon's soldiers. After a brief word with the wide-eyed proprietress, Mercedes was led through the back and up the stairs. Two chambers branched off a corridor that smelled strongly of mint. The proprietress knocked once and opened a door, waving Mercedes inside with a murmured, "Lady."

Galena was Mistress of the Royal Household. Twice a month, on the first and fifteenth day of the calendar, she visited an apothecary to have her head plucked, raising her hairline to the very top of her head. The practice had gone out of fashion years ago, for which Mercedes was grateful, but many of the older women clung to their rituals. Galena's habits, at least, made for a predictable routine. Mercedes preferred to speak to the woman privately, away from the castle. And today was the fifteenth day of the calendar.

Galena lay on a narrow bed in the center of a sparsely furnished chamber. Light filtered in from small round windows set high in the wall. A strip of white cloth covered her eyes, and a crisp blanket shielded her robust form from the neck downward. Jorge, her pet monkey, curled up fast asleep by her toes. An attendant stood by her head, pulling hairs one strand at a time with pincers. At Mercedes's appearance, the girl dropped into a curtsy and offered a whispered, "Lady."

Galena stirred, mumbling, "What? Who?"

The attendant whisked the cloth from her eyes. Galena blinked at the sudden light before focusing on Mercedes. Abruptly she sat up, the sheet clutched against her. Long gray strands spilled about her shoulders. "Lady Mercedes!"

"Forgive me for spoiling your day of rest, Mistress Galena." It was difficult not to stare at Galena's freshly plucked head, though she tried. "This will not take long." One glance had the proprietress and the attendant hurrying from the chamber. The door shut behind them. Mercedes waited, ear cocked, but heard no retreating footsteps.

Mistress Galena glared at the door. "Be off!" she hollered. At last, the sound of footsteps in retreat.

"Very effective," Mercedes said, looking about for a place to sit. There was no chair. She settled on the bed by Galena's feet and lifted the sleeping monkey onto her lap. Today, Jorge wore a blue tunic and a matching hat secured beneath his chin with a strap.

"Has something happened at the castle? A mishap? I will fix it immediat —"

"It is nothing like that." Mercedes straightened the monkey's hat. "I'm looking for information only. And your discretion."

Galena's confusion deepened. "Always, Lady."

Mercedes had already decided to trust her. Mistress Galena had always been kind to her and, more important, to her mother. Demanding of the castle servants, but fair. Also, she did not tolerate idle chatter and telltales. "You've been in my family's service for many years now. . . . How many?"

"Forty, Lady. Since I was ten. I started in the scullery."

Jorge stirred, and Mercedes stroked his back. "Then you were in Cortes the day the princes disappeared?"

Mistress Galena pulled the sheet higher. Whatever questioning she had expected, this had not been it. "I was not," she said. "Back then, I managed the king and queen's summer home."

Mercedes was surprised. "You're from Esperanca?"

"Yes, Lady. I was summoned here to replace Madame Fe after the . . . great tragedy."

"Replace her? Why?"

Mistress Galena was somber. "Fe was a widow with three children. Two girls and a boy. They were in service that day, sent with the princes."

Mercedes's hand stilled on the monkey's back, struck with horror. "All three?"

"Yes," was Galena's quiet response. "Not one of them reached their eighteenth year. Fe lost her wits that night. That is why I was sent for. No one else was qualified on so little notice."

"Is she alive?"

"No, Lady. The king and queen showed her every possible kindness. They gave her a home and a nurse in the parish of St. Michel. She died ten years ago."

The murky waters surrounding the missing servant girl cleared a little. Mistress Galena waited patiently as Mercedes worked through her thoughts. The monkey woke, yawning and stretching on her lap. "Hello, Jorge," she said absently. To Galena, "Would there be a record of the servants who traveled with the entourage that day?"

Mistress Galena looked thoughtful. "Certainly. I will look at once. Though it may take a little time."

"Do what you're able, and take my thanks with you." Here it became tricky, siphoning off information that she would prefer to keep close. "I'm looking for a female who would have gone on the picnic and disappeared in the chaos afterward. Someone who might have been missed."

Mistress Galena stared. "You think . . . ? I don't understand. The servants were all buried by their families."

Mercedes wanted to say, *Were they? Who says? Madame Fe?* She said only, "It was a confusing time. For everyone. I would like to know for certain."

Elias did not try to find Judge Piri at his home. It was midmorning already, late hours for a maritime judge. Instead, he went to look for him at the waterfront.

Del Mar's harbor was a vast, sprawling affair, shaped like a half-moon, thick with people and commerce. Every ship one could imagine was anchored here: sleek galleys and tubby cogs, fishing vessels and pearling dhows. Sturdy, battered junks. A crane rose above a carrack, with its forecastle and sterncastle, hoisting heavier goods from the ship and lowering them onto the dock. Elias eyed the crane wobbling in midair and prudently moved out of harm's way. Better not to tempt fate. Out of habit, he searched for his own ship, unsurprised to find it missing. The *Amaris* would have sailed north already for repairs at the royal shipyard near Esperanca.

He wound his way past market men and women doing brisk business. This one selling the cheap tin trinkets that turned one's fingers green, that one hawking fried fish, mussels, and prawns. A row of beggars crouched against a wall, bowls extended and flies buzzing about tattered robes. Just past them, three imposing buildings rose from the very center of the harbor: the Guild of Mariners, the House of Trade, and the Court of Sea Affairs. Elias headed toward the last.

People flowed in and out of the courts like the tide. No one ever looked happy to be here. Not the stern-faced men in robes or the ships' officers with their ramrod postures. Not the shipman leaning against a stone pillar and biting his fingernails down to nothing. The court oversaw all manner of legalities involving the sea: missing cargo and stolen cargo and spoiled cargo. Insurance claims and counterclaims. Complaints leveled against captains, accusations of mutiny. Elias had just passed beneath the center archway when he saw Judge Piri hurrying his way.

The judge was in his middle years, short and fat; rolls of excess flesh hung from his chin. His robes were more crimson than red. The judge did not see Elias at first. He was too busy barking at his clerk.

"What do you mean, he's not here?" the judge demanded. "Where is he? Why am I paying a translator who is not here to translate?"

"My lord judge," the harried-looking clerk said. "Master Duarte's father died two days ago."

"And?"

"And? Er . . . and he's gone to be with his mother. To comfort her during her time of grief."

The judge's sigh was long and irritated. As he drew closer, Elias heard him say, "Families. Such a nuisance."

"Judge Piri," Elias said before the judge could walk past.

Both men stopped. The clerk bowed. Judge Piri took in Elias's wounds, new and old. And leaped to conclusions. His scowl deepened. "Lord Elias. Another fight, I see. Whose fault was it this time?"

"Not mine, sir," Elias said, and, when the judge snorted, "May I have a word?"

"You may," the judge answered. Elias and the clerk fell into step beside him. They headed directly toward the water. "But it will have to wait until I've found myself a translator, as it is far beneath the capabilities of my clerk."

Elias spared a sympathetic look for the red-faced clerk. He thought fast. If Judge Piri slipped away now, he might lose his only chance to question him today. He asked, "What sort of translator?"

"The ship is from Caffa," the judge said. "There's some dispute with the cargo, which must be seen to at once, I'm told. No one understands a word the captain is saying."

"I speak Caffeesh," Elias said.

The judge glanced at him sidelong. "Fluently?"

"Yes. I can translate, if I may have a word afterward."

The clerk sent Elias a grateful look, and, mollified, the judge said, "Agreed."

Elias surveyed the vessels rocking at the water's edge. "Which ship is it?"

"It's just there, Lord Elias." The clerk pointed to a handsome caravel with triangular lateen sails and a name painted near the prow in a flowing, womanly script.

"The *Flying Stag*," the judge read, and grimaced. "Ridiculous."

The cargo was ruined. The captain was, too, though he did not know it yet. It was all because of the rats.

Elias stood in the *Flying Stag*'s cramped hold and tried to breathe through his mouth. The chamber had room enough for two shipmen to work comfortably among the barrels and crates. At present, he shared the space with five others on a day growing rapidly hotter: Judge Piri and his clerk; the *Flying Stag*'s captain and *his* clerk; and William the Spicer, a del Marian whose family had traded in spice and pepper for generations. The pleasing scent emanating from the spices was overpowered by nervous, stinking sweat and the unmistakable presence of Coronad rat droppings.

Judge Piri was the first to speak, in del Marian. "Lord Elias, ask this puppy how long he's been in command of this ship." The judge's clerk had turned the top of a cask into a temporary desk, complete with inkpots and quills he'd requisitioned from the captain's quarters. He scribbled away, recording every word spoken, stopping occasionally to dab away at the beads of perspiration on his forehead.

Elias turned to the captain. He was younger by a year or two and looked near collapse, his face the color of salt, his formal captain's attire drenched in sweat and lost dignity. Elias translated the judge's words, leaving out the puppy reference and repeating the question twice before the captain finally stammered a response.

Elias tried not to let his surprise show. "He says three months," he said, and, ignoring the oaths spewing from William the Spicer, added, "He inherited the captaincy after his father and brothers died last winter. He was not intended for the sea."

"Clearly," the judge said, his expression severe. "What was his livelihood before this disaster?"

Elias winced at the captain's answer. "He was studying to be a sculptor."

"A sculptor!" This outburst came from William the Spicer. He was only a handful of years older than Elias, but his face was so red and the vein ticking at his temple so pronounced that Elias worried for his heart. The spicer's rage was understandable. He had likely waited many months for this shipment to arrive, and it was a common practice to pay for the whole order in advance. The spice crates filled the hold floor to beam, full of clove, nutmeg, mace, and others that would have been worth a fortune . . . had Coronad death rats not found their way into the crates and left behind enough droppings to fertilize the royal orchards of del Mar.

Master William sputtered, "This is contemptible! I've sunk a fortune into this shipment. A fortune! My lord judge, I demand recompense! I demand—"

"I'm well aware of why we're here," Judge Piri said. "There's no need to shout it at me. Lord Elias, tell the captain to show us the cats."

Elias's heart dropped when he translated the order and saw the blank look on the captain's face.

"Cats?" the captain repeated. "What cats?"

Despite the barrier of language, his words needed no translation.

"Is he simple?" Judge Piri asked no one in particular.

William the Spicer sagged against an open crate filled with pepper and rat droppings and moaned.

"I think he just doesn't know our laws," Elias said, adjusting the carrier on his shoulder. His shirt stuck to his back. "Should I explain?"

Judge Piri nodded. Elias turned to the captain. "Sir, all ships sailing within the Sea of Magdalen must carry a minimum of two cats on board."

"But why?"

"They keep down the rat population," Elias said. "It's very important when you're transporting perishable goods. The animals must be officially documented by the ship's clerk" — he glanced at the captain's terrified clerk, who clutched an oversize sea register to his chest — "before departure, with the rest of the cargo. If your man can show that you brought the animals on board at the start of this voyage but the cats subsequently died, then you will not be held responsible, as the damage did not occur due to your negligence. The law is written in the Magdalen Sea Codes, Article 20."

The captain swallowed several times. "And if there are no cats?"

Elias was very careful not to look at the spice crates. "Then the captain of the vessel will be held liable for all loss."

The captain swung toward his clerk and spoke in low, urgent tones. Like the captain, the clerk was just a boy. In fact, everyone on this ship was uncommonly young. Where were the more seasoned sailors? The officers? Elias wondered if the captain had replaced them with younger men who would not question his lack of experience. He had seen it done before.

While the spice merchant fumed and the judge sighed his impatience, the Caffeesh captain ordered the clerk to examine his book and produce evidence of cats. The clerk kept shaking his head and repeating himself: *There are no cats on board, Captain. There never have been.* Both men looked ill.

Finally, the captain turned to Elias. He said softly, "The cats . . . we did not know."

William the Spicer was incensed. He shouted, "That is his defense? Every fool knows you need rat catchers —"

The captain interrupted in a flurry of rapid Caffeesh.

"What did he say?" Judge Piri demanded.

Elias paused long enough to give the captain a disgusted look. All pity for him vanished. "He says the droppings can be removed. His crew will pick them out and the spices can still be used. No one would have to know, outside this ship."

A tense silence fell. Realizing his error, the captain backed up against a wall of crates. Judge Piri's expression had turned thunderous. He said, "Tell this puppy this: St. John del Mar is not some savage outpost. We do not give our people food touched by rat filth. Particularly Coronad rat filth, which is poisonous."

Elias translated. A rat made an appearance just then, emerging from behind a crate. For a Coronad death rat, it was average only, its length roughly equal to Elias's forearm. The rat's eyes were cloudy, like an old, old man's, and its fur was the dark, matted green of seaweed. The rat, bold and curious, sniffed at the Caffeesh clerk's boots, and the clerk, already rattled, screamed. The rat scuttled out of sight, claws scraping against wood.

"I've seen enough," Judge Piri said. Heat and anger had turned his face the same color as his robes. "Ignorance of the law is no defense in this kingdom. It is the court's decision that the captain will reimburse Master William what is owed for the cargo. Master William, what is your loss?"

Elias's mouth fell open at the figure William the Spicer named. The captain swayed, then said, "Sirs, I do not have it."

The judge heard Elias's translation and was unsurprised. "Can you send for it?"

The captain shook his head. He met no one's eyes.

The judge said, "There's no choice, then. The . . . *Flying Stag* will be sold, immediately. Proceeds will go first to pay wages to the crew and their passage home. What remains will go to Master William."

"It is not nearly enough," the spice merchant whispered. "It is a fraction of what I paid."

Judge Piri gave him a pointed look. "Have you insurance?"

The merchant's answer was to close his eyes. When he opened them a moment later and leveled a malicious look at the captain, Elias guessed his intent. He shoved Judge Piri out of harm's way as William the Spicer grabbed a crate full of worthless, sullied pepper and flung the contents across the hold, directly into the captain's face.

196

The morning had not gone as Elias had intended. There was some delay and screaming as fresh water was located to flush out the captain's eyes, which had taken on a grisly appearance. The whites had gone red with inflammation, much like Judge Piri's robes. William the Spicer had been hustled from the *Flying Stag* by the harbor guards and thrown into a cell in the lower reaches of the Court of Sea Affairs. The judge might have overlooked the merchant flinging pepper at the sea captain in a fit of rage, but if Elias had not acted quickly, Judge Piri would have suffered the same fate. And for that, he was far less forgiving.

"Well, Elias," the judge said now, "what is this about?"

They were in the thick of the harbor, waiting for a food seller to prepare their lunch. The woman made a living selling baby molluscs. The sea creature resembled a miniature octopus, roughly twelve inches in length from the top of its head to the tips of its sixteen tentacles. Its color rivaled that of a pure stone emerald, and while the mollusc was firmly impaled on a sharpened stick, it was so fresh as to be not quite dead. The eyes had drifted shut, but the tentacles rose and fell in a slow, lazy motion, as if it believed itself to be under the water still.

Elias exchanged payment for three molluscs on skewers, offered two to the judge, and said, "I wanted to ask about Felip of Mondrago."

The judge leveled a sharp glance at the food seller, but she had already turned away to help the next customer. He studied Elias, frowning, then said, "Let's walk."

They wound their way past numerous languages and

dialects; past Lunesian shipmen disembarking from a ship, trunks carried on their shoulders; past an old gypsy woman sitting on a crate, smoking a pipe with her face tilted upward, basking in the warmth of the sun.

Judge Piri was in no hurry to speak. He bit off the end of a tentacle. The mollusc emitted a short, sharp squeal, then fell abruptly silent, every tentacle falling limp. The judge swallowed, made a satisfied sound, and finally said, "The infamous Felip of Mondrago. A curious topic. An old one. What is your interest?"

Elias thought of Lady Esma: *Mondragans? Those men weren't from Mondrago. They were del Marian.* He knew he would not endear himself to Judge Piri with a lie. How many did a judge have to listen to in a single day? No, an outright lie would not do. But a half-truth was not the same thing.

"I never knew my father," Elias said. "I suppose I'd like to know as much about him as I can. Including how he died. It's not something I can ask my mother."

"No. But there's not much I can tell you."

Elias said, "I've spoken to the king. I'm to say you may speak freely here."

The judge was silent for a time, concentrating on his mollusc, never a simple creature to chew. He asked, "How old were you then? Two years?"

"A year."

"Only a year." Judge Piri looked off toward the ships. "A pity. A child should know his father."

There was an odd note to the judge's voice. Elias tried to

recall what he knew of him. Not very much. Only that he was a widower. No children.

The judge tossed his stick, licked clean, to the ground and said, "Felip of Mondrago confessed. He knew details only the guilty would know."

"What details?"

The judge made good headway on his second skewer before answering. "He was a soldier in the Mondragan army," he said. "Not high-ranking. One night he, along with several other soldiers, were summoned to a secret meeting with their king, who made them an offer. Gold and estates, more wealth than they could dream of, in exchange for one simple task."

Elias's mollusc remained untouched. "Kidnapping our princes?"

"Yes," Judge Piri answered. "They were to sail to del Mar and keep to themselves until they heard from a fellow countryman here. Country*woman*," he corrected. "A Mondragan within the del Marian court who would give them further instructions."

"That would have been their ambassador?"

"Yes," Judge Piri said. "She was suspected even before Felip's confession. Her family had been living in the castle for years."

Elias could not imagine it. Full-blooded Mondragans living within the castle along with their entourage, fully accepted and enjoying diplomatic privileges. Eighteen years later, Mercedes continued to be spat on in the streets.

The judge might have read his thoughts. "It was different then," he said. "Our kingdoms were cordial, if not overly friendly.

King Andrés had admired the previous Mondragan king greatly. He was not as impressed with his son, I believe. But they were allies."

"Was the ambassador ever questioned?" Elias asked.

"No. She'd fled by the time Felip was captured."

They paused to allow a queue of women to pass. They were women of the Bushido, dressed plainly in varying shades of brown. Each balanced a rush basket on her head without having to use her hands to hold it in place. The baskets were filled with cherries. One of the younger women winked at Elias. She reminded him a bit of Luca—broad shoulders and a distinct row of black hair above her lip—and he smiled and offered a small bow in return. They disappeared into the House of Trade.

The judge frowned after them, distracted. "Are you certain that was even a woman?"

Elias laughed. "The mustache is a symbol of fertility among the Bushido women. A sign they're searching for a mate," he explained, then turned the conversation back. "What happened when Felip reached del Mar?"

It took Judge Piri a moment to recall what they were speaking of. "After several weeks, the men were contacted and told to act quickly. A picnic had been planned for the princes the next day. With your father. They were to follow the party at a distance and wait until the wine had been consumed. All they had to do was listen for the screams, for this particular poison was a painful one. Then they were to take the boys off, as well as the nurse and your father if they were living. Lady Esma and Lord Antoni would have fetched sizable ransoms as well."

Elias said, "And your prisoner did this? He confessed to taking the boys, my father, and Lady Esma?"

"He did," the judge confirmed. "The plan was to take the del Marians to an island off Mondrago to await the ransom payment. But there was a storm. Felip only survived because he'd found a piece of wood to cling to. A Hellespontian ship sailed by and rescued him." Judge Piri tossed his second stick, frightening some chickens pecking away in the dirt. "That is all I know. It was an ugly business."

Elias was silent. Felip of Mondrago had lied even while being tortured. Lady Esma had been left behind. Why would he say she'd been taken?

And something else: everyone connected to the crime was long dead. Poisoned, drowned. In Felip of Mondrago's case, hanged, his body left for the crows. Mercedes had been furious with Lady Esma for staying hidden. But he asked himself if Lady Esma would still be here, among the living, if she had left the safety of Javelin.

And another thing. "How long have you been a judge?"

"Nearly eighteen years." The judge eyed Elias's skewered mollusc. "That will go bad soon."

Elias offered him the skewer, which was accepted with thanks, and said, "A judgeship is a lifetime appointment, isn't it? What happened to your predecessor?"

"Killed at Mondrago."

Commander Aimon, Judge Piri. Who else? How many others had catapulted to positions of power, out of necessity, far earlier than they should have? "Why did he go to Mondrago? I've never heard of a judge fighting in a war."

"They murdered our princes." Judge Piri looked grim. "The king is your friend. What wouldn't you do, if harm came to him?"

It was a fair point. Piri tossed his third stick. As he did, an object fell from his red robes and landed, sparkling silver, on the ground. Elias bent to retrieve it. It was a miniature painting set inside an oval frame. The portrait fit into his palm. He studied the image: a woman, slender and dark-eyed, with straight black hair parted in the center and left to flow in loose waves to her waist. Seated beside her was a child, a girl of six or so with a marked resemblance to the judge.

A hand clamped around Elias's wrist.

"Give it to me," the judge ordered.

As though Elias had intentionally snatched the portrait and tried to run off. Wordless, he offered the miniature, feeling as though he had intruded on something very private, had seen something he was not meant to see. He had never heard of the judge having a daughter, but that did not mean she had never existed.

"They are very beautiful," Elias said quietly.

The judge snapped the miniature closed and shoved it deep into the folds of his robes, his expression remote.

"They were."

FOURTEEN

THERE WAS NO avoiding Commander Aimon. Elias returned to his chambers only to hear a terse message relayed to him through Reyna, who had taken over his worktable with the second map. The commander wanted a word. At once. Elias sighed inwardly. Aimon would never berate Ulises or Mercedes for riding off yesterday without escort. But Elias, as usual, was fair game. He ignored the *at once* part of the order, lingering in the tower long enough to share a meal with Reyna — mussels and fried clams — and to make her promise not to spend her entire day indoors. Then he headed off to answer the commander's summons.

From the arena's darkened tunnel, he emerged into blinding sunlight. Off to one side, soldiers practiced military drills; marching in time, hundreds of boys and men in green and silver. To his left, a catapult lay fully dismantled. Various parts littered the ground: beam, counterweight, sling, wheels, framework, what looked like a thousand iron bolts. Commander Aimon instructed a swarm of apprentices on how to reassemble the catapult as quickly as possible. A skill they would have to master in a real war, during a real siege. Elias walked toward them, his steps slowing as the smell of rotting animal flesh assaulted him. A long trough sat just outside the circle of apprentices. Normally, rocks would have been set within for swift placement in the slings. But Elias did not see any rocks, only severed pigs' heads piled in the trough.

Commander Aimon caught sight of Elias. He motioned for one of the older boys to take his place, then joined Elias, crossing his arms and regarding him with a stony expression.

Commander Aimon could hold a silence better than anyone. Elias did his best not to shift and squirm under his scrutiny. When that failed, he said, "Commander, I didn't ask them to come. I couldn't get rid of them."

"I don't doubt it." Was that amusement in the commander's voice? He couldn't tell. "There's no need to quiver. I'm not going to throw your head in with the pigs' today."

"I'm grateful." Elias eyed the heads. No one could accuse him of having a weak stomach, but he had just consumed his fair share of mussels and clams, and the smell wafting from the trough was not sitting well. "Why are these heads here? Have we run out of rocks?"

"Oh, we'll still use the rocks," Commander Aimon said dismissively. "But a rock causes only physical pain." He reached into the trough and held up a head by one ear. The pig stared back at Elias with a gaping mouth and half-closed eyes. The commander said, "Tell me, how would you feel, after months of siege, low on food and water, to have rotting heads flung at your feet?"

"Pigs' heads?"

Commander Aimon didn't blink. "Whatever heads are available."

That unleashed several morbid images: horse heads, dog heads, human heads. Elias did not have to think about it long. "I would want to cling to my *maman*'s skirts."

The commander appeared satisfied with the answer. "That is what I want. For grown men to cling to their *mamans'* skirts." He tossed the head back into the trough. "To win any war, it's not enough to draw blood. We must hurt them here." He tapped his head twice, transferring blood from his hand.

Elias looked at the blood on the commander's temple and felt the hairs rise along his nape. This felt like a warning. He said, "We've not been to war for years."

"True," the commander acknowledged. "But we're always prepared for it." An apprentice appeared and offered him a rag. The commander cleaned himself off, his expression assuming more normal lines. "I didn't ask you here to discuss war strategy. I'll tell you the same thing I told the king. A reminder, if you will, that he is the only surviving son of del Mar. Whatever anyone thinks of your maps."

"You think they're fakes? Even now?"

"Who can say? Riddles on maps. Grand ladies living in the woods." The commander tossed his rag to another boy running past, who caught it without stopping. "What I do know is that this puzzle is for you to solve. *You*, Lord Elias. Not the king, not the lady Mercedes. Neither one of them has an heir. What happens to this kingdom if they fall?" He shook his head. "Stealing away like you did to Javelin without a single guard to watch your back was a child's act. You are no longer children."

The words stung because he knew they were true. "Peace, Commander. You've made your point."

Commander Aimon sighed. "Why do you look at me that way?" he asked quietly. "As if I'm your enemy. You are not the only one who lost a father."

Elias's head came up. He thought of the spirit in the meadow, a twin to this man. "I'm sorry."

Neither was accustomed to having anything in common with the other. They both looked away. Commander Aimon's words were gruffer than usual. "I think they're dead. There's something else at play here, but whatever it is, I believe . . ." He paused as a triumphant cheer emerged from behind them. The catapult had been reassembled. "I believe in an eye for an eye. A life for a life. I'm here if you need help. My men are here. *Use* us. You are not the only one who wants to see this put right."

"You told me once that Aimon was made commander right there in the meadow," Elias said to Lord Silva.

"Yes, by King Andrés."

"How old was he?"

"A few years older than you." Lord Silva spoke from behind his desk, where he watched Elias pace from one end of the chamber to the other. On the desk was a wooden sphere twelve inches in diameter, braced between two weighty manu-scripts to prevent it from rolling away. A world map had been cut into curved strips, or gores, and laid out on the desk. Soon they would be glued, piece by piece, to the sphere. Lord Silva was building a globe. "Just a boy. But there was no one left in front of him."

Elias pictured the soldiers at their dice game, one in par-ticular. "His father died that day."

"Yes. And he lost two younger brothers at Mondrago."

Elias stopped pacing, horrified. "Two?"

"Yes." Lord Silva steepled his hands before him. A window had been left open, and through it came the low, sustained horn from a departing ship. "Elias, he's the most powerful man on this island, after the king. What you're thinking is dangerous."

"I don't really think it. I think . . ." Elias set his carrier on the desk and dropped into a chair. "I don't know what I'm thinking."

Commander Aimon was stern and humorless, but he was not only these things. The commander had taught Elias how to fight when he was a boy. He had dragged him away from his maps and paints and into the royal arsenal. Sword, dagger, bow and arrow, crossbow, Elias had learned how to use them all, right alongside Ulises. What was it the commander had said to him? *For whatever reason, the prince has chosen you as a friend. You will learn to keep him safe. One can't fight off the enemy with a compass divider.* And to Elias's amazement, he had been a good teacher, a patient one. Aimon had never shown much appreciation for the geographic arts, but what he had taught Elias had saved his life. Many times.

Elias told all of this to Lord Silva, who, after a lengthy pause, said, "Bad men are capable of generous acts. It's a rare person who is completely evil. The reverse is also true. A good man may commit a terrible thing and spend the rest of his life trying to set things right." Lord Silva pinched the bridge of his nose, a sign that he was tired. "We humans are complicated creatures. There are so many in-betweens within us."

Elias said, "You think I'm being foolish."

But Lord Silva surprised him. "I wish I could say so with absolute certainty." At Elias's startled look, he mused, "Is Commander Aimon capable of murder? Of course; he's killed plenty. But always for the good of del Mar, so far as we know. You were one of my finest apprentices, Elias. What have I always taught you?"

Elias was silent. Then, "To trust my instincts."

"Yes. Your reasoning has always been sound. Trust yourself."

Elias was always surprised by the faith Lord Silva showed him. "I'm glad you were here. This is not something I can speak to anyone else about."

"No," Lord Silva agreed. "Your friends will not thank you for your suspicions."

"I know it." Mercedes in particular. After a minute, Elias asked, "Have you ever wondered what your life would have been like if none of this had happened?"

It could not have been a simple thing for Lord Silva. To step down as Royal Navigator after his son, Vittor, had died. Only to be summoned back for another eighteen years.

"I imagine it would have been very quiet," Lord Silva responded with a small, sad smile. "Perhaps too quiet. I don't regret returning. I only wish it had not happened the way it did."

Elias was starting to feel gloomy, and he could see its effect mirrored on Lord Silva. Very deliberately, he changed the subject. "Have you seen Reyna? I'm hoping I'll go upstairs and find she's solved this entire riddle for us."

Lord Silva's smile was indulgent. "It was good of you to let her help with the Hellespontian maps. She delivered them to the captains yesterday with Luca."

"I told her she could if she helped."

"And she'll never forget it. Those captains are a colorful lot."

Elias had not intended to broach the subject of Reyna today, but since he was here . . . "What will become of her?"

Lord Silva's eyebrows rose. "That sounds dire. What do you mean?"

If you could sail off today, where would you go?

I would go everywhere.

"I think she would like a chance on one of the ships."

Lord Silva's smile faded. "Has she said so?"

"She doesn't need to."

Lord Silva stood and walked to the open window. Distinguished as always in his dark robes, hands clasped behind his back. Without turning, he said, "When the child comes of age, she will marry. One of our geographers, preferably. Maybe even you." He glanced over his shoulder and laughed at Elias's expression. "Your face, Elias. She won't be nine forever."

Elias waved aside his teasing. "Marrying a geographer is not the same as being one."

Lord Silva turned fully to face him, sober once again. "Women are different from us. Here," he tapped his temple once, "and physically. Their minds and bodies cannot endure the hardships of an extensive sea voyage, or the rigors of living in the wild. It would break them."

Privately, Elias wondered what Mercedes would say to being described as inferior to men in mind and body. He shied away from that image and asked, "Why couldn't Reyna train with the boys? She could be made strong. As for her mind, forgive me, but I disagree. She's smarter than all of them already."

"It's not possible," Lord Silva said abruptly.

"But—"

"That will be all." Lord Silva's expression said the matter was closed.

As much as it gnawed at him, Elias would have to respect his decision. "Yes, sir." He rose and made for the door.

"Elias." When he glanced across the chamber, Lord Silva's gaze lingered on the carrier strapped to his back. "Be careful. Of what you say and who you say it to."

"I will."

"Why would Felip do it?" Mercedes wondered. "Confess to kidnapping, to *murder* even, if he didn't do it?"

"Oh, who knows?" Elias frowned into his empty glass. They had gathered in her chambers after supper. He had scorned her too-dainty armchairs, choosing instead to sprawl across deep blue rugs, his back resting against her chair leg. The windows had been left open. A cool sea-salt breeze drifted in, along with the strumming of a lone guitar from the courtyard below.

Mercedes reached down and plucked the glass from his hand. She offered her own in exchange. He murmured his thanks and looked up at her. Neither had changed clothing after supper; they wore their formal attire still. Her dress made of white lace, the skirt full and pouring to the rugs beside him, the blouse cut off her shoulder to expose a delicate collarbone. He watched her, forgetting all about maps and false confessions, distracted by her loveliness.

She pushed a strand from his forehead and said, "You're not sleeping."

"No," he admitted. "Are you?"

She shook her head.

"Come to the tower next time," he invited. "We can be sleepless together."

Green eyes widened. She sat up very straight in her chair. Before she could say anything, another voice intruded.

"I'm right here," Ulises said, his tone mild. Only a few feet away, Elias's map was spread across a low table where the king had been studying it for the last quarter hour. "I can hear you."

"And?" Elias smiled slightly. "What are you both thinking I meant? Reyna is there. And Basilio never leaves. Mercedes would be in good company."

Ulises snorted, and Mercedes said crisply, "It sounds like a party. I will tell Commander Aimon. He will want to come, too." Which amused everyone in the chamber except Elias. He threw back the rest of his drink and frowned into that glass, too.

Ulises asked suddenly, "What is this here? Is this something?"

Elias set his glass on the table and scrambled to his feet. He and Mercedes crowded in beside Ulises, who had his finger on a bend of the Francoli River, which flowed east of Cortes. The map showed two miniature stone bridges spanning the river at its widest point. In unison, the cousins pressed their noses right up to the map, then turned to Elias with brimming excitement.

"Two bridges!" Mercedes exclaimed.

Two bridges on the map, when there was only one now standing.

Elias hated to disappoint them. "There *were* two," he said, and watched their faces fall. "One was much older than the other. It rotted through sixteen . . . seventeen years ago? It was never rebuilt."

"Oh," Ulises said. Then, "Seventeen years? How do you know so many tiresome facts?"

Elias shrugged. Mercedes returned to her chair, chin

propped on fist, while Elias stayed where he was, both he and Ulises scowling over the map.

Mercedes stirred. "It's a convenient story, isn't it? Piri questions a foreign soldier, who conveniently confesses to kidnapping and murder. Who is conveniently hanged the day of his confession."

Elias started. "The same day?"

She nodded. "I looked up the records."

"What are you saying? You think Piri forced him to confess? Made everything up?"

"He's done it before," Ulises said bluntly. "He would be left alone with prisoners, who would admit to committing whichever crime they were accused of in the end. But by the time they did, they would be missing a hand. Or a foot."

"Their eyes sometimes," Mercedes added as Elias looked from one to the other, aghast.

"Mercedes put a stop to it after Father died," Ulises said. "They're not on friendly terms."

"He's a cave dweller," Mercedes said.

"Why didn't you tell me this yesterday?" Elias demanded.

Mercedes looked defensive. "It would have been all you thought about," she said. "I didn't want to cloud your judgment, in case there was another reason he was on these maps."

His judgment? He was a terrible judge of character. He *liked* Judge Piri, had always liked him. He'd even bought him a meal, he remembered, thinking of the skewers. Turning back to the map, he studied the gold cicada on the grassy knoll where Judge Piri's home should have been. He said, "What other reason could there be?"

A knock sounded on the door, followed by a voice calling out, "My lady? It is Galena."

Mercedes rose, alert, and crossed the chamber. Ulises shot Elias a glance. Both men rose, Elias quickly rolling the map and returning it to the carrier. The women spoke softly at the door, and then Galena, Mistress of the Royal Household, appeared beside Mercedes. Her pet monkey, Jorge, trailed after them, dressed in green and silver with a white ruffled collar. A miniature sword hung from his belt. Galena carried a large register bound in leather and was clearly discomfited by their presence.

"My king, my lord Elias, forgive me. I did not mean to intrude. I will return —"

"They know what I've asked of you." Mercedes gestured toward a chair. "You may speak freely here."

They sat. Elias held out his hand in invitation, and Jorge streaked across his arm, making himself comfortable on his shoulder. "What are you eating, Jorge?" he asked in greeting. The monkey popped a sticky, half-eaten sweet from his mouth and offered it to Elias, who laughed and refused. The sweet went back into Jorge's mouth.

Galena's gaze went back and forth from the king to Elias. Noting the bruises, the scratches, the cut lips. She would have heard about their mysterious outing yesterday. News traveled swiftly through the castle. Elias said, "We've known each other a long time, Mistress. You've seen us look worse."

Galena smiled a little and, prompted by Ulises's "You found something for us?" answered, "Yes, my king." She placed the register on the table, opening it to a page filled with columns and names and numbers. The ink had faded to gray. Yellowing had begun its creep along the parchment edges. She said, "Lady Mercedes asked if I would look over the names of servants from . . . from the picnic to see if anyone had been unaccounted for."

"Yes?" Mercedes asked.

"There were ten in service that day." Mistress Galena showed them a list of names on the left-hand side of the register. "I found this among Mistress Fe's belongings and went through the names one by one." She skipped through five or so pages and said, "I found burial fees paid by the castle. The king and queen" — she glanced at Ulises — "also ordered pensions paid to the families."

As Madame Galena spoke, disappointment rose in Elias. Another dead end. "So they are accounted for."

"Yes, Lord Elias. All but one."

Silence fell.

"Who?" Ulises asked.

"I only know that her name was Eve," Mistress Galena said. "There's no record of a burial or pension. There's nothing about her at all. Not her city of birth, her parents' names, siblings." She looked at each of them, her brows drawn together. "I have no excuse to offer for such record keeping. Forgive me for not being of more help."

Mercedes said in a distracted tone, "No, you've helped tremendously." Soon after, she ushered Madame Galena from the chamber. And then pressed her back against the closed door and looked at them. Elias could almost see her mind working, like the inside of a clock, the wheels turning and clicking into place.

Lady Esma had not been mistaken. The murderers had been assisted from the inside, by a royal servant.

Someone named Eve.

FIFTEEN

WAKE UP, ELIAS."

Elias opened his eyes, starting violently at the candlestick hovering an inch away and the large figure leaning over his bed.

"It's just me."

Luca.

Elias rose to his elbows, groggy and irritated. "What are you doing, looming like some reaper . . . ?" Through the window, the sky reflected the muted shades of dawn. "What hour is it?"

Instead of answering, Luca said, "I need a favor. Will you see to the boys this morning?"

"With what?"

"They're swimming in the cove."

Elias cast a suspicious eye at the window. "When?"

"Within the hour."

Elias groaned. Learning to swim was a must for any child who wished to become a royal geographer. Older boys like Elias and Luca usually taught the younger. An uncommon practice, but Lord Antoni had insisted on it long ago after a boat had capsized within sight of the western shoreline and every man had drowned because he could not swim.

It was too early for favors. "Ask Madame, why don't you? She's up already."

Everyone knew Madame Vega rose before the sun, toiling in her work chamber while the tower slept for hours more.

"She's gone off," Luca said. "I just saw her horse in the courtyard."

That was interesting enough for Elias to sit up and ask, "Gone where?"

"How should I know?"

Luca's tone was brusque, which did nothing for Elias's level of charity. "Why can't you do it?"

"It must have been the fish at supper," Luca admitted after a long sigh. "I won't be of use to anyone today. Will you get up and help me or not?"

Luca *did* look terrible, waxy-skinned, with beads of sweat on his forehead. Commiseration won out over the desire for more sleep. There was nothing worse than eating bad fish. And Luca rarely called in favors, though Elias owed him plenty. He fell back onto the bed.

"Fine. But this means we're even."

A brief smile broke through his friend's misery. "We're not even close." Luca turned away, taking the light with him. "Have a care with Hector. The water terrifies him."

Mercedes found Elias on the beach with a dozen near-naked boys. Most swam about in the blue-green waters of the cove, the fish having likely fled to Lunes by now from all the splashing and shrieking. Elias was by the water's edge trying to coax the Grecs' son into the water. She heard him say, "It's safe, Hector. There are no monsters in the bay." The child was having none of it.

"I think you'll lose this battle," Mercedes said, torn between sympathy for Hector and amusement over Elias's plight. She spoke in Oslawn, as a courtesy to the man who had accompanied her here, her words safe from the child's ears.

Elias glanced over, his expression rueful and sleepy-eyed. He answered in the same language. "I think so, too. Reminds me of someone I know."

He hadn't troubled himself with a shirt, and he wore what might charitably be called trousers, ragged linen carelessly held up at the waist with a rope. She studied the image that had been inked onto his left shoulder: del Mar's symbol, two serpents entwined and glaring, with long, slithery tongues. A rogue wave served as a backdrop. When had this been done? Where? She imagined him on Hellespont, in some dissolute tavern thick with smoke, gritting his teeth as a sullen character with an eye patch did his work. Elias's brows lifted, his lips twitched, and with a start she realized she'd been staring at his chest longer than was polite.

Mercedes lifted her chin, even as she felt her cheeks turn hot. She would not be flustered. One faced many uncomfortable moments in front of others. The key was to pretend you did not notice them. And if Elias's smile only widened, and his eyes grew mischievous, she ignored that, too. She turned to the man waiting patiently beside her. The Oslawn ambassador was in his middle years, bearded, with tufts of gray hair that stood straight up in the breeze. He was as tall as she, which meant he was not tall at all, and like her, he held a bow in one hand and carried a quiver of arrows on his back.

She made the introductions. "Lord Ambassador Greger of Oslaw. He arrived just last evening. My lord Greger, may I present Lord Elias?"

Elias returned Lord Greger's greeting, adding, "You'll forgive our dress." He spoke courteously, still in the ambassador's native tongue, but Mercedes saw that he never lost sight of the boys. He kept a particular eye on Hector, who was content to form sand cakes a few feet away. The water was shallow for only ten or twelve feet before the sea floor dropped sharply. She knew this intimately.

"It seems we're the ones overdressed," Lord Greger said, smiling. "We were practicing in the arena when we heard the boys." Behind them were the sea walls, with stone steps leading up to the arena. "I was convinced there were baboons afoot, and I have come to see with my own eyes."

Elias laughed. "No baboons. Though the sound is similar."

The scent of fish frying drifted their way. Farther down the beach, a trio of men sat around a small fire. Fishing poles leaned against a nearby boulder.

Lord Greger watched, bemused, as one of the boys ran past,

hollering what Mercedes recognized as an ancient del Marian war cry, and jumped into the water with a tremendous splash. The ambassador remarked, "I've always understood seawater to be unhealthy. Won't they fall ill?"

"I've lived half my life in the water," Elias said. "And I'm rarely ill." He called to one of the older boys, Jaime, to mind Hector before continuing. "These are del Mar's next explorers, my lord Greger. They'll spend much of their time aboard ships, and they'll face plenty of dangers. But drowning won't be one of them."

"I see," Lord Greger said. He asked Elias another question, but Mercedes was only half listening.

She found herself straying back to Elias's face. She had been trying very hard not to think about his upcoming journey. Two years gone, at least. It felt like forever. What if he was seriously hurt? He could be stabbed. Or catch a horrible, wasting disease. If anything happened to him, she would not know of it for a very long time. She heard Lord Greger ask, "What is that around the child?"

Hector had grown brave enough to sit beside Jaime in three inches of seawater. Tied around his waist was some sort of pink tubing filled with air.

"A life belt." She answered Lord Greger's question, very familiar, after all, with the contraption. Elias had taught her to swim in this very cove when he was nine and she eight. "It helps them stay afloat when they're just learning to swim."

"What is it made of?"

"Cow's bladder," Elias said, his smile widening at the older man's expression. "You blow into a piece of bladder, like Jaime is doing there, and tie the ends off." They watched as Jaime blew into a flattened length of bladder, his cheeks puffing and the bladder gradually inflating.

Mercedes said, "It's disgusting, I know, but very effective."

"I'll take you both at your word," Lord Greger said with good-natured skepticism. He turned to Elias. "I met your father many years ago, my lord Elias. He's not someone easily forgotten."

"He isn't," Elias agreed. "I'm sorry you missed him. He and my mother are in Esperanca for the summer."

Confusion settled over Lord Greger. "Forgive me. I meant Lord Antoni."

This time Elias looked away from his charges. He glanced first at Mercedes, then Lord Greger. He was no longer smiling. "Of course. That would have been a long time ago."

"Twenty-five years," Lord Greger confirmed. "He was passing through on the way to the Inner Jangas. We had a very interesting conversation over supper about cannibals." He smiled at the memory, then said, "The resemblance is a striking one. I suppose you've been told that before."

"Yes." Elias looked out over the water, his forehead creasing.

Mercedes saw what had caught his attention. A swimmer alone at the mouth of the cove. Arms lifted high as he glided through the water. She could not make out who it was. He was too far away.

"One of yours?" she asked.

"It better not be." Elias looked over the boys again. She could almost hear him counting them off in his head, one by one. "No, they're all here."

"Elias . . ." She drew his gaze toward the two boys sitting in the shallows. Jaime was also watching the unknown swimmer. He was a handsome boy, dark haired and slender. And very guilty-looking about something.

"Jaime," Elias called, switching back to del Marian as he asked, "do you know who that is?"

"Ah . . ." Jaime scratched the back of his neck. He looked down the beach toward the fishermen. "Who?"

Elias's voice took on a warning note. "Jaime . . ."

The boy's shoulders drooped. "I think it's Reyna."

Elias uttered a word in Oslawn that caused Lord Greger's mouth to fall open. Alarmed, Mercedes brought her hand up to shield her eyes from the sun. *Was* it Reyna?

"Who is Reyna?" Lord Greger wondered.

"She's in no danger." Jaime scrambled to his feet. "She swims better than —"

But Jaime spoke to air. Elias was already gone, running past him and diving into the water.

"You will explain yourself," Elias ordered.

An arm's length separated him from Reyna, who, to his immense relief, did not look to be in any danger of drowning.

She wore a simple linen shift. Her hair was coiled above her ears in ram horns so tightly wound that only a few strands had escaped. Her arms skimmed the surface while her feet kicked expertly beneath the sparkling turquoise of the water. Someone had taught her to swim. He refused to be impressed. It did not excuse her recklessness.

"I'm enjoying the water like everyone else," Reyna said, stormy-eyed. "I've done nothing wrong."

"Is that what you think?" Turning aside, he spat out a stream of water and tried to catch his breath. He'd never swum so fast in his life, terrified at the thought of her slipping beneath the waters before he could get to her. "Does your grandfather know you're here?"

"No."

That was it. A simple, defiant *no*. Where had the sweet child gone? The girl he knew was quiet and obedient. No one ever had to worry about Reyna. Now she glared daggers at him, and there was something about her mutinous expression that reminded him of Mercedes. He swam backward, putting several feet between them, and tried to rein in his temper.

"Reyna, swimming this far out is dangerous."

"And where am I to swim? In the bathing pools? With the women? The water is three feet deep there. It's ridiculous."

"With the boys." He swiped salt water from his eyes and scowled at her. "Surely Master Luca explained the rules?"

"I'm not allowed to swim with the boys!" she cried, slapping one palm against the surface and splashing them both in the face.

"Madame Vega says it's indecent." Her tone took on a disdainful note. "As if it matters to me what a naked boy looks like. As if there's anything of interest to see." Before he could think what to say, she was a child again, with her lower lip trembling. "It's not fair, Lord Elias. I've done everything I'm supposed to do. It's not fair that they will all be chosen and I will not. Even Hector."

His anger left him. He had stepped into an adder's pit of hurt and injustice, and there was nothing to be done about it. Lord Silva's words were fresh in his mind. "Have you spoken to your grandfather?"

A sniffle. "He says choosing an apprentice is a master's privilege, and that he will not influence their choice. He says . . ."

He waited and, when she remained silent, prompted, "Reyna?"

A single tear dropped, becoming part of the sea. "He says if I do not marry, I may take over for Madame Vega one day. Or join the royal painters."

"We couldn't do without them," was his gentle reminder. "Would that be so terrible?"

A sea worm looped around her, bumping a shoulder, wanting to play. She nudged it aside with her hand and said, "I don't want to stay home, painting someone else's adventures."

How would he feel, to be in her place? They were not so different, he and Reyna. "Who taught you to swim?"

Reyna glanced toward shore. "Jaime. He owed me a favor."

Plenty of favors being repaid these days, Elias thought sourly. "Listen to me. I —"

He nearly missed it before it disappeared beneath the surface. Beyond them, in even deeper waters, was the unmistakable, undulating form of a sea serpent. Swimming their way. It should not be here, so near to the shore. Reyna had seen it, too. Her gasp was cut off when he grabbed her by the arm and propelled her toward dry land. Fear made his voice sharp.

"Go! Fast as you can. Don't look back."

She was gone, her small arms and legs taking her as quickly as they could toward shore. For all her speed, she could not match the swiftness of the serpent that approached. He would have to distract it.

They were not the only ones who had spotted the creature. The calm waters were no more as the boys splashed frantically toward safety. Lord Greger had waded in, pulling them from the water. Mercedes was a blur of sky blue as she raced down the beach. Away from the children. Away from him.

"Mercedes," he said aloud, her name still on his lips as he turned away, swimming toward the serpent and open sea.

It could have been cast in gold, so pure was its color; its eyes were blood-red garnets. Elias would have thought it a thing of beauty, from a distance.

For the last several minutes, the serpent had been content to swim loose coils around him. Not touching him. Not yet. The cove had become a fearsome, whirling pool. The churning of the water could not drown out the roaring in his ears.

A mariner's harpoon protruded from its neck. Six feet of forged steel bounced hideously from an open wound. Someone had shot it. That was the reason it was here. The creature was dying, and its actions had become unpredictable.

He heard his name carried on the wind. A glance behind him showed Reyna stumbling onto the beach. *Good girl.* Now there was no one left to save but himself. Trying to appear as small as possible, he sank into the water and swam for shore.

The serpent hit him, hard enough to send him spinning down toward the sea floor, where there was no air to breathe and his lungs burned. His attempts to claw his way to the surface failed; his fingers scrabbled uselessly against smooth scaling. In desperation, he wrapped arms and legs around the serpent and held tight. It reared back, spiraling out of the water, and Elias found himself hundreds of feet in the air, clinging to the serpent's neck, the harpoon lodged directly beneath his feet. The serpent twisted around to pin him with glowing red eyes. Its mouth opened wide to reveal rows of iron-gray teeth and a black gaping hole.

A single arrow flew straight into the serpent's open mouth, a moment before its head exploded into devil fire. Elias tumbled into the water in a shower of gory serpent flesh. He resurfaced, coughing up the sea and worse, relief threatening to swamp his vision. He looked toward shore.

The boys were there with the ambassador and Reyna. Another man holding a lit torch. And standing beside him, with her bow still raised high, was Mercedes.

SIXTEEN

Lord Ambassador Greger waded into the shallow waters and hauled Elias to his feet.

"Good God, boy. I've just lost ten years of my life. Are you hurt?"

"No, I —" It was all Elias had time for. The boys closed in around him, everyone speaking at once. Reyna flung her arms around his neck and cried, "I'm sorry! I'm so sorry. It's my fault!"

"Stop." He pried her fingers loose so that he could inspect her. She was trembling. So was he. "You've all your fingers? Your toes?"

"I have them."

Jaime was just behind her, an arm around a whimpering Hector. *Perfect,* was Elias's fleeting thought. There went Hector's final swim lesson.

"We'll speak of this later," Elias said to Reyna. Slimy bits of serpent clung to his hair. He pulled a stringy piece free and tossed it onto the sand, distracting and delighting the younger boys. "From now on, you'll swim with me, or Jaime. Never alone. Do I have your word on it?"

"Yes, Lord Elias," Reyna said.

He looked over her head. "Jaime?"

"I'll make sure of it, Lord Elias."

The man holding the torch approached him. He wore rough, salt-stained clothing and a strip of red fabric across his forehead — one of the fisherman from down the beach. Elias knew him.

"Too close, chart maker." The fisherman spat onto the sand. "You could have been food for the fish."

"How is it here, Mungo?" Elias's heart was still racing. Across the cove, the serpent's corpse had slipped entirely beneath the surface, leaving the water calm once again. "Who would risk killing it?"

Serpents that swam within the sea boundaries of del Mar belonged to the king. They were hunted by the king's fishermen, their skin traded for gold and their meat considered a delicacy. To steal from the kingdom was to risk what all thieves risked: fingers, or a hand, and a lengthy stay in the castle dungeons.

"Some idiot shipman." Mungo the fisherman shrugged. "A Coronad, maybe. Lucky for you, your lady is a good shot."

His lady.

Mercedes stood at the edge of the crowd with her bow pointed to the ground, the hem of her blue dress soaked with seawater and coated in sand. And the look on her face . . .

"Mercedes." He walked toward her, the lump in his throat painful and sudden. He knew how he would have felt if she had been the one in the water.

She asked faintly, "What sort of person swims *toward* the snake?"

He slowed his steps. Spread his arms wide and said, "I'm in one piece. See?"

"For now you're in one piece!" she burst out, and flung her bow at his feet, sending up a spray of white sand. All went silent with shock around them. The lady Mercedes never, ever shouted. Or threw things. She cried, "What of tomorrow? What of tonight? One day you're going to find yourself in trouble, Elias, and I won't be around to save —"

He kissed her. Cupped her face with both hands and touched his lips to hers. He had not thought he would make it, not this time, and the kiss was full of fear, and relief . . . until a fisherman's chuckle reminded him they were not alone.

Mercedes stumbled back, wide-eyed, her chest rising and falling in time with his. And then she turned and ran off. Leaving him staring after her with children and fishermen and a foreign ambassador at his back.

Elias could not follow her. Not right away. First he had to see a pack of overly excited children back to the tower and deliver the ambassador safely to Ulises. Both took time and much explanation. Then he had to endure Basilio's horrified rantings while he sat in a tub and scrubbed off the remainder of the serpent's guts from his hair and skin. And when finally, *finally,* he was able to look for her, he discovered she was nowhere to be found. Not in her chambers, not in the castle. No one he asked knew where she was. He stalked across the grounds, gnashing his teeth in frustration, before one of her attendants finally took pity on him. Lady Mercedes had gone off with Commander Aimon, but she was expected to return for supper.

Elias spent the remainder of the afternoon in the tower with both maps. Or tried to. Fellow geographers Luca, Martín, and a handful of others interrupted frequently. They had heard of the serpent — and the kiss! — and wanted to know every detail, grousing when Elias sent them packing. By the time he dressed for supper, his mood was dark. It would have looked odd to wear his carrier to eat, so he left it in his chambers, hidden within a secret niche in the wall that he had discovered by accident years ago.

The ambassador's presence meant supper was a grander affair than usual. Long tables spanned the great dining hall, weighed down by their bounty: roast pigs on copper platters, a pomegranate shoved into every mouth; fried fish and boiled octopus; great round bowls of rice blackened with squid ink; and endless plates of olives, figs, grapes. The cheese stank beautifully.

Elias spotted Luca at a table and headed in that direction, stopping often to greet those he hadn't seen in months. Conversation was loud and lively, nearly drowning out the trio of guitar masters occupying a corner. The musicians dressed in flamboyant embroidered red, their feet tapping on the stone. Elias had nearly reached Luca when a hand snaked out from one of the tables and grabbed his arm.

"Elias." Lord Braga pulled him down to be better heard over the noise. He was a tall man, bald, with an extravagant mustache. When Lord Braga was ashore, he taught navigation and astronomy. "Madame Vega says you're considering an apprentice."

Exasperated, Elias looked for Madame Vega, but she was nowhere to be found. "Ah. I am. That is —"

"You'll consider my Jaime." Lord Braga gestured down the table to where the children sat. Jaime with Reyna, Hector laughing. Hector appeared to have fully recovered from the incident with the sea serpent. "He's more than ready. As a favor to me."

Directly across from him, Madame Grec straightened, lips pressed thin. She told Lord Braga, "You should not influence him. There are others to consider."

Lord Braga gave her a pitying look. "Hector's not meant for the seas, Genevieve. You're better off sending him to Isidore."

Elias looked at Hector in a new light. His stepfather was always complaining about how hard it was to find good apprentices for the Exchequer. He asked, "Is he good with figures?"

"I think so," Lord Braga answered. "A little young to say for certain, but —"

"Hector will be an explorer!" Madame Grec snapped. "Like his father. Not some coin counter." Madame and Lord Braga exchanged narrow-eyed looks over the roast pig.

Elias was offended on his stepfather's behalf. Lord Silva came to the rescue. "Lord Braga, leave the boy alone," he said mildly, and Elias sent him a grateful look. "Elias is capable of making his own choices, in his own time. And Madame Grec," he said with a warning look, "this is neither the time nor the place."

Madame Grec stabbed a slice of pig with her knife. Lord Braga sighed and released Elias's arm, and Elias gratefully made his escape.

Luca greeted him with a "They won't leave you alone until you decide."

"I feel like a cornered rat." Elias elbowed a place for himself along the bench between Luca and Martín. Luca looked almost like his old self. He must have felt better to be risking another plate full of fish.

Martín said, "Choose anyone but Mateo. I've decided to take him on."

"Fine," Elias said absently.

Ulises and Mercedes sat at a table on a dais, Lord Greger between them. He had never seen her in that dress before. It was as green as the Javelin palms, trimmed in black lace. She wore no jewelry, a simple black ribbon around her neck her only adornment. Ulises spoke pleasantly with the ambassador. Elias wondered how the king had explained the bruising beneath his eye, then decided he didn't explain. Only Commander Aimon and Mercedes would be brave enough to ask, and they already knew what had happened. Mercedes caught Elias's gaze. Her smile faded to nothing, and she looked away.

She was avoiding him.

The conversation continued around Elias as he thought about Mercedes and maps and the upcoming voyage. He had been looking forward to this expedition. Now two years felt like a very long time to be away from home. He glanced again toward the dais, then scowled at Luca, who elbowed him in the side and said, "You'll get nowhere sitting here and brooding, Junipero."

Elias ignored the unflattering reference to del Mar's fabled romantic hero, who jumped from the southern cliffs to his death after his true love, also his sister, married another. It dawned on him that the chair beside Mercedes was empty. Lady Aimon dined on the other side of it, which meant the commander had not yet arrived.

An opportunity.

Elias abandoned his companions with a hurried "I'll see you later," and made his way to the raised table. When he pulled back Commander Aimon's seat, he was rewarded with a frown from Mercedes and a smile from Lady Aimon.

"What handsome company," Lady Aimon said after he had kissed her on each cheek. She glanced at Mercedes, who dissected the fish on her plate with great care. "I'll not flatter myself into thinking you're here on my behalf." Lady Aimon turned to speak to her other supper companion, offering them what privacy she could.

Elias greeted Lord Greger. The ambassador endeared himself to Elias by also turning aside and striking up a conversation with the king.

Food and wine were placed before him. The wine was half drunk before he said in a low voice, "Mercedes."

She did not look up from her plate. "Lord Elias."

Lord Elias, he noted. Not a promising start. "I left your bow in your chambers. Did you see it?"

"Yes. Thank you."

He happened to catch Ulises's eye at that moment. Elias had never been good at reading lips. He could not tell if his friend had mouthed *Good luck* or *Do not bother.*

He tried again. "Lord Greger is pleasant."

"He is. Very pleasant."

Elias drank more wine. "Mercedes, do you remember Lady Antonella?"

She looked over at that, startled. "Of course I do."

Lady Antonella had been a distant relation of his stepfather's. A year ago, she had sailed for Caffa to visit her ailing sister, who had married a nobleman there. The ship had been set upon by pirates and everyone aboard murdered, from the captain down to the cabin boy.

Elias said, "I was in Coronado at the time. When the news came, we were told only that a del Marian noblewoman and her party had died off the coast of Caffa. No names were given. I thought it was you."

Finally, she met his eyes. He said, "For two weeks, I thought you were gone. Luca will tell you I was ... poor company." Her hand rested beside her plate. He reached out, touched the back of his hand to the back of hers. "I'm sorry I frightened you this morning. But you are not the only one who worries. You are not the only who has stayed up at night, imagining the worst."

Once again, Mercedes concentrated on her plate. He waited, frustration mounting. "Nothing to say? That is unlike you." And then he wished he had not pushed her. The words she spoke were far worse than silence.

"It does not matter."

He breathed in his hurt, breathed it in deep. It felt as though she'd kicked him. "If you say so," he said, and made to push back his chair. Her hand covered his, stopping him.

"You're misunderstanding me." She turned into him, their heads nearly touching, and spoke quietly. "You've been dreaming of this expedition since you were a boy. Do you remember, years ago? We were at the cove, and you were talking about sailing past the Strait of Cain at last. You spoke of it for so long that I fell asleep right there on the sand. And when I woke, you were still speaking of it."

He smiled despite himself. "I remember."

She smiled, too, a little. "You'll be away for years, Elias, and I think of everything that can go wrong. I have trouble sleeping sometimes, thinking of it."

A small sound from Lady Aimon, though her back was still turned. It sounded like a sniffle. He was past caring who heard them.

He said, "Then don't think of it. Come with me." The words were out before he could consider them further. And even then, he did not regret speaking them. At her stunned look, he said,

"There's nothing strange about an emissary joining an expedition. It's been done before. Come with me."

She took a deep breath. "I can't come with you."

"Why not?"

"Because I'm going to Mondrago."

That silenced him. Mercedes glanced over her shoulder at her cousin, who was laughing over some story with the ambassador, then said, "We've been discussing it for some time. You know this. Someone must go there and find out what needs to be done."

She would oversee the rebuilding of Mondrago. It was not something that should have surprised him. "Ulises asked you to go?"

She shook her head. "I asked. Today. This . . . it feels right to me, Elias. That I should go."

He understood how she felt. Especially now, after what they had learned at Javelin. "How long will you be gone?"

"I've no notion. Truly, I don't know."

"*When* will you go?"

This time, she took more care of her words, and of who might be listening. "After we're done here." She spoke of the maps. Mercedes would leave for Mondrago once the riddle was solved. "When I said it does not matter, I only meant . . . when this is over, I will go one way, and you will go the other. And that is all."

Her hand still covered his. Everything he needed to say was trapped inside of him. All he managed was "Is it?"

Behind him came a loud *"Ahem."* Commander Aimon had come to claim his chair. When Elias looked back, the commander regarded him with raised eyebrows and asked, "Are you quite finished?"

"Oh, Aimon," Lady Aimon said under her breath. She dabbed at the corner of her eye with a napkin. "What timing."

"Yes, Commander." Elias stood. He could feel his face burning. Mercedes once again had eyes only for her plate. He took small comfort in seeing that her cheeks were as red as his must be.

He didn't bother to return to Luca and Martín's company, but left the great dining hall with his appetite lost.

In his chambers, a single candle burned on a table, casting shadows upon charts and stone. There was no sign of Basilio. Elias placed his sword and dagger on a large chest. His coat fitted like a second skin; it took some effort to remove it without help, but after much cursing and struggle, he managed to set it aside. His thoughts were occupied, and because they were, he had only a second of warning. Against a wall, one long shadow split into two, and a figure sprang forward with his sword raised high.

His own weapons were across the chamber on the sea chest, sword and dagger of no use to him now. Sheer instinct had him twisting away; in the same motion, he seized a globe off a table and hurled it at the masked intruder, dressed head to foot in black.

A grunt of pain emerged as the globe made contact. The man staggered backward. Elias had time to see another shadow emerge before he heard a loud crack and his nose exploded with pain. He dropped to his knees, hands clutched to his face. Another blow, this time to the back of his head, and he was on the ground, face pressed against stone. A knee dug into his back. His attacker's breath was hot against his ear.

"A message for you, mapmaker." The man's voice was soft, gentle even. "You are curious like the cat, my lord Elias. It serves you well in your profession. But there's such a thing as being too curious, hmm? The cat has only so many lives. And then what happens to it?"

As Elias fought to stay conscious, his hand closed around a familiar object trapped between the floor and his hip. His pouch. He worked the brass compass divider free of it and stabbed backward, blindly, deep into flesh. He heard a sharp, satisfying cry of pain before darkness rolled over him and he felt nothing.

SEVENTEEN

Eve, Lady?"

Katalin, Cortes's Royal Tax Collector, wore a baffled expression. She was a trim young woman with a neat, tidy appearance: a single braid down her back, her robe the color of sand and unadorned by fur collar or cuffs or jeweled pins. Like Mercedes, she was half Mondragan and half del Marian. Unlike her, Katalin's hair was a magnificent flaming red. "Is there anything else you can tell me?" Katalin asked. "Her father's name, perhaps? Or his guild?"

"I've next to nothing," Mercedes confessed. She was perched on the edge of Katalin's worktable in the castle's tax chambers. She had fled the dining hall as soon as she was able and come here. Ulises, merciful cousin that he was, had invited Ambassador Greger on an evening stroll through the menageries. Her presence had not been required.

These chambers were part of the Exchequer, or treasury, a long, cavernous space lined with shelves that nearly buckled under the weight of scrolls and ledgers. Empty moneybags hung from hooks on the wall. Tables displayed scales at their centers.

In the light of day, the chamber would be filled with taxmen and their apprentices. At this late hour, Mercedes had found only Katalin working by candlelight and surrounded by orderly towers of gold squid and silver double-shells. She said, "All I know is that her name is Eve. Even that may be misleading, given all the possible variations."

"Eve will be a nickname, likely," Katalin agreed. She sat back in her chair, her expression turning thoughtful. "She could be an Evalin or an Eva-Jean or a Genevieve. . . ."

"Eva-Mari," Mercedes offered.

"Exactly so."

"The Eve I'm looking for may not live in Cortes any longer," Mercedes said. "She may not even be alive. My thought is that she's between the ages of thirty-three and forty-three . . ." Katalin's expression brightened at that bit of knowledge, and then fell once again when Mercedes finished with ". . . though I cannot say for certain."

They turned as one to regard the ledgers on the shelves, ledgers that held the names of every tax-paying citizen of del Mar for centuries. It did not help that women took their husbands' names when they married. Elias's mother, for example, went from the unmarried Lady Sabine to Lady Antoni to Lady Isidore. And once married, their names disappeared from the tax records altogether; only their husbands' names were recorded.

But.

If a woman was unmarried and her wages paid to her alone,

she would be in these records, somewhere. A slim chance was better than no chance at all.

Mercedes said, "I know what I ask. It will be like searching for a ring dropped into the sea."

"It's daunting," Katalin admitted. "But not impossible. If I may make a suggestion?"

"Of course."

Katalin gestured toward the shelves. "Lord Isidore knows these ledgers better than anyone. I could send a messenger to him in Esperanca —"

But Mercedes was already shaking her head. Lord Isidore would have questions. And she would not want to lie to Elias's stepfather after all the kindnesses he had shown her over the years. Simpler to leave him out completely. She said, "I can't have anyone knowing of this except you. I'll have your word on it."

Katalin was quiet for a time. "Lady," she said, "I know you spoke to Lord Isidore on my behalf. After my father passed on. I know I'm here because of you, and I'm grateful."

Mercedes had met Katalin a year ago, through Elias. Katalin's father had worked at the harbor collecting the custom duties on imports and exports. His daughter had worked by his side, but after he died, a new customs officer was put in place. Katalin was left with no employment. At the same time, the position of Royal Tax Collector had become available. The council had balked at naming a woman to the position, thankless job though it was. Particularly one who was half Mondragan, though no one said so in Mercedes's hearing. She had nearly run out of breath arguing on Katalin's behalf. But in the end, she had won.

As Royal Tax Collector for Cortes, Katalin rode throughout the parishes, gathering taxes on the king's behalf. Always with an armed escort, because she was a woman, a Mondragan, and someone who carried around bags of gold. And because no one liked the taxman.

Mercedes looked around the gloomy chamber with its scales and ledgers and endless monotonous work, or so it seemed to her. "You're thanking me for this?"

Katalin's smile dimpled. "I am." She turned to the wall of ledgers with a thoughtful, determined expression. "I'll start immediately. If there are Eves in these tax rolls, I'll find them for you. You have my word and my silence."

Mercedes thanked her and left, and thought: *Nothing to go on but a name.*

Four hundred steps led up to Elias's tower chambers. Years ago, Mercedes had taken it upon herself to count them. She climbed them now, around and around the winding steps, the torches on the wall lighting her way through the darkness. Her courage faltered on the twentieth step.

Her outburst on the beach had mortified her. A display like that, in front of the children, in front of *Ambassador Greger*. She wanted to clutch her head and groan every time she thought of it. And then the kiss. And then supper.

What would she say to him?

You always know what to say, Mercedes. That is your gift.

It was not true. She was not the sort of person who spoke easily of what she felt in her heart. She could not put into words her fear, watching the serpent turn its gaze to Elias, and knowing that if her arrow failed, he would be lost. And she would be lost. She could not *say* these things.

Someone was coming down the stairs at a fast trot. Mercedes did not want to startle anyone. She called out, "Basilio?"

The footsteps stopped. No one answered. Mercedes placed her slipper on the next step, and whoever was there turned tail and ran back up the stairs. Or maybe two people; she could not say for certain. She could hear the scuffling of feet like rats across stone. A door opened and closed.

Mercedes continued upward, cautious. There were many chambers in the lower levels of the tower, rooms for the other geographers and their servants. People passed through this stairway regularly. Why would anyone feel the need to hide from her?

Her ears twitched at another sound. A whimper? A moan? Very faint and coming from above. She drew her dagger from her belt, lifted her skirts off the steps, and ran.

There were crows in his bedchamber. Elias heard the cawing as he came to, and felt agonizing pain behind his eyes. The sound grew louder and more frantic.

"Crows," he said, and opened his eyes.

"Hush."

Mercedes. He was lying on the floor with his head cradled in her lap. Worry clouded her face, and over her shoulder, he saw that the shrieking was coming not from crows, but from Basilio, wringing his hands in the corner and wailing.

Mercedes said, "Basilio! You hush, too! Find help." Basilio fled. Mercedes helped Elias sit up. She kept her arms around him.

"What happened?" he mumbled. "My nose —"

"Looks very bad. Don't speak." She fished a handkerchief from her sleeve and wiped his face, slow and careful. The cloth came away bloody.

He closed his eyes and held himself very still, trying to keep the sickening dizziness at bay. His nose throbbed painfully. He must have drifted off, because when he looked up, Basilio had returned, Madame Vega on his heels. Her face was white and shocked. She knelt beside them.

"Look here," she commanded of Elias. "Now look there. Hmm. There's a knot on your head the size of a serpent's egg. What have you been up to?" Madame had brought with her a wooden box with a handle on top. As soon as she lifted the lid, the pungent aroma of lavender ointment filled his nostrils.

Mercedes asked, "Are *you* well, Madame?"

Madame Vega paused with her hand in the box. Elias tried to focus on his geography mistress, saw a face more tired than usual, eyes rimmed in red.

Madame Vega murmured, "A speck of dust in the eye only, Lady. Thank you." She turned to Elias. "Are you hurt anywhere else?"

"No, Madame." A thought struck him; he bolted upright, startling Mercedes, and looked across the chamber. "Basilio, the map?"

Reyna's map had been left on the table. Basilio shook his head. "It's gone, sir."

Elias could see Mercedes struggling to hold her tongue, even as her eyes clearly asked, "Where is the other one?" Before he could answer, young faces gathered in the doorway, whispering. Reyna was among them. The children fell to the side as Ulises stalked into the chamber with Lord Silva.

Ulises demanded, "What happened?"

Elias tried to clear his head. "He was already here. They were."

"Who, Elias?" Lord Silva asked.

Madame Vega reached down and picked up his brass compass divider. The points were red with blood, still fresh.

Elias shook his head. He didn't know. "He had a sword —"

From Basilio: "It wasn't a sword." He pointed a shaky finger toward the far side of the chamber, beneath the window.

Lord Silva crossed the chamber and picked up something that looked like a club. He appeared flabbergasted. "Well, we know the weapon, at least. Where did this leg come from?"

A horrified gasp from Mercedes, a sound that echoed

around the chamber. Ulises grew very still. Elias squinted through the dimness. Lord Silva held a wooden stump. It was covered in blood, but Elias could make out the seahorse, intricately carved. Just as he formed the thought *Lady Esma*, the screaming started.

A child's cry, pouring in through the open window.

EIGHTEEN

THEY FOUND LADY Esma in the geographer's courtyard, her body tossed upon the southernmost point of the mosaic compass. The tiles beneath her shimmered green and silver. On any other evening, a work of art to be admired beneath a full planting moon.

But not on this night.

Tonight, a tight-lipped Commander Aimon crouched beside her body directly across from Elias. Mercedes stood nearby, alongside Ulises and Lord Silva. Onlookers kept to the edges. They crowded every inch of covered passageway. Hector was one of them. Elias could hear him wailing in his mother's arms.

"She was just there! I was running, and I tripped, and she was just there. Maman, she did not have a leg!"

"Shhh, my darling."

No one dared approach. Not with the king looking as he did, cold and remote, until one peered a little closer and saw his eyes full of rage and the pulse ticking wild at his throat. As for Elias, he knew he was disturbing in his own way: a face bruised and mottled, his nose set at an odd angle . . . and hands that weren't quite steady as he reached down to close Lady Esma's eyes.

Closed for the last time. Never again to see the stars in the sky, or the moon riding low among them.

If the commander noticed Elias's trembling hand, he did not say so, but sat back on his heels and said gruffly, "She was beaten to death."

"Yes," Elias said.

Lady Esma wore the same clothing he'd seen her in days ago. Shirt and trousers, one leg rolled up to accommodate a wooden stump that was even now in his chamber under Basilio's watchful eye. Every inch of her that he could see was battered purple and black. Beaten until she died, likely with her own leg. His mind reeled from the cruelty of it.

He felt a hand on his shoulder. Mercedes, eyes filled with a terrible guilt. Her last words to Lady Esma had been angry ones.

"What will we tell everyone?" he asked her.

Because they must be told something. The curiosity pulsed around them. Like a heartbeat. Like a living, breathing thing. Better they were fed some tale than to have someone nosing about, discovering what they should not discover.

Her answer came quietly. "No one can know who she is. We will say . . . we are unable to identify her, though her features suggest she is of Lunesian descent. Perhaps a mariner. Commander Aimon is looking into it. The king, of course, is outraged that such a crime would occur in his kingdom, in his castle. He will not rest until her murderer is apprehended and made to answer for this crime . . . or something similar. I will think of more later."

"I remember when she was nearly a child herself," Lord Silva said, stricken. "Always with a little prince by her side. Who would do such a thing?"

"She was safe in that forest," Ulises said. "The girls would never have let anyone harm her."

Elias said, "Which means she left. Freely."

From Mercedes, an angry whisper: "*Why?* She would not leave Javelin for anything. Why now?"

Just then, a hush fell over the crowd. A horse and cart appeared beneath an archway and made its way, slow and plodding, across the compass toward them. A robed woman drove the cart; two burly men walked beside it. It was over in minutes. When the cart stopped, the woman exchanged brief words with the king and the commander. Lady Esma was covered in linen and placed in the cart. It rumbled off as quietly as it had come.

"Lord Silva," Ulises said abruptly.

The Royal Navigator had been staring after the departing cart. He jumped slightly. "Yes, my king?"

"Two strange men entering your tower. Someone might have noticed."

"Three," Elias said. They turned to him in question, and he clarified, "There were three. Someone stayed in the shadows and watched. He didn't say a word."

"You're certain?" Mercedes asked.

"Yes." Just before Elias had lost consciousness, he'd seen a third figure. In the corner, eyes glittering beneath a dark hood.

Lord Silva's mouth pressed into a thin line at the revelation. "I'll look into it at once," he said, and then hesitated. "My king, may I speak?"

"Of course."

"I worry about the boy," Lord Silva said.

Elias glanced over at Hector before he realized Lord Silva meant him. He felt his cheeks flush hot with humiliation. The commander was listening. And Mercedes. As he was reduced in height, in width and breadth — a child to be protected still.

"Elias could have been killed today," Lord Silva continued. "Right under our noses. I wonder if we should rethink his role in this."

Elias's response came flat and angry. "No."

Ulises studied Lord Silva, expressionless. "You would have him walk away?"

"This was a warning," Lord Silva said. "A very clear one. I don't wish to lose both father *and* son, and have to explain the loss to his mother."

"*No,*" Elias said again. "Don't ask it of me."

Support came from an unlikely source. "He's rattled a cage, my lord Silva," Commander Aimon said. "He's scared whatever's in it. It's a little late, I think, for him to just walk away."

Ulises turned to Elias, who glared back and silently dared his friend to do as Lord Silva asked. "Well, Elias. It looks like someone is trying to frighten you."

"Ulises —" he began.

"*And?*" Ulises interrupted softly. "*Are* you frightened?"

The look Elias sent him showed everything he felt. Ulises studied him, then said, "Good." He turned to Lord Silva, "We'll continue as we've been."

Lord Silva's expression tightened. "My king . . . As you wish." He bowed, stiff and correct, and walked off. Mercedes turned to watch him go.

"Mercedes," Ulises said, bringing her attention back around, "I want her buried in her family crypt. She will not rest in a stranger's pit."

A pause. Mercedes asked, "Without her family knowing?"

"Yes."

After a moment, she said, "I'll see to it."

A brief glance as she passed Elias, a promise they would speak again before the night was over. And she was gone, taking Commander Aimon with her.

There were just the two of them now. Ulises said, "Find out who did this. Bring them to me. I have plans for them."

"I'll see to it."

Ulises clapped him once on the shoulder. And then he, too, was gone.

Elias strode across the courtyard to Hector, who had his arms wrapped around his mother's waist. Madame Grec opened her mouth to speak, took a closer look at Elias's face, and snapped it shut again.

Elias crouched before the boy. Was it only this morning he had been at the cove, trying to coax him into the water? "It's been quite the day for us, Hector."

The boy sniffled. "Yes, Lord Elias."

"Are you all right?"

"Yes, sir. Are you?"

The smile came involuntarily. "Just. What were you doing out here?"

Hector said, "Cook said I could have an extra sweet if I went to the kitchens. She said I could choose."

"Ah," Elias said, understanding. "What did you choose, then?"

Hector pointed to the far end of the courtyard, where a small object lay on the tiles. "I tripped over her and dropped my cake." A tear dropped to the ground. "I did not mean to scream."

Elias said, "There's no shame here, Hector. Anyone would have been afraid." He tried to think past the vicious pounding in his head. "Did she open her eyes at all? Did she say anything?"

"No. She was . . . she was not there." Hector's face crumpled.

A hand came down on the boy's shoulder, and Madame Grec said quietly, "Enough."

Elias thanked Hector and made his way to his chambers, ignoring those who tried to speak to him. His mind was plagued by doubt and suspicion. Why had Lady Esma left the forest? Had she remembered something else and come to Cortes on her own to tell them? By coincidence, had she been spotted by her killer and done away with before she could speak with them? It was a large and unlikely coincidence.

Or.

Had someone gone into the forest and lured her out? As a warning. As a threat. He hoped it was the former, because if it was not, he would have to think hard about what that meant. Very few people knew how to safely navigate the forest of Javelin, beside himself.

Basilio had been busy. Everything was tidied, the broken glass swept up, the tables righted. On one of the tables were the contents of Elias's pouch: stones, tin, key, coins. His compass divider was also there, the brass wiped clean of blood.

"I'm fine, Basilio," Elias said when the servant tried to fuss about. Elias set his carrier on the table and lowered himself into a chair. Slowly. Everything hurt. "Why don't you go to bed?"

"Madame Vega left the salve." Basilio hovered, eyes filled with concern. "I'm to tell you to use it. Before you go to bed, again in the morning, or she'll know." The air reeked of lavender ointment.

Elias closed his eyes. "Fine."

Silence followed. He thought Basilio might have gone on his way until he heard him ask, "What shall I do with this?"

Elias opened his eyes. Basilio held Lady Esma's leg, cleaned of her blood and his. Wordless, he held out a hand; Basilio gave it over. Elias traced a fingertip along the seahorse's carved dips and whorls. Someone had killed her, but only after they had hurt her in a way he had never seen another person hurt before. Not in all his years, not in all his travels. With deliberate, indifferent cruelty. And what of his own part of it? He had led someone right to the borders of Javelin and shown them the way in.

What was he missing?

"I heard it was a woman," Basilio said. "Did you know her?"

"A little. That's not what we're telling others."

"I understand. I am very sorry, Lord Elias." Basilio bowed and would have left him to his solitude. He stopped when Elias said, "There were only two keys made for this chamber, weren't there?"

"Yes."

"What about the molds? Did we keep them?"

Basilio was frowning, understanding why Elias asked. A key could be easily copied from impressions, and all sorts of mischief done, which is why most locksmiths kept their molds and impressions under lock and key. Basilio said, "I had the locksmith break them in front of me before I would pay him. I'm sure he was offended."

The answer was not surprising. Basilio had always been cautious. Elias picked up his key from the table. It was made of iron, the bow and stem plain and functional, the bit a complicated pattern of grooves and teeth. He held it up to the candlelight and studied it, turning it over, bringing it close and sniffing it. Basilio had come to stand by his side.

"Where is yours?" Elias asked, tossing his key back onto the table.

Basilio fished an identical key from the pouch at his belt. Elias took it, sniffed, and glanced sharply at Basilio, who leaned close and asked, "What is it?"

"Wax."

Astonishment showed on Basilio's face, followed quickly by ire. Elias pointed out the tiniest bit of yellow wax, no larger than a dot of ink, left to cling onto the bit. Someone had made a wax impression of the key and had been careless with their cleanup. Basilio muttered something very nasty and un-Basilio-like.

Elias tried to work through a puzzle. "It would not take long to make an impression. But how would they use your key? It's always with you."

Basilio was silent, and then with a sudden stricken look said, "The baths."

The castle baths were enjoyed by men and women, their chambers separated. To enter, one had to first disrobe completely, leaving clothing and other belongings on open shelves that were nominally guarded by attendants. Elias had been to the baths countless times. It would have been a simple thing to wait until an attendant was called away and make a quick wax impression, returning the key within seconds.

"When did you last go?"

Basilio looked wretched. "Yesterday. In the morning. I'll have new ones made immediately. I am so very —"

"Don't," Elias ordered. "This is not your fault." He

drummed his rage along the table. "Listen to me: You'll go to my parents' house tonight. Stay there until I send for you."

"What about you?"

Elias looked at the carrier he'd set on the table. The second map had been safely accounted for in the niche. "I'm not going anywhere."

Basilio looked at the key in his hand. He squared his shoulders. "Forgive me, Lord Elias, but neither am I."

It was well past midnight by the time Mercedes returned to her wing of the castle. A lone torch on the wall cut through the gloom. Two guards followed her. They had dogged her steps ever since she had left the geographers' courtyard, but a glance over her shoulder had them halting abruptly at the far end of the corridor.

Elias was there, sitting outside her chambers. His back against her door, his legs stretched out across the corridor, fast asleep. He opened bleary eyes when she sat by him. Her green dress covered the stones and billowed about his legs. Even in the dim light, he looked terrible. *His poor, poor face.*

He managed a crooked smile. "That bad?" he asked.

"No, it's worse," she said with feeling. "What are you doing here? You should be in bed."

"Later," he dismissed. "When will you leave?"

"At first light."

Absently, Elias smoothed the green silk covering his legs. "How will you do it?"

"Oh, who knows?" It was a two-day journey to Lady Esma's ancestral home in the mountains. Despite what she had promised her cousin, she had no notion how she would go about burying her in the crypts without anyone else noticing.

Another small smile. "You sound like me." He glanced down the corridor to the soldiers. Both were very carefully not looking their way. "You'll take guards?"

"Yes."

"How many?" he persisted.

"More than enough. Elias, listen to me." She placed a hand along his cheek. She needed him to *hear* her. "I'll take guards tomorrow, and I won't go anywhere alone. I promise you I will be very, very careful, if you will."

Meeting her eyes, he said quietly, "I promise, Mercedes."

She kissed him, lightly on bruised lips, and she did not care who saw. For the rest of her life, she would remember him sprawled face-down on his chamber floor, unmoving. "I won't be gone a week," she said, after. "And I'll see you when I come home."

It looked to her as if he had forgotten to breathe. He exhaled in one great big rush. "I'll see you when you come home."

Even then, she was not comforted. She knew he meant what he said. He would be careful. At least he would try. Elias rarely sought out danger. He didn't need to. Danger had a way of finding him, regardless.

Elias did not have to knock on Lord Silva's work-chamber door. It stood wide open. The Royal Navigator was at his desk, working away with parchment, ink, and compass divider. A stubby candle flickered by his elbow and sent wisps of smoke trailing toward the ceiling.

Elias remained in the doorway, uncertain of his welcome. "Sir," he said quietly, not wishing to disturb Reyna, who curled up on a chair by a floor globe, fast asleep.

"Yes? What is it?" Lord Silva did not look up from his work. No invitation was made to enter.

"I'm sorry for earlier."

"Don't think on it," was the curt response. The quill scratched across parchment. Then, "Was there something else?"

He should go. Come back later, when Lord Silva's displeasure had a chance to cool. It always did. But he didn't want to leave things as they were. Lord Silva had only ever had his best interests at heart, and he didn't like to think of him humbled in front of others. "I wanted to say thank you."

Lord Silva's hand stilled. He regarded Elias. "For what?" he asked softly. "Embarrassing you in front of your friends? In front of that humorless commander?"

"For watching over me," Elias corrected. "Even when I don't need you to."

An expression he could not decipher flashed across Lord Silva's face, there and gone in a blink. "Good night, Elias. Close the door behind you."

"Good night," Elias echoed. He bowed, even though every

inch of him hurt, and Lord Silva did not see. He had already turned his attention back to his work. Just before the door closed, Elias discovered that Reyna was no longer asleep, if she ever had been, but watched him from across the chamber, her eyes wide and troubled in the candlelight.

Elias spent the rest of the night and all the next day in front of the map. Sleep eluded him. Food repelled him. He leaned back against his chair, rubbed bloodshot eyes with his knuckles, and considered all that he knew.

Someone with an intimate knowledge of del Mar had painted both maps, a knowledge gained by many years living here, or at least years studying charts of the area. Or both.

That same person had been alive as recently as ten years ago, when the southern beacon of Alfonse had been erected.

The artist knew that the lady Esma had not been captured along with the princes and Lord Antoni. He had known there was a chance she was alive and hiding within the boundaries of Javelin.

The lady Esma had pointed a finger at her own countrymen. Judge Piri had contradicted her, claiming that the prisoner, long buried, had confessed. But could Piri's word be trusted?

And if there was a third clue on this map, Elias was damned if he could find it.

He could no longer deny the possibility that his father was alive somewhere, sending hidden messages that might never have been seen by him but for fate, and chance. The least Elias could do was search the map again. And again, as many times as necessary.

He started where all things must start. From the beginning:

Adventurer, two princes lost but not gone.
Follow the path of the ancient mariners, Tramontana to Ostro.
Look not to what is there but to what is not.

NINETEEN

HERE WAS NOTHING to be found on the map that
night or in the days that followed. Elias was not alone
in his frustration. Determined to unmask the three intruders in
Elias's chamber, Lord Silva had questioned everyone within the
Tower of Winds — every geographer, every artist, every student
— without success. No one had noticed anything suspicious
until Hector, poor Hector, had started screaming in the courtyard. And even that had not been so very unusual. Commander
Aimon's luck in questioning was no better. A one-legged woman
with silver-and-black hair flowing down to her waist? No one
who fit that description had entered through the city gates. The
guards would have remembered.

A brief discussion ensued about Elias simply returning to
Javelin to *ask* the spirits what happened. Ulises said no. Not even
if he waited for Mercedes to accompany him, for if the spirits did
not already know that Lady Esma had been murdered, did Elias
truly want to be the one to tell them of it?

Ulises made a good argument.

After two days of huddling over the map and slathering on

Madame Vega's cloying but effective salve, Elias had had enough. He bolted from his chambers and headed down to the harbor.

It was morning. A mild wind had kicked up by the waterfront, scattering chicken feathers across his boots and filling his nostrils with smoke from the food stalls. The geographers' booth stood among a hundred others at the eastern edge of the harbor. Here, geographers met with all manner of travelers, from humble shipmen to prosperous merchants, gathering information that could prove useful. They purchased sketches of unfamiliar lands roughed out by mariners. They learned which kingdoms were at war or on the verge of war, and what that meant for diplomatic relations and land boundaries.

Geographers took turns at the booth whenever they were in Cortes. Even Lord Silva could occasionally be seen behind the tables. It was a way for them to keep their knowledge of the world sharp, and to continue to meet the diverse people who flowed in and out of del Mar like the tide.

Today, Madame Vega and Luca manned the booth. Reyna was there recording a transaction in a ledger. All three glanced up as he entered the booth. All three winced. His face showed even worse in the light of day.

"Madame." Elias leaned close to Madame Vega so he could be heard over the din. "I can take over."

"Absolutely not," Madame Vega said. "You should be resting. Have you been using the salve I left?"

"Buckets of it" was his grim reply; at the same time, Luca said, "Elias, go home. You'll scare everyone away with that face."

At least twenty men waited in front of their booth in a straggly queue. More than a few were recognizable; the majority of them were far uglier than Elias. In his personal opinion. He called to a Lunesian mariner who balanced a wooden chest on one shoulder.

"Is my face frightening to you, Noah?"

Noah stepped from the queue to consider him. His response was amiable. "Frightening? No. It's an improvement, I think."

There was laughter all around as men contributed their thoughts on Elias's looks. None of it was kind. Madame Vega conceded with a sigh, gathering up her things and preparing to leave.

Reyna appeared by Elias's side. A sensible apron protected her dress. "I can take your carrier."

He hesitated. Understanding, Reyna added quietly, "I won't leave the booth, and I'll wear it myself. It will be uncomfortable to sit with."

It made sense. She slung his map carrier behind her — it was nearly as tall as she was — then went to help Luca. Madame Vega had not yet gone. She lingered at the edge of the booth, watching the carrier pass from one to the other. Madame was no fool. She knew enough to suspect something in his carrier was dangerous. And by the look on her face, she did not like how close that danger had come to Reyna.

"Master Luca?" Madame Vega said.

"Yes, Madame."

"Reyna is your responsibility. See her home safe when you are done here."

"Of course," Luca said after a quick glance at Elias.

Then Madame was gone. She had not given Elias the responsibility, though he was slightly older than Luca, the more senior. Keep Reyna safe? Everyone knew he could not even keep himself safe. He tried not to let it sting.

The next man in the queue was exactly the sort of distraction Elias needed. Javier was a del Marian mariner. Wizened, his skin like cracked leather, and the most prolific storyteller Elias had ever come across. Javier traveled widely, had fascinating stories from foreign lands: a strange race of people with a single eye in the center of their foreheads; a kingdom no one had ever heard of overrun by black rabbits as tall as men. The old man never had anything that could be verified, but today it did not matter.

Elias sat in his chair and folded his arms. "What story do you have for me now, tale spinner?"

The hours passed. Elias immersed himself in the stories told and in the maps and charts spread out before him like a feast. For a sea chart was never solely a sea chart. On the surface, it was simple parchment: sheepskin transformed into vellum, paint, and gilt; a work of art. But he had learned never to mistake the importance of a good map. It could show the most efficient trade routes, the safest harbors. A rival kingdom's most vulnerable entry points. Also the capes and coves where pirates were known to lurk, waiting to pounce on the unsuspecting.

"Tell me, Elias," Lord Silva had said years before when he was very young, younger even than Reyna. "If you were aboard a ship filled with women and children and were set upon by pirates, what would you do first? Throw the maps overboard, or save the women and children?"

"Women and children?" Elias had repeated, wondering if the question had been asked to trick him.

"*Infants.*"

"Well, surely the infants, at least . . . ow!" Lord Silva had cuffed him, not gently, on the side of the head. "The maps first. Of course the maps!"

"Excellent answer," Lord Silva had replied. "Remember, our maps show our trade routes. Our trade routes are our livelihood. We protect them always."

Reyna stood beside Elias now, entering figures in her ledger. Elias waited until she finished writing, then said, "Tell me, Reyna: If you were aboard a ship filled with women and children and were set upon by pirates, what would you do first? Throw the maps overboard, or save the women and children?"

Luca glanced over and grinned. He, too, had had his head smacked once upon a time by Lord Silva.

"Women and children?" Reyna asked.

"*Infants.*"

Reyna set her quill aside, her expression thoughtful. "I'd

throw all the maps overboard first. But I would try to do it as quickly as I could."

She'd not hesitated. Elias beckoned the next man forward in the queue, surprised he could still find something to laugh about.

It was the middle of the afternoon when the Mondragan appeared. Young like Elias, his hair the color of wheat, he carried four beautifully painted maps of Mondrago.

Elias took his time, ignoring the line, grumbling and impatient, that snaked before him. He glanced at the Mondragan. Before Lady Esma's death, he would have sent him on his way, for he'd no real interest in Mondragans besides Mercedes. And Elias could tell from the man's expression that he expected to be sent away. The Mondragan's map carrier hung from his back; he gripped the strap that lay across his chest and stared straight over Elias's head, his expression remote.

Elias saw something else. While the paints used on the maps were of the finest quality, ones he used himself, this man's clothing was showing wear. Unraveling at the shirt cuffs and collar, the fabric nearly worn through. He was thin for his frame. He'd not had enough to eat. What funds the Mondragan had were going toward his supplies. It was a choice Elias could understand and respect. He would rather starve than use inferior paint.

"Do you speak del Marian?" Elias asked.

The stranger couldn't hide his surprise. The question had been asked in Mondragan. "Yes," he replied in del Marian.

Elias switched back to his native tongue and gestured to the maps. "What is your price?"

"Ten gold squid. Apiece."

There were hoots from the queue. One man said something particularly rude. Reyna's ears turned pink, though she didn't look up from the ledger. Frowning, Elias glanced around the Mondragan. He did not know the rude man, with his pocked skin and the whites of his eyes a disturbing shade of yellow.

Elias returned his attention to the Mondragan. "This is not Alaattan's cave, sir," he said, provoking laughter from the crowd.

The Mondragan held his gaze. "Ten gold squid," he said quietly. "No more, no less. That is my price."

In the queue, the jaundiced stranger spat. "You'll be lucky to leave this island with your arms unbroken. Filthy Mondragan."

The Mondragan mapmaker stiffened; the hand around his strap clenched. He said nothing.

Annoyed, Elias looked around him once again. "Be silent," he ordered. The man's rants slowed to a grumble. Turning back, Elias said, "It's a ridiculous amount for a simple chart." A pause. "One gold squid. Apiece."

"They're not simple charts, I think you know." The Mondragan tapped the first map. "I've used only the highest-quality vellum and inks. The blue is made from the indigo plant. The red from hematite. And the green —"

"Is from malachite. Yes, I know."

Something that was almost a smile flickered across the Mondragan's face. "Then you know it will last. And they were drawn after the earthquakes."

Elias's interest was piqued. "I've just come from Hellespont. Was Mondrago affected?"

"Yes," the Mondragan said. "The entire eastern coastline has been altered. I've redrawn it, as well as marked the new shoals and sandbars. It's all here."

Where had this man gained his skill? Not on his native island, certainly. "Where did you apprentice?"

"With Master Abner. A chart maker on Lunes."

"I know of him."

Elias did not need four maps of Mondrago. But Mercedes would, one day soon.

"Reyna?" When she turned to him, he said, "Give this man ten gold squid. Apiece."

Elias was looking at the Mondragan as he spoke. Saw his stunned expression, followed by immense relief, before his neutral expression returned.

"Elias," Luca hissed, "that beating must have turned your brains. Ten squid! To a Mondragan! Madame Vega will have your head."

Elias shrugged. "Then let her have it." There were more than a few mutters in the crowd. Well. It was time for him to go, anyway. He would leave the disgruntled men for Luca to manage.

Reyna dipped her quill in an inkpot. "Your name, sir? It's not on the maps."

Hearing that, Elias looked at one map, where, instead of a cartouche, a *T* in the bottom right-hand corner served as signature.

"My name is Tycho," the Mondragan said.

Reyna copied his name into the ledger, then counted out forty gold squid and poured them into a leather pouch. She handed over the coin. A smile flashed across his face when she said with perfect seriousness, "Del Mar thanks you. This is fine work, Master Tycho."

Elias gathered the four maps and rolled them together. "You may bring additional work to me at the castle if you choose. I'd be glad to look at them." And then in a move that had everyone around them but Reyna gaping, he stuck out his hand. "I am Elias."

Even the Mondragan looked at him as though he were deranged. Elias kept his hand extended and waited. Finally, the other man clasped his hand and said, "My thanks."

That should have been it. Tycho likely would have disappeared into the crowd without incident, but his self-control was not without limits. The man with the yellow eyes could not keep his mouth shut. As Tycho walked past, the heckler said something crude and explicit about the Mondragan's mother. Reyna's mouth fell open. Tycho punched him in the face.

The heckler went down. To make matters worse, the other men in the queue had grown bored with waiting and joined the fight. Someone swung a fist at Tycho. There was a sharp crack as knuckle connected with chin.

Chaos ensued.

"Stay here," Elias ordered a wide-eyed Reyna. He vaulted over the booth into the fray. Out of the corner of his eye, he saw Luca do the same. Elias shoved his way through the crowd, dodging blows, trying to get to Tycho, knowing the man would be beaten and robbed of forty gold squid if he didn't. He cursed himself. He should have been more discreet about offering that much coin.

"Why are we helping a Mondragan again?" Luca shouted. He ducked, narrowly missing a fist. "We have the maps. To hell with him!"

"Just do it, Luca!"

The Mondragan was holding his own, fists flying, his map carrier jostled behind him. Someone reached for Tycho's coin pouch. Elias elbowed him in the face. The Mondragan glanced at the foiled thief, then at Elias. A brief smile conveyed his thanks.

The next few minutes passed without clear thought, in a blur of fists and cracks and laughter. A sharp whistle pierced the air — soldiers — and the crowd dispersed as if by magic. Luca, his ear bleeding, gave someone a final kick.

Tycho stood with his palms on his knees, panting. He eyed Elias. "You seem to like fights, del Marian."

Elias wiped the blood from a cut on his knuckle. He was going to need more of that awful salve. "I'm as peaceful as a monk. I know it's hard to believe."

Tycho looked disbelieving. He glanced past Elias, his eyes widening. "The girl," he said sharply.

Elias turned, and what he saw nearly stopped his heart. Beside the mappers' booth, Reyna lay curled on the ground, trying desperately to hold on to Elias's map carrier as a man — the turd with the yellow eyes — tried to pull it from her.

Elias raced toward them, shouting. Reyna cried out as a boot connected with her back. She let go of the carrier. The man looked up, saw Elias, Tycho, and Luca bearing down on him, and took off running. Elias skidded to his knees beside Reyna. Luca was only a second behind him, full of shock and wrath.

"Her ribs," Elias said, breath faltering. He was afraid to touch her, move her. Thinking fast, he said to Luca, "Go find —"

"No!" Reyna's words came on a gasp. "He's getting away!"

The man was halfway across the harbor with Elias's carrier. And the last map. Torn, he met Luca's eyes over Reyna's head.

"Go," Luca said.

Elias took off; he ran faster than he ever had before, his eyes trained on the stranger. Who had provoked a fight, and when Elias was distracted, had gone straight for his map carrier. Someone had planned this. Elias dodged a man holding an ape on a leash, narrowly missed two merchants having some sort of disagreement over salt barrels. And realized suddenly that the man he chased was favoring his right leg.

Elias had stabbed an intruder just days ago. With a brass divider. In his right leg.

At the opposite end of the harbor, a fire burned in a barrel.

A vendor stood by it, frying up his wares, and as Elias watched in horror, the map thief flung the carrier into the blaze. He turned to look at Elias and grinned. Teeth as yellow as his eyes. He ran off.

Too far away to be caught. He would get away, this man who would kick a little girl until her ribs snapped. And who very likely had beaten Lady Esma to her death.

A red haze settled over Elias's vision. He grabbed his dagger and dropped to one knee, his gaze never leaving the man's retreating back. He threw his weapon. The knife lodged in the man's neck. Elias heard him cry out, saw him stumble, before the crowd closed in around him.

His carrier was alight in the center of the barrel. Elias felt the flames as he approached. In desperation, he swung his leg out, overturning the barrel. The vendor had been frying fish. He was incensed as they went flying to the ground. He came at Elias with a long fork but was forced to stand aside when Tycho held a sword to his jugular.

Elias's flaming carrier had also fallen. He stomped on it, then yanked off his vest and used it to protect his hands as he twisted the cap off and pulled the map free. Relief coursed through him. The parchment was singed about the edges, but largely unharmed. All around him were shouting and whistles, along with the curses from the fish vendor.

Tycho's eyes were on him. "That must be a very important map, Elias of del Mar." The Mondragan sheathed his sword. He looked at the map thief, sprawled face-down in the dirt. "I think you killed him."

TWENTY

IN THE LOWEST chambers of the castle, the air smelled of death and damp.

"I don't recognize him," Ulises said. "He's a del Marian, clearly, but other than that, who knows?"

The king stood with Elias and Commander Aimon. Reyna's attacker lay on the stone slab before them, his yellow eyes staring up at the ceiling. No one reached to close them. A robed attendant, the same woman who had removed Lady Esma from the tower courtyard, hovered in the doorway, awaiting instructions.

Elias said, "I've seen his face before."

"Have you?" Commander Aimon eyed the dead man with contempt. "I'll ask about. Maybe someone will come forward and claim him," he added with skepticism. And then, to Elias's surprise, the commander placed a hand on his shoulder briefly and said, "The first one is always the hardest."

Elias had never killed a man. He worried that he should feel horror, or at least some sense of guilt, but he could think only of Lady Esma and Reyna, and all he felt was numb. "I don't feel much of anything, Commander. Is that normal?"

Commander Aimon was quiet. "You will."

"Elias," Ulises said, "he beat a child without thinking twice, and I doubt he was a saint before then. I think your eternal soul is safe for now. I just wish we knew who he was."

"It wasn't just Reyna," Elias said, and slid his dagger from its sheath.

Ulises asked sharply, "What are you —?"

Elias ripped the dead man's trousers, his right pant leg, from waist to knee, exposing a hairy thigh wrapped in dirty bandaging. Both Ulises and the commander stared at the wound.

"From you?" Ulises asked, his expression hardening.

"Yes." They knew he'd injured one of his attackers in his chambers, stabbing him in the leg with, of all improbable weapons, a compass divider. The dead man was not only Reyna's assailant, but Lady Esma's, at least one of them.

A look passed between Ulises and the commander, who beckoned the attendant over. "Keep him for three days," Commander Aimon ordered. "We'll see if someone claims him."

"If no one does?" she asked.

"Feed him to the dogs," Ulises said quietly.

It was the kind of order Elias expected from the commander. Not Ulises. And he discovered Commander Aimon had been right. Elias would feel something. It came, quick and merciless. He doubled over, emptying the contents of his stomach onto the stones until there was nothing left inside him.

Reyna had a black eye, two cracked ribs, and three broken fingers on her left hand from where her attacker had stomped on them. She was asleep in her bedchamber. Her door had been left open, and directly outside, well-wishers had gathered in the hall and on the adjacent staircases.

Madame Vega was just inside the door, stiff with outrage and worry. She spoke in low tones with the physician who had just seen to Reyna's injuries. Lord Silva sat by his granddaughter's bedside, haggard.

"Sit, Elias," he ordered. "It's exhausting to watch you."

Elias had been pacing at the foot of the bed. He had not come here directly after visiting the morgue but had gone to his chambers first to bathe and change. He had not wanted to enter Reyna's chambers smelling of death and sickness. At Lord Silva's words, he took a chair opposite him. He could barely look at Reyna. There was something wrong, something profoundly unnatural, about seeing a small girl with a bloody and blackened eye.

Instead, he studied the curious object that had been placed on her bedside table: a miniature wooden catapult, only a foot in height, an exact replica of the siege weapons in the arena. Lord Silva saw him looking and explained, "Aimon sent it over earlier. It's his own work. She was quite taken with it when the children visited the armory last month. He thought it might cheer her."

Nonplussed, Elias asked, "Commander Aimon carves children's toys?"

Lord Silva's weary shrug said, *To each his own interest.*

Madame Vega came to stand beside Elias. He half rose, offering the chair, but she shook her head and waved him back into his seat. She kept one hand on his shoulder, and he reached up and held on to it, letting go only when he felt its trembling subside. It was then that Reyna opened her eyes.

She looked at the worried faces around her. "The map?"

Something shifted inside Elias, very close to his heart. Of course, the map would be her first concern. "It's safe."

"Don't think of it, my dear child," Lord Silva said. "You must rest."

Reyna tried to move her left hand and gasped. A moment later, the fingers on her right hand wiggled. "Not my drawing hand. Good."

"Not your drawing hand," Elias agreed. "Only everything else. You're looking more like me every day, Lady Reyna."

She managed a smile, which faded as she said, "I've seen him before."

Madame Vega's hand slid from his shoulder.

Elias leaned close to Reyna, excitement creeping over him. "That's what I thought, too. Was he a mariner, do you remember? Has he been to our booth?"

"This can wait, surely?" Madame Vega asked.

"Enough, Elias," Lord Silva said. "She needs to rest."

"Not from the harbor," Reyna said. "Not from Cortes . . ."

"No?" Elias thought hard. "A villager, maybe? Or a farmer —"

"I said enough!" Lord Silva came to his feet. The bite in his voice surprised the onlookers, who went silent and watchful in the doorway.

Elias also stood, trying to hold back his frustration. Everything he did lately displeased Lord Silva. Every step he took was the wrong one. "Forgive me."

Madame Vega had gone around to Lord Silva's side. The warning look she gave Elias was clear. It hardly mattered, because Reyna's eyelids had grown heavy. Elias leaned over the bed and dropped a light kiss on her forehead. She didn't stir.

Lord Silva returned to his chair. "We all want to know who did this. I, most of all. For now, I want her out of Cortes. As soon as she can travel, I'm taking her back to Alfonse. She'll be safer at home."

Safer at home.

Home.

Home was where you went to rest your head after a long and weary day. It was where your family lived, if you were fortunate enough to have one. Elias had not visited Judge Piri at his home, had not spoken to the man of family. A mistake. It was Piri's home that was missing from the maps.

Footsteps echoed on stone as he hurried down the tower's endless steps. Judge Piri lived in the parish of St. Cruz of the Mountain. The day was winding down. If the judge was not yet there, he would be soon. Elias would go to him and ask . . . what?

"Careful." The warning came around the final bend in the stairwell and saved Elias from tripping over Luca, who sat on the bottom step.

"How is she?" Luca asked. He looked wretched.

"Awake for a little while." Elias sat beside him and told him what the physician had confirmed: the cracked rib cage, the broken fingers. Luca had seen the black eye for himself. It was he who had carried Reyna back to the castle.

Luca flinched. He asked, "What are you up to?" and when Elias did not, could not, respond, he said, "Madame tells us to leave you alone, that whatever you're doing, it's not our concern." Luca turned his head, looked at Elias directly. "Someone attacks you in your chambers, and we're not to ask you about it. A dead woman ends up in our courtyard. Reyna is upstairs with her ribs kicked in, and you —" He broke off. "You don't even like to kill spiders, let alone . . ."

Elias hung his head. "I threw up all over the morgue," he admitted.

After a moment, Luca handed over a waterskin that was not filled with water. The sweet burn of Kaska made its way to Elias's empty stomach and left him lightheaded. He handed the skin back and said, "If it was only about me, I would tell you."

It was the answer Luca expected. He set the skin on the step, and they sat for a time in companionable silence. Elias's thoughts drifted back to the harbor, before everything had turned ugly. He said, "The Mondragan mapmaker . . ."

Luca frowned. "What about him?"

"How many people do you know who can draw charts like that?"

Luca shrugged. "Plenty."

"Luca."

"A few," Luca conceded, grudging. "What of it?"

Voices drifted from above. Still faint, but they would not be alone for much longer.

Elias said, "If he were anyone else, a Lunesian or a Caffeesh, we would have offered him the hospitality of our tower. Offered him our friendship, asked about his travels. Instead, we send him on his way, even when it's clear he could use our help."

Luca was unsympathetic. "You gave him forty gold squid," he reminded Elias. "He'll be fine."

Elias picked up the waterskin but did not drink from it. "Someone tried to spit on Mercedes."

Luca's head snapped up. "What? Who?"

"An old woman in the courtyard," Elias answered. "In front of everyone. It wasn't the first time." For all his prejudice against Mondragans, Elias knew Luca held a soft spot in his heart for Mercedes. It did not hurt that she was only half Mondragan. Or that she was beautiful. He said, "That mapmaker, Tycho, he's like us, Luca. Just a baby when it happened. Mercedes wasn't even born. How much longer are we going to spit on them?"

Luca looked away, scowling at the wall. "My grandfather died at Mondrago."

"I know it," Elias acknowledged. Luca's grandfather;

Commander Aimon's brothers. Countless others. It felt a hopeless thing, trying to set things right. The voices above grew louder; the footsteps, closer. He got to his feet, handed back the skin. "I have to go."

Luca's sigh lasted a full five seconds. "There's an empty chamber next to mine. I'll find your Mondragan. I suppose he can use it."

Elias smiled down at his friend. "I owe you one."

"You owe me twenty," Luca corrected, but there was a smile in his voice.

Elias turned to go, then stopped. "Do you know Judge Piri?"

The change in topic took Luca a moment. "The harbor judge?"

"Yes."

"Sure," Luca said, "My father makes his shoes. I used to go with him to the judge's house when I was a boy. His left foot is larger than his right. Did you know that?"

"No," Elias said. "Did you ever meet his wife? Or his daughter?"

Luca frowned, shook his head. "They were already gone."

"How? Was it fever? An accident?"

A strange expression crossed Luca's face. "They're not *dead*, Elias. Why are you asking?"

"He said they were . . ." In his mind's eye, Elias was back at the harbor. He saw the miniature, set in silver, of a woman and a child.

They are very beautiful, Elias had said.

They were.

What had Piri meant, if not death?

"Luca, what happened to them?"

Luca told him. And just like that, the truth caught up with him. He stood there, on the bottom step in the Tower of Winds, conscious only of a great spiraling horror.

Elias told no one where he was going. To Basilio, he said only that he was riding south, that he would be back when he was back. Basilio had time enough to throw some clothing in a pack before Elias snatched it from him and left.

The journey would take all night. For that reason, he left Pythagoras behind. His horse was fast, but riding him the whole way meant they would have to stop and rest. Quicker to take one of the castle horses and replace it with fresh ones along the way.

It was dusk when he rode beneath the castle portcullis and tore down streets lined with palms. He caught a glimpse of Madame Vega leaving a church. He nearly ran over Commander Aimon and Lazar. He heard his name shouted but did not stop. Later, he would see how foolish his actions had been. To go off without telling a soul where he was bound. But in the shocked turmoil of his mind, it made sense that he should stay quiet. He could not speak to anyone of what he suspected until he was certain. And though he knew what he would find at the end of his journey, there was a desperate need in him to *see* it.

He reached behind him for his carrier, assuring himself that the map was safe, and rode on.

The landscape flashed by him in a blur. Bustling city gave way to towns and villages that grew fewer and farther between as he rode south. Night brought the mosquitoes in droves. He took the shortest route he knew, at times bypassing Marinus Road in favor of the coastal roads, which were less crowded and not as popular with thieves. Supper was a hurried affair at an inn. His horse was exchanged. And later, when exhaustion threatened to topple him from his saddle, he snatched a few hours' sleep under an outcropping of rock with a view of the sea. Sometime in the hours before dawn, he remembered where he had first seen Reyna's attacker. He felt cold inside.

Another piece of the puzzle, suddenly clear.

He arrived at Alfonse in the early morning hours. Rather than enter the gates, he rode past until he reached the very tip of the island, where the cliffs dropped straight into the sea. Exhausted, sore, he slid from his horse. He left the animal by a tree and walked as close as he dared to the cliff's edge. He was utterly alone here. The wind was at his back. The surf churned below. To his right was the southern beacon, only ten years old.

He unrolled the map onto the dirt. South of del Mar, a cluster of islets had been painted. Cali, St. Carlo, Olivos. He looked up, eyes traveling south, and felt his heart break all over again. How had he not seen it?

A fourth island was visible, though it had not been painted on either map.

Adventurer, two princes lost but not gone.
Follow the path of the ancient mariners, Tramontana to Ostro.
Look not to what is there but to what is not.

The answer had been there all along, hidden in plain sight. He heard a low moan and realized it came from him.

Where could you hide two royal princes and a lord of del Mar without fearing their discovery? Where could you condemn someone to death without killing them? You hid them, across the waters, on a desolate land, a place where even the great sainted angels feared to tread.

Valdemossa.

The Island of the Lepers.

TWENTY-ONE

ELIAS DID NOT know how long he stayed there by the cliff's edge, weighing what few choices he had. What was he to do? Return to Cortes with his suspicions? For as long as he stayed here, the sea separating him from Valdemossa, that was all they were: suspicions, theories. Nothing proven, as insubstantial as the air.

Or keep silent? Tell no one. Take his thoughts to the grave, and why not? He no longer wished to know. The three were dead in everyone's eyes: Antoni, Bartolome, Teodor. Why not keep them that way? Dead and whole and beloved.

His conscience called him an unpleasant word. It stared at him wide-eyed, appalled that he would even consider it. His conscience looked like Mercedes.

He argued with her.

The truth would bring no one peace, Mercedes. The answers would make things worse. For Ulises, for del Mar. If they are alive, they will be horrors, men who exist in a living, breathing death.

And what of his own family? His *maman* and Lord Isidore

labeled bigamists, his brother and sisters scorned as bastards. There were many excellent reasons to hold his tongue.

Mercedes argued back. *Elias, they are people still, and they have begged for your help through these maps. Would you turn your back on them now?* And then she fell silent, her voice replaced by the sound of approaching riders.

He did not rise, did not turn to see who it was riding through the copse of trees behind him. He knew who led them. The others mattered not at all.

But he listened. To the horses that came to a stop, their nickers low and rumbling. Only one man dismounted and walked toward him, slowly, the crunch of stone beneath boots nearly drowned out by the surf below.

The footsteps stopped.

"You should not turn your back on an enemy," Lord Silva said quietly. "I must have taught you that, once or twice throughout the years."

The sound of the Royal Navigator's voice sent a tremor through Elias. Of rage, and grief, and the small part of him that had believed a mistake had been made died a quick, silent death. He rose and turned in one fluid motion, pulling his dagger free of his belt.

Lord Silva stood twenty feet away. Not in his robes, but dressed for travel in browns and greens, the cape at his back fluttering in the wind. He looked terribly old and tired. Keeping pace with Elias had taken its toll. Behind him, three men remained on their horses, blocking any possibility of escape.

They were younger than Lord Silva, strong, well-built men his stepfather's age. Two were only vaguely familiar, but the third was Belos, Lord Silva's steward from his home in Alfonse.

With difficulty, Elias asked, "Is that what you are to me, my lord Silva? My enemy?"

Lord Silva's gaze dropped to the dagger in Elias's hand. "I wish I could say no."

Even now, Elias found he could never harm this man. Shoving the dagger back in his belt, he said, "I'm not."

"Can I trust you to keep silent?" Lord Silva asked. "Not a word to your lady or the king? Not a hint to Commander Aimon?" He studied Elias's expression. "I did not think so."

Elias's mind spun as he tried to find a way out of this predicament. Never in his life had he been so aware of his surroundings. The cliff's edge behind him, the sheer drop into the churning waters below. "What am I, then? Another loose end to be tied up? Like Lady Esma?"

"Do you think I wish to be here?" There was a harshness to Lord Silva's question. "I've done everything possible to keep you safe—"

"Safe?" Elias repeated, scornful. "Is that what you call it? Look where we are!"

"Yes, safe! My quarrel has never been with you. I've given you warning after warning—"

Lord Silva broke off as one of the horses sidestepped nervously and whinnied, picking up on the tension, and had to be soothed. Deliberately, Elias called to its rider, "Hello, Belos."

The steward's head came up quickly, though his voice was even as he returned the greeting. "My lord Elias."

"You'll give my regards to your lady?" Elias kept his voice pleasant, even as the anger burned inside him. He had known this man and his family since he was five years old. "And Rosamund? I heard she was recently married. My felicitations."

This time, Belos looked away and said nothing. A dull flush crept up his neck.

"Enough," Lord Silva ordered softly.

"No," Elias said in agreement. "I would not want to embarrass your fellow assassins. You've kept them close, I see. But you're missing one of your tenant farmers."

That is where he had remembered seeing the yellow-eyed stranger from the harbor. A chance encounter when he was twelve or thirteen, riding along the eastern edge of Lord Silva's estate with Luca. The man had returned their greeting with a scowl, and when Elias had glanced back, the farmer had spat in their wake.

From that memory came others. Lord Silva encouraging him to solve the riddle, but not for very long. Only until he discovered the first clue. The map stolen from his chambers when very few knew of its existence. A hooded figure in the corner who never spoke because Elias would have known his voice. Lord Silva speaking to the king, worrying for Elias's safety. Looked at on their own, they meant nothing. Together, they had given him pause. Made him consider things too horrible to consider.

Surprise had registered on Lord Silva's face. "I did not realize you'd crossed paths." He was quiet, then, "You're young,

Elias. And to the young, there is only good and bad and never anything in between. I am not a bad man —"

"You can say that without choking on your words?" Elias could no longer pretend any sense of calm. "You slaughtered the king's guards." He jabbed a finger toward the sea. "You sent two boys and my father to rot on a leper colony. You started a *war.* Show me what a bad man looks like, my lord Silva, if you are not one."

"Don't stand there and shout at me," Lord Silva snapped, "when you don't know the truth of it! *The great sainted Antoni.*" His voice was filled with a bitter loathing. His eyes blazed. "I loved that boy. I took him in, trained him. *And he killed my son!*"

Elias stared at him. What, in the name of every saint who ever lived, did Lord Vittor have to do with any of this? "An avalanche killed your son."

"You know nothing," Lord Silva replied, contemptuous. "I went to the king, who would not punish Antoni. He did the opposite. He commended him for his *bravery*, for bringing home Grec and Braga. So I showed them both . . ." He trailed off, gazing across at Valdemossa.

Elias felt physically ill. "What did you show them?"

Something bleak moved across Lord Silva's face. "I showed them what it felt like to lose a son."

"I don't understand."

"And you won't. There's no point in speaking of it. Belos?" Lord Silva beckoned. All three men dismounted and approached with their swords drawn.

Elias tried desperately to buy time. "Do you really think you'll be able to walk away from this? Mercedes will find —"

"Nothing." Lord Silva's gaze never left Elias's. "There won't be anything left for her to find. Forgive me."

Elias stepped back; pebbles fell away at his heels into air. He could try to fight his way, though he had only a dagger. And the odds were against him, four to one. He glanced behind him at the deadly, churning surf.

Deadly, but not unfamiliar.

He had mapped this coastline as part of his apprenticeship, by boat. He knew the jagged rocks were present, but most did not press up against the island, and they were far below the surface. If he jumped, he might be able to avoid impalement. And if he could manage that small miracle, it was a matter of swimming around the tip of the island to the beaches along the southeastern edge. It could be done.

As long as the waters were free of serpents.

Lord Silva said, "Elias, there's nowhere else for you to go. Do you think I want you to feel pain? Take the sword; it will be quick, I promise you. Or will you end up food for the water snakes?"

Elias pulled his gaze from the waters below. His heart was pounding. "An excellent suggestion."

Lord Silva frowned. "Which one?"

"I'll take my chances with the snakes." Elias saw the shocked realization on Lord Silva's face as he stepped back, into nothingness.

Elias hit the water feet-first, the impact felt within his entire being. The Sea of Magdalen called him deeper into its depths, but as he sank lower and lower still, relief filled him. He'd escaped the rocks. Just then, a hazy image formed in the distance. Serpentine and growing larger. He kicked in the opposite direction, but his efforts were in vain. Something coiled around him, tightening, loosening, and pain sliced up his leg. His silent cry was met by a powerful rush of water. As the serpent pulled him farther out to sea, and his lungs filled with water, he thought, *Mercedes*.

"What do you mean, he's gone?" Mercedes demanded, still in her dusty traveling dress. She had not been home half an hour. "Gone where?"

Ulises shoved the crown onto his head. "No one knows." They were in his private chambers. Her cousin wore pale green robes hemmed in ermine, an enormous emerald ring on one hand. More emissaries had arrived, this time from Caffa, and he was already delayed in meeting them. "He left three days ago, alone. He didn't tell anyone where he was going. Basilio knows only that he was heading south and that he looked . . . upset."

There was an odd note to his voice.

"I've not been gone a week. What has happened?" she asked, and then covered her mouth with both hands when he told her.

"Reyna will be fine." Ulises answered her wordless question.

"I thought Elias would just need time to himself after . . . but something else is wrong — Where are you going?"

She was halfway to the door. "To find him. What else?"

"Cousin."

She looked over her shoulder, ready to argue if he told her not to go. But Ulises asked, "Where is Lady Esma?"

The details of the last few days were not something she wanted to dwell on. Not ever again. "We buried her with her mother."

Ulises studied her. "There were no difficulties?"

She shook her head. "I know the priest who watches over the crypts. He owed me a favor."

"Good." He crossed the chamber, kissed her on both cheeks. "Take men. Be safe."

"I will."

Mercedes delayed leaving long enough to change into fresh clothing, question Basilio, and visit Reyna.

Who was awake, but not alone. Across the chamber, the language master, Madame Grec, played a game of chess with Lord Braga. By the sound of it, Madame was winning and Lord Braga was not taking it well. Her son, Hector, had given up his place by Reyna's bedside when Mercedes appeared. He sprawled about the window seat with parchment and lead, drawing in a patch of sunlight.

Even knowing what had happened to Reyna at the harbor,

Mercedes was unprepared for what she saw. The bandages, the bruises, one eye blackened. Anger was a white-hot coiling of serpents inside her. Reyna looked so small and helpless lying in that bed.

"It doesn't feel as bad as it looks," Reyna said, reading her thoughts. "At least I don't think it does. No one will give me a looking glass."

Mercedes slid a hand onto the bed, palm up. Reyna placed her right hand in hers. Her left was wrapped in bandages. "You'll look like yourself again soon," Mercedes said. "Better to save the looking glass for then." She eyed the catapult on the bedside table, recognized Commander Aimon's work, and took in the flowers filling the room. "You've had many visitors."

"There's always someone here. Madame Vega makes sure of it." In a much quieter voice that did not carry across to the others, Reyna said, "Lady Mercedes, where is he?"

The worry in Reyna's eyes matched her own. "I don't know, dearest. I'm going now to find him."

"It's not like him to leave without telling anyone. Something is wrong."

A glance across the chamber, but no one paid them any attention. Mercedes said, "I've known Elias since we were very young. Younger than you, younger even than Hector. And do you know how many times he's found himself in some sort of trouble?"

A small smile emerged. "A hundred?"

"Oh, more than that," Mercedes assured her. "More like a thousand. And of that thousand, do you know how many times he has walked away perfectly safe?"

Reyna said, "Every time?"

"Every time." Mercedes squeezed her hand. "This will be no different." She glanced up, startling Madame Grec, whose ears were very clearly straining. Quickly, the language master dropped her gaze, her cheeks coloring slightly as Lord Braga groused, "Stop daydreaming, Genevieve. It's your turn."

Mercedes was back in the stables within the hour, along with the six soldiers who would be accompanying her. She had just swung onto her horse when she heard her name called.

Katalin the tax collector hurried over. "I know this is important, Lady," she said, holding up a scroll tied with red ribbon. "I thought to find you before you left. But I can deliver it to your chambers if you prefer."

"No, I'll take it with me." Mercedes took the scroll. "Eves?"

Katalin stepped back. "Yes. An interesting assortment."

Madame Grec's birth name was Genevieve. It was a simple thing to forget when one rarely heard the name used. She pushed her questions to the back of her mind. So many of them; so few answers. For now she would concentrate on riding south and try to pick up Elias's trail.

A soldier on horseback stopped beside her. "When you're ready, Lady."

"I'm ready now." Mercedes reached behind her and tucked the scroll into her bag. To Katalin, she said, "I won't forget this," and left to find Elias.

Rough hands pulled Elias from the water. He landed on his side, his leg burning, coughing up an endless amount of seawater. Above him was a confusion of voices, loud and flapping, like warblers bursting from the trees.

"Did you see that? Boy jumped right off the cliff . . ."

"Helped along, from what I saw," was the grim response. Someone jostled Elias's leg, and he cried out.

Another voice broke in, sharp-like, "Have a care with that leg, Fermin."

"That's a nasty bite. And look, it left a tooth behind. Shall I pull it out, Brother?"

A brief, considering silence. "Leave it in for now or he'll bleed to death all over this boat."

It was the last thing Elias heard before he lost consciousness.

When Elias came to, his mind was a muddle, but he could see the sun low in its descent. And palm trees. Someone had tossed a blanket over him. He was on dry land, being carried on a stretcher by four people. Three wore forest-green robes with their hoods pulled low, so he could not see their faces.

The fourth man, hoodless, glanced down at him. "I don't know who you are, or why someone was tossing you from a cliff, but friend, you must have the luck of the devil."

Elias saw black hair and a full, bushy beard. Older than he, but not old, and dressed in the plain brown robes of a monk. He said, "Ulises?"

The stranger stiffened. A warning look came into his eyes before he reached beneath the blanket and pressed down on Elias's injured leg.

Elias screamed. Two palm trees swam before him, then four, six, and, once again, he knew nothing at all.

Elias smelled the sea air before his eyes were fully open. He found himself in a strange bed in an unfamiliar chamber. Light flooded in through the open door, causing him to turn away from its painful glare. It was then that he saw the bearded stranger sitting by the bedside, observing him. Elias struggled to sit up. His bones felt like water. Something was wrong with his leg.

"Best to go slow," the stranger advised, and reached out to help him. Elias stopped him with a black look.

The stranger retreated. "My apologies for before." He indicated Elias's leg. "I couldn't risk your words being heard by others, Elias of del Mar."

"What words?" Cold sweat dried on Elias's skin. He would have flung the covers off, but he wore nothing underneath except a tight linen binding around one leg. The stranger offered a cup. This Elias would not refuse, for his mouth felt like a dry desert road. Once the water was gone, he demanded, "How do you know my name? Where am I? Alfonse?" Shielding his eyes, he turned once again to the open door.

And froze.

Not far beyond the doorway was a sandy beach and the Sea of Magdalen. In the distance, he could see the southern cliffs of Alfonse and, off to the side, the Peninsula del Sud. If the peninsula was there, and he was here, then . . .

"I see you've worked it out for yourself," the stranger said quietly.

A shadow fell across the doorway, followed by a woman holding a tray. She wore a green robe, her dark hair braided and wound atop her head. Sores covered her face.

Elias reared back, cracking his head against the wall. The cup hit the floor and rolled away.

The bearded stranger got to his feet, sighing. "Thank you, Mari. Put it there. I'll see to our guest."

"Forgive me," the woman murmured, and disappeared.

Once she'd gone, the stranger said, "Be still. Before you undo my hard work."

Elias burst out, "Valdemossa! How long—" Lightheaded, he felt the bile rise sharp within him. The man snatched a bowl from the table and held it out. Elias swung—the bowl went spinning across the chamber, and he went tumbling off the bed in a tangle of sheets. Face-down on the floor, his leg in agony, breathing through his mouth. When he was certain he would not be sick, he rolled onto his back, groaning.

The stranger did not try to help him up. "You're on Valdemossa; it's true. We pulled you from the water just before a sea serpent tried to eat you for breakfast. I'm not a leper, and I have been the only one caring for you. Mostly."

Elias felt a crawling along his skin, but when he lifted his arms, there was nothing there. Even Rafael's scratch on his wrist had vanished, healed completely.

"You're right to be concerned." The stranger sat on the bed and eyed Elias on the floor. "You should not be here. But you must grow stronger before we can think how to move you. You're as safe as you can be, under the circumstances."

Elias's eyelids felt suddenly heavy. Difficult to keep open. The stranger's face wavered above him. "What did you put in my drink?"

"Nothing harmful. Your leg would hurt worse without it."

His eyes had fallen shut. "How long have I been here?"

"Ten nights," the stranger answered. "The cut on your leg is not deep, but there was poison in the tooth."

Elias's eyes snapped opened. *Ten nights.* So long. Lord Silva would have returned to Cortes by now. Mercedes, too. He had promised her he would take care. "How do you know my name?"

"One of the residents here recognized you. He said you were kind to him some weeks ago. In Cortes."

Rafael. The leper in the alley. "Who are you?"

There was a brief silence. "I'm known here as Francis of Valdemossa. I'm a Brother of the Order of Saint Lazarus, a monk and the caretaker of this island. But a long time ago . . . I was known as Teodor." He knelt by Elias's side just as his eyes fluttered closed and said softly, "Teodor of del Mar."

TWENTY-TWO

ELIAS WAS ALONE the next time he woke. He found he could sit up without feeling lightheaded, and when he inspected his wound, there was only a dull throbbing along his leg, rather than the blinding pain he remembered. How much time had passed since he'd last spoken to . . . Brother Francis? Prince Teodor? Had he even been real? Or had the man in the monk's robe with the face of a king merely been part of a bad fever dream?

Clothes lay folded on a chair. Not his own. A loose shirt and sand-colored trousers, both soft from use. Uneasy, Elias wondered who had cleaned them, who had handled the cloth that would touch his body. But what use, wondering? What had Mori said? *No one knows how the leper's curse is spread, and for every claim, there's argument against it. And . . . There's no use in worrying. Unless you wake up one day and your arms and legs have gone numb. Then I would start to worry plenty.* The only other choice would be to wander the island naked. He struggled to his feet, placing most of his weight on his good leg, and dressed with a painful slowness. No shoes had been left; there was no sign of his boots. He went barefoot.

Food had been placed on a table by a window. He stuffed himself full of bread, cheese, honey, and berries until there was nothing left on the plate. Through the window, he saw Brother Francis standing at the water's edge with his back to the cottage. He wore a brown robe, his hands clasped behind him in a way that reminded Elias of Ulises. Not a dream, then.

A walking stick leaned against the wall with a smooth cradle to rest his arm. He made use of it. A story lay before him, all that he had been searching for since he'd learned of the maps. And now he felt as he did standing alone on the cliff top, uncertain he wanted that knowledge.

He stepped out into the crisp morning. And went perfectly still. His cottage was the first in a row of cottages that lined the beach. To his right, wraithlike figures in hooded green robes went about their day. Most huddled on stoops outside their doors, alone or in groups. The silence was eerie, given the number of people about. At least fifty, and as Elias looked on in consternation, the hoods turned as one to watch him.

Only three had dispensed with their hoods. At the cottage nearest his, a woman stood in her doorway, watching two children play in the sand. All three displayed signs of the leper's curse. The youngest child was a boy about six years of age. Unsettled, Elias thought about his sister Lea, who was the same age, safe at home and healthy. He recognized the woman who'd brought the tray to his cottage when he'd first woken. She glanced over at him, her expression having turned wary.

He already felt like a horse's ass for his behavior, and when he attempted a bow with a walking stick, he felt like a clumsy horse's ass, too. "Apologies," he said, and gestured toward his leg. "Fever, you know."

Surprise flickered on her face, and then a shy smile emerged. She dropped into a low, formal curtsy. "I do. I'm pleased to see you're better, Lord Elias."

She knew who he was as well. The boy and girl had stopped playing and stared at him as if he were the oddity among them, which he supposed was true. And he wondered again if it was already too late for him. He had been on this island, mostly unconscious, for more than ten days.

He asked, "Are these your children?"

"Not by blood. We care for them now because their parents cannot." She made a shooing motion with her hands. The children turned from Elias and resumed sand building. "I'm Mari. Wife of Fermin of Valdemossa." She stopped before adding, "Daughter of Piri of Cortes." The last sounded like a question.

Elias nearly dropped his walking stick. "Judge Piri?"

"Is he a judge now?" A pleased look came into her eyes. "He was an officer when I was a girl. Do you know my father? Is he well?"

Elias pictured the judge holding the silver miniature, a portrait of his lost family. "He is, though it's clear you're missed. And your *maman?*"

Mari's expression turned grave. "She passed on seven years ago."

"I am sorry."

Mari glanced past Elias toward Brother Francis, then smiled again and said goodbye. She called the children in and closed the door to her cottage.

Elias hobbled over to the monk. He would have fallen over without the stick. They looked across to the big island, where the beacon was a lone sentinel outside Alfonse.

"I'm grateful to you," Elias said. The waves lapped at his bare feet.

Brother Francis dipped his head, once. "You have questions, I imagine."

"Hundreds."

"I'll do my best to answer them." Brother Francis gestured toward the long stretch of beach. "We'll walk, if you're able. It will help you grow stronger."

They walked for a time in silence, past more cottages. Ulises's elder brother was well-liked here, whatever name he chose to answer to. Every leper they passed called out in welcome to Brother Francis. Or lifted a hand in greeting. Some hands were mere stumps. Through an open cottage door, another monk knelt before a woman, wrapping her arm in white bandaging. Elias looked away quickly, feeling like a voyeur.

"I'll not drag at the truth, Lord Elias. Your father is dead."

Elias stopped. He had known it in his heart, for if Lord Antoni were alive, would he not be here? Prince Bartolome, too? Still, the monk's words, so simple and direct, were a knife to the gut. Blinking rapidly, Elias looked at the beacon across the water.

Brother Francis followed his gaze. "He died nine years ago, just after that beacon was completed."

Elias wavered. The monk grabbed him, holding him upright. "I'm fine," Elias said, though he was not. When he was five years old and his mother remarried, his blood father had been alive. He straightened, and Brother Francis dropped his hand.

"Prince Bartolome?" Elias asked.

"My brother is dead." The monk's face was expressionless. "Shall I start from the beginning?"

"Please."

"Then sit. You look as though you're about to fall over."

They found a dry patch of sand. And Brother Francis began his tale. Some parts familiar; some parts not. He spoke of Bartolome's interest in navigation and of his adoration of Lord Antoni. He spoke of the picnic. Elias kept silent and let the story unfold.

"I had no interest in maps and compasses." A smile flickered across the monk's face. "But I wasn't about to be left behind while they went on their adventure. I badgered our nurse, Lady Esma, until she agreed to take me along.

"Someone had poisoned the common barrels. I'd taken a sip, just enough to sicken me, before the others started falling. My brother realized and knocked the cup from my hand. Still, I lost consciousness. And when I woke, the three of us were on a boat, gagged, our hands bound, headed here."

Elias asked, "What do you mean? They just left you on shore?"

A half smile, with not an ounce of humor in it. "Not on shore." Brother Frances pointed behind them. "There's a keep through the palms there. A simple structure, but the locks on our doors were sound. That's where I lived for years."

King Andrés had searched everywhere for his sons. They had been here all this time, a day's journey from their city of birth.

"Our jailer was a man named Hugo. It's not how you imagine," Brother Francis added. "We were placed in separate cells, but we were allowed to visit on occasion. Hugo did not beat my brother or me."

Elias heard what the monk had left unsaid. "He beat my father?"

"In the early years, yes. When he tried to escape."

Elias looked away, and after a time, the monk continued. "We were treated differently from Lord Antoni. We weren't shackled. Our meals were decent. . . ."

His father had been shackled. His father had been starved.

". . . We were allowed books. It did not feel like someone wanted to punish us. It was more . . ."

"Someone wanted to punish my father," Elias finished.

A pause. "Yes. Later, even Lord Antoni was allowed his paints and parchment. We had been here a year when Bartolome first showed signs of the leper's curse." Brother Francis turned aside from what he saw on Elias's face. "He grew weaker and died several years later. It was your father who kept me in my right mind during that time." He stopped. "I don't wish to speak of Bartolome. You may imagine what you will."

Elias tried very hard not to imagine it: a small boy, a future king, dying a leper. "You're not behind a locked door now."

"No. The lepers at Valdemossa are cared for by the monks of the Order of Saint Lazarus. The monastery is just over there." He pointed. "The three brothers who lived then knew of the strange recluse who lived in the keep. Sometimes, they would see Hugo walking near the water. He never sought their company, which didn't surprise them, for their calling was to care for the lepers. They left him alone."

"Who was he, your jailer?" What could Lord Silva have possibly offered to entice someone to spend years as a guard on a leprosarium?

"I've no notion." Brother Francis lifted a handful of sand and allowed it to drift between his fingers. "Eventually, the monks noticed that Hugo no longer roamed the shores. One brother went to look in on him. Hugo had died in his sleep. When he searched further, he discovered us."

Elias found he'd been holding his breath. "Did he know who you were?"

"Oh, he knew."

It made no sense to him. "Then how were you not returned home?"

Brother Francis turned to look at him. "What reason had I to return home? To claim my place in the castle? I grew up in a prison, Lord Elias, on a leper colony."

"That wouldn't have mattered."

"Oh, no?" Both eyebrows rose in skepticism. "What sort of

prince would I have made? What sort of king? Not one del Mar would have been proud of, I assure you."

Elias heard the awful truth of his words. "And my father?"

Brother Francis looked away. "It was the same for him. We do get news here when the supply ship comes. It's how we heard what happened at Mondrago. How your father learned of your mother's marriage to Lord Isidore, and of their daughter. He would not have the charge of bigamy laid at her door, or have her child branded a bastard. Even if it meant giving you up." Several moments passed in silence. "Lord Antoni remained at the keep. He died soon after."

"How?" Elias steeled himself for the answer. Already he felt a sickening weight at the thought of it.

"It was his heart," Brother Francis said quietly, understanding. "He showed no signs of leprosy. I promise you."

Elias covered his face with his hands. His father had been allowed that small dignity, at least. The monk sat beside him for a long time, not saying a word, until Elias's shoulders stopped shaking and he lifted his head.

Brother Francis said softly, "I lived with the monks, learning all that I could. They were old men, gone now, and others have taken their place. To everyone here, I am Brother Francis." He looked over his shoulder. "This island is my responsibility. No one knows my secret except you."

Elias dashed his tears away with the back of his hand. "What about the maps?"

"What maps?"

Elias explained, and watched as the monk's calm demeanor turned to astonishment. "Is that how you found me?"

"Yes."

Brother Francis unearthed a pebble, skipped it viciously across the shallows. "I never knew about the riddles. Your father asked if he could be allowed paint and parchment to pass the tedium. He suggested that Hugo send the maps off to foreign markets through the supply ships. They could be sold, and Hugo could keep the coin. Hugo agreed. There was little risk to him, since they were unsigned. Two maps, you said?"

"Yes." Both lost now, one to theft, the other somewhere in these waters when he'd jumped from the cliff. His map carrier was gone.

"Only two," the monk said. "He painted hundreds. Why would he do it? He knew I wouldn't have left here."

Elias did not think he was expected to answer the question. He kept silent.

The monk said, "To this day, I don't know why we were taken."

"I know a little. Not all of it."

Elias told him everything, starting with his return to del Mar from Hellespont. Brother Francis interrupted several times. *Lady Esma lived in Javelin? All this time? And I know that story. But Lord Vittor was killed in an avalanche. An accident.*

"That's what I thought, too," Elias said. "Lord Silva blamed my father, and he blamed yours for not punishing him. He said he wanted to show them what it would feel like to lose a son. Did my father ever speak of it?"

"Never." The monk's only sign of emotion came from the pulsating vein at his temple. "What it would feel like to lose a son. Two sons, in my father's case. My poor, poor brother."

He meant Bartolome.

"You have another brother," Elias reminded him. "And Mercedes, your cousin. You have family."

Brother Francis stood. His closed expression warned Elias to tread lightly. "I've tired you out, Lord Elias. You need your rest."

He *was* tired, and heartsore, but there was something he needed to do first. "May I see their graves?"

Brother Francis said nothing at first. And then he held out his hand to help Elias to his feet. "Of course."

"This is where you were kept?" Elias asked.

"Yes."

Deep within a cluster of palms was a stone keep surrounded by yellow oleander trees. A figure at a window stepped from view.

Elias asked, "Does someone live here?"

Brother Francis followed his gaze to the window. "No, it's empty."

"I thought —"

"The graves are just there." Two crude wooden crosses had been erected nearby. While the monk knelt in prayer before his brother's grave, Elias stood beside his father's. This marker was far simpler than the memorial on the outskirts of Cortes. Sorrow filled him, and something else.

Rage.

"Why aren't you angry?" Elias asked.

Brother Francis looked over. "What good would it do? It harms us more than our enemies."

"Not always."

"Lord Elias, sometimes we must simply forgive for our own sakes." Brother Francis looked at the crosses. "They're at peace now."

"That may be." Elias turned away from the cross. "But I am not."

TWENTY-THREE

AS SOON AS they left the graves, Elias said, "I need to get off this island."

Brother Francis was in agreement. "You're not safe here," he said as they retraced their steps along the beach, making their way toward Elias's cottage. "No one knows why some are afflicted and others are not, and every hour you're here puts you at risk. But as to how . . ."

To Elias, the solution was simple. "All I need is a boat."

"A boat will do you no good." Brother Francis pointed to the beacon across the water. "The guards are there to keep intruders out. That includes us."

"No, it will be fine," Elias assured him. "They know who I am."

"You'll not make it close enough for them to recognize you," Brother Francis explained patiently. "There are rules that must be followed. We're allowed to fish our waters, including serpents, but our vessels must not pass beyond the boundary rock." A large triangular stone jutted out from the sea halfway between

Valdemossa and Alfonse. "When the supply ship arrives, we meet it at the rock. Our supplies and any new arrivals are lowered into our boats."

Elias was distracted by the mention of the water snakes. "You're allowed to hunt serpents?"

"Yes. Within our boundaries."

"Did you lose one recently? And a harpoon?"

Brother Francis stopped in his tracks. "How could you know that?"

"Your serpent turned up near a beach in Cortes. Still alive." Even then, there had been a connection. Plenty of time to reflect on that later, when he was off this island.

Brother Francis was aghast. "Was anyone hurt?"

Elias shook his head. "There were children swimming in the cove," he said, deliberately adding, "but your cousin, Mercedes, was there. She killed it with an arrow."

Brother Francis resumed walking, leaving Elias to follow. The row of cottages came into view, along with their quiet inhabitants robed in green. Seeing them only intensified his desire to escape.

As if he could not help himself, Brother Francis asked, "A single arrow?"

Elias heard the skepticism and shrugged. "I would not lie to a monk."

A sideways glance, amused. "I've heard she's an unusual lady."

Elias smiled involuntarily. "That is one way to describe her." *Mercedes.* He needed to find his way back to her. He asked, "How often do the supply ships come by?"

"The first week of every season. We'll not see another until autumn."

Elias was dismayed. "I'm not waiting until autumn, I assure you." He considered his options. "What happens if you sail past the rock? Has anyone tried?"

"More than once." A crease appeared between the monk's brows. "The Order cares for its people, Lord Elias. They are clothed and fed and given the opportunity for a decent life, despite their afflictions. But don't forget that most were forced to live here, separated from their loved ones. Not everyone is content."

No. He imagined not. "What happens when they try?"

"Archers," Brother Francis said. "Once a boat crosses the boundary, fire arrows are launched from the beacon, and whoever is on board is burned to death. If they jump, they either drown or are eaten."

Elias was nearly silenced by the horror of it. "I'll sail at night. No one will see me."

"It's been attempted. They have wolf eyes, those archers. We must find another way for you to leave."

Elias was starting to feel desperate. They had reached his cottage. He lowered himself onto the stoop outside his door, glad to rest his leg. "What if I were to leave from another part of the island, out of sight of Alfonse? I'll sail out, toward deep sea, then make my way around del Mar, bypassing the archers."

Brother Francis dashed that plan, too. "Soldiers are stationed on each of the outer islands. Cali, St. Carlo, and Olivos. A boat can be seen departing from every point on Valdemossa."

Feeling thwarted, Elias flung his stick to the sand. Hoods swiveled in their direction. He repeated, "I'm not waiting until autumn. There must be another way."

Someone called for Brother Francis. Another monk from down the beach. Brother Francis waved back in acknowledgment. He said to Elias, "If there is, I think you'll be the one to find it. I must leave you." He nudged Elias's walking stick with his sandal, moving it within reach.

Elias raised a hand in wordless farewell. In one of the cottages, someone coughed endlessly. A painful, hacking sound. He quelled the instinct to seek the person out, to offer any assistance. He must keep his distance here.

Soon after, a school of sea serpents appeared in the waters. There were at least ten of them dipping and gliding past the boundary rock in blues and reds and greens and golds. One of the serpents, a red one, lifted its head high and turned toward shore. Almost, it felt as though it looked directly at him. A forked tongue slithered out and flapped one long, lazy flap before the creature's head dipped beneath the surface and the school swam past. The lepers watched silently. More than a few crossed themselves.

Elias did not want to become serpent food. He'd escaped that fate twice. Foolish to tempt it a third time. And he had no wish to be pierced by a fire arrow, or to drown. He would have to think of something else. He dropped his chin onto his fist.

And brooded.

Midday found Elias scavenging among the palm trees behind his cottage when he heard Brother Francis call his name.

"I'm here!" he called back.

The monk appeared. He watched as Elias hobbled around the trees, pausing before one shrub, then moving on to another. "What are you doing?"

"Looking for something," Elias answered, distracted. "Does the indigo plant grow on this island?"

Brother Francis looked blank. "Which plant?"

"Indigo," Elias repeated. "It's a shrub, about this high" — he demonstrated — "with small blue flowers."

"Why do you need it?" When Elias explained, Brother Francis looked thoughtful. "I've no notion if it does. But I know someone who might. I'll ask, if you'll stay off that leg. You're not at full strength."

"I will. My thanks to you, Brother." Elias caught Brother Francis's smile and wondered at it. It was only after he returned to the cottage that he realized it was the first time he'd referred to the monk by his holy name. By any name. He had avoided using either King Teodor or Brother Francis, utterly ignorant as to what to call a king who did not want to be a king but chose instead to be a monk.

Brother Francis had left him a meal. Elias ate, waiting impatiently for his return. But the day's exertions had tired him out, and within a half hour of his meal, he had crawled into bed and fallen asleep.

By early dusk, Elias had begun to wonder if Brother Francis had forgotten him when he appeared in the doorway.

"Is this what you're looking for?" Two indigo bushes were presented, dirt clinging to the roots.

Elias snatched up his stick, delighted. "Where did you find them?"

"Not far inland," Brother Francis said with a smile. "One of the men here knows of plants and herbs. He knew what you asked for."

Grinning, Elias took one of the plants. Dirt rained all over the floor. "You'll give him my thanks?"

"Of course. There's more where they came from." Brother Francis glanced outside. "Do you need anything else?"

"Yes. Please. I need fire."

They built a fire on the beach directly outside his cottage. Elias worked in a frenzy, piling driftwood and sticks gathered from the woods. He ignored the monk's orders to rest and let him take care of it. The lepers stood in the gathering shadows of dusk, watching. He felt their curiosity. Such a fire? In the middle of summer? Brother Francis set it ablaze, and when the flames were at their highest, Elias flung the two bushes into its midst.

Nothing happened.

The bushes crackled and crumbled, and Elias felt a terrible doubt. Had he been mistaken about the indigo? Could the Caffeesh have used another plant for their beacon fire? He'd been so sure. After a time, Brother Francis glanced at him, saying nothing. Just as Elias was about to admit failure, the flame changed color.

Slowly, from a vibrant orange-red to a brilliant vivid blue. Elias looked at Brother Francis; they grinned at each other. Elias could just make out three royal guards atop the watchtower. Were they turned toward Valdemossa? Wondering at the strangely colored fire? Would they ignore it, or would a diligent sort at least send word to Commander Aimon? Elias would know one way or another. One day on horseback to Cortes; one day back. Surely Ulises or Mercedes would remember their conversation about beacon fire in the forest of Javelin.

As the days passed, life took on a steady, predictable pattern. When Elias woke, Brother Francis was there to share his breakfast and tend to his wound. It made Elias uncomfortable to have Brother Francis serve him, and he told him so. He might look like a monk and speak like a monk, but that did not change the blood that flowed through his veins. Elias could manage to spear his own fish from the shallows. Or olingohot fruit from a tree. Francis had agreed when Elias suggested it, and then continued to do as he always did. Stubbornness — the trait ran strong in that family. Afterward, the monk disappeared for a day of prayer, solitude, and service. Elias started another fire and kept it burning throughout the day.

As for his neighbors, Elias nodded in greeting, and they nodded in greeting. Everyone kept their distance. He had asked after Rafael, whom he'd met in Cortes, and learned he was being cared for on the opposite side of the island. Elias did not seek him out. Supper was a simple meal with Brother Francis.

He learned that Valdemossa was home to more than two hundred lepers. The monastery consisted of sleeping quarters for the monks, as well as a school, a chapel, a graveyard. There was even a prison, for the few who were violent and could not be trusted to live among others. It was a strange thought — what must it feel like, to be considered a leper among lepers?

"Do the monks ever get sick?" Elias asked one morning over breakfast. It was his fifteenth day on Valdemossa.

"Since I've lived here, no," Brother Francis answered. "In the last hundred years, there have been four."

Elias didn't know how anyone could be so calm about it. "You've managed this long to escape it. Have you never thought of leaving?"

"My place is here." At Elias's disbelieving look, Brother

Francis smiled slightly. "Is it so hard to understand? That I could be content here?"

"Yes," Elias said bluntly.

Another smile. "When I first studied to become a monk, I was taught that each of us is exactly where we should be, that life unfolds for us precisely as it is supposed to."

Elias didn't believe him. No man could be so at peace with himself, not after what he'd endured. He said, "Lord Silva is not where he should be."

Brother Francis reached for the bread. He broke it in two, offered half. "Was he a good teacher to you?"

The wound was still too raw. A betrayal Elias could not yet understand, let alone forgive. But he answered honestly. "He was."

No butter on the monk's slice, only a drizzle of honey. "Then can you not remember his goodness, and forgive his . . . shortcomings?"

Elias stabbed a grape with his knife. "Why would I?"

Brother Francis was quiet for a time. "Do you consider what would have happened if Lord Silva had not done what he did?"

Elias spoke around the grape in his mouth. "What do you mean?"

"You would have known your father, yes," Brother Francis said. "But not your stepfather. Not your brother and sisters. They would not exist. Would you wish them away?"

Silence. Elias's answer was to stab another grape. "It's too early for philosophy, monk."

Brother Francis smiled. "Then we'll speak of something else. Tell me about your travels."

The next morning, Elias woke to a sound outside his cottage. He dragged himself from bed, pulled on trousers, and poked his head out. A heap of indigo plants had been left beneath his window. Newly uprooted, for he smelled the soil, sharp and pungent, and saw the worms wiggling among the roots. A figure in a green robe was on the beach, walking away.

"Hello!" Elias called out.

The figure paused but did not turn and, after a moment, hurried off.

When Brother Francis arrived at breakfast, he looked at the indigo plants, frowning. "When did you gather those?"

"I didn't," Elias said. "One of your people left them at dawn. He didn't stay to talk."

Brother Francis looked down the beach. An odd expression crossed his face.

"What is it?" Elias asked.

"Nothing. It's nothing."

Sleep eluded him that night. He found himself tossing and turning and thinking of Mercedes. Worrying for her. Wondering where she was. By dawn, he had given up on sleep. He was dressed, his bandage wrapped, waiting impatiently for the time when he could light the fires.

When he heard the indigo plants falling outside the door, he was off the bed and across the chamber. He flung open the door. The hooded figure froze on the stoop, outlined by the dawn sky, then spun around and walked away. The disease hadn't yet crippled his lower limbs. His stride was fast and sure.

"Wait," Elias said.

The stranger ignored him.

Elias grabbed his stick and went after him, slow and clumsy on the sand. "I said stop!" he ordered, breathless.

The stranger stopped ten feet away and turned halfway toward Elias. Dark gloves shielded his hands. "What will happen if I don't?" His voice was like gravel, rough, older than the trees in the forest. "You're hardly in a position to give chase, my lord Elias."

Elias was mystified by the man's unfriendliness. "I only wanted to say thank you. To offer my respects, Grandfather."

The stranger made a sound that might have been a laugh. "I'm not so old as that." A pause. "Though maybe soon. I would not know." He looked at the pile of sticks waiting to be set alight. "Brother Francis told me of your plan with the fire. You've put much faith in your friend."

"She'll find me."

A pause. "She?"

"He," Elias corrected, and felt his face grow warm. The stranger had been referring to the king. "Ulises will come. As long as he's told of it. I don't know if they've sent word."

A small silence. Then, "You've traveled to Caffa?"

Elias was startled. The stranger recognized the origins of blue fire. "Many times. I have you?"

"Oh, many times."

"Are . . . were you a shipman?" Elias asked.

But the stranger was done talking. His answer was to walk off. He stopped almost immediately. "You're overusing the plants," he informed Elias without turning. "One should be enough for four hours. You don't need to throw in more." He continued walking.

"My thanks . . ." Elias trailed off. The stranger was too far away to hear, striding down the beach and disappearing around a copse of palms.

Curiously, Brother Francis never asked after his younger brother. Until one night over supper, on Elias's twentieth day on Valdemossa, he said, "What sort of king is Ulises?"

"A good one," Elias said immediately. "I think he'll be a great one, in time. He's still feeling his way since his . . . since your father's passing."

Elias's plate was nearly empty. The monk's, in contrast, was barely touched. "You're good friends," Brother Francis said.

"Since we were boys." More like brothers, but Elias kept those words to himself.

Brother Francis said, "A king whose elder brother is alive is in a . . . tenuous position."

Elias stopped with his fork halfway to his mouth. He set it aside. "In some kingdoms, maybe."

"In most kingdoms." Brother Francis sipped wine from his cup. "If I were to ask you to keep my existence to yourself, how would you answer?"

They regarded each other across the small table. Elias said, "I won't keep this from him."

The monk's hand tightened around his cup, then slowly relaxed. "You trust him with your life, it sounds like."

"I do," Elias said.

"Do you also trust him with mine?"

Elias shook his head vehemently, knowing what the monk suggested. "He would never . . . you don't know him."

"That's true." Brother Francis studied the contents of his cup as he spoke. "I remember an infant in my arms. I remember trying not to drop him. And failing once when Lady Esma was not looking. I don't know him like you do, Lord Elias. But no man can serve two masters. That I do know."

"Ulises showed me the maps," Elias reminded him. "I'm here because he sent me to find you."

"I wonder if he truly understood the risks?"

Elias was not proud of what he was about to say. He nearly held his tongue. "I offered to stop looking."

Brother Francis was startled. "For us?"

"Yes." Elias found it hard to meet his eyes. "After we left Javelin, when we realized that one of you, maybe all of you, might still be alive, I offered to forget about the riddle. To forget about you. Ulises said no."

The silence filled every corner of the cottage, every corner of the last eighteen years. At last, Brother Francis said softly, "So be it. You trust him. I will trust you."

"Good."

Some time was spent concentrating on their meal before Elias spoke again. "You're content here, Brother. I see it now, though I did not believe it could be true. After your jailer died, was my father also content?"

Now it was Brother Francis who had trouble meeting his eyes. "No. He was not. He missed his family."

That night, sleep escaped Elias entirely. He sat outside with his back against the cottage, one knee drawn up, watching the stars and thinking of Mercedes. Black hair down to her waist, eyes green as sea glass. A smile that could stop his heart if he was not careful. He saw her in Javelin, calming the spirits. He saw her standing at the water's edge with her bow raised high. He remembered their kiss outside her door.

Wherever you are, Mercedes, please be safe.

He fell asleep near dawn, coming awake only when he felt something hit his side. Indigo plants. His mysterious hooded helper had not seen him.

Only half awake, Elias mumbled, "Thank you."

The stranger started violently, spinning around and tripping on the hem of his robe. Without thinking, Elias lurched to his feet and grabbed the man's hand. They both toppled over onto the sand. After the first shooting pain in his leg, Elias felt nothing.

In the gray light of dawn, he saw the stranger's hands, ungloved. Not stricken with leper sores, as Elias had pictured, but as blue as his own.

Holding his robe together beneath his chin was a gold compass pin.

His hood had fallen back. The face that Elias saw was his own. Many years from now, after a hard life lived. Bearded, hollow-eyed, not a leper.

Not a stranger.

Elias could not say how long they sat there sprawled in the sand, the only sound the lapping of seawater along the shore. He let go of his father's hand. Lord Antoni stumbled to his feet, doing nothing to hide his tears. His father was gone, racing down the beach until he was lost from view.

TWENTY-FOUR

ERCEDES HAD TRACED Elias's route south. He had made no effort to conceal himself; stealth had not been his goal. An innkeeper and stable master had recognized him. *Lord Elias? Certainly, he was here. Didn't stay long, though, wasn't as friendly as usual, and he looked like he'd been in a fight.* Nothing she did not know already.

She lost him in the last town before Alfonse. There were no more sightings, of Elias or his horse. His trail had gone as cold as this feeling inside her. She refused to call it terror.

Where are you, Elias? Where did you go?

Time was spent in Alfonse. She questioned the king's soldiers, but they were of no help. Nothing outside the ordinary had taken place, just the normal routine of petty thievery, tavern brawls, and bickering neighbors. And, oh, a lost soul had thrown himself off the cliffs some days back. Tragic, but it happened sometimes. She did not interview the soldiers only, but plowed through the rest of Alfonse until the entire city was turned inside out and every contact questioned, bribed, and threatened. She had burned bridges there, with nothing to show for it. And when finally she had left, it was with the unshakable feeling that she was leaving him behind.

Regretfully, her entourage encountered no bandits or others of bad character along the roads. They at least would have offered a distraction. The tears came only once, late at night, on the return journey to Cortes. But it was only that once.

Because she'd had plenty of time to think on the ride south, and then north. And she had taken a very close look at Katalin's tax scroll. Mercedes had no proof. No motive. Only a hunch, a theory pressed up against her heart, keeping company with her fear.

In the castle's great dining hall, life went on as usual. There were no foreign dignitaries to entertain, and the king's table was crowded with the everyday assortment of noblemen and noblewomen. Ulises spoke with Lords Pistorius and Bernat. Mercedes watched them laugh at something he said and thought her cousin could have been an actor on a stage. No one would guess how upset he was behind that smiling facade.

The lords were accompanied by their wives: Lady Pistorius; also Lady Bernat, who would never know that until recently, her younger sister had been alive and well within the forest of Javelin. One could fill an entire world with all the things we did not know.

Mercedes had chosen to dine at a table among the castle women, which she did on occasion. Katalin was there, along with Mistress Galena, her pet monkey, Jorge, chattering happily on her lap as she fed him morsels of octopus from her plate. Madame Vega sat directly across from Mercedes.

"Where is Lord Silva this evening, Madame?" Mercedes glanced past the geography mistress to a nearby table crowded with boisterous geographers. Always the loudest table in the hall. Elias and Lord Silva were noticeably absent. "I hope he's well."

Madame Vega smiled, though her eyes were tired. "Perfectly well," she said. "He's gone to Esperanca to inspect the expedition ships. He did not want to leave Reyna, but . . ."

"I understand." Mercedes pushed the octopus around on her plate. "Reyna looks better."

"Much better. The doctor expects a full recovery. My prayers have been answered."

"My prayers as well."

Perfectly pleasant conversation. A graceful back and forth, like a dance. The wine was heady tonight. Mercedes took a few sips only.

Around them the conversation had turned to babies.

"They have not decided on a name," Madame Julián was saying, disgruntled. "And they will not take seriously my suggestions, when I am only trying to be helpful." Master Julián served as the king's tailor. The Juliáns' eldest daughter was to give birth soon. The infant would be their first grandchild born.

"Which suggestions, Madame?" Katalin asked.

"If it is a girl, perhaps Chastity," Madame Julián said. "Or Charity, Prudence, Patience — what is wrong with those?" she demanded over the laughter.

Mistress Galena was blunt in the manner of old friends. "You'll curse the child with those names, Rowena. She's bound to fight it, and then they will have to rename her Feckless, Impertinent, Greedy, or . . . what is the opposite of chastity?"

From there, a string of possibilities poured forth.

"What of Olivia?"

"Or Tanis?"

"Julieta?" came another suggestion.

There were murmurs of agreement for the last.

"What of Evangeline?" Mercedes asked. "That is your name, is it not, Madame Vega?"

Katalin made a small choking sound. Both Mistress Galena and Jorge fell silent. Mercedes did not look at them.

Madame Vega had just taken a bite of octopus. She stopped chewing, her eyes settling on Mercedes, before continuing. A napkin raised, a dab at the corner of a mouth that no longer smiled. "It is my birth name, yes."

"Evangeline," Madame Julián tried. "It is lovely. I will suggest it, as long as you don't object?"

"Of course I do not." Madame Vega spoke to Madame Julián.

Her eyes, however, never once left Mercedes, who smiled and said, "Perhaps the baby will be called Lena for short, or Eve. You have used both names before, Madame. They are so pretty."

Nothing more was said about Madame Vega's birth name. Supper continued, and the conversation turned from babies to

husbands to the terribly high prices demanded by the cloth merchants at the harbor. Mercedes laughed when she was expected
to and added her own observations here and there, even as her
heart pounded and her hands slicked with sweat. She could turn
the actor too when needed. She could play any part, for however
long it took, if it meant finding Elias.

The next course included thin slices of sea serpent served
alongside a bed of rice and topped with a single fish eye. Red fish
eyes were considered a delicacy, though she had never been able
to stomach them. The texture, the taste, the slippery feel in her
mouth, horrible. Her eye had been shunted off to the side of her
plate, hidden beneath a piece of bread so that she would not have
to look at it.

Madame Vega's fish eye was proving to be a worthy
opponent. Her hands trembled as she tried to slice through
it. Mercedes watched with grim pleasure as the eye continued
to thwart, darting across the plate as Madame Vega tried and
failed to spear it with her knife. *Good. Let her be nervous. Let her
be off her guard.*

It was not long before others noticed. "Gracious," Madame
Julián said with a small laugh. "Just pick it up with your hand.
We will not judge you too harshly."

Katalin, her eyes first on Mercedes, then on the geography
mistress, asked carefully, "Are you well, Madame?"

"A sudden headache," Madame Vega murmured. "I believe
I'll retire early."

And Mercedes took this to be her cue. She pushed her chair

back. "The noise cannot be helping. I must leave as well. Come, I'll see you to the tower."

At that, Madame Vega looked up and met Mercedes's gaze. Mercedes had seen that look before. In the eyes of a wild pig, trussed with leather ties, right after it had been captured. They stood in unison, which caused the conversation to drop slightly as the men in the hall rose to their feet. Ulises raised his eyebrows as they walked past the high table.

"A slight ailment," Mercedes explained with a sympathetic look in Madame Vega's direction. "Please don't trouble yourselves."

"Be well, Madame," Ulises said to Madame Vega, though his sharp eyes were leveled on his cousin, who was not known for her caring bedside manner. "It's dark. Take escort, Mercedes."

"Of course." Mercedes smiled pleasantly, tucking Madame Vega's limp arm into hers. When she tried to pull away, Mercedes dug her nails into the woman's arm. A small gasp followed, but there was no more resistance.

Commander Aimon dined at a table full of soldiers. Mercedes did not look at him on the way out. She did not have to. He watched them go, his expression arranged, as always, in a scowl.

Mercedes did not send for an escort. The moment they left the dining hall, she released the older woman's arm.

"Somewhere we may speak," Mercedes said. "Privately, or with an audience, it matters not to me."

Wordless, Madame Vega led them across the courtyard and down a set of stairs, to a chapel tucked away by the orange groves. There were a handful of religious sanctuaries within the castle walls. Never barred, so visitors could find prayer and solace at any hour of the day and night. The chapel doors were studded with iron bolts. Inside, the pews were empty, the altar absent of any priest, though the walls were torchlit and offered a welcoming light. The scent of oranges lingered, mixed in with an oppressive, cloying incense.

Mercedes swung the doors shut behind them. "An appropriate place, I suppose, for a confession."

Madame Vega's face was white and stark. "There's no punishment you can order that will make me feel worse than I already do."

"Then you don't know me well, Madame. I assure you, I can make you feel far worse. Where is Lord Elias?"

"Dead by now. I'm sorry." And with that, Madame Vega walked down the aisle and entered a pew halfway down. She knelt and bent her head, hands clasped before her in prayer.

How long Mercedes stood there, she could not say. Her hands gripped the back pew so hard, her veins stood out like the rivers and creeks on a map.

Dead by now. I'm sorry.

She forced her fingers loose and willed herself forward, one slipper in front of the other. She took the pew directly across the aisle from Madame Vega. Sitting, not kneeling. The silk of her midnight-blue skirts rustled about her. Madame Vega continued to pray, too low for Mercedes to make out the words, but she thought she recognized the rhyme and rhythm of the *Sinner's Lament.*

How tempting it was to reach out, grab the woman by the hair, and smash her face into the next pew. A terrible thing to consider in a chapel, but she, too, knew the *Sinner's Lament.* She could pray for forgiveness later. But that would not do. Force would not work here. It would not bring her closer to finding Elias, who was *not* dead, whatever Madame Vega said. Mercedes would have to be patient, and she would have to think. And so she sat, dark spots hovering at the edge of her vision, and waited.

The walls were decorated with the frescoes of saints. Famous ones, obscure ones. Mercedes studied them in detail. There was Master Mori's Appolonia, with her pliers and bowl full of teeth. Also Saint Matthew, patron saint of stonemasons and military engineers, a fierce-looking man holding a miniature cathedral and standing alongside a battering ram. He reminded her a little of Commander Aimon. She had moved on to Saint Christopher when Madame Vega spoke at last. Very few people could tolerate a silence stretched so thin.

"I am so tired of secrets."

"Then do not keep them," Mercedes advised, studying her. Madame Vega's gaze had not wavered from her steepled fingers. "You reminded me of someone, that day in Reyna's chamber when we looked at dresses. You wore no paint on your face. Do you remember?"

"Yes."

"Until yesterday, I could not think who. And then it struck me. You look like Reyna."

A quick inhalation of breath was the only sign Madame Vega had heard her. Mercedes prompted softly, "Tell me, Madame, who is Lord Silva, to you?"

"He is my father."

Mercedes was unsurprised. Too late, she had seen the resemblance between Reyna and her aunt. Lord Silva's secret illegitimate daughter, for, given Madame Vega's age, she had been born when Lord Silva's wife was still living. Another story entirely.

Mercedes asked, "Where is your *maman?*"

"Dead many years." Madame Vega's words were brusque. "A farmer's daughter from Alfonse, swept off her feet by a wealthy nobleman. It's a common tale, Lady."

"True," Mercedes agreed. "But helping one's father poison a royal party, kidnapping the king's sons . . ." — here Mercedes had to fight to keep her voice steady — ". . . and returning eighteen years later to finish off Lady Esma, well. That is not quite so common."

Out of the corner of her eye, Mercedes spied movement. Commander Aimon in a small alcove, listening. He must have entered through a side door, as silent as a turnip. She shook her head, a warning for him to keep silent. His scowl deepened.

Madame Vega had buried her face in her hands, and Mercedes had to strain to hear her words. "I did not want to do it."

"I know you did not." Mercedes tried not to choke on her

words. "What did you say to Lady Esma? How did you get her to leave Javelin?"

Still speaking into her hands, Madame Vega answered, "I told her you sent me."

Mercedes stared at her, horrified. "Me?"

"I said you needed her help. Urgently, and that you would explain once she returned to Cortes."

"And she agreed?"

"She did not hesitate."

Mercedes closed her eyes briefly and tried not to think of the bitter words she had flung at Lady Esma's feet. Words she could never take back. "Where is Lord Elias?"

"I don't know."

"You do know. Tell me."

"I will not speak out against my father."

Mercedes slammed a fist onto the arm of the pew. Madame Vega jumped.

"He's finished already!" Mercedes swept an arm toward the alcove. It was then that Madame Vega saw Commander Aimon with his arms folded and his face set in stone. Mercedes had not thought it possible for her face to lose any more color. "Surely you understand that? There's no going back from this for Lord Silva. But you have a chance. Exile, maybe. And perhaps . . ."—she grasped at carrots she could offer—". . . you may see Reyna in time. I know you care for her. She is your niece."

"Reyna." Madame Vega laughed, a horrible, high-pitched

sound that ended on a gasp. She doubled over; her forehead struck the pew in front of her.

Realization came too late for Mercedes.

"No!" She leaped across the way, catching Madame Vega as she slumped sideways. A knife, a supper knife taken from the dining hall, protruded from her belly. For Mercedes, shock gave way to panic. "It won't be this easy for you! Where is he?"

"Give her over." Commander Aimon nudged Mercedes aside. He gathered Madame Vega in his arms and laid her out in the aisle upon the stone. They knelt beside her. One look at the wound and Mercedes knew there would be no more questions for Madame Vega.

Who blinked at the candelabra directly overhead. Blood trickled from her mouth. Her eyes rolled back once before focusing on Mercedes. "Elias is gone. Reyna . . . is gone. We are all gone." Her eyes fluttered closed. They did not open again.

Mercedes saw the stunned look on Commander Aimon's face, and cold prickles rose along her forearms. She had not misheard.

Reyna is gone.

Commander Aimon said, "I'll stay here. Go now!"

Mercedes's hands were covered in blood. She wiped them on her dress. And then she ran.

The hour had grown late, and the corridors were sparsely populated. The few servants about pressed up against the walls, eyebrows raised, as Mercedes flew past. She rounded a corner and nearly ran into Ulises.

He reached out to steady her. "I've looked everywhere for you. What's happened?"

In response, she grabbed his arm and dragged him along. Across the castle grounds, into the Tower of Winds, up the stairs toward Reyna's chamber. He listened as she spoke, interrupting once. "She's *dead?*" And again when she came to the part about Reyna. "No, she's safe, Mercedes. There's a guard at her door."

It was as Ulises said. A soldier, Lazar, bowed when he saw them. "Mistress Galena is sitting with her. She came just after supper." He opened the door and stepped aside to let them pass.

Mistress Galena sat by Reyna's bedside, reading from a book as the child listened sleepily. Jorge was tucked beneath her arm. A small hearth fire had been lit, and a candle flickered on a table beside Commander Aimon's toy catapult. All three looked up when the door opened.

Smiling, Madame Galena set the book aside and rose. "We'll finish tomorrow. Look who has come to see you, dear."

Ulises glanced at the book, then smiled at Reyna. "*The Travels of Antoni, Lord of del Mar?* You must know this one by heart."

"It's my favorite," Reyna said with a smile. She looked past him to Mercedes, brows crinkling. "Are you well, Lady?"

Mercedes found her voice. And could only be grateful her dress was so dark that Madame Vega's blood was unnoticeable. "Certainly I am." She settled at the foot of the bed and studied the small glass dish on Reyna's table. It was empty. "What was in that bowl? Sweets?"

Madame Galena answered. "I'll fetch a fresh bowl, Lady. There *were* sweets, but Jorge would not touch them, and he eats everything." She scooped up the dish. "I knew they must be off, so I threw them out."

Mercedes looked at her cousin, who appeared thunderstruck. Poison once again. It had been Madame Vega's weapon of choice.

Ulises swallowed before managing a parody of a smile. He reached out and patted Jorge on the head.

"Good monkey," he said.

The following morning, Mercedes rode out as soon as the portcullis had lifted. Not far, only outside the city walls and across the fields where the castle walls did not feel as if they closed in upon her.

The news had spread quickly. Sometime in the night, Madame Vega, del Mar's beloved geography mistress, had fallen down the stairs and broken her neck. A horrific, tragic accident. The morgue attendant was one of Commander Aimon's trusted few. She would keep Madame Vega's knife wound to herself and ask no questions. Already, the servants hurried about, draping the Tower of Winds in black.

As for Lord Silva, a messenger had been sent to Esperanca to inform him of the terrible news. Commander Aimon had made sure to send an even faster messenger to find the Royal Navigator before he learned of his daughter's untimely death and decided it would be prudent to flee.

The ride did nothing to ease Mercedes's gnawing fear. She was afraid to face the truth. That she was too late. That Elias was gone, and she did not know where to find him.

When she returned to the castle gates, a soldier on horseback was speaking to the guard. Neither looked happy. They paused to greet her, resuming their conversation as her horse cantered past.

She heard the castle guard say, "You'll have to wait, I said. Go to the kitchens and find something to eat."

"But —"

"The commander is busy. He doesn't have time to hear some strange tale of lepers and blue fire. Go . . . Lady? Is something wrong?"

Mercedes had whirled her horse around, and whatever showed on her face caused both men to fall silent. The soldier on horseback had removed his helmet and cradled it beneath one arm. Sweat matted his hair; his face was weary. She knew this man, had seen him only days before. He was one of the king's messengers.

A soldier from Alfonse.

TWENTY-FIVE

Brother Francis found Elias sitting on his stoop with his head in his hands.

"I didn't know monks were allowed to lie," Elias said without looking up.

Brother Francis stopped a few feet away. His sigh was a long one. "I don't think we are," he admitted.

The glare Elias sent him would have scared off most men. "Why did you?"

"I would do anything for your father. He asked for silence."

"You weren't silent," was Elias's bitter reminder. "You told me he was dead. I am told again and again that he is dead." And when Francis said nothing, Elias asked, "What is he called here? Robert? Matías? Does he hide behind a false name, too?"

A sudden, painful grip on Elias's arm. Brother Francis's face was inches away, his eyes narrowed. No longer the benign monk.

"Don't think of being unkind to him." The warning was low and fierce. "Every choice he's made has been for you."

"Get your hand off me."

They had drawn an audience. Elias's neighbors stood by,

watchful, men and women and children. One man holding a shovel stepped forward, stopping only when Brother Francis shook his head.

The monk released Elias's arm. "He's known as Antoni. It's a common name here, and he keeps to himself." Once again he was Brother Francis, who straightened and calmly dusted the sand from his robe. "Your father lives in the keep. I think you remember the way." He walked away.

"Brother Francis," Elias said.

Francis didn't turn around, but he stopped.

"Whose graves did you show me?"

Quiet. "Bartolome's. And Hugo's."

The door to the keep was open. Elias hovered by the threshold, winded from the walk. His first thought was that the chamber looked like any other in the Tower of Winds. Paint and parchment on a table, maps on the walls. The skin of a white hog lay flat across the table surface, its bristles washed, dried, and ready for plucking. A good number of painter's brushes would be made from that unlucky beast. Even Lord Antoni, watching him quietly beside the skin, would have blended in with his white shirt and ancient trousers streaked with paint. Only the small gold hoop in his left ear would have raised eyebrows. Especially from Madame Vega. Royal explorers were not encouraged to look like pirates.

One more thing out of place. Behind Lord Antoni was a

life-size painting of Elias's mother holding an infant high in the air. Mother and child appeared in profile. She wore an emerald dress; Elias was without a stitch of clothing. They were both laughing. If he could force the words past his throat, still he would not know what to say.

His father spoke first, the same rough voice as before. "Your *maman*. She's in good health?"

Elias turned away from the painting. "Yes."

Lord Antoni kept busy with mortar and pestle, grinding a stone with water. Elias was fairly certain the stone was hematite, for his father's hands were now a cardinal's red. "And your . . . Lord Isidore. He's been good to you?"

"Yes." Then, helpless, "I don't know what I'm supposed to say to you."

The grinding stopped. A small smile emerged. "I've spoken to you a thousand times in my mind. Now that you're here, I find that I, too, am tongue-tied." Lord Antoni swiped his cheek with one hand, transferring the red paint. "Francis has told me all of it, but I don't wish to speak of such ugliness just now." He gestured toward a chair opposite him. "Sit. You should not tax that leg. We'll talk of small things, perhaps, and make our way from there."

Elias was grateful to give his leg a rest. He leaned his stick against the table and sat, wondering what small things they would begin discussing.

Lord Antoni said, "You've earned master status," and when Elias looked surprised, pointed to his robe, tossed on a bench near the door. The compass pin was visible. "You wouldn't have worn it otherwise."

"It was sold to you?" Elias had thought the pin lost forever when he'd offered his cloak to Rafael that long-ago day in Cortes.

"Traded," Lord Antoni said, "for a heavier cloak. They catch chill easily, even in summer, once their condition progresses." He spoke in the same matter-of-fact tone used by Brother Francis. Two men long accustomed to living among the lepers.

Elias wondered aloud, "How are you not sick?"

Lord Antoni shrugged. "Who can say? Maybe something else was meant for us. Certainly, Francis has a calling. Me, I'm not so sure." He'd resumed grinding. Beneath his hands, the blood-red stone was slowly turning to paste. "If you're a master geographer, you must have an apprentice."

Elias could have been on del Mar, speaking to Madame Vega. "I'm considering one, but I can't see how to make it work." A small knife lay within reach beside several unsharpened quills. Absently, he picked up a quill and began trimming it with the knife. He caught himself — he was not in the tower, and these were not his supplies — and looked up to find Lord Antoni watching him.

"No, it's fine," Lord Antoni said when Elias would have put them aside. "This almost-apprentice of yours. What is wrong with him?"

"Her," Elias said. "There's nothing wrong with her except that she's a girl. And Lord Silva's granddaughter." He explained about Reyna discovering the first map. How she had brought it to the king's attention. He described her attack at the harbor, and her attacker: Lord Silva's faithful, callous servant, who must have known who she was even as he robbed her.

Lord Antoni had stopped grinding. "Was she hurt badly?"

Elias scowled at the memory. "Her ribs were cracked. Three fingers broken. Her face is black-and-blue."

"My God," Lord Antoni breathed. "How old?"

"Nine," Elias said. "The doctor says she'll be her old self, eventually. She's stronger than she looks." She would have to be, to weather the coming storm. Lord Silva would not go unpunished this time. And then what would happen to her?

They did not speak for some time, and their work continued, until Lord Antoni said, "Most people are content never to leave their place of birth. And others, it is all they can think about. Sailing off, discovering new places, meeting different people. It's part of who they are. You would know this, I think."

"Yes."

"Then don't think of her as Silva's granddaughter. Or even as a girl."

Elias was sitting here, with his father, and he was amused. "She wears dresses. Her braids are three feet long. How else am I supposed to think of her?"

Lord Antoni smiled. "As an adventurer, just like you. Think of the good you can do her."

Elias caught his likeness in the knife's surface. He made an effort to smooth his frown. "It's not that simple."

Lord Antoni shrugged. "If you say so."

A child cried out in the distance, a reminder of where they were and why. Elias set the knife and quill down. "Would you have let me leave this island without a word?"

Lord Antoni looked away. "I'm a danger to you. You're better off forgetting I'm here." He resumed his grinding, but not before Elias saw the slight trembling of his hands.

Small things, and we'll make our way from there.

Quietly, Elias left his walking stick by the table and went to study one of the maps on the wall. This one was of Cortes, fine and extremely detailed. "You painted this map from memory?"

"I did."

"It is extraordinary."

Lord Antoni glanced over at the map, pleased by the compliment. "Archaic, maybe. I imagine it looks nothing like that today."

"Cortes hasn't changed as much as you think. Though" — Elias pointed — "that brothel in St. Mark's burnt down seven years ago. They built a church in its place. It's not as popular, I think."

It worked. Amusement flickered in his father's eyes. He looked at the map. "What else?"

But his questions could not be postponed indefinitely, and Elias found himself asking, "Why would Lord Silva say you killed his son?"

By now Lord Antoni had finished with the hematite and had scrubbed the red from his hands as best he could. He was drying them with a rag when he heard the question. His answer was quiet. "Because I did. Vittor died because of me."

Not *I killed Vittor*, but *Vittor died because of me*.

Elias said, "I don't understand."

Lord Antoni dried the mortar and pestle as he spoke. "I was a boy when I first saw a map of the Bushido Territories. It was bordered in the north by mountains, mountains so tall their peaks were never without snow, even in high summer. But beyond the mountains, the map was empty. And for me, for any geographer, there is nothing more thrilling than a blank space on a map."

Elias selected a new quill to sharpen. "I know it."

Lord Antoni smiled slightly. He set the mortar and pestle on a low shelf, then brought the skinned hog close and began plucking its hairs, quick and efficient. "No one knew what lay beyond the mountains. Not for certain. But there had been stories. Some said that at the end of a dangerous and narrow road, part of the Blue Horn Pass, was an unusual door. One made of iron, that rose hundreds of feet toward the heavens. And through that door was . . ."

When Lord Antoni trailed off, Elias took over. "A kingdom that had turned its back to the world a thousand years ago. One that had hoarded its gold and treasures. The richest kingdom in the world. Or so the stories went. No one had ever made it through the Blue Horn Pass. Until the del Marian expedition."

"Vittor led us," Lord Antoni said. "He had dreamt of finding the Iron Door since we were boys. There were thirty in our camp. Myself, Vittor, Braga, Grec. The Bushido guides and servants." His fingers were a blur on the hog skin. The bare patches grew rapidly wider. "The first days were uneventful, but as we drew farther into the pass, it all started to go wrong. Our guides vanished one night, along with most of our food and supplies."

"Do you think they left on their own?" Elias asked. There were some who believed the Bushido guides had known what lay ahead of them and had fled, leaving the rest of the expedition to their own sorry fate.

"I do," Lord Antoni said, with a hint of grimness. "We decided to take turns guarding the camp each night, but the men of the first watch also disappeared. It was clear they had not left by choice."

Great pools of blood had remained, Elias knew, and tracks. It looked as if the men had been dragged straight up the mountain. By something large and horrible.

Lord Antoni said, "Several of us followed the tracks, but we turned back before nightfall with nothing to show for it." By now, a small mountain of hog bristles had amassed on the table. "Vittor and I argued. I wanted to turn back. We were low on food. We were losing men. I said no expedition was worth the lives lost. The lives we would continue to lose if we did not turn back."

Elias set aside the sharpened quill, chose another. "Lord Vittor disagreed."

"Yes. Part of me couldn't blame him. Vittor was Silva's eldest son, and the only one of the three who showed promise as a navigator. He had always been his father's favorite. Our sendoff from Cortes had been tremendous. There were fireworks over the harbor. It looked like the entire kingdom was there to wish us well. To return home and admit failure . . . I understood his decision, though I could not agree with it. The next night, we lost the boys."

Elias looked up from his quill, saying nothing.

Lord Antoni said, "Four apprentices had accompanied the expedition. Vittor's, Braga's, Grec's, and mine. When we woke the next morning, there was no sign of them. Jonas was gone."

"Jonas?" The name was out before Elias could think to hold his tongue. The names of the four apprentices had not appeared in his book.

"My apprentice. He was twelve."

Lord Antoni waited until Elias admitted reluctantly, "Jonas is my brother's name." It was only because Elias looked directly at his blood father that he saw it: the flash of pain in Lord Antoni's eyes, quickly gone.

"Yes. Well. Jonas lived in our home. Sabine was fond of him." Lord Antoni looked at the painting of his wife and son before he picked up the thread of his story. "A key had been left on Jonas's pallet. It was as tall as a grown man. By then, the morning mist had lifted and we saw the Iron Door only a short ride away. It had not been there when we had stopped to make camp a day earlier."

"Vittor and I fought even worse than before. I told him he was a fool to fall for such a trap. He told me I was a coward for wanting to turn back when we were so close. And I—" Here, Lord Antoni broke off, took an unsteady breath. "I said better he had been taken first and the rest of us spared.

"Those were the last words I said to my friend before he swung open the door. That was when we discovered it had been lined with bells along the very top. Large ones. Imagine a hundred church bells being rung at once with the mountains all around us packed tight with snow. I had never seen an avalanche before."

Elias's glass of water was half full. He held it out. Lord Antoni took it with thanks and downed the contents.

Elias said, "I still don't see how Lord Silva can blame you. How is an avalanche your fault?"

Lord Antoni said, "Vittor did not die right away. By some miracle, I found myself clinging to a large rock. I thought everyone else was gone until they burst through the snow and swept right by me." Lord Antoni's hand curved around the empty glass. "I was able to pull Grec and Braga onto the rock, and a few others, but by the time Vittor was close enough to reach, I could not hold on. Silva might have heard about our arguments. They were ugly. He might have been told how I held his son's hands in mine . . . and let him go."

Elias spoke into the quiet. "The story said one of your arms was broken, but you still saved six men."

"Not the one who mattered," Lord Antoni said. "Silva was devastated when we returned. He left Cortes and would not see anyone. I didn't know he'd gone to the king. Andrés never said. I never realized, until now, how much he hated me."

Mari had directed Elias to a cottage at the far end of the beach. It was larger than its neighbors, easily three times in length, and when he poked his head in the doorway, he saw that it was a hospital.

One cloaked in sickness and incense. Pallets lined the floor with lanterns glowing gold between them. Brother Francis was among the monks tending to patients. He knelt beside an old man, and something painful lodged in Elias's belly as he watched Ulises's elder brother dip a cloth into a bowl and wring it out before cleaning the leper's feet. When he was done, both feet were wrapped in binding cloth. Brother Francis rested a comforting hand on the patient's shoulder and moved on to the next person, a woman this time. He caught sight of Elias in the doorway. His expression gave nothing away, and he turned back to the woman.

Elias went to sit on the beach. The sun rode low on the horizon. Soon torchlight would appear across the way. The light had nearly gone by the time Brother Francis settled beside him. They looked out upon the water and the gently lapping waves.

Elias greeted him quietly. "Brother Francis."

"Lord Elias."

Elias rested his elbows on his knees. "He's not like I imagined."

"No?" Brother Francis tossed a stone into the water. "The same could be said for you."

A slight edge beneath the mildness. Their last encounter had not been a pleasant one. Elias said, "I won't apologize."

A small reluctant smile from the monk. "That makes two of us. Neither will I."

"That's not very monk-like," Elias observed.

"As you say."

There they were, the torches at Alfonse. "I have two sisters," Elias said. "Nieve is twelve. She's most like our father . . . Isidore. She has a head for numbers. And Lea is six. She's interested in many things. It changes, really, with the tide. My brother, Jonas, is a baby." He found his own stone and tossed it into the shallows. "I don't see them very much anymore, but we are a happy family, Brother Francis. I grew up in a happy family."

Brother Francis was watching him, and frowning. "Do you think I would begrudge it of you? I'm glad of it. I am."

Elias believed him. "I wish it were different. But you've said it yourself. I could not have one family without the other." He breathed in the night air and said what he'd come here to say. "I'm sorry for what happened to you, and to Prince Bartolome. But part of me, the selfish part, is very glad you were here for my father. I'm grateful there was someone here, to love him."

For the next two days, Elias limped to the keep after manning his fire. Brother Francis joined them sometimes, never staying for very long. They spoke of pleasant matters. Elias's voyages, mostly. When he broached weightier topics, like his mother, Lord Antoni would close in on himself. Much like Brother Francis did when he tried to speak of Ulises.

"May I ask you something?" Elias said to Lord Antoni. He never found himself idle at the keep. Today, he'd been tasked with assembling the hog bristles for the paintbrushes. First, he gathered together bundles of freshly plucked bristles. Some bundles were slimmer than his smallest fingernail, others twice as fat as his thumb. Some were tapered; others, even — brush heads for a painter's every whim or need. He tied each off with waxed thread.

Lord Antoni sat across from him, binding the finished bundles onto wooden handles. He glanced up at Elias's question. "Ask," he said.

"I found the cicada on your map. In place of Mari's house. Is she the reason you painted it?"

"Yes." Lord Antoni looked genuinely puzzled. "What other reason would I have?"

Elias told him of Mari's father, Judge Piri, and his role in questioning the prisoner, Felip of Mondrago. Lord Antoni, somewhat paler than he'd been a few minutes earlier, shook his head. "I knew nothing of that. Please don't mention it to Mari."

"I won't." Elias fell silent, thinking of a hundred other things he wished to know when Lord Antoni said again, "Ask."

"Did you really rescue a village girl from a crocodile?"

A startled silence, followed by a question threaded with amusement. "Is it so hard to believe?"

Elias snipped a length of waxed thread with his shears. "I was told you had a particular fear of crocodiles. . . ." The slight narrowing of Lord Antoni's eyes said he knew exactly who had shared that bit of information. "Forget I asked."

"Are *you* afraid of crocodiles?" Lord Antoni asked.

Elias shrugged. "Of course."

"Of course," Lord Antoni repeated dryly. "Who isn't? I did save her. If I had stopped to think about it, I might have run in the other direction. But there was no time." He cinched a brush head to its handle with more force than necessary. "Silva was there that day. He saw me do it."

Lord Silva had lied to him. A petty, unnecessary lie. "Why would he take me on as apprentice? He must have hated the sight of me."

"It would have looked strange if he had not, perhaps," Lord Antoni said. "But he could have moved you off to another navigator after a year or so. No one would have thought it odd. I imagine he kept you on because he saw your potential." When Elias was quiet, he added, "Whatever he has done, it does not change the fact that he was an excellent teacher. To both of us."

"You're kinder than he deserves."

"Oh, I know it," was the grim response.

Elias no longer wished to speak of Lord Silva. "How did you know Lady Esma was in Javelin?"

"Esma." Lord Antoni closed his eyes briefly. "I didn't," he admitted. "We hear things when the supply ships come in. And from the new arrivals. I only knew she never returned to Cortes. And she wasn't here. The last time I saw her, she was a stone's throw from Javelin." He raised his eyes to Elias's. "I never thought someone would see the riddle and actually solve it."

"You must have had some hope."

"Very little."

Elias snipped another length of thread. "I will get you off the island. Not immediately. We'll be recognized on a royal vessel, especially standing together. But I'll come back on my own. I don't want you to think I'd leave you here."

Lord Antoni only looked at him, unsmiling. "To what end?"

"What do you mean?"

"Elias, I won't return to del Mar."

"You don't have to." Elias's hand swept the chamber, toward the maps. "You could make a new life, anywhere else. I can help you."

Lord Antoni did not look at his maps. Only at his son, with a look on his face that said he would not be swayed. "I'm an old man."

"Not that old."

"Come, let us speak of —"

"I don't wish to speak of small things!" Elias snapped, getting to his feet. "Why the riddle, if you didn't want to be found?"

"I did it for Teodor . . . for Francis."

"The riddle was for Brother Francis." Elias still held the

shears. He tossed them onto the table. "This secret life you live, this is for me, and Maman. What about you?"

Nothing.

Elias said, "You're spoken of still, by everyone. I met the ambassador of Oslaw, who remembers you well. They talk of your adventures and your bravery. . . . What do you imagine they'd say if they could see you now? Would they recognize you?"

Lord Antoni flinched. He lowered his head.

And Elias felt ill. Frustration had loosened his tongue, had made him cruel and thoughtless. When would he learn to *think* before he spoke? "Forgive me."

Lord Antoni addressed the table. "I'm no longer that man," he said, his tone fierce. "I can't turn back the sand glass and *be* that man. No matter how I wish it."

"Forgive me, please. I wish it unsaid."

Lord Antoni laid a hand over the finished brushes. "We've done quite a bit today. Perhaps tomorrow."

A dismissal. Silently, Elias gathered his walking stick. When he left, he carried his shame with him, black and ugly, perched like a crow on one shoulder.

He returned to the beach in a filthy temper. Flinging plants into the fire, far more than were necessary. They were useless, anyway. So were those cursed soldiers in Alfonse. He fumed, pacing on the sand with blue fire blazing directly behind him. His leg *hurt*. He cursed it, too. He could not stay here any longer.

Mercedes . . . He beat at the sand with his stick, then raised his hand high in a rude gesture aimed at the soldiers. Giggles emerged behind him. Mari's children peeked at him from behind the trees. Brother Francis also approached. He sent the children scattering with one look.

Elias said, "I need a boat."

Brother Francis stopped a safe distance from Elias's stick. "No."

"I'll take the risk, monk. It's not your decision."

"It's not a risk. It's a certainty. They'll fire on you."

Elias snapped, "Better to be fired on than to rot here! How do you stand this life?"

Remorse filled him when he saw Brother Francis's expression. Elias dropped to the sand, holding his head in his hands. "Forgive me. I'm offending everyone today, Brother. I'm a horse's ass."

"As you say."

Elias laughed and did not raise his head. A minute later, the monk's sandaled feet appeared in his periphery. "I know your frustrations," Brother Francis said quietly. "And I'll miss our conversations, Lord Elias, when you've gone."

"What?" The sudden switch in tone brought his head up. "Then you'll give me a boat?"

"I don't need to." Brother Francis looked beyond him.

Elias turned and, a second later, stumbled to his feet, ignoring the pull in his leg, aware only of a sharp, painful sensation in his chest. A caravel had sailed into view, the royal flag of del

Mar raised high. The ship did not come from the direction of Alfonse, but from deeper waters. It headed directly for the boundary rock. He could see a figure at the helm, the wind blowing her hair behind her, and knew without a doubt that it was Mercedes.

TWENTY-SIX

ELIAS WAS ALREADY hobbling for the boats. Brother Francis called to someone, and another monk in his middle years appeared by Elias's side.

"My name is Brother Lorenz. I will row for you, Lord Elias." He dragged a small rowboat into the water.

Elias thanked him. When he looked back, Brother Francis was gone.

The boat pulled up alongside the ship. Peering over the side at Elias, with identical expressions of wariness, were Mercedes, Ulises, Commander Aimon, and the captain and crew of the *Desdemona*. And no wonder. Elias knew what he looked like. Nearly a month's beard growth, dressed in a brown robe, he was twin to the silent monk by his side. Also, he had just come from a leper colony.

"Elias!" Mercedes said.

"Elias?" Ulises called down, doubtful.

"What took you so long?" Elias yelled back, and Ulises grinned.

Commander Aimon did not look as happy to see him. "Are you sick, boy?" he shouted down.

"No, Commander."

"Then *what*, in the name of *Saint Matthew's mother*, are you —" The commander would have said more but was distracted by Mercedes swinging over the side of the ship. She clambered down the ladder, ignoring his shouting and threats.

Elias watched her. Her dress was the color of spring leaves. Her underskirts, which he could see clearly from where he stood, layer upon layer of black lace. He nudged Brother Lorenz with his elbow without saying a word. The monk, who had been gazing upward with his mouth hanging open, whipped his head around, his face having turned an alarming shade of purple.

Elias nearly fell back into the water when she threw her arms around him. The boat rocked precariously. He buried his face in her hair. "Mercedes." He said her name over and over again, and it was some time before he heard the hoots from above and saw the scandalized expression on Brother Lorenz's face.

"You're hurt," she said between kisses. "Your leg —"

"Is better than it was. Truly, love. Don't —"

She smacked him in the chest. "I've looked everywhere for you! Everywhere! I thought you were dead! And then a messenger arrives, and he's going on and on about blue fire. Elias, what are you *doing* here?"

"Oy!" Commander Aimon yelled. "That can wait. Get up here, both of you!"

Elias took her hand, pressed a kiss to her knuckles. He glanced at Brother Lorenz, then at Mercedes, and shook his head once. She frowned, understanding the need for silence, though not the reason behind it.

All ears were cocked Elias's way, waiting for a response. He looked behind him toward Valdemossa, where he knew Brother Francis watched from some hidden vantage point, waiting to see what he would do.

You trust him with your life, the monk had said. *Do you also trust him with mine?*

Far easier to keep what he'd learned to himself. He could spare Ulises the burden of knowing how Bartolome died. He could honor Brother Francis's request for peace and anonymity.

Except it was Ulises who had asked him to solve the riddle. And Elias had made a promise to his king.

"My king," Elias said, "you must come with me."

Commander Aimon looked incredulous. "You have lost —" He fell silent when Ulises placed a hand on his shoulder.

Ulises knew. He was no longer smiling, his face having paled to moonstone. He looked at Valdemossa for a long moment before he swung over the side of the ship, climbed down the ladder, and jumped into the monk's boat.

The boat ride was a silent one. The monk beside them barred any meaningful conversation. Commander Aimon had joined them, dropping into the smaller boat with a face full of thunder. Elias focused on the western end of the island, where he saw a figure standing alone upon a rocky ledge. Ulises saw him, too. He stiffened, his eyes filled with curiosity and dread.

"My thanks to you, Brother," Ulises said when they reached the shore, and the monk bowed. Elias scooped his walking stick from the sand. They kept to the water's edge as he led them to Brother Francis. The island's residents looked on in silence.

"Don't take offense," Elias said quietly. "A bow would be painful for many of them."

"I understand." Ulises raised a hand in greeting. Mercedes did the same. They were met with bows from those who were able and, from the children, wide eyes and whispers.

"So many," Ulises said. "Some so young. I did not realize."

Commander Aimon crossed himself.

When they had passed the last cottage, Ulises stopped. "Elias. Tell me."

A short time later, Ulises learned the full measure of Lord Silva's treachery. As long as Elias lived, he would never forget the look on his king's face.

They stayed back as Ulises joined his brother. Elias resting on the sand, Mercedes beside him. The commander standing a short distance away beneath a palm. The brothers faced each other; words were spoken. At one point, it looked as though they argued. Elias caught his breath when Brother Francis, once a prince named Teodor, knelt before Ulises and bowed his head. Brother Francis didn't see what Ulises did next, but Elias did. His friend took a step back, nearly stumbling. His hand hovered in the air above the monk's head before it finally settled on his skull, a formal acceptance of loyalty.

Mercedes turned her face into Elias's shoulder. "Elias, I'm so sorry. There's more. Madame Vega was our Eve."

"Was?"

After Lord Silva, he had thought nothing else could hurt him. He was wrong. She had always been *Madame* to him. Never Lena, never Eve. Kind in that stern way of hers. *And so you are Elias*, she had once said to a boy dazzled by the Tower of Winds. *You are most welcome here.*

He recalled small details, insignificant at the time. On the day Lady Esma's body had been discovered in the courtyard, Madame was nowhere to be found. Not in her work chamber, not at supper. Luca had seen her ride off in the small hours of dawn.

At the harbor, Madame had watched Elias give his map carrier to Reyna. Not long after, a brutal stranger had turned up, intent on stealing it. Even if it had meant harming an innocent girl.

I've seen him before, Reyna had said. She would have

remembered her attacker eventually, recognized him as a farmer on her grandfather's property. Madame had known this. Lord Silva had known this.

Elias could barely speak past his fury. "Where is he?"

The commander answered. His response was brief and ominous. "Esperanca. I've sent someone for him."

Mercedes asked, "Do you wish to see him?"

"I want to kill him," Elias said.

Commander Aimon said, "You're not the only one."

When Elias and Mercedes arrived at Lord Antoni's keep, they found it empty.

"Oh." Mercedes stood riveted before the painting of Elias and his mother. She surveyed the rest of the chamber slowly. "That poor, poor man."

Elias searched the keep, calling out. He found a bedchamber and a small kitchen, both empty. He checked out back, nothing. On a hunch, he looked behind the large painting. There it was, a door. They followed the steps downward. Small rectangles had been cut into the stone walls, letting in enough sunlight to guide their way.

At the bottom of the staircase was a chamber bare of any furniture. The dust lay thick beneath their feet. To the right were three smaller chambers. No, not chambers. Cells. The doors had been torn from their hinges and left in a mangled, splintered heap in a corner. Beside the heap was an axe, also covered in dust.

Mercedes entered the first cell. She turned full circle, said quietly, "I can scarcely breathe in here."

It was the same for him. He entered another cell, identical to the last. A high window barred with iron allowed a sliver of light in. All those years. His father painting maps in such a place. After only a few minutes, Elias felt the stones closing in, the dust threatening to choke him.

"Elias."

In the first cell, Mercedes was on her knees in the grime with a palm pressed flat against the wall. "Look."

He crouched beside her. Someone had carved deep into the rock, one word only.

Bartolome.

Brother Francis said, "It's difficult, sometimes, to say goodbye."

"I'll come back. Will you tell him that for me?" They had waited for some time for Lord Antoni to appear. Commander Aimon had finally put his foot down. They were going *now*. Elias hated that his last conversation with his father had been a hurtful one.

"I will tell him," Brother Francis promised.

They stood outside Elias's cottage. The rowboat was down the beach, waiting for its last passenger. For weeks, all he had wanted was to leave Valdemossa, and now that he could, his feet had turned to lead.

"She's lovely, your lady," Brother Francis said. He had met

Mercedes within Brother Lorenz's hearing, and for that reason, the introduction had been formal and impersonal, a monk thanking a member of the royal family for honoring the colony at Valdemossa with a visit. Lorenz could never know of the blood ties between Mercedes and the man he called Francis.

"She is," Elias said, hearing the slight wistfulness in the monk's voice. Perhaps the cousins would meet again one day, forge some sort of bond. Only time would tell. "How do I thank you, Brother? I don't know where to start."

"You don't. I'm glad to have met you, Elias of del Mar."

"I'm glad to have met you. If there is ever anything you need . . ."

"I'll send word with the supply ship," the monk promised, and smiled. "Or with blue fire, if I'm in a hurry."

Elias returned his smile and started down the beach, stopping when Brother Francis called his name.

"I meant to say . . ." Brother Francis trailed off. Elias was not used to seeing the monk at a loss for words. "that I, too, wish it were different. But I'm grateful that you are there for my brother, and my cousin. I'm thankful there is someone there, to love them."

After a minute, Elias bowed. "Brother Francis."

"Lord Elias."

There was nothing more to be said. Elias passed one last glance over his cottage and the people gathered by it. And then he turned and walked away.

TWENTY-SEVEN

THE CELL WAS a pleasant one, as far as cells went. Through iron bars, Mercedes saw rugs on the floor and maps on the walls. A bed, a chair, a table covered with books. Two fat candles gave off a warm glow. Commander Aimon had not been stingy with the light. She was astonished, and then immediately ashamed of her astonishment. But she had not expected such graciousness from the commander. Not for this prisoner. Not even if the king had ordered it so.

"I'll wait here," she murmured to Elias and leaned against a rough stone wall directly opposite the cell. Elias was outwardly calm, but she knew how much he had dreaded this visit. Obligation had driven him to this prison south of Esperanca. A secret prison, hidden deep underground beneath the ruins of an old fort. This was where the kingdom's more inconvenient captives lived. Often, it was where they died.

Elias waited as Lazar produced a ring of keys and unlocked the cell door. It swung inward on creaky hinges. Mercedes held out a hand as the soldier passed her by; he gave her the keys and left. He would join the commander and Ulises, who had gone to inspect other parts of the prison. Ulises had not confronted Lord Silva since his capture, not yet. She wondered if he ever would. Or was it enough for her cousin to know that Lord Silva would remain underground always? It wasn't enough for her. She bitterly resented the comforts this man had been granted. He did not deserve it.

Lord Silva had risen from the chair when he saw them through the bars. He stood rooted in place. Shock rippled over his features. He had thought Elias dead. Food for the fish and the water snakes.

"Elias," he breathed. "Elias."

And along with shock, she saw relief, and hope. How dare he feel these things? As if Elias's affection was something always to be expected. No matter what Lord Silva had done. Despite all he had destroyed.

Elias stood just inside the cell. Lord Silva had not missed the slight hitch to his walk. The doctor had said Elias would recover fully. Still, it would be some time before he could walk without being reminded constantly of a serpent's tooth slicing through his leg.

Elias said, "Commander Aimon insisted you were being treated well. I wanted to see for myself." He shifted, so that Mercedes could see his profile. Unhappy, a muscle pulsing along his jaw. "I see now I should have trusted him."

The disgraced Royal Navigator was dressed simply — a white shirt and dark trousers — but the clothing was clean and of good quality. He looked terrible, of course. Dark circles under his eyes, lines of grief and defeat etched deep into his skin. But he did not look malnourished. He was being fed regularly. Allowed to wash. Another unexpected mercy from the commander.

"Elias, please." Lord Silva stepped forward, freezing at the sound of keys clinking together. Mercedes had moved away from the wall, the ring of keys in one hand, her dagger in the other. Their eyes met. He knew Elias would not hurt him, but Mercedes was a different matter. *Not too close*, her expression warned. Anger flashed in Lord Silva's eyes before he turned to his former apprentice. "Please. I cannot stay here."

"Are you being mistreated?" Elias asked, his tone distant.

"There are no windows!" Lord Silva gestured toward a solid wall, growing visibly agitated. "I'm not allowed outside. I can't breathe in here. I can't see the sky."

Elias said, "I'm sorry for it."

"You could ask the king —"

"For what?" Elias demanded, very softly. "What favor would you have me ask him, on your behalf?"

"Exile." Lord Silva gripped the back of his chair. "Banishment. I'll leave del Mar, and no one will ever see me again. I swear it."

Mercedes cursed this hateful old man. Lord Silva did not know it, but Elias had already gone to the king. Having reconsidered his initial impulse, Elias had begged for imprisonment, not death. For mercy, not torture. *He's an old man*, Elias had reasoned. *Let him live out the rest of his days in a cell, alone. It will be punishment enough.* Elias had argued hard for these concessions. Ulises had not wanted to give it. Bitter words had been exchanged. But in the end, Lord Silva had been brought here to live out his sentence in relative comfort.

Elias repeated thoughtfully, "Exile."

"Yes," Lord Silva said. "The king is your friend. He would do this for you, if you asked him."

"But mine is not the only family you've harmed," Elias reminded him. "I came to tell you this: You were returning to Cortes on horseback when you were attacked by brigands. In your shock over Madame Vega's death, you traveled carelessly. Alone, without escort. The brigands robbed you of your coin and burned your body in a ravine. What was found was nearly unrecognizable. Your funeral was a splendid, somber affair." He watched as Lord Silva lowered himself into his chair. "This story was not invented for your sake, my lord Silva, but for Reyna's."

Lord Silva had blanched as Elias relayed the details of his death. His head was bowed; his arms hung between his legs.

Elias said, "You've not asked about Reyna. Not once." Lord Silva's only reaction was a stiffening of his shoulders. "Tell me, when Madame tried to poison her, was she following your orders? Or was it her own decision?"

Lord Silva lifted his head. "Her own. Of course I would never harm the child —"

"You're lying," Elias said quietly. "And I'm done with it."

Elias left the cell without looking back. Mercedes turned the key in the lock. They walked away as Lord Silva shook the iron bars behind them and cried, "Come back! Elias, please! You cannot leave me here!"

They sailed for Cortes on a galley with a minimum of crew. Men capable of both manning the smaller oars and guarding the king. Commander Aimon had remained behind at the prison, but Ulises spoke with Lazar on the opposite side of the galley. It was late, the moon and stars bright against the night sky. Mercedes heard the oars slapping against the water, felt the galley surge beneath her feet.

She joined Elias at the steering oar as he guided the boat from harbor. He smiled when he saw her, made room between himself and the oar.

"Do you know what I think?" she asked after settling in, her back against his chest.

His answer was to press a kiss against her hair. "Tell me."

"I think if he had not tried to harm Reyna, we would not be here tonight," she said. "The commander would have gone to Lord Silva's cell and found it empty. He would have escaped in some mysterious, improbable way."

Elias was quiet for a time, until they had left the harbor behind them. "I can steer this ship home blindfolded," he said finally. "I can steer it in my sleep, Mercedes. And I know every inch of this kingdom like the back of my hand. I know these things because . . ."

"He taught them to you," she finished softly. She could feel his sadness and his anger.

"He's two different people, almost. Even when I'm standing in front of him, and *I know he's lying to me*—" His hands on the oar tightened. "I can't forget the good he's done. Am I a fool?"

"You're not. We can't help who we love."

"I suppose not." A small silence. "We? Who can't you help but love? Don't say Ulises."

She smiled. Perhaps it was easier to say because she was not looking at him but out at the sea and the night sky covered with stars. "I love you, Elias. I've loved you all my life."

Elias tipped her chin, looked into her face. He was smiling, the first real smile she had seen in a long time. Very quietly, he asked, "How much do you love me?"

"Not that much," Ulises said.

Mercedes jumped, her head cracking the underside of Elias's chin. He cursed. Ulises had appeared from nowhere, six feet away with his elbows on the railing, looking out at the water. She moved hastily out of Elias's arms.

Elias rubbed his chin. "You're always around," he accused.

"Do not forget it," Ulises advised. And, "We're going the wrong way."

Elias said, "I'm going south. To Cortes."

"But Esperanca is north. Your family is still there, are they not?"

Understanding, Mercedes smiled at her cousin. She did not think she could love him any more than she did right now. Even with all that had transpired, and the angry words exchanged regarding Lord Silva's imprisonment, Ulises had proven himself a friend. He knew what would help Elias most of all, quickest of all.

She said to Elias, "Your mother has been expecting you all summer. And Jonas is probably riding a horse by now, he's growing so fast. You should go."

Elias looked north. As though he could see through the darkness and the distance to his family home. Excitement crept into his voice, replacing the melancholy. "She's expecting you, too," he reminded her. "Come with me. Both of you."

"I've things to take care of," Ulises said. "But we'll drop you off, and I'll see you in Cortes before the ships leave."

"What things?" Mercedes asked her cousin.

"Many important things," Ulises said, a smile in his voice. "That I can manage without you. Go with him."

"Come with me," Elias said.

Mercedes laughed. It was not such a hard decision after all. "I'll come."

And she was glad she'd said it. Because Elias grinned and looked almost like his old self. He called out orders to the men at the smaller oars before steering the boat north, toward Esperanca, and home.

TWENTY-EIGHT

WHERE ARE HIS companions?" Brother Francis asked.

"Dead," Ulises answered.

They had gathered in the hold of a ship near Valdemossa's boundary rock: Ulises, Commander Aimon, and Brother Francis. At their feet was Lord Silva. A sack had been tossed over his head. The disgraced Royal Navigator lay on his side, hands and feet bound with rope.

Commander Aimon yanked the sack off. Lord Silva flinched at the sudden brightness, though it was only a single torch in an otherwise dark hold. He had fallen far in the days since Elias had last spoken to him, in his comfortable cell with his precious maps on the walls. Hair and beard shorn off. Clean clothes replaced by something the commander must have dug out of a rag heap.

Lord Silva struggled to a sitting position. His gaze darted around the cramped hold. Looking for mercy, Ulises suspected, but there was none to be found with the commander. None to be found with himself. And then Lord Silva spotted Brother Francis in his monk's garb. A holy man. Ulises forced himself not to look away from the hope he saw in Lord Silva's eyes.

Brother Francis crouched before Lord Silva without expression. "Do you know who I am, old man?"

Not a very pious or respectful question, for a monk. A moment of confusion passed before Lord Silva's eyes widened; his head swung from Brother Francis to Ulises and back. Even with the monk's beard, the resemblance was a disconcerting one. Silva opened his mouth; what emerged was a strange gurgling sound, like a man choking.

Startled, Brother Francis asked, "He can't speak?"

Ulises's gaze flicked right, to an unrepentant Commander Aimon. He had been tasked with guarding Lord Silva while Ulises saw Elias and Mercedes to Esperanca. When Ulises had returned, Lord Silva had no longer been in possession of his tongue.

"No," was all Ulises said.

He had lied to Elias. Made a promise he had no intention of keeping. He despised himself for it, but not enough to stay his hand. How long had it taken Bartolome to carve his name so deep into the stone?

"You'll say nothing to Lady Mercedes?" Commander Aimon had asked when Ulises had shared his true plans for Lord Silva.

"No," Ulises had said. "If I do, she won't be able to tell Elias. She's kept enough secrets for us, Commander."

"True. But I don't think she would keep this one from him."

"Mmm." It had been his thought as well. "Then there's that."

Now Brother Francis asked, "He's to be killed, then?" They ignored the sudden thrashing his words provoked. "It's just as well, I suppose, for death pays all debts."

"Not always," Ulises said. "And not this time, Brother."

Brother Francis rose slowly. "What will you do?"

Lord Silva had stopped gurgling to hear the answer. Commander Aimon was a forbidding statue with a torch in one hand, an empty sack in the other.

Ulises did not take his eyes from his brother's face. His brother, whom he did not know. His only living brother, because of what Lord Silva had done. Even now, the thought left him breathless with rage. "Elias spoke of a prison here."

Shock registered. Brother Francis was beginning to understand. "It's for our violent criminals."

"That will do," Ulises said.

"It . . . would be kinder to kill him."

"Kind?" Ulises repeated. "Yes. But I would have him live, as my brothers once lived. I would have him remember his crimes for many years. As a leper, or not." His voice did not tremble, but his hands, clasped behind his back, did. "But I'll see him dead, quickly and painlessly, if that is your wish."

The silence was broken by a low, keening moan from Lord

Silva. Brother Francis watched him, his fists clenching and unclenching at his sides.

"Teodor, is that your wish?" Ulises held his breath, until Brother Francis stepped back, out of the torchlight and into the shadows.

"No, my king. It is not."

TWENTY-NINE

THERE WAS COMFORT in tradition, in the rituals and words that bind one to a people. Like the mariner's blessing, given by the king in the castle's great hall.

It began with the drums. And the drummers, twelve men in del Marian green and silver with their backs up against the wall. A steady beat, soft at first, then louder, and joined by the rhythmic clapping of hands and pounding of feet upon the stone. This went on for some time, until Elias could feel the thrumming within his entire being.

As del Mar's newest Royal Navigator, Lord Braga held a place of honor beside Ulises. Mercedes was also seated at the high table, her dress the green of seafoam, her hair loose around her. Half the city was here, it seemed, the hydrographers, astronomers, and geographers packed in beside the sea captains, instrument makers, and navigators. Elias and Reyna were among them. Most wore black, in formal mourning for Lord Silva. But today was not one for grief, only celebration.

Tomorrow, five ships would sail west past the Strait of Cain on expeditions expected to last anywhere from six months to three years. The *Aldene*, the *Amaris*, the *Nina*, the *Palma*, and the *St. Clementina*. On every ship, in addition to captain and crew, would be a pilot major to navigate the vessel and a geographer to survey the coastlines and interiors.

Ulises stood, a signal for the drums to slow and stop. He spoke the mariner's chant; his deep voice carried easily across the hall:

> *"You, adventurer who boasts of being*
> *quick-witted and a good troubadour,*
> *would you make me a song*
> *that the eight winds call?"*

Ulises paused, expectant. And everyone joined in:

> *"Levante, Scirocco, and Ostro,*
> *Libeccio, Ponente, and Maestro,*
> *Tramontana and Greco:*
> *Here you have the eight winds of the globe."*

There were cheers. People drank. They pounded on the tables and drank some more. The cats and dogs were in ecstasy, licking up the spillage beneath the tables. And monkeys, Elias amended, when he spotted Jorge under a bench, working his way through half a melon.

Smiling slightly, Ulises raised a hand. The hall quieted. He said, "Not every man can leave his home. Leave all that is familiar, his family and his friends, the buildings and streets he has learned to navigate by heart, and journey to parts unknown. It takes a man with the soul and spirit of an adventurer...."

An impressive opening to a speech, one Elias had heard practiced numerous times in the past few days. He had suggested that last part himself. There were more cheers and pounding, and as the glasses and utensils rattled the tabletops, his thoughts wandered.

To Lord Silva in his secret prison in the north. Elias would not see him again. He had done what he could for his old teacher, and he understood what it had cost Ulises to grant his request. It had humbled him. Never again would he take his king, or their friendship, for granted.

Ulises had spoken at Lord Silva's funeral. Paying homage to a man he would sooner have drowned in a river. A necessity, for to proclaim Lord Silva a villain was also to admit that King Andrés, Ulises's father, had made a grievous error. To cast St. John del Mar in a terrible light in the eyes of its neighbors and the world. It was to turn curious eyes in the direction of Valdemossa and expose truths best left alone. Ulises would do what he could to make things right for Mondrago — that was where Mercedes came in — but not at the expense of his father's legacy.

Elias's leg was healing nicely, leaving only a scar to add to his many others. To his relief, he did not have to explain his absence from Cortes to anyone. Basilio had told anyone who asked that Elias had been sent on a mission on behalf of the king. It was the sort of explanation that discouraged questions. And if, on occasion, he now caught a curious look from Luca, or a quiet, thoughtful frown from Lord Braga, nothing ever came of it.

Then there was Reyna. Lord Braga had not only taken on the role of Royal Navigator but had welcomed the girl into his home, where she had been nursed back to health by his wife, Lady Braga. Her friend Jaime would not be around. He would sail with Luca. But Jaime had five brothers and sisters, and a loud, loving family was just what Reyna needed to distract herself from her grief. It was the best place for her. Elias told himself this. Over and over, until he nearly believed it.

He had intended to keep the truth from her, a plan that had crumbled to dust when he'd walked into her chamber and found her at a window seat. No longer bruised, at least not on the outside. Lady Braga had granted them privacy.

As soon as the door closed, Reyna had said, "I remember where I saw him. The man from the harbor."

Elias had come to a halt in the middle of the chamber. Several seconds passed before he could trust his voice. "Reyna . . ."

Softly, she had said, "Please tell me the truth."

No girl of nine should ever look so serious. He had done as she asked. Settled beside her on the window seat and told her everything — about Lord Silva, Madame Vega, the long-ago avalanche that had started it all — and watched a solitary tear make its way down her cheek. She'd said, "You must hate me."

"Look at me." He'd waited until she looked him in the eye.

"You are not your grandfather's keeper. Not your aunt's. Do you understand? We are responsible for no one's conduct but our own."

Her face had crumpled, and he'd held her in his arms as she wept.

Ulises was nearing the end of his speech. "We are grateful for your courage and fortitude. We commend you for your service." He raised a cup high. "For the glory of del Mar, go safely."

Elias looked to Mercedes and found her eyes on him already, the hint of a smile about her lips. He raised his cup toward her as Ulises's words echoed across the chamber. *For the glory of del Mar, go safely.*

A new adventure. For both of them.

Tomorrow, the *Amaris* would be sailing west past the Strait of Cain.

Elias would not be sailing on it.

"Mondrago," Lord Braga had said, incredulous. "Are you absolutely certain?"

"It needs to be done." Elias stood before Lord Braga's desk in what was once Lord Silva's work chamber. Already the signs of the former Royal Navigator were disappearing. Lord Silva had kept an orderly space. No one could ever accuse Lord Braga of tidiness. Great teetering stacks of parchment covered the desk. Globes and scrolls crowded the shelves and littered the floor.

The most glaring change was the absence of Lord Vittor's world map, a father's prized possession. It had been removed from the wall and replaced with a larger, more current version drawn by Braga himself.

"Yes, yes, it needs to be done," Lord Braga said from his chair, his scuffed boots propped on the desk. Shoes on the furniture. This was also new. "But by *you*? I can send —" A sharp hiss followed. He whipped his head around, glared at the boy standing by his side. "Jaime!"

"Apologies, Papa," Jaime said, a needle in one hand. They looked at each other in mutual exasperation. "But I've asked you twice now not to move."

Elias almost smiled. It turned out Lord Braga had always secretly desired wearing an earring, a practice previously frowned upon, and now that he was Royal Navigator, there was no one about to refuse him. Jaime had been enlisted to pierce two holes in his father's left earlobe.

Lord Braga harrumphed, though he sat perfectly still as Jaime prepared his second piercing. To Elias, he said, "It's a good idea, not leaving that island to rot any longer. The king makes a wise decision."

"I think so, too."

"But *Mondrago*." Lord Braga's mustache was a bushy, splendid thing. It drooped to his chin when he frowned. "There's no mystery there. It's been discovered. With this expedition, there is a chance for glory."

"I'm not looking for glory."

Lord Braga's eyebrows rose. Even Jaime paused, glanced sidelong across the desk. Both knew his words were a lie.

"Elias," Lord Braga chided, his voice soft, "come now. We are all looking for glory."

Elias amended, "I'm not looking for it just yet. This is important to me."

Lord Braga opened his mouth to respond, flinched. "Boy!"

"I'm finished!" Jaime jumped out of his father's reach, both palms raised as though he'd been caught stealing something.

"Oh." Lord Braga lifted a hand to touch his ear, then thought better of it. He angled his bald head toward Elias. "How do I look?"

Elias studied the small gold hoops and thought of a similar one worn by his own father. "It suits you."

"Good." Mollified, Lord Braga swung his boots to the floor. He rummaged around his desk, found some coins beneath a pilot book, and tossed a double-shell Jaime's way. The boy caught the silver and grinned. "Make sure you're back in time for supper," his father ordered, and Jaime was gone.

Once the door had shut behind his son, Lord Braga turned back to Elias. "Don't think I don't see right through you. I know who else will be on Mondrago. You're not the first person to lose your heart, and your good judgment, because of a girl."

This time Elias smiled. "But what a girl."

Lord Braga laughed. "Fine. Go. At least if I send you, I know the work will be done well."

"Thank you, sir."

"*But*" — Lord Braga swung his boots back onto the desk — "don't take too long there. No settling down. No growing fat and comfortable in some castle by the sea."

"I'm nineteen only. Little chance of that."

"I'm glad to hear it. I have plans for you, Elias."

Elias felt his curiosity stir. "What plans?"

"What else?" Lord Braga eyed the chart on the wall. "Look there. It won't do, not even a little bit. There are too many blank spaces on that map."

The festivities had not ended in the great hall but had poured into the courtyard, with its grand sprawling olive tree. There was dancing and music — the castle musicians had taken their place beneath the tree — and tables laden with more food and drink. Lanterns hung from hooks on the walls, so many of them that it appeared almost daylight.

Elias was too distracted to enjoy any of it. Frowning, he inspected the crowd from the courtyard's second-floor balcony. "Well, they don't look too menacing."

Beside him, Mercedes smiled. A mass of children gathered directly below. Necks craned in anticipation, the smaller ones clutching their *mamans'* hands. Elias's own mother was there with Jonas and Lea. But many of the faces were unfamiliar, children from outside the castle walls. Their parents. Their grandparents. Who knew what darkness rotted their souls?

Mercedes said, "You're worrying too much."

"No."

She touched his arm lightly. "Why don't you go find Ulises? Or Lord Isidore? My, look at all that food."

His lips twitched at this involuntarily. "Are you trying to be rid of me?"

"Yes," she said and laughed. "Stop worrying. There won't be any trouble tonight."

She sounded so sure. And far more enthusiastic than she had on the road to Javelin, when Ulises had first broached the subject. Tossing sweets to children. Bringing back an old tradition. Still. He thought of the old woman who had spat at her. "If there is, I'll wring their necks."

"Whose necks?" his cousin Dita demanded. She looked over the balcony at the children, then back at him, askance. "Have you been drinking?" She didn't give him a chance to respond. "Elias, what are you still doing up here? You're in our way."

"I'm going." He knew when he wasn't wanted. All around him, females gathered armfuls of wrapped sweets from the massive burlap sack he had lugged over from the kitchens. Lady Aimon was here, and Mistress Galena. His sister Nieve and Reyna and even Katalin the tax collector among them. Mercedes had surrounded herself with friends.

He scooped up a handful of sweets from the sack, ran the back of his hand across Mercedes's cheek, ruffled Nieve's hair, and grinned at the outrage that followed. Ulises was at the back of the crowd, talking to Lord Isidore. Nearby, guards scowled at the merrymakers.

"What are they doing?" Ulises asked, meaning the females on the balcony.

Elias tossed a sweet at him. Ulises caught it. Puzzled at first, and then not. A startled smile broke across his features.

"She wanted to surprise you," Elias said.

"It nearly killed me to give her the coin for it," Lord Isidore added. "But she assured me it was for special occasions only, not every Tuesday."

Ulises asked, "She went to you for a sack full of sweets? How much could it possibly cost?" As Lord Exchequer, Lord Isidore approved any significant castle expenses.

Lord Isidore laughed. "My king, she is throwing more than that." He handed his cup to Elias, said, "I'd better help your mother." He waded into the fray toward his wife and youngest children.

Elias shrugged at Ulises's questioning look. He'd no notion what his stepfather had meant. Just then, Mercedes leaned over the balcony, arms full, and called out a greeting. Were they certain they needed more sweets? Absolutely certain? It looked like they had plenty already. And the children jumped up and down at her teasing and insisted, yes, they needed more. Smiling, Mercedes looked across the courtyard, eyes touching on Elias, who lifted his cup, and then to her cousin, who mouthed the words "Thank you."

Mercedes flung her arms wide; her companions did the same, and the sweets came raining down. Predictably, the children erupted in a mass of squeals and grabbing hands. Lord Isidore's laughter boomed above it all.

Elias's cup froze halfway to his lips. Beside him came a shocked inhalation of breath. Ulises asked, "Is that —?"

Yes, it was. Elias found himself laughing. He had forgotten completely.

It doesn't have to be just sweets, does it? Make it so they can't say no to you. Make it so they have no wish to.

Bribery? You think I should throw coins along with the sweets?

I would never turn down silver.

Mercedes had listened to his counsel and gone one step further. Not just sweets, not just silver, but gold as well. Delicate treats wrapped in paper. Copper sand dollars and silver double-shells. Squid cast from solid gold. All of it, together, falling from the sky like starlight.

EPILOGUE

Father and son stood side by side on the shores of Valdemossa.

"You should not have come back here, Elias."

"My lord father, please. May I speak?"

Halfway down the beach, Brother Francis and Reyna conversed beside a small boat. Farther out to sea, an even larger boat anchored by the boundary rock.

"Who is the girl?" Lord Antoni asked.

"Reyna," Elias said. "You heard they imprisoned him? Outside Esperanca?"

"Esperanca?" Lord Antoni repeated, then added hastily, "Yes, Francis told me. What did you come here to say?"

A thousand things needed to be said between them. Elias would start with this. "The fleet sailed two days ago."

A sidelong glance. "And you are not with them."

"No. Ulises . . . the king has his heart set on rebuilding Mondrago. He's gathering stonemasons and artists and . . ."

"Surveyors," Lord Antoni finished.

"Yes."

"You were looking forward to this expedition."

"There will be others." True, it had stung to watch the ships sail from the harbor. But it felt right that he should be part of Mondrago's future. Mercedes was already there. He planned to follow, but there was something he needed to do first. "I hoped to see you settled somewhere before I go. The ship is waiting."

"What?" Lord Antoni stared at him, incredulous. "Now?"

"Why not?" Elias asked. "You don't belong here. There's another place for you. A real home with friends, travel, whatever you wish for." When there was no response, he added, a bit desperately, "I brought gold. It's still your gold, if you think about it. I don't see why you should not use it to make a new life for yourself. Anywhere but here."

From Lord Antoni, nothing.

Elias pressed on. "I would like to know you," he said. "If you won't go, then I'll come here. Again and again, I'll come back. I hope I don't fall ill. But if I do, please don't feel that you're in any way to blame."

A sharp laugh. "You'll have to work on your subtlety. It's a low thing, threatening one's parent."

"I know it," Elias admitted. "I don't have time for subtlety."

Lord Antoni looked down the beach. "She's your apprentice?"

"No." Here was where his plans could unravel. "I hope she'll be yours."

Lord Antoni gaped at him. Maybe Elias was asking for too much, all at once. He had to try. "She has no one," he said. "I'll gladly take her with me if you say no. But I thought she might be good for you. An apprenticeship —" He shrugged. "It's only seven years. It's nothing." And when that elicited no response, "Think of the good you can do her."

At that, Lord Antoni's eyes narrowed. "You would throw my words back at me?"

"Yes." Elias pulled the leather strap over his head. The map carrier was only days old, the leather a rich mahogany, a small *A* the size of a thumbnail embossed on the side of the cap. He had made it himself. Offering the carrier to his father, he said, "It will be an adventure."

Elias waited; the silence went on forever.

Lord Antoni took the carrier with both hands, holding it as carefully as one would an infant newly born. He brought it close and inhaled the rich leather scent of it. Then, "Reyna, is it?"

"Yes."

"An adventure, you say?"

Elias smiled. "Yes."

Lord Antoni gave a last, considering look down the beach before he slung the leather strap over one shoulder and said, "She is going to need her own carrier."

ACKNOWLEDGMENTS

With all my heart, I would like to thank my agent, Suzie Townsend, who keeps me focused on the one thing I can control, which is to try to tell a good story.

My wonderful editors, Elizabeth Bewley and Nicole Sclama, who love the world of del Mar as much as I do and helped ensure my final draft was a hundred times stronger than my first.

Danelle Forseth and Erika Baker are the busiest moms I know, but they still found the time to come by the house so that I could practice for book readings, helped brainstorm villain names, and answered strange and random book-related texts at all hours of the day and night.

Before she moved to Montana, Kelly Murray made sure I saw the sun occasionally, meeting me halfway up the hill for our walks and offering much needed encouragement during early drafts. I am very lucky to have friends such as these.

Elias's story takes place on an island, which is no coincidence. I was born on an island, raised on another, and as I look back over this manuscript, I realize how much my childhood has shaped both my setting and my story. The food, the sea, the relatives, even the ghosts in the forest. To everyone back home on Guam who has cheered me on, wished me luck, bought a stack of books to force on family and friends: *Si Yu'us Ma'ase*. Thank you. The map at the front of this book is for you.

Speaking of maps, my daughter, Mia Evangeline, sketched the original back in the fifth grade and she didn't even ask for payment. The finished map you see is the work of the brilliant illustrator Leo Hartas. Many thanks!

And finally, and with much love, there's Chris, who really deserves a thank-you page of his own.